Paciencia Perdida

An Anthology of Peruvian Fiction

Translated & Edited by

Gabriel T. Saxton-Ruiz

Dulzorada Press

PACIENCIA PERDIDA: AN ANTHOLOGY OF PERUVIAN FICTION

© 2022, Dulzorada Press
Editor-in-chief: José Garay Boszeta
Email: jose@dulzorada.com
Book design and layout: Miguel Garay Boszeta
Email: miguel@dulzorada.com
Dulzorada logo design: Bidkar Yapo | @nacionchicha.pe

Library of Congress Control Number: 2022921222

ISBN: 978-1-953377-18-0 (paperback)
ISBN: 978-1-953377-19-7 (hardcover)
Published by Dulzorada Press
http://Dulzorada.com

Printed in the USA

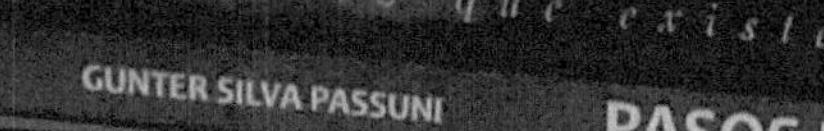

Una voz que existe
GUNTER SILVA PASSUNI
PASSOS PESADOS
Claudia Salazar Jimenez
El Inventario de las Naves
¿Qué tengo de malo?
MAD
BAR
Premio ALFAGUARA de novela 2006
DE LOS ESCRITORES ASESINOS
Juan Ma
Santiago Roncagliolo
ALFAGUARA
Eduardo Benavides
ALFAGUARA
Forasteros en tu
Carlos Dávalos
Dios es peruano
DANIEL TITINGER
ÓSCAR COLCHADO LUCIO
32
4
ROSA CUC
DIEGO TRELL
SAN MARCOS
L

To Beatriz, Lucas & Leo (los frikis) + Winston

CONTENTS

Introduction: Who Killed Mario Vargas Llosa?

By Gabriel T. Saxton-Ruiz

In the fall of 2010, I was starting my second year of teaching at the University of Wisconsin-Green Bay. Like most junior faculty, I said yes to any and everything that was asked of me—well, that's called paying your dues, which happens in any profession. One particular "yes" that I remember fondly was agreeing to teach an upper-level class for the history department, a course titled Political History of Modern Latin America. While the content clearly fell in my wheelhouse, I still felt much trepidation at the prospect of stepping into a classroom full of history and poli sci majors accustomed to riveting, thought-provoking lectures courtesy of my rock star colleagues. The history department, housed in two different academic units, Humanistic Studies and Democracy & Justice Studies, typically won the end of the year teaching and scholarship awards, constantly appeared on NPR, often provided on-air commentary for programs on the History Channel, and every semester dazzled the local community with projects analyzing the linothorax, an ancient linen body armor; examining blacksmithing techniques in a Viking-age replica farmhouse; and educating the public on the rich cultures of the First Nations peoples, including the Menominee, Ho-Chunk, Potawatomi and Ojibwe, upon whose traditional homelands the campuses of the different state universities of Wisconsin reside.

But hey, my fellow professors of modern languages and literatures and I were no slouches by any stretch of the imagination. However, by virtue of not teaching in English, our classes tended to be much smaller than the history ones. In fact, many of our sections had an enrollment of ten or twelve students, and we'd routinely arrange the chairs in a circle to help stimulate discussion and foster community. The apprehension I felt regarding the history class involved both the space I'd be using (picture the classic scenes depicting academia on cable TV shows and those large, tiered theater halls jam-packed with over a hundred students) and the lecture-based format of the course. I suffered from an extreme case of impostor syndrome as the semester started, running my lesson plans and lecture notes past colleagues who were extremely generous with their feedback and support. I was so caught up in creating PowerPoints with pie charts and bar graphs documenting poverty rates or data on victims of political violence, that when it came time to teach, I felt as though I had been reducing complex histories to mere statistical figures.

After a few weeks under my belt, I reached out to a senior faculty member and asked that she sit in on my class to get her perspective. As the students shuffled out of the lecture hall, my colleague suggested we grab a coffee to go over the "dumpster fire" I called my class. Her comments were concise and blunt, boiling down to the question, why didn't I replicate how I normally taught my Spanish culture and civilization classes? "Where are the stories? Where's the poetry? Where's the humor? You're boring your students to tears!"

She was right of course—I had changed my entire pedagogy and teaching style to fit what I had assumed was the "proper" way to teach a class on Latin American political history. Moving forward, I included short fiction by Luisa Valenzuela and clips from Adrián Caetano's 2006 film *Crónica de una fuga* (*Chronicle of an Escape*) to describe Argentina's infamous Dirty

War; Pablo Neruda's poem "La United Fruit Co." to discuss that American corporation's oversized and exploitative influence on Central American and Caribbean nations; and I used the Zimbalist brothers' documentary *The Two Escobars* (2010) to present crucial moments of twentieth century Colombia and the link between fútbol and narcotrafficking.

By the time we were scheduled to talk about Peru, I felt more comfortable embedding cultural productions to introduce major sociohistorical themes from the different countries and subregions we were covering in class. That's not to say I was completely at ease lecturing to the masses, and every now and then, I'd get the feeling I was overcompensating for my insecurities by resorting to gimmicks for cheap laughs. I guess that may explain the choice to begin our unit on Peru's recent history with a line from the opening paragraph of Mario Vargas Llosa's 1969 novel *Conversación en la Catedral* (*Conversation in the Cathedral*).

On the lecture hall's gigantic screen, I projected an image of the book's cover and both the original quote and its translation by the irreplaceable Gregory Rabassa: "¿En qué momento se había jodido el Perú?" ("At what precise moment had Peru fucked itself up?"). As might be expected, the slide was met with mixed results: several students found it comical, many rolled their eyes probably thinking the professor was trying too hard to impress, and others felt the need to whip out their smartphones and capture the moment to post on social media after class. (Pathetically, I even photobombed their pictures while throwing up a Nixonian double peace sign.) The F-bomb notwithstanding, the sentiment expressed in Vargas Llosa's novel accurately reflected the material we were going to explore in the following three or four classes.[1]

Here was a book from the late 1960s fictionalizing episodes from the Manuel Odría dictatorship of a decade earlier, but the pessimistic outlook could easily have applied to the country's contemporary history, a period marked by political and social upheaval; a bloody internal conflict waged by the armed forces, the Maoist terrorist organization known as *Sendero Luminoso* (Shining Path) and *Movimiento Revolucionario Túpac Amaru* (Túpac Amaru Revolutionary Movement, commonly referred to by its initials MRTA), a Marxist-Leninist guerrilla group; and of course, enduring financial crises.

I shared with the class what Vargas Llosa meant to me, telling students he was the writer I'd read and re-read the most in my lifetime. In high school, I'd been blown away by his debut novel *La ciudad y los perros*, first published in 1963 (*The Time of the Hero*), only to later dissect it in grad school while learning all about the Faulknerian techniques of nonlinear narration and shifting points of view. A few years later I laughed and laughed reading *La tía Julia y el escribidor* (*Aunt Julia and the Scriptwriter*, 1977), and then realized Hollywood had adapted the work in a feature-length film starring Keanu Reeves, Barbara Hershey and Peter Falk, the quirky 1990 comedy *Tune in Tomorrow*. I told my students people often quote the first lines of novels, but hardly anyone talks about a book's last few sentences—perhaps to avoid spoilers, although I submit that the real reason is because endings frequently let us down. Not so with Vargas Llosa's *La guerra del fin del mundo* (*The War of the End of the World*, 1981), the last two lines of which still give me goosebumps just thinking about them. I droned on and on like a fanboy, going so far as to disclose that in college I used to make mixtapes for friends and give my compilations titles lifted from the Vargas Llosa section of my school library. A collection of mellow tunes perfectly curated for a make-out session was called "The Perpetual Orgy," taken from the Peruvian author's essay on Flaubert; another mix, "The Green House," stolen from his second novel, featured songs I considered environmentally conscious like REM's "It's the End of the World as We Know It," Marvin Gaye's "Mercy Mercy Me (The Ecology)" and "Beds are Burning" by Midnight Oil; and lastly, "Story of a Deicide," had a whole bunch of dark, classic doom metal songs (nothing to do with Vargas Llosa's analysis of Gabriel García Márquez's *One Hundred Years of Solitude*).

I concluded the brief trip down memory lane and my relationship with Vargas Llosa's books by saying if ever there was a more deserving candidate for the Nobel Prize in Literature, it was him. But, I added, he'll never win; as a public intellectual, his political writing frequently ruffled too many feathers. I declared with confidence that he'd be a perennial contender, but the secretive jury of the Swedish Academy would never risk presenting him the award lest it find itself embracing the "prophet of neoliberalism," as Spanish author Manuel Vázquez Montalbán once described Vargas Llosa.

Two days after that class, I took my one-year-old son to the cardiologist in the morning and didn't bother to check my email. Doctor visits with my youngest child were always emotionally daunting since he'd had open-heart surgery seven days after birth and a medically bumpy first year, including a couple of trips to the emergency room. The check-up went really well. I was ecstatic and headed straight to campus, eager to continue the conversation about Peru's tragicomic political farce with my students. With a few minutes to spare before I had to navigate the underground tunnels connecting different campus buildings to reach the lecture hall, I opened my inbox to find over sixty new messages. More than twenty of them were from students repeating a variation of the same comment/question, along the lines of, "Didn't you say this guy would never win the Nobel Prize?" The rest of the emails were from family, friends and colleagues, all mentioning their surprise upon hearing the news. "Can you believe it? ¡Viva el Perú, carajo!" Yes, Mario Vargas Llosa had won the Nobel! I was already on a high after my kid's doctor's appointment, and the unbelievable announcement from Stockholm took my mood to another level. I walked into class and had a blast celebrating with my students, who took pleasure in ribbing me about my atrocious forecasting skills. Since we were in Green Bay, the Mecca of professional football of the American variety, I decided to have fun with my newfound Anti-Nostradamus special powers and offered the class another prediction: the Packers were *not* going to reach the Super Bowl that season, much less win it. Feel free to google the 2010-11 NFL standings at your leisure to see how I fared.

As to be expected, Vargas Llosa's Nobel win sparked a renewed (or brand-new) interest in his work the world over. It also shone a spotlight again on Peru's literary scene, which years earlier had been the subject of a lengthy profile in *The New York Times* penned by Simon Romero, "Past War and Cruelty, Peru's Writers Bloom," a piece highlighting the country's burgeoning independent publishing houses, the hip narrative journalism magazine *Etiqueta Negra* and the international success of novelists Santiago Roncagliolo, Alonso Cueto and Daniel Alarcón, whose works recreated the period of political violence in the 1980s and 1990s.

In my little corner of academe, I was beseeched by colleagues and students alike to recommend titles by Vargas Llosa and newer, younger Peruvian writers. Since many of them suffered from that most American of afflictions called monolingualism (ha!), my list of suggestions was pretty inadequate. Most of Vargas Llosa's oeuvre was readily available in English—that was easy—but going through my office bookshelves I only managed to find the following books of "contemporary-ish" Peruvian narrative in translation: Alfredo Bryce Echenique's 1970 classic *Un mundo para Julius* (A *World for Julius*, translated by Dick Gerdes); *La palabra del mudo*, a collection of stories spanning 1952-1975 by Julio Ramón Ribeyro (translated as *Marginal Voices*, by Dianne Douglas); José María Arguedas's masterpiece *Los ríos profundos* (1958) (translated by Frances Horning Barraclough); *From the Threshold: Contemporary Peruvian Fiction in Translation*, an anthology published in 1987 featuring several notable authors from the 1970s and 1980s, edited by Luis Ramos García and Luis Fernando Vidal.

For those interested in exploring newer writing from Peru, I also shared Santiago Roncagliolo's award-winning novel *Abril rojo* which had just been published in translation a year earlier (*Red April,* rendered into English by the inimitable Edith Grossman, one of my personal idols, and the translator of minor works such as Cervantes's *Don Quixote,* García Márquez's *Love in the Time of Cholera* and many novels by Vargas Llosa), and a special issue of the literary journal *A Public Space.* Edited by Daniel Alarcón and Juan Manuel Chávez, it contained a brief yet compelling portfolio of Peruvian short pieces from the early 2000s, showcasing multigenerational talents, including the previously mentioned Roncagliolo, Julio Durán, Óscar Colchado, José de Piérola and Miguel Gutiérrez. I can't say for certain how many of my students and colleagues actually read the novels I recommended, but I did receive very positive comments on the short collection from *A Public Space*—a World Lit professor even added the stories by Colchado and de Piérola, along with a Vargas Llosa essay, to his course reading list that semester. After finding out about that World Lit class, I had what is popularly referred to as an aha moment, a project that has taken me forever and a day to complete: this anthology of contemporary Peruvian fiction you hold in your hands.

The evolution of this book is riddled with many false starts, beginning with a host of working titles I discarded for different reasons. At one point, I had settled on *Bajo un nuevo sol: Peruvian Fiction in the Twenty-First Century*, an attempt to capture the feeling of a new dawn (*nuevo sol* = new sun), the rise of a group of contemporary writers, but I was also referencing the currency of Peru.[2] When the Peruvian government changed the name of its money in 2015, I felt the need to brainstorm other possible titles. None of the ideas I came up with thrilled me all that much, so I resorted to pilfering Vargas Llosa's works for inspiration again. His 1986 novel *¿Quién mató a Palomino Molero?* (*Who Killed Palomino Molero?*, translated by Alfred MacAdam) was always a favorite of mine as it combined elements of a popular genre (hardboiled detective fiction) with the technique of overlapping narratives, dubbed "communicating vessels," while at the same time offering commentary on social class, race and corruption—I've always been a sucker for that juxtaposition of low and highbrow styles in cultural productions.

So, I thought, what if I were to call my book "Who Killed Mario Vargas Llosa?" With this tongue-in-cheek riff, I attempted to suggest a literary patricide; a way to introduce the English-reading world to recent writing that was both indebted to the Peruvian Nobel, but also trying to break away and create new artistic projects. Nowhere near as elegant as Harold Bloom's *The Anxiety of Influence* (1973), but hoping to convey a similar perspective, I still thought my title could work given the monumental presence of Vargas Llosa among his writerly compatriots. In fact, two of the authors featured in this anthology, Diego Trelles Paz and Francisco Ángeles, have explicitly highlighted Vargas Llosa's impact on their published fiction.

In Trelles Paz's first novel, *El círculo de los escritores asesinos* (*The Circle of Assassin Writers*, 2005), his character "el Chato" heads over to Vargas Llosa's house in Lima, but the writer never appears. The only thing the up-and-coming young author encounters is a building casting a shadow over him, and he wonders what would happen if he were to actually run into the Nobel laureate sans bodyguards, only to conclude that he'd probably punch him.[3] The scene clearly illustrates both how Vargas Llosa's influence looms large and a desire to break free from it, as the symbolically violent act suggests.

For his part, Ángeles published a short story in 2009 (one year before the surprise win!) titled "Mario Vargas Llosa, Premio Nobel de Literatura" about a group of friends who'd get together each year on the first or second Thursday in October, to watch the live transmission of the Nobel Prize for Literature announcement, waiting in eager anticipation for Vargas Llosa's name to be called. This annual meet-up is described with all the trappings of a soccer tailgate full of finger foods and alcohol, but each time the Peruvian friends' hopes are dashed when the elder Swede declares the victor, an author they'd never (or barely) read.[4] As evidenced by this brief summary of Ángeles's story, Vargas Llosa's literary hero status among his fellow Peruvian writers is undeniable. And I could go on with more examples underscoring the effect Vargas Llosa has had on contemporary writers: from stylistic concerns (the first few novels by Jorge Eduardo Benavides have been described by critics such as Robert Ruz and Álex Lima as building on techniques of the *novela total*, including the use of assimilated dialogue and multiple fragmented plot lines associated with Vargas Llosa's *The Green House* and *Conversation in The Cathedral*) to more personal matters (like Pedro Novoa naming his son "Mario" after his cultural idol).

But in the end, I opted to keep "Who Killed Mario Vargas Llosa?" for my introduction as opposed to the book because I wanted the title to center on several aspects I believe unify this collection and help describe my overall translation style. The alliterative *Paciencia Perdida* which gives title to this anthology means "Patience Lost," a feeling that permeates many of the pieces. These short stories tend to display a loss of patience and faith in Peru's institutions, the disappointment of unrealized expectations or unrequited love, frustration at the lack of economic opportunities, indignation at violence against women and condemnation of the country's systemic racism and inequality.

By the same token, I left *Paciencia Perdida* in Spanish because I'm a card-carrying member of "Team Foreignization" when it comes to translation preference. Susan Bernofsky describes "foreignizing" translations as those that "preserve all of the ethnographic details and explain them or footnote them or 'stealth gloss' them [...] to handle unfamiliar things in translation.

That sort of translation is respectful of the foreign culture." On the other hand, Bernofsky uses the following example to explain a "domesticating" style, "instead of having people eating what they were eating in a foreign country and explaining the customs around the food, you Americanize the food or tradition." As the reader will notice, I have kept many words in Spanish, especially for certain landmarks, street names, terms of endearment for family members and, of course, expressions related to cuisine. I want my readers to be transported to Peru (or the other settings of these texts) and to be fully aware that these stories reflect other social realities. Plus, as anyone who has ever met a Peruvian surely knows, food is an extremely serious matter. I couldn't possibly reduce items such as the lovely sounding mondonguito to a mere stew or the mouthwatering butifarra to a plain old ham sandwich as the in-demand star translator George Henson once quipped in response to one of my Facebook comments. There are numerous Spanish words throughout this collection of stories; however, the majority of them should be easy to comprehend given the context or the gloss I provide. If not, a thirty-second Google search should do the trick.

For me, *Paciencia Perdida* also suggests an attitude many Peruvians view as a national idiosyncrasy. According to Spanish journalist Juan Cruz, the author Alfredo Bryce Echenique used to share an anecdote comically summing up what it felt like to be Peruvian. The story goes something like this: during a soccer match between Peru and Brazil broadcast on the radio, the commentator providing the play-by-play, a rabid fan of Peru's national team, excitedly describes, "PERU IS ADVANCING, PERU IS ADVANCING, GOOOOOOOOOOOOOOOL, BRAZIL!"

Similarly, in the Romero article I mentioned earlier, the editor of *Etiqueta Negra*, Julio Villanueva Chang, remembers how his publication was first received by his countrymen saying, "[m]any people still tell me the magazine doesn't feel Peruvian. […] The return of self-esteem in Peru, the overcoming of a feeling of defeat, is something recent." The tension between that pervasive undercurrent of defeatism and the urge to rise above it is also noticeable in several of these stories. And perhaps it's precisely because of these competing stances that Peruvian writers and their works have often been in the limelight in the first two decades of the twenty-first century. Even before Vargas Llosa's Nobel, Peruvian novelists and short story writers were already making waves on the international stage by winning some of the most prestigious Spanish-language literary awards.[5] Over the last fifteen years or so, as the visibility of contemporary Peruvian literature increased outside of the country, so too did my interest in studying and translating it.

Although I'd always been a voracious reader, it wasn't until the early and mid-2000s, while in grad school, that I became obsessed with all things related to Peruvian narrative. My daily routine revolved around reading several literary blogs including Ivan Thays's *Moleskine Literario,* Gustavo Faverón's *Puente Aéreo,* Javier Ágredas's *Libros* and Gabriel Ruiz Ortega's *La fortaleza de la soledad,* just to name but a few (because there were many, many blogs back then and I tried to read them all!). Through these I was able to explore recent trends in Peru's cultural scene, especially the rise of independent publishing houses such as *Estruendomudo, Ediciones Altazor, Mesa Redonda, Editorial Casatomada* and, later on, *Animal de Invierno* and *Pesopluma.* Soon I'd begin emailing my aunts, uncles and cousins in Lima, begging them to track down titles reviewed in the blogs; not only books from the indies, but also the venerable national publisher Peisa and the multi-national behemoths like Alfaguara and Grupo Planeta. And every time my parents made a trip to Peru to visit family, they'd graciously agree to visit bookstores and return to DC with excessive baggage fees thanks to me. I'm forever grateful for their willingness to be my personal chasquis, the name given to important messengers during the Incan empire.

In the years since my proverbial aha moment back in 2010, this book-length translation project has been a dream of mine, but I had doubts about my ability to complete it. Although I was active as a scholar and considered myself an unofficial ambassador of Peruvian literature in the United States, publishing a book which analyzed representations of political violence in contemporary narrative, editing and translating a special issue on international alternative histories for *Words Without Borders* and taking on the role of editor-in-chief at the online portal *Stories from Peru* founded by London-based writer Gunter Silva, my life changed in early 2016 and I almost left the profession altogether. That year I got divorced and took a job at the largest Catholic university in Texas, the University of the Incarnate Word (UIW) in San Antonio. It was meant to be a stop-gap gig since, in my depressive state, I had somehow allowed myself to be recruited by a government agency looking to hire people with language abilities and international experience. I was only supposed to be at UIW for a year while my security clearance went through its lengthy process.

But a lot can happen in a year. For starters, Donald J. Trump became the "leader of the free world," and there was no way I could work for his administration. Truth be told, I probably wouldn't have been that great of an asset for any government no matter its ideology or lack thereof. And after a disastrous first semester at UIW, in which my survey of Latin American literature class was miraculously not canceled, even though it had an enrollment of two students, I fell back in love with teaching and writing. The following term, a ninja nun by the name of Sister Martha Ann Kirk took me under her wing and allowed me to participate in a grant she had just received to educate students and the community about human trafficking. I didn't know Sister Martha Ann all that well, so I googled her. It turns out the nun had spent a considerable amount of time in Peru and, just before I arrived on campus, she had published an op-ed in the *San Antonio Express-News* titled "The real shining path in Peru: Incarnate Word sisters," a beautiful piece describing the vital mission work her fellow sisters undertook despite the real threats of violence of 1980s and 90s Peru. I was inspired by Sister Martha's words and her passion, and dove into my projects with a renewed sense of purpose.

One year later, I had politely declined the government job, published another book (a co-edited monograph with my friend and mentor César Ferreira, on the collected works of Jorge Eduardo Benavides) and, on a personal note, I had gotten engaged to the beautiful and brilliant Bea in a secluded spot over-looking the mystic and majestic Machu Picchu ruins. My life had certainly gotten back on track. It was by no means perfect; I missed my two sons Lucas and Leo (aka los frikis), who lived in another state, but we always made the most of it when we were together. Nevertheless, I felt as though I reached a good place in every sense of the expression, and decided to get this labor-of-love anthology underway.

So, who's in this collection and why? That's the $64,000 question, isn't it? As someone who has spent almost two decades studying the ins and outs of the Peruvian literary scene, I'm more than aware of debates regarding who has access to the country's (or even international) publishing networks. Every time a new anthology comes out, accusations of argollismo, the practice of favoring one's friends, get levelled at the editor. For transparency purposes, I'm happy to declare that this book features tons of friends of mine: friends on Facebook and Instagram; some I've hung out with and shared a meal and one too many pisco sours; some I've never had the pleasure of meeting in person, but we've chatted online for years; and still others whom I've only just gotten in touch with to ask permission to translate their pieces. I consider them all my friends because they were kind enough to believe in this project and allow me to include their work here.

My main goal with this anthology is to share a stylistically-eclectic mix of wonderful short stories that provide a snapshot of some of the new writing coming out of Peru in the first two decades of the twenty-first century. I wanted the group to be diverse, showcasing authors who are both established and up-and-coming, and hailing from different parts of Peru, including those who stayed in the country and others who left to cast their luck in Europe or the United States.

In terms of themes, this collection explores a wide array of topics ranging from ruminations on the years of terrorism and state oppression (Diego Trelles Paz, Oswaldo Estrada and Jorge Eduardo Benavides); intimate portrayals of migration and its impact on individuals (Nataly Villena, Julia Wong, Francisco Ángeles and Carlos Yushimito); varying depictions of inequality and institutional crises (Gustavo Rodríguez, Claudia Salazar, Richard Parra, Fernando Ampuero and Luis Hernán Castañeda); pieces speaking out against the negative treatment of women (María José Caro, Karina Pacheco, Bethsabé Huaman and Romina Paredes); works exploring emotional and psychological trauma (Alexis Iparraguirre, Katya Adaui, Jennifer Thorndike, Yeniva Fernández and María Luisa del Río); stories that examine fragile masculinity (Juan Manuel Robles, Hemil García Linares, Gunter Silva and Pedro Novoa); and richly ambiguous and allegorical texts (Miluska Benavides and Gimena Vartu).

When selecting these stories, I didn't focus on whether the authors all belonged to the same generation, but the bulk of them are part of what we generally refer to as Generation X (born approximately between 1965 and 1980) and millennials (born between 1981 and 1996). The one major outlier is Fernando Ampuero, who was born in 1949 and is considered by many of the writers in this anthology to be an important mentor.

As with all collections, there are of course several notable absences. I wanted to translate all of the pieces myself, so if a work was already under contract or published elsewhere, I excluded it. Another arbitrary rule I imposed on this anthology dealt with the desire to only include self-contained short stories and not excerpts from novels. All the same, there is one glaring omission in the anthology that I want to highlight: I am missing authors who write in the other languages of Peru like Quechua, Aymara, Asháninka and more. Here's hoping my fellow San Antonio transplant and Indigenous Literature correspondent for *Latin American Literature Today* (LALT), Christian Elguera, will take on the challenge of compiling a collection of Peruvian stories from these traditional native languages.

Another testament to Peru's success on the world stage is the fact that it was the guest of honor at last year's Feria Internacional del Libro (FIL) in Guadalajara, the largest and most important Spanish-language literary festival. When it was announced that Peru would be the invited country, the outgoing government assembled a delegation of novelists, poets, illustrators, critics, historians, and other prominent intellectuals and cultural promoters. This group consisted of various familiar names, award-winning writers who'd not only achieved critical and popular success at home, but also abroad. Nevertheless, after the extremely divisive national elections and Pedro Castillo's administration took power, it quickly moved to modify the list chosen to represent the country in Guadalajara.[6] In so doing, Castillo's Minister of Culture, Ciro Gálvez, removed recognizable figures such as Renato Cisneros, Cronwell Jara and Jorge Eslava, and most importantly, he disinvited a trio of women writers who that year had published critically-acclaimed books: Karina Pacheco, Gabriela Wiener and Katya Adaui. The ensuing controversy caused several of the writers on both lists to decline the invitation in protest, leading to much public debate, especially on social media. The government held firm and released a statement standing by its decision, explaining that the second list was more representative of the country's diversity. As expected, the backlash persisted until Gálvez resigned and a new minister was named. In one of her first acts in office, Mirtha Vásquez offered up a third list in the hopes of repairing the damage the controversy surrounding the delegation had unleashed. For his part, Vargas Llosa decided to chime in, making some rather ill-mannered comments indicating that Peru would be sending a "pathetic" group that didn't contain any "real writers." The rollout and decision-making process for who would make the cut or not certainly involved incompetent missteps on behalf of both the previous and current governments, but Vargas Llosa's hyperbolic statements were scurrilous.

I wasn't part of the official Peruvian delegation, but among various activities in which I participated at FIL, I had the pleasure of moderating a panel with the last two Premio Nacional de Literatura (National Literature Prize) winners: Teresa Ruiz Rosas (2020) and Richard Parra (2021). Other prominent authors in attendance included Miluska Benavides, the only Peruvian selected in last year's Best of Young Spanish-Language Novelists chosen by the magazine *Granta*; Óscar Colchado, a prolific author who has won numerous prestigious international awards; and Jennifer Thorndike, a novelist who a few years earlier at FIL had been honored as one of the best Latin American writers born in the 1980s.

The anthology you hold in your hands features many of the authors on one or all three of these Peruvian delegations although I couldn't add every single big name possible, this is still a very selective group of writers.

I am excited to finally share these amazing authors and my interpretations of their work with the world. I hope it serves as an introduction to their compelling stories and that it spurs readers to explore other works and writers coming out of this Andean nation. Lastly, another goal of this anthology is to help the Peruvian diaspora in English-speaking countries (especially my fellow Peruvian-Americans, or as Daniel Alarcón famously said "100% Peruvian, 100% American") reconnect with the rich literary tradition of their roots. ¡Viva el Perú, carajo!

Gabriel T. Saxton-Ruiz

~~Green Bay, July 28, 2011~~
~~Lima, July 28, 2021~~
San Antonio, July 28, 2022

Notes

[1]   I still use the quote in classes because it's almost too perfect a description of the legacies of Peruvian presidents from 1985 to the present. Every elected president from then until now has been prosecuted since leaving office! Alan García (1985-1990, 2006-2011) committed suicide in 2019 right before being arrested on bribery charges. Alberto Fujimori (1990-2000) was convicted of corruption and human rights violations and has been in prison serving a 25-year sentence since 2009. Alejandro Toledo (2001 -2006) is currently living in exile in the United States, but Peruvian authorities have been trying for years to get him extradited to stand trial for collusion and money laundering. Ollanta Humala (2011 -2016) was detained along with his wife, Nadine, and placed under house arrest for several months on conspiracy and money laundering charges (their trial began in early 2022). Pedro Pablo Kuczynski (2016-2018) abruptly resigned from office and was later sentenced to three years of house arrest for corruption and bribery. Kuczynksi's Vice President, Martín Vizcarra, became his successor, lasting almost two years as president before being impeached and removed from office. His ousting and the naming of Manuel Merino as interim president, which many political observers labeled a coup, was met with mass demonstrations in the streets resulting in the tragic deaths of two protestors, Inti Sotelo and Bryan Pintado. Merino's short-lived five-day "administration" ended before it began, and Francisco Sagasti was designated president until the 2021 general elections. Sagasti, a dead ringer for the Dos Equis "Most Interesting Man in the World" pitchman, known for quoting César Vallejo's poetry in his speeches, had the unenviable task of leading the country at a time when Peru had the highest per capita mortality rate in the world from COVID-19. And then came the 2021 elections…

2   From 1863-1985, Peru's monetary unit was called "sol," but with inflation the government introduced the new currency "inti" which was equivalent to 1,000 soles. As luck would have it, this monetary policy change didn't produce the desired results and the inti only exacerbated the hyperinflation crisis. When Alberto Fujimori came into power in 1990, he instituted extreme austerity measures known as "Fuji shocks," lifting subsidies and price controls on many everyday items. *Peru: A Country Study*, edited by Rex A. Hudson for the Library of Congress, described the moment in the following manner, "[o]vernight, Lima became a city which had [...] 'Bangladesh salaries with Tokyo prices.'" The government changed the name of its currency to "nuevo sol" in 1991 and it stayed that way until 2015, when it dropped the "nuevo."

3   Here's the original quote from Trelles Paz's novel, "[...] lo único que veo es esta imponente edificación que me ensombrece por completo. Lo curioso es que espero sin saber qué voy a decirle si un día asoma y, a veces, he llegado a la conclusión de que, si alguna vez veo a Vargas Llosa sin uno de sus perfumados y atractivos guardaespaldas europeos, voy a agarrarlo a golpes."

4   And here are a few lines from the original Ángeles piece that summarize a key component of the plot, "una vez al año, el primer o segundo jueves de octubre. Año tras año, a partir de las diez de la noche, los siete u ocho de toda la vida llegábamos con botellas de vodka, quesos y cervezas, el anfitrión de turno encendía la pantalla con mucha ceremonia y, como si fuera un partido de fútbol, nos sentábamos a mirar la transmisión de la ceremonia de entrega del premio Nobel. [...] Y siempre teníamos la esperanza de que por fin el nombre elegante y sonoro de Mario Vargas Llosa fuera el que surgiera nítido de la garganta escandinava del viejito de pelo blanco y alisado. Y entonces sería el momento de saltar y abrazarnos y de hacer barras tribuneras y después ya veríamos qué hacer. Como sea, eso nunca ocurría y nosotros repetíamos las conversaciones del año anterior, siempre iguales mientras el viejito pronunciaba sin gestos el nombre del ganador (pasaron Coetzee, Le Clezio, Naipaul y tantos otros que nunca habíamos leído o de los que llanamente nunca habíamos escuchado hablar)."

[5] Among the more high-profile examples, Bryce Echenique's *El huerto de mi amada* (*My Lover's Garden*) won the Premio Planeta in 2002; Alonso Cueto, winner of the Premio Herralde in 2005 for his novel *La hora azul* (*The Blue Hour*, translated by Frank Wynne); the previously mentioned *Abril rojo* by Roncagliolo which won the Premio Alfaguara; Jaime Bayly's *Y de repente, un ángel* (*Suddenly, An Angel*) was a finalist for the Premio Planeta in 2005; and Iván Thays, too, ended up as a finalist in 2008 for the Premio Herralde for his novel *Un lugar llamado Oreja de Perro* (*A Place Called Oreja de Perro*). In the post-Peruvian-Nobel years, notable award-winners include Claudia Salazar and her novel *La sangre de la aurora* (*Blood of the Dawn*, translated by Elizabeth Bryer) with the Premio las Américas in 2014; Trelles Paz received the Premio de novela Francisco Casavella and was a finalist for the Premio Rómulo Gallegos for his 2012 novel *Bioy*, and his 2016 novel *La procesión infinita* was a finalist for the Premio Herralde; and lastly Jorge Eduardo Benavides won the Premio Torrente Ballester in 2013 for his novel *El enigma del convento* (*The Mystery of the Convent*).

[6] Peru's general elections in 2021 resulted in a runoff pitting Pedro Castillo, a leftist yet socially conservative teacher with Keiko Fujimori, the daughter of disgraced former dictator Alberto Fujimori. Vargas Llosa who had been vehemently opposed to the Fujimoris for three decades, implored his countrymen to not vote for Castillo believing his government would erode Peru's democratic institutions and ruin the economy. "Peruvians should vote for Keiko Fujimori because she represents the lesser of two evils and, if she's in power, there are more possibilities of saving our democracy," he wrote in the Spanish newspaper *El País*. Replicating the playbook of Republicans in the United States, Fujimori's supporters claimed voter fraud and launched several investigations that came up empty. Ultimately, Castillo was sworn in as president after winning by a slim margin of less than 1% or roughly 44,000 votes.

Morgana's Night

By Jorge Eduardo Benavides

Resignation, sighed Morgana as she arrived at the Plaza de Armas. From there she contemplated the yellow flash of the floodlights arranged in front of the Government Palace, the light and shadow effects weaving a sinister mesh above the menacing armored cars which slowly patrolled the perimeter of the square. A few soldiers smoked as they made their rounds between the army jeeps, green and motionless like lizards. Still hesitating on the corner, and rejecting the shiver of fear running down her back, Morgana zipped her light jacket and sighed again before deciding to continue. Bad move on her part to decline María Luisa's offer of a ride—do you want us to take you?—as she got into her husband's tiny blue car. Morgana could only manage a polite smile, no, she'd responded, it's just five minutes to the bus stop. Actually, she wanted to be spared the couple's predictable ensuing bickering. More than once she had seen María Luisa suddenly run to take refuge in the bathroom, and when she'd come out with swollen eyes, the annoying Señor Martínez would approach her desk, rest his bony fingers on the table as his face widened in a surly smile, more relationship problems, señorita? My God, shameless old creep, they'd remark among themselves as Martínez left, furious at the impudence. But the truth was things were not going so well for poor María Luisa and Antonio, they fought daily. In any case, it was rather enviable to focus on those fights and intermittent reconciliations, which turned out to be foolish in the grand scheme of things, but that for better or for worse seemed to distance them from that other thing that had begun to grow like a tumor in the country for a little over six months, captivating the public's attention, with no chance of respite from the cycle of explosions and blackouts and car bombs.

Morgana instinctively squeezed her purse when she passed a group of soldiers smelling of sweat, the features on their olive faces chiseled as if by a knife because of the tension. One of them flirted with her and the rest exploded in laughter, better to ignore them, they could ask for her letter of safe-conduct and cause problems, what had happened to Andrés was an abhorrent violation, she recalled somberly, but she couldn't avoid that damn sensation again when faced—unavoidably, as if it were not up to her—with the soldier's salacious gaze. She felt herself blush, the things you think about, idiot, and hastened her pace until she reached the edge of the square, leaving behind the voices, whistles, burning laughter. It was her own damn fault, what had been going on with her lately, that in a man's presence, sudden and seething bursts made her blood boil with something that could crudely be called…lust? At first, she had convinced herself that her body simply felt nostalgic for Andrés because Carmelo, well, what could you ask of a love that felt like it was made of butterfly wings? But after those solitary nights, the memory of which still made her suddenly blush, she realized it wasn't sex her body was asking for (or her soul, hell, what does it matter?). It was something else, violent and sweet like sex but more urgent, more…but whatever, the silly things you think about, Morgana, she said to herself, annoyed, as she glanced at the Government Palace, which seemed to be engulfed in flames due to the floodlights. What could be happening over there? Ever since the problems had worsened, that was all anybody talked about, in the newspapers, on the radio and television, on the buses and in the cafés, even at the office. Initially, she didn't give it much thought, she was still adrift in the crushing pain of what losing Andrés had meant to her, why would she care about what was happening in the world? She regarded the general commotion the country was experiencing from a distance, and only became darkly aware of what was really happening when her Tía Nena, so soft, so white, so indifferent to life for who knows how many years, said the other night that this would be the end, that there was nothing to do but wait, that you had to accept this with resignation, and her heart had shrunk like a fist because Tía Nena was stranded in the labyrinth of a silent and gelatinous senility she seemed to surface from on rare occasions.

When she reached the square with the statue of a motionless Pizarro mounted on his horse, the street was completely dark, not a single car in sight. Morgana could swear she saw shadows scurrying about then dissolving into the doorways of old houses that leaned against one another as if overcome by tedium. Behind her, the cathedral bells began to ring. No way could she cross the Plaza de Armas again and backtrack to Abancay. The soldiers would bother her again, they would get riled up at seeing her pass by once more, think she was attempting to excite them. Damn Señor Martínez, she thought out loud, how he'd insisted the two women conduct a pointless, time-consuming, last-minute inventory. Given what was happening in the country, why did he need that fucking inventory done? It had all been a sly trick to get her alone, because when they left the office, after María Luisa had gone with her husband, the old man caught up to her at the first corner, solicitous, a hint of that revolting smile of his, which Morgana had come to detest since she began working there, and offered her a ride, it was dangerous for her to walk the streets alone, the president was addressing the nation tonight and Lima would be completely shut down. Morgana looked him right in the eyes, disorienting the old man. No thanks, she said, unable to cloak the harshness of her words: she would catch the bus on Avenida Tacna and be home in no time. She could still hear Martínez's spiteful voice saying she'd never find a taxi, the city had shut down, she'd have to go on foot, anything could happen to her, it was dangerous to walk alone even with a letter of safe-conduct. She should have accepted the ride from Martínez, his stupid, inappropriate familiarity, his innuendo-laden chitchat, his covetous glances at her neckline whenever he approached her desk with some trivial request. This bothered Morgana at first, but later, and begrudgingly, she had to admit to a moist, hot flash that would leave her breathless as she made her way to the filing cabinet or María Luisa's desk, and Martínez's eyes would follow her with idle desire glinting behind his plain-rimmed glasses. It was uncontrollable, and she would be furious at herself for provoking it, but the heart of the rancor she reserved for herself, pulsed the suspicion that she wasn't provoking Martínez, it was that other uncontainable thing that took over her body, keeping her confused and irritable. Only Carmelo accepted her fits of rage, and that infuriated her even more.

Reaching the end of the first block, she had to contain her laughter because she'd been walking on tiptoe as if afraid she might wake the balconies and doorways from their dilapidated slumber. Unable to restrain a childish fit of curiosity, she pushed open a door to glimpse the entrance, for some reason she was drawn to those run-down old buildings converted into wretched, promiscuous tenement houses. A dense, distant mist floated in the air, and if not for the muffled whispers that reached her, she might have thought the place was abandoned. In the dark of the humble courtyard, two attentive yellow eyes shone brightly, following her with interest. Here, kitty, kitty, Morgana whispered as she approached the animal. The cat stealthily jumped onto the staircase landing and, from there, continued to observe her with utter calm. In the vast depths of those attentive eyes, Morgana thought she caught a glimpse of eternal life, and suddenly, she felt captivated, faraway, fragile. She had no idea how long she stayed there. From afar, she could hear spluttering tanks slowly converge on the Plaza de Armas, like caterpillars. She rose sluggishly (not realizing she'd been squatting), walked through the entryway door and continued along the deserted street, thinking how late it had become and how hard it would be to find a bus or taxi; Mamá and Tía Nena would be waiting with dinner ready, anticipating the president's address about to be broadcast on all radio stations and television channels. She pictured her mother sitting in front of the TV with a bowl of soup she'd hardly touch, the meticulous looping of a crochet hook in Tía Nena's hands, her incessant old-lady mumbling, her gaze devoid of color and the almost abstract smile she'd offer when Carmelo would greet her, because by this time he'd already be home, Morgana thought, annoyed, as she crossed the short street that ends at Santo Tomás de Aquino school. A pay phone stood on the corner, and Morgana thought about calling home to say she was on her way and under no circumstances should Carmelo come to pick her up. But she walked on by, it wasn't that much farther to the bus stop at Avenida Tacna, to that other familiar darkness after the fifteen-minute trip to her house, where Carmelo would be waiting with his small, red, ex-seminarian mouth, how horrible, and his lethargic mannerisms, his love of lace and mothballs (what did she see in him? My God, what did she see in him?). Always smiling and polite as he languidly sweetened the cup of tea Mamá would offer, fussing over him, before sharing the story of her misfortunes: how Papá left us a thousand years ago, the hardships that trapped us in that tiny house on Avenida Francisco Pizarro some five hundred years back, surrounded by criminals and other lowlifes, the widow's pension that barely afforded enough to eat, the helpless bundle Tía Nena had become after her second stroke, she'd been like a mother, like a grandmother, and now she was more like a sack of old bones, she'd never say that but still. What must you think of us, Carmelo, all I do is bother you with my sad tales. Carmelo would trip over himself like every other identical evening, please señora, the things you say, we must resign ourselves to the situation, resignation above all else, you see what's happening in this country. And he'd clasp her hand warmly, sweetly, as she pretended to watch television. I detest you Mamá, I detest you Carmelo, I hate that complicit resignation in which they burrow like worms. But she wouldn't say anything, she'd remain silent until Mamá would say, oh my, how time flies, it's time to put Tía Nena to bed. Between the old woman's trembling footsteps and my mother's humming while washing the dishes, that act rehearsed to the point of abomination will end and the next will begin, Carmelo's prudishness, his innocent eyes, the kind-hearted smile he gives Morgana when her mother comes to say goodnight and no staying up too late watching TV because we've got an early start tomorrow. They're young and can stay up late, while she, on the other hand: well, see you tomorrow, Mamá, Morgana would say, huffing, as the echoes of the spiritless house melt away. Her mother's predictably sad undressing. Tía Nena's coughing, throat clearing, and endless chirping whispers from a room laden with images and dripping candles. Then another type of silence would emerge between them, and Carmelo wouldn't even try, he wasn't capable of it, never has been, oh, why bother, Morgana muttered as she clutched her purse to her body. A white rage ambushed her, imagining how she'd have been only too happy to toss the ring, which María Luisa openly admired after noticing it glint on her finger, into the trash. She'd almost rather have Martínez's fixed gaze on her cleavage for all eternity.

But today will surely be different, Morgana thought while slowing her furious pace. Today, just like every other day since this madness that nobody could explain and that has the country on tenterhooks, she put herself in the government's hands. Her mother will alter the tenor of her trivial complaints, venting the myriad fears that chase and harass her like everyone else. She'll seem relieved upon hearing the doorbell and will announce in a gentle, full voice that Carmelo has arrived, what news does he bring, my oh my, and she herself will go open the door, come in, come in. And poor Carmelo won't know how to console, he won't know how to transmit that steely calm, with which he usually relates to things, but now, for the first time, seems to have vanished, ever since the news began to come out on TV. They're not telling us the whole truth because chaos would erupt, things are never as they seem, he said a few nights ago after the news broadcast, and upon hearing that banal cliché that betrayed a hint of cryptic know-it-allness, Morgana became infuriated like never before. She grabbed a past issue of *Vogue* from the magazine rack and absentmindedly thumbed through it, I hope the chaos comes, she said spitefully, but in this country, people no longer have the guts to even take to the streets, despite what's going on, everybody's talking about resignation, and that disgusts me, you know? She turned to him, still at the other end of the sofa, and as she gazed at the doglike stupor in his aquamarine eyes, she felt her chest shake with joy: there'll be civil war or worse, she continued almost gleefully, ignoring Carmelo's babbling. What does civil war have to do with this, honey? Why is what's happening the government's fault? But Morgana had already let a damn grudge take over her body, as if what was happening in the country had something to do with Carmelo and his larval love, with Mamá's rusty litanies and Tía Nena's trembling shuffle through the dark corners of the entire house, with old Martínez and his lascivious attention, which made her feel hot all over, just like the fleeting glances from the men she'd passed lately. But it had nothing to do—and that was the strange, curious and amusing thing about it— with sex: her body lit up like a torch, that was all, and even though, after crying incessantly over Andrés's desecrated corpse, she thought at first it was the urgency of wounded, isolated desire, she was now certain it was something else, almost like the opposite of desire, a different hunger that left her fatigued morning, day and night: the need to be a different Morgana, to usurp her own identity, to rail at herself, like Carmelo said could now happen to the country at any time. Nobody was to blame for what was happening, and that was dangerous in the long run.

Morgana reached the last block of Conde de Superunda almost without realizing it. No lights shone on Avenida Tacna either and suddenly, the unnerving sensation of being the only person out on Lima's deserted streets shot through her chest. By now the president would be addressing the nation, yet another anodyne message urging calm and useless civility, which has until now been deployed to deal with events of the past few months. She found it odd though, the complete absence of patrols, not a single soldier on Avenida Tacna: starting at Santa Rosa bridge, the street was stunningly desolate. The unusual spectacle of the absence of traffic didn't disturb her as she first thought it might, rather it felt like an unknown sort of freedom that propelled her to walk into the middle of the road and stop, fully aware of her solitude.

Walking home didn't bother her in the slightest. She was almost glad she had to, knowing that Carmelo and her mother would soon begin to check the time, over and over, calming each other with comforting words incapable of disguising the panic that the clock had by now struck ten and she still hadn't arrived. Her mother would be the first to break down, Carmelo would offer to go look for Morgana, but of course, that was nonsense, he didn't own a car. They'd have to wait until the president had finished his message for the city to slowly resume its routine of fear, the nighttime traffic would start to flow, little by little, and the buses and taxis would return. People would begin to file into the streets to comment on the speech, on the useless precautions the president had repeated before the cameras and microphones of every media outlet, the directives that'd already been circulated ad infinitum by the National Security Council, established when things started to occur. Resignation, bah.

Back on the sidewalk, Morgana reassured herself she wasn't scared, but accepted she'd have to call home to let them know she was fine and to just sit tight. The first pay phone she found a few blocks away ate one of the tokens she kept in her purse, and she could barely make out her mother's broken voice on the other end of the line. Morgana, is that you? You won't believe what happened… She didn't have time to utter a complete sentence, and blurted out a profanity when she realized she was abruptly disconnected. What was her mom trying to tell her? One of those trivial matters that always flustered her, I'm sure. Having only one token left, she walked several blocks in search of another phone, and finding none in working order, she begrudgingly decided to head back to Santo Tomás de Aquino. She didn't care at all for that open alleyway several doors down, and though the street was also quite dark, at least she didn't feel the dull suffocation that seemed to await her when she reached Conde de Superunda.

After a few minutes of walking, she spotted the pay phone and mentally rehearsed how she'd respond to her mother's worried reprimands: no, Mamá, she'd wait patiently until the traffic was back to normal to grab a taxi; if Carmelo insisted on coming to get her, she'd stop her cold, she was a big girl and knew how to take herself, it made no sense for him to grab a cab when it would be easier for her to just get one on Avenida Tacna rather than Francisco Pizarro.

Morgana would never have been able to say whether she saw the man before she reached the corner or not until she was at the phone booth. In any case, she'd remember he was neatly dressed and had the confused air of someone unfamiliar with the area. With no hint of alarm—for she's sure this is how it occurred— she heard the man address her. Receiver in one hand, the other grasping the sharp edge of a comb she found in her purse when she took out the token, Morgana turned to him. He wasn't very tall, black hair flattened against his skull by an old-fashioned pomade, eyes shining with embarrassment that foolishly moved her, forced her to smile as he confessed to being lost: yes, it was his first time in Lima, he was staying at the Savoy, had gone out for a walk and couldn't find his way back, he said contritely. His warm voice contained a hint of roughness or virility that momentarily unsettled Morgana. He smelled of fine cologne and wore a sport coat that was certainly expensive. A foreigner, she assumed upon hearing him speak. Yes, of course, Morgana heard herself say, she'd walk him to the hotel, it wasn't too far, she'd just make her call and they'd be on their way.

And then the first peculiarity occurred: unexpectedly— or rather, yes, of course it was expected that her mother's and Carmelo's nonsense would ridiculously come together, she just wasn't prepared to deal with it—Tía Nena answered and said they'd left without saying where they were going. "They fled," the old woman added as if thinking out loud, but what else could be expected in her state. After a pause in which Morgana couldn't find a thing to say, Tía Nena asked did she want something, hijita, and then who was calling and for whom. Don't worry, Tía, she said, but the old woman had already hung up. Her mother never left Tía Nena alone, something was wrong.

The second peculiarity, after distractedly responding almost in monosyllables to the stranger's chatter as they made their way to the hotel, was finding the lobby empty, and no matter how often they rang the doorbell, the mirrored wall at the entrance only returned their own bewildered reflections. It was as if all of a sudden everyone had fled, Morgana thought, then quickly dismissed the idea, what idiotic thoughts came to her mind, she was beginning to feel frantic. If you'd like, you could use the phone in my room, the man suggested most awkwardly, which Morgana appreciated. I don't know much about what's happening here, the man added gently, but if it's anything like the interior, it might be dangerous for you to go without getting in touch with family first, señorita. Thank you very much, but no, she said, knowing she was blushing, and couldn't make eye contact because, damn it, that strange heat was coursing through her body again. But it wasn't sex, she calmly repeated to herself, it was that other thing howling inside of her without respite, rhyme nor reason. Thanks, but don't worry, she said with a polite, firm handshake.

Back on the street, Morgana felt her shoes grow exceedingly tight and after thinking about it for a bit, she decided to take them off. On the corner, shoes in hand and no more telephone tokens—she did have money on her, but it wasn't much use at the moment—she felt helpless for the first time that night. She pictured Carmelo and her mother, his fear tawny and soft, Mamá's sobbing in the taxi, they must have gotten one by now, almost an hour had passed since she left the office and the presidential message would've likely ended by now. The awful silence of fading night felt odd, she thought. The most logical thing would be to walk back to the office, where else would her mother and Carmelo go. She continued barefoot for one block and then another before putting her shoes back on. She decided to head toward Avenida Emancipación, but halfway there, abruptly changed her mind, figuring that route would be longer and she was already tired. The absolute silence in the streets seemed unreal, as if the entire city had up and left, like thousands were rumored to have done in recent days, avoiding border patrols and strict airport controls. It was absurd, things in Lima weren't as serious as in the more remote provinces. And that was a crazy thought anyway: a city doesn't move just because, out of the blue and in silence, as if the inhabitants had sworn a vow of stealth. She was exhausted and stopped for a moment not far from the Plaza de Armas. To her surprise, the arrogant glow of floodlights pointing at the Govenment Palace, which had escorted her when she passed by the soldiers over an hour ago, was gone. She thought it'd be better to cross Jirón Ica and head back toward Conde de Superunda, it was always preferable to walk on a familiar street.

She barely had time to be frightened when she noticed a shadow zigzagging furtively on the opposite sidewalk. The hand buried in her purse registered the comb's tiny teeth stabbing her sweaty palm. She stood there not daring to move, looking obstinately towards the place where she'd noticed—or thought she noticed, no longer sure of anything—the shadow disappear.

She kept walking, sticking as close to the wall as possible without changing her pace, but after a minute or an hour, she'd lost sense of time, she was certain of being followed. Don't turn around, Morgana, she said to herself, don't turn around, but the fear or whatever it was that had stifled her breathing was stronger than reason and she whirled around. This time she clearly saw the shiny polish on a pair of shoes in that flash before the shadow appeared to plunge into an alleyway. She immediately thought of the man from the hotel, and asked, her voice cracking, is that you? Please, tell me it's you, she insisted, about to scream when she realized a response would not come. Absurdly, she thought about Tía Nena rocking herself in front of the television that had been turned off, immersed in her crocheting, mumbling, this would be the end, you had to accept this with resignation. Carmelo and her mother must be at her workplace by now, realizing their foolishness. It would've made more sense to slowly retrace her likely route home. But how could they know she was now far off her usual path? She pictured an intricate gameboard of alleyways, the patient series of trial and error that chance would have maliciously mapped out, and gave up looking for them.

With hysterical hands, she pulled the comb out of her bag, gripping it as if it were a razor and looked down the alleyway where the shadow had disappeared. It couldn't be that peaceful, old-fashioned foreigner, he seemed so courteous, so incapable of something like this. Carmelo would've gently told her things are never as they seem. She'd have wriggled away from his chaste caresses, only to wonder why she'd accepted him, why she'd given in to that anodyne love, to the promise of a life she was sure would involve more abnegation than satisfaction. Lately, everything had the fate of resignation, people didn't talk about anything else but abnegation and resignation since news of what was happening in the country began to spread, since all of this madness had begun to grow and grow. Even in the overwhelming silence that enveloped Morgana when she started to run, she thought she could hear herself scream at an ominous feeling of guilt, without receiving any answer. At some point, she suspected she might be back on Conde de Superunda, but her crying and the turbulence of blood rushing to her ears didn't allow her to think. She banged on several doors, but nobody answered. She almost wanted to face her attacker out in the open, but when she turned to listen to footsteps inching closer, she found only the dark end of the deserted street. She'd never know how far she ran or down which streets, but after an exasperatingly elastic stretch of time that seemed to rotate on its axis, at long last, she felt the hinges of a decaying door give way, catapulting her into an entryway where time seemed to stand still and filthy. She realized she was back at that desolate house where she'd stopped earlier, who knows how long ago, thanks to the cat. She called for help, whispering through each of the worm-eaten doors flanking the colonial courtyard. She covered her mouth to contain the sobs that were growing louder and louder. No one was around. Feeling light-headed, Morgana thought Tía Nena must have been telling the truth, her mother and Carmelo had also fled, how else could she explain they hadn't come for her. And how could she explain that no one had heard her screams as she raced through the dead streets knowing she was being followed? As she leaned against the rotting wooden staircase, a dizzying wave of fear crept over her again, forcing her to stand and stumble. Feeling the damp steps under her feet (she'd lost one shoe while running and violently tossed the other), she reached the second floor of the rundown tenement, the faint clarity from the street filtering through the open courtyard door. No one was on that floor either, the doors boarded up, just one more staircase left, even more rickety and narrower. From it, as slim as an Assyrian effigy, the cat spied her.

Hunched against the second-story railing, not daring to look down into the cobblestone courtyard, Morgana heard stealthy footsteps treading through the dark. Yes, she thought, trapped in the absurdity of it all, as she climbed the staircase that led to the rooftop, the president must have finished his address by now, but nothing would change, nothing would alter the never-ending resignation that hit her like the night wind as she emerged from the staircase: the clean slice of Lima sky that received her was almost a relief. But she could still hear footsteps approaching.

Hand Tricks

By Karina Pacheco Medrano

With their backs to the sun, they had pedaled for almost two hours before reaching the detour, which took them away from the paved road and the horns of cars heading to the countryside that Sunday in March. As they advanced along the dirt trail, noon light filtered in through the trees, hurting the cyclists' eyes, making the path unfold like a snake tattooed with light and shadowy stripes. Every now and then, Elsa and Jano would hold hands; they'd let go at the potholes as their eyes focused again on the chiaroscuro route. They were close to their destination when a great thrush's droppings landed on Elsa's head. Although most of it fell on her helmet, a few greenish droplets slid down her forehead. She braked suddenly and was about to skid into a pine tree, but immediately took control of the handlebars, and overcoming her laughter, began to look for a tissue.

"Gross! It smells horrible!" she cried out and poured water from her bottle onto the tissue to wipe her forehead.

"Consider it a good luck omen," Jano said, laughing.

"Yeah, good luck, sure," she replied and, while taking out another tissue to clean her helmet, recalled her upcoming trip.

Jano suggested they relax for a bit under the tree where he rested his bike. Elsa hesitated for a second, then noted they'd be at the secluded water hole in no time. She was still on her bike, supporting it between her legs, opening and closing her hands and fanning her fingers. After gripping the handlebars, sweat had soaked through the mesh of her gloves.

"Are you sure you don't want to stop here for a while?" Jano insisted.

"No, no. It would be better to get there in one go."

"Okay."

Jano got back on his bike and began to pedal furiously. Elsa stayed put, observing the flexibility of his legs, the strength of his buttocks. She took her time before setting off.

When she thought she was near the water hole, she spotted the trail Jano's bicycle had left in the grass and followed it, making her way through drooping willow branches. At the water's edge, he was already undressing. Elsa got off her bike, laid it on the grass and let her backpack fall to the ground.

"Slowpoke!" Jano yelled and jumped in the water.

She hurried to take off her clothes. Both of them began to swim, but didn't dare dive. Despite the sun and heat at that time of day, the water was cold, almost freezing because of its glacial source. Trying to keep their heads afloat, they embraced, feeling the current carrying minnows that brushed and nibbled their legs. Elsa shivered, not knowing whether it was because of the cold or contact with these odd creatures.

"They're too small to be afraid of," Jano said, trying to put her at ease while holding her by the elbows.

"They're annoying."

"We're not going to let them annoy us, right?"

Elsa could see waves in his eyes. She hugged his neck and kissed him, treading water and kicking the minnows that hadn't stopped bothering her.

"I think I'm going to explode," she said upon pulling back from Jano's mouth.

"Well, explode then," he replied and began kissing her breasts.

"Should we go ashore?" she whispered.

"Not before we go under," he dared her.

Elsa didn't want to be left behind. She never wanted to be left behind. She liked that Jano saw her as always ready to meet and exceed his challenges, and took pleasure in pushing her body to its limits.

"One, two, three!" Jano counted.

They took a breath and dove. In the deepest water, they could make out the almost transparent minnows that had been lurking around them. The fish seemed blind, and on their bodies was a single, snowy white dorsal fin that swayed erratically every time Jano or Elsa tried to catch them. The two were running out of air. Elsa couldn't last any longer, her head resounded with pain. Resurfacing, she began to swim to shore. She was about to touch the brownish dirt when she felt Jano climb on her back.

"Let's do it like turtles," he proposed, and without letting go, pushed her forward until her jaw rested on dry land.

Elsa adjusted to receive him. He squeezed her breasts as if wanting to bite them with his hands. She groaned. Jano covered her mouth and began to penetrate her. In three days, she was set to board a plane that would keep them apart for six months. Elsa wanted to cry. She wasn't sure if it was their impending distance from one another or the pain she was enduring at the moment. As if he could interpret her feelings, Jano muttered:

"Pleasure has to hurt you, honey."

Elsa thought she saw bushes in the forest shaking, and believed she heard footsteps moving away. Rabbits with big ears came to mind; she imagined the rabbits had been spying on them and had now run off in search of a small cave to copulate. Jano removed his hand from her mouth.

"Now I want you to squeal like a pig," he said.

Elsa stopped thinking about the rabbits, lost herself in the roar pounding on her back; she felt as though a stranger were on top of her, and though he was hurting her, she didn't complain. She just wanted to please him, allow that turtle man to break her resistance. She squealed.

"More," he commanded.

"I no longer have a shell."

"Don't talk," Jano said and pulled her back by the hair.

Elsa tried to move at his pace, but found it difficult. Her feet were frozen, still in the water. She fixed her gaze on the bushes, slightly swaying despite the absence of a breeze. Tears ran down her cheeks.

As if he could see her face, Jano ordered her to close her eyes. She didn't understand how he knew her so well. Although she obeyed him, embarrassed because someone might be watching them, she couldn't stop thinking about those withered bushes, moving as if they were healthy and fresh. Jano let go of her hair and began to kiss her shoulders, neck and ears. Elsa started to laugh, her insides inflamed. A scream. She wasn't sure if it came from her throat or if it had been Jano. He collapsed on top of her.

"I can't escape from you," Elsa confessed, raising her jaw.

"Of course not."

She began to feel suffocated, but made no effort to break away from him. The feeling of her crushed breasts overwhelmed her, and she worried they'd remain flaccid. He rolled over beside her.

"I'm sorry," he said. "I've been a bit tense."

"You've never been scared I won't want to return from my trip?" Elsa asked, turning around.

"At first, yeah. Not anymore."

"And you've never been scared I might fall in love with another man?" she added.

Jano put his hand on her vagina.

"And you're not scared I might start a life with someone else?" he responded. She shivered. "If you come back, I'll wait for you. If not, well, no. In the end, it all depends on you."

He said that and got up, took the towels out of the backpacks and lay down on his. Elsa rinsed off in the water to remove the dirt and pebbles that had stuck to her body. She then stretched out beside him. They held each other's hands and gazed up at the sky.

There they were again, in the hidden water hole where they had met a year ago. Jano had been coming down the hill at full speed and his bike skidded off the curve. His chain flew in the air. As he looked for it in the bushes, he spotted a swelling pond that was probably just a shallow spring in the dry season. He made his way through the brush and reached the shore. It didn't take long for him to remove his shoes and wade into the water up to his knees. Those clear waters, although quite frigid, seemed to him ideal for swimming or even scuba diving. As he returned to the dirt path to secure his bike, he spotted three cyclists approaching. They weren't wearing helmets; when they got closer, he saw there were two women and a man. From a distance, he fixed his attention on Elsa, on her tan legs pedaling with purpose, unlike her companions. When they were in front of him, he recognized the other girl and greeted her as if they were good friends. He wanted to stay with them, wanted to stay with Elsa. He didn't care that the guy had been introduced as Elsa's boyfriend. He told them about the accident, but preferred not to tell them about the water hole he'd just discovered. The three got off their bikes and began to look for his chain. It was Elsa who found it, tangled in a ball at the base of a cactus. When she handed it to him, Jano took advantage to stroke her fingers.

Once the chain was repaired and in place, he went back up with them to the esplanade stretching out at the top of the hill. There they settled under a tree and shared a meal. A short distance away, a plane was descending into the city. Elsa and her friend commented how impressive it was that the place remained so rural, despite being in an urban sprawl zone. Jano pointed out that the area was untouched due to its proximity to some archaeological ruins.

"Really?" asked Elsa, attentively.

"Yes, there's a tower and several other ruins up there. Let's hope they stay protected," he answered keeping his eager eyes on her.

Elsa grew troubled and turned to her boyfriend, but he'd fallen asleep with a hat over his face. "He went to bed really late last night, poor thing," she explained.

The three of them had just started the second year of a Master's program, but her boyfriend worked nights, so the bike ride had worn him out.

Elsa suggested they head up to that tower. Jano immediately stood. Ada, her friend, looked at them strangely, as if she could sense in the air that she'd be a third wheel, and indicated she'd stay behind to read.

"I haven't studied for tomorrow's exam," she added.

The hill wasn't steep, but Elsa could feel the man's increasingly heavy breathing behind her.

"This isn't Incan. It's probably more than a thousand years old," she noted when they reached the foot of the tower.

"How do you know?"

"I just know," she replied.

He ran his fingers over the moss that covered the stone base; he looked up and noticed the top of the tower was crumbling.

"Elsa, when we head down that slope, I want you to look at where we were this morning, and I want you to remember it well because I'm as certain about something as you are that these stones were placed here more than a thousand years ago. There," Jano signaled with his arm, "hidden in the forest, is a secluded water hole. I tell you that a year from now, I'll be there with you. You're going to be mine. And I'm never going to be too tired for you."

Elsa didn't answer. She stared at the outline of the forest, turned and hurried down the path until she reached the tree where her boyfriend was.

Within three months, she had begun dating Jano, secretly at first, then openly. One early morning in late August, they set off on their bicycles to the water hole, but by then the dry season had come and water was scarce, barely up to their waists. They made love on the towel Jano spread on the grass. Elsa shivered; they'd been together a short time, but already she felt she couldn't live without him. He always showed that he knew her like no one else, always pushed her to experiment more with sex. That morning, he'd put a handful of grass in her mouth and hadn't let her speak until, between gasps, she ended up swallowing it.

Her ex-boyfriend had dropped out of the Master's program, and she felt guilty. Lying next to her, Jano told her to stop.

"He must've had several reasons for dropping out when he was almost done," he argued. "And, in any case, Elsa, we're not kids anymore. We've all had to deal with breakups."

He gave her a kiss and stood up. He took dry dirt in his hands, mixed it with water and formed clay. He made two little figurines, a man and a woman, and had them walk along the shore, jumping up and down. Then he threw them into the water.

"They should go diving," he said. "We'll come back when the backwater rises."

Elsa began to laugh. He kissed her again and, with the clay that was left on the ground, began to smear it on her breasts. "I'm going to mold you too," he said. "You're going to be more delicious. Ready for the oven." "You can kill me if you want." Elsa heard herself utter those words and shivered. But Jano was already on top of her.

That morning, she told him she'd been awarded a scholarship for an internship in Mexico. He stayed silent. For the first time, she detected vulnerability on his face.

"It'll be six months, right?" he asked.

"Yes, I start in March. We still have seven months."

He grabbed a handful of dry grass and dropped it to float on the water.

* * *

And there they were again at that same water hole, March again. The rains had been abundant, and they found the backwater wider and deeper than they'd imagined. In three days, Elsa was to fly to Mexico.

"When you come back, if we pass the long-distance relationship test, we could think about living together," Jano proposed.

She smiled, put the towel around her shoulders and walked over to the backpack to get something to eat. She was sprinkling salt on the avocados she'd brought as a snack, when again she thought she heard strange noises coming from the bushes.

"Did you hear that?" she asked.

He lowered his soda can and listened for a moment. Taking another sip, he walked over to her as she stood still.

"It could be the wind, it could be rabbits; in the end, it could be ten thousand curious onlookers, but what does it matter?" he said, taking an avocado. "We won't see each other for a long time, let's enjoy the moment."

She hugged him, was going to kiss him, but Jano turned her face down and began to smear avocado all over her. He tossed the remains into the water and penetrated her without pause. It hurt, but she didn't complain. She didn't want any fights to ruin their farewell days. He'd told her that perhaps he could schedule his vacation three months early to go visit her. That plan made her happy.

Suddenly, in the distance, she thought she could make out two outstretched hands in the grass. She tried to raise herself up on her arms.

"Jano, stop for a second," she said.

He didn't seem to hear her.

"It looks like there are hands back there," she insisted.

"Stop it, Elsa," he said, clearing his throat and pushing her head down to the ground.

Again she felt numbed by his weight, but after spilling into her with a cry, he kissed her hands. Jano smelled her hair and fell asleep. Slowly, shifting her shoulders, Elsa got him to turn over and covered him with a scarf.

Sitting on her towel, she stared out at the water. A blue-tailed bird flew over the water hole. She turned her head to follow its course, and then she saw them again. She got up, took two steps and realized she was in great pain. She took two more steps. She screamed.

Jano jumped to her side. The sun shone on a woman's bruised, outstretched hands. As they got closer, they discovered her face down, messy hair covering the side of her face; even so, they revealed a swollen cheekbone, a black eye.

"Is she…sh-she dead?" asked Elsa, stuttering.

He took the woman's pulse.

"She's dead," he confirmed.

"Maybe she was alive just a minute ago!" Elsa sobbed.

"Don't say that. We would've heard her."

Elsa recalled the rabbits she'd imagined earlier. White, black, green, pink rabbits, with very long, pointed ears and short, round tails, were fleeing through her mind.

"Jano, I told you there were hands!"

"Calm down, Elsa. Touch her skin; it's cold. She was certainly dead before we got here."

"Maybe she was dying, and we were fucking like nothing was happening!"

"Stop it now! How could we have imagined something like this?"

She was a twenty-nine-year-old woman from a minor shantytown just over an hour away. The district police recognized her right away and immediately issued an arrest warrant for her husband. The night before, their neighbors had heard another one of their fights, and in the morning they took care of their three children, who were crying, not knowing where their parents might have gone. In recent years, she'd filed several abuse complaints, but later withdrew them.

"Don't feel guilty. This was bound to happen sooner or later," the officer in charge of the case told Elsa.

"See?" Jano remarked as they left the police station.

She looked into his eyes, and again he seemed like a stranger.

"Stop blaming yourself for everything," he said once more at the airport.

"No, I won't blame myself." She gave him a quick kiss and went to her boarding gate.

The plane began to climb above the city. From her window, she could make out the southern highway full of cars mid-week, and bridle paths, forests, some ponds and backwaters. Her breasts were scratched and the touch of her bra hurt them. Her jaw was injured, too. She hadn't realized it until she saw herself in the mirror at the police station. The girl traveling beside her pointed to the wound.

"Who did that to you?" she asked.

Elsa blushed, squirming in her seat.

"I did it without realizing," she replied and went back to gazing out the window. The city was already far away. She began to say goodbye. Her hands played against the glass, waving from left to right, right to left.

The Artist

By Gunter Silva

After teaching my classes at the university, I usually took the Tube and went home, but on that sunny day I felt like grabbing a coffee at an outdoor café. That was when Isabel approached my table and, with those eyes the color of carbon, asked if she could join me.

"The seat's free," I said.

She sat down and crossed her legs, and with one hand picked up her cup of espresso. It seemed as though she didn't like me watching her.

"Espresso," she explained, raising her cup as if making a champagne toast. "When I want coffee, I want coffee, and when I want milk, I want milk."

I nodded and, just when I was about to start reading again, she began talking.

"So you're the professor…"

"Santisteban," I said. "Santiago Santisteban."

"I'm Iza. I'm guessing you teach art."

"Pleased to meet you, Iza," I replied, and held out my hand. "Yes, that's right. I'm an art professor. How'd you know?"

"Well, not many people read *Domenico Ghirlandaio: Artist and Artisan* at two in the afternoon."

Iza was young and beautiful. She could've been one of my students in the "Renaissance Sculptures, Paintings and Drawings" course I was giving at Goldsmiths. Similarly, this meeting at the café could have been by chance, but Iza wasn't my student and the meeting that afternoon was not by chance, as I would find out much later.

Summer

Iza belonged to the generation of Peruvians who believe that if they take an English or IT course, they will rise out of poverty. She spoke English perfectly and dressed in such a daring fashion that I thought I was looking at a European girl and not a compatriot.

"I'm from Lima," she said the second time we saw each other.

We had met in downtown London to see a film, as part of a Spanish film festival. The plot was about two newlyweds who buy an apartment in a building still under construction, but the work gets delayed because they were building it illegally. This causes problems between the couple.

"The people are very caricatured," she said as we walked to the bar.

"I thought they were very real, they were done well," I replied. It had been a while since I'd been out with a woman; perhaps I said that just to say something. To make conversation.

"The director of the construction company was portrayed as this villain, but nobody's all bad. Woody Allen films are the best," she announced, her index finger pointing straight in the air.

"Neurotic."

"'Neurotic' is the only thing you can think of to say, Mr. Professor. Woody makes his films from such a personal viewpoint, so intimate, so philosophical…"

"If you've seen one Woody Allen film, you've seen them all, Iza."

"Jazz, anti-intellectualism, the city as a concept, irony, love, humor," she went on. Listening to her talk with such passion, I wanted to tell her that it would've been a pleasure to have her as a student in my class. Instead, I said:

"There are only two themes in his work, Iza: religion and sex. And they repeat ad infinitum."

We went into the bar we'd been looking for and ordered drinks and a bag of salt and vinegar chips. Sitting on a sofa covered in cherry-colored velvet, Iza started talking about art. I was surprised of how much she knew about the topic and how passionately she expressed herself. On my fourth beer, I felt as if a violent storm were rising in my stomach, then moving into my veins until my hands felt like ice. Later I noticed my shirt was soaked with cold sweat. That was the night I realized I was falling in love with Iza, when the words froze in my throat and my mouth couldn't find the right things to say. I attempted various moves, but all were frustrated attempts at seduction. At one point I tried to get her on the dance floor, but she shook her head. I felt like a novice schoolboy. Like a man who goes to a pub, throws six darts and ends up finding all the darts have landed on the floor.

Patrons were coming in and out of the pub all the time, but luckily the shadowy bar hid my shame and my wet shirt. After a while, I saw Iza look at her watch and then jump up.

"Sweetie," she said, rubbing my shoulder. "I've got to meet someone…but we have lots to talk about."

She said goodbye with a kiss on my cheek. I stayed for one last beer. After a while, it occurred to me that I was a man sitting alone at a table full of empty bottles. The remains of a date.

* * *

Iza called just a few days later. I was in the middle of teaching, so I put my cellphone on silent and carried on talking about the importance of portraits in Venice during Paolo Veronese's time. The cell vibrated twice more like a cicada trapped in my jacket pocket. I felt a strange happiness. At noon, I called her from the university cafeteria.

"Is that how you treat your friends, Mr. Professor?' she scolded me. "Not answering your phone is very bad manners."

"I'm sorry," I said. "You called right in the middle of lecture."

"Imagine if I'd had an accident and was calling to tell you my last words," she replied.

"Iza, don't be so dramatic."

"You'd have missed my last words, Mr. Professor. The things you only say when you're at death's door."

Much later, I suggested we have dinner at my place on the weekend, and she promised to forgive me for not answering her call. I thought for a few moments about what I'd make for dinner, and her voice brought me out of my daydream.

"Agreed, Mr. Professor?" she asked in a solemn voice.

"It's a deal," I said and gave her my address.

* * *

As it was already late, I went shopping. I'd decided to bake salmon with vegetables and boiled potatoes. I also had a bottle of white wine chilling in the fridge. After shaving, I put on Gillette moisturizing cream. I never used aftershave, but at that moment I thought about buying some. I looked at the clock and realized I was running out of time. I then ran to the bedroom and decided on a polo shirt, thinking that a button-down would make me look too formal and old. Obviously, I wanted to look younger.

At five minutes past seven, the doorbell rang. In all my thirty-seven years, I'd never met such a punctual Peruvian. I opened the door, and there was Iza with four white roses wrapped in paper. I improvised and put the roses in a Coca-Cola bottle.

"Water, Mr. Professor," she said.

"Water?" I asked, surprised, "I have red or white wine."

"No, I meant water for the roses. You don't want them to wilt, do you?" she asked, raising her eyebrows. "And a beer for me, thanks," she added right away.

Iza took the bottle of beer and started exploring the apartment. "Nice place," I heard her say somewhere behind me. I poured myself a glass of wine and turned on the oven, making sure I set the right temperature. When I got to the living room, Iza was examining my library.

"There's an obsessive order here," she said, without looking away from the shelves. "Your books are painstakingly organized by subject, author, date…"

I took a sip from my glass.

"In fact, Mr. Professor," she continued, "this whole place is laid out like a museum."

"It's a small space," I said, trying to find an excuse, as if I were embarrassed for keeping my own apartment tidy.

"I didn't know you liked poetry," she said, and right away demanded I read her something. Her eyes were as deep as wells and her lips were moist like humid air.

I walked toward her and picked out a book of poetry by José Watanabe I had been thumbing through that very morning, and began to read in a low voice.

> *Its dissolution*
> *traced svelte and primordial beings*
> *with the fleeting density*
> *of quartz crystal*
> *and suddenly they were pure forms*
> *like a mountain or a planet abruptly ravaged.*

How impossible to love what so quickly fades.
Love swiftly, said the sun.
And I learned, in her perverse and ardent kingdom,
to honor life:
I am the guardian of ice.

I wanted to tell her, with the poem, that life flies past you. That we were there to enjoy every moment of our existence, that if we were going to love each other it had to be at this very moment, that what I most wanted was to have dinner with her, get drunk with her and end up in bed, submerged in her body.

"Watanabe," she said, unsurprised.

"Have you read it?" I asked.

"Yes, but he's not my favorite poet," she said. "There are two types of poets, Mr. Professor. Those who write like adolescent girls and those who write like the gods."

"Watanabe is a god."

"No, adolescent girl," she said.

"Dylan Thomas."

"Another adolescent girl," she replied.

"César Vallejo," I said at last.

"Like the gods," she said.

After a while, we ate dinner. Iza said she loved fish, claiming she was very Mediterranean in that way.

"You mean you're a typical girl from Lima?" I corrected her.

"I can't live without eating seafood and salad with olive oil," she said, then raised her beer and drank from the bottle. "The food in Lima isn't as light as Mediterranean cooking," she added.

That night we talked not only about food, but also about painting and art. It was clear those were her favorite topics. On those subjects, she seemed as comfortable as a fish in water.

I remember asking whether she had an art degree. She said no, she'd never stepped foot in a university classroom, which I found odd.

While I did the dishes, she headed for my study. When I went in, I found her with a pile of books on Giotto, Rubens and Rembrandt; she also had a few old essays I'd written some time ago. The essays were on drawings from the thirteenth through the eighteenth centuries.

"You're going to have to let me borrow all of this, Mr. Professor," she said.

By then, I'd gotten used to being called *Mr. Professor.*

I told her there was no problem as long as she looked after them and gave them back once she was done.

"Cheers," she said, looking at some books which had grown discolored with the passing of time. Then she opened one and showed me a few of Rembrandt's drawings. It was a large book and she held it with both hands, like someone carrying a baby.

"The best poems, Mr. Professor, were written like each stroke by one of the great masters," she declared.

Autumn

Iza disappeared like a puff of cigar smoke, until one day she called and arranged to meet up. She gave me an address, 33 Sumatra Road in North London. It was a beautiful street, affluent, with cherry and magnolia trees losing their leaves with the change of season.

Once there, I was surprised to find that Iza had a husband; she'd never mentioned that detail. After so many years in London, I'd gotten used to people being honest. When I confronted her, she said, "I never lie, Mr. Professor. I invent truths and hide information." The husband was slim, with the nose of a wise man. His name was Alejandro, but she called him *The Artist*. Apparently, Iza had a thing about giving people nicknames. Alejandro seemed to be a sad man; he had the look of an artist whose work doesn't sell, who hasn't achieved fame and suddenly realizes his creativity is rapidly consuming itself, like wood on a bonfire.

I spotted my books, spilled across a table. I tidied them up and found amongst them a newspaper cutting. It was dated one week before I met Iza. My photo was printed alongside an interview I'd given to a reporter from *The Guardian* for the cultural supplement they published on Sundays. My name had been highlighted in green. I understood then that my first meeting with Iza hadn't been by chance.

I've never thought life is governed by fate, that everything is part of a plan to which we must submit.

Standing in that flat in West Hampstead, I felt like a pawn waiting to be moved to the next square.

"Are you all right?" Iza asked.

I was sure that if I said no, she'd disappear from my life forever.

"Yes, I'm fine," I said. "A beer would go down well right now, Iza."

"Mr. Professor, your wish is my command."

She returned from the kitchen after a bit with three beers, and we toasted. I don't remember why we toasted, but that was the least of my worries. Right away, Iza showed me the drawings Alejandro had done. They were copies of the Old Masters.

To be honest, they were good copies. His sense of harmony was sincere and noble. I imagined I was there to assess his work, that this was the game I was destined to play. I looked at Alejandro. His skin was hard and cracked like wood left out in the sun for a long time. Until then, Alejandro hadn't said much. He had settled for following me with his gaze.

"They're very well drawn," I told him. "But for them to be Rubens originals, you'd have to make these dark lines as fast as you can. That'll make your drawing more expressive."

Alejandro took a Giotto drawing out of a file.

"What about this one?" he asked, timid.

"Shorter, sharper movements will give the body more volume," I said.

That afternoon we had a few beers and chatted about art. They showed me fourteen drawings in total, which I analyzed and gave my sincere opinion. I don't know if Alejandro began to trust me because of how openly I spoke to him, or if it was the beers that had relaxed him, but suddenly he began talking to me as if we were old friends.

"If you put a piece in a museum, after a while it becomes authentic," he said.

"But if the drawing is a fake, you'd be committing a crime," I pointed out.

"No, Mr. Professor," Iza chimed in. "It's not a crime to draw in another artist's style. It isn't, as long as you don't sign it as Giotto or Rubens."

"I must admit, they are very good copies, Alejandro," I said, looking him in the eye. "Your sense of harmony is that of a true Old Master."

"It's thanks to patience," came his answer to my praise, adding, "nothing to do with talent."

As I was getting ready to leave, three of Iza and Alejandro's friends arrived. They were Russian, with scruffy three- or four-day beards, but expensive clothes. They also brought a case of vodka.

"Don't go," Iza said. "The party's just getting started."

Everything that happened next is terribly hazy. I remember having danced with Iza a few times, the vodka going down our throats like water. I wasn't used to drinking just vodka on ice, and my head started to hurt.

Alejandro lay down on the sofa with a book on painting, looked at the images and drank slowly. I guessed he was thinking about the details, trying to understand the meaning of those paintings.

"The glory of art," he mumbled from the sofa. At that very moment, I saw the Russian named Kuznetsov put his hand on Iza's inner thigh. Her red dress was pulled up, and I could see her underwear, the delicacy of her thighs. Iza was wearing jewels and festive accessories; she resembled a flamenco singer. I looked back at Alejandro and he was asleep, or pretending to sleep. He seemed like a man who'd never experience life with faithful women and sensible men.

I got up and went to find my coat. I couldn't stay a minute longer after what I had witnessed. I felt as if a hard pit had lodged in my throat and my chest began to hurt.

I opened the door, and Iza appeared behind me.

"Why are you leaving?" she asked, making a sad face. "Perhaps you're bored, Mr. Professor?"

I didn't answer, kept walking.

"The Artist's work will steal the show," I heard her say from a distance.

"Losers," I muttered as night fell and the city slept.

Winter

At the beginning of November, I went to a temporary exhibition on Goya at the National Gallery. There I met Stephanie, a Ph.D. in Baroque art from the Sorbonne. Stephanie was a kind woman who enjoyed looking feminine and loved shoes. She owned as many shoes and books as would fit in her apartment, and luckily for me, she shared my interests in art and poetry. I thought we would make a good couple and, even though I had never believed in love at first sight, things seemed to work out for us both.

I started travelling to Paris every two weeks. I stayed at her place near Rue Duperré. She had an apartment with balconies and planters full of lilac flowers that cascaded over the window sills.

She lived there with her cat Loulou and all the little plants she kept. We'd often go to museums, cafés and bookshops until our feet wore out or night descended; afterward, we would make love in silence, and she would fall asleep with her glasses on, trying to read a novel.

Stephanie never grew overexcited debating philosophy or having intellectual conversations, like the other French women I knew, nor did she try to stir up revolution in some third world country. She was enthusiastic about looking at paintings and sculptures, and found it emotional to contemplate the things we take for granted, such as walking or breathing.

By the end of January, thanks to Stephanie, Iza had become just a vague memory. Stephanie might never have Iza's lavish beauty and sensuality, but she was a strong, faithful woman.

One Sunday, when I was returning to London by train, I came across a photo of Kuznetsov in the paper. The article said that three Russians had been arrested in Madrid, responsible for selling seven fake drawings—five Giottos and two Rubens—to the Prado museum. I read the whole article with my heart pounding a thousand miles an hour. I didn't find any mention of Iza or Alejandro. I felt calmer.

Days later, I mentioned the incident to Stephanie. It was six in the evening and the sky still held its bluish hue. We were having dinner at a little café in Montmartre.

"How could they sell fake drawings to the Prado?" I wondered aloud.

"We live in a world where originality doesn't exist. Only authenticity," Stephanie answered, opening her mussels in a wine and scallion sauce.

* * *

Two years later, I was invited to a conference at Columbia University in New York, where I'd present my latest paper on the philosophy of light in Caravaggio's works.

That summer afternoon, I dressed plainly, in a white shirt, black tie and jacket. After my presentation, which lasted almost two hours, came applause, followed by cocktails and hors d'oeuvres. One of the waiters, a Colombian, came and filled my empty wine glass.

"If you're looking for a good time, Doc," he said, holding out a card bearing an address, "this is the place to go."

I had achieved an important milestone in my career and that night I felt I deserved to celebrate in a big way, as one should. My ego had inflated like a hot-air balloon with all the congratulations from people I knew and praise from various colleagues at American universities. For the first time in my life, I didn't want the night to end.

At two in the morning, quite drunk, I found the little card in my jacket pocket. It said that in addition to sex, they offered massages. The place wasn't far from where I was on Seventh Avenue in Manhattan. I decided to walk there on that starry night; for some strange reason, I didn't want to return to the solitude of my hotel room.

I arrived at the building and looked at the card again to make sure I was at the right address. I didn't want to wake up some hysterical New Yorker in the middle of the night. I pressed the button for the right apartment number, and the electric door opened with a click.

"Eighth floor," someone said through the intercom.

I took the elevator. My reflection in the mirror revealed a wrinkled face, creases that gave my face an air of class, a certain status.

The doors to the floor-through apartment opened, and Iza stood there to welcome me.

"How nice to have you here, Mr. Professor," she said with a smile on her lips.

That night, Iza confessed that The Artist was not her husband. They'd met at a brothel in La Victoria, a poor neighborhood in Lima. Alejandro paid her to sit for him once or twice a week. He drew Iza's naked body as if he were insane, like a man in a trance.

"He never spoke much," she said. "He took his work very seriously."

With the money from the Prado, she'd set up this business, an ancient and noble one. She had seven girls working for her, said she'd started a while ago with only two.

"Manhattan isn't just a set for Woody Allen films," she said. "It's the perfect place to take money off rich guys, Mr. Professor."

We made love in a room with red lights and ceiling mirrors. On one wall was a poster of *Annie Hall.*

"Want to do it without a condom?" she asked.

A long silence ensued, then Iza stopped and turned on the regular white lights.

"You're not a client," she said, pointing at me with her index finger, adding, "We don't need the red lights anymore."

She must've thought it was the bright lights that caused my eyes to fill with tears.

Here, We Survive

By María Luisa del Río

I used to work with indigenous groups on the Cenepa River, and one time a young couple passed through the mission. They were nomads, who stopped in our village so the woman could give birth, and then be on their way. But two babies were born, and that worried them. The father walked in front of the mother, with blowpipe and arrow, and looked out for which bird or mammal he'd aim at to feed his family. He couldn't carry his children because he needed to hunt to provide for his family, or be on alert, day and night, to protect them from jaguars. The mother needed to keep going while breastfeeding, and had to keep both babies in front because if she carried one on her back, that child could die from a venomous bite from some animal she couldn't see. So, the parents decided to leave one of the babies behind, the smaller of the two, the skinniest one. The baby they saved had a better chance of survival because he was stronger.

We saw how the mother abandoned the weaker child on the path, laid out on a bunch of large leaves, with no clothes or diapers, as they belonged to an uncontacted tribe. Little by little, we approached to pick him up. But she turned and yelled at us in her language: "Leave him there, he's my son! If you want a baby, have your own! Don't take him!" And we had to leave him. We cried, prayed, and ultimately obeyed.

A Picture with Rocky Balboa

By Francisco Ángeles

The only thing I want, Rocky told me, the only thing I want in life is for a Peruvian journalist to come to Philadelphia and film a television report about me. I want everyone in Peru to see me dressed up as Rocky Balboa, hat to one side, and jacket, tight-fitting across the chest, as I climb the steps of the Museum of Art with Bill Conti's "Gonna Fly Now" playing in the background, and the sounds of violins and drums, *trying hard now, it's so hard now*, I'll raise my arms as I reach the top and gaze at the city from above, Rocky said that afternoon, over a couple of beers at the decaying Pasqually's Bar & Pizza.

I had met him thirty minutes earlier, while absent mindedly watching a baseball game I wasn't really interested in, since I've never been interested in anything remotely linked to what they call "American culture," I don't even like getting drunk and staring at the TV on a depressing Sunday like that one with the mild weather of a typical mid-April evening. I was drinking my second mojito at the bar, they'd put less alcohol than the first, and was about to leave, check in hand, but took too long to pay because I had no idea where to go next, my only distraction the last few days had been reading all about the robberies at cafés in the area, where they still hadn't apprehended the suspect in this peculiar and captivating case. I took one last sip of the mojito and was finally about to leave when this guy dressed as Rocky entered the bar and immediately identified me as Peruvian, something in my features or posture giving me away. "Peruvian?" he asked in Spanish, alluring and smiling, pointing at me while waiting for my response. I gave a slight nod, suspicious, like someone who's about to get scammed, perhaps that's what gave me away as Peruvian, the unassailable gesture of one who knows the importance of being on the defensive because you could get scammed at any moment. Rocky winked at me, satisfied by my response, and said he'd buy me a beer. I accepted on the condition that he let me get the next round. Rocky smiled again, at ease, relaxed, in control of the situation, adding that we should grab a table to talk more comfortably. He turned to the girl at the bar, a curvy blonde jiggling a cocktail shaker with tattoo-covered arms, winked at her and asked her to bring two Budweisers to a table in the back. And soon we were sitting across from one another, I felt a little tense despite the two mojitos, which hadn't fully taken the edge off or left me firmly on my axis, the only position from which I seem to exercise some control, though I know that deep down you never exert control over anything, much less me, a nameless employee at a pet grooming salon, an immigrant who has given up the ambition that never really existed, an immigrant who didn't leave his country to do better but to fail quietly away from Peru, without anyone fucking with him. The next morning I would have to get up early to spend another day grooming animals that had a better future than mine, cleaning their snouts and brushing their fur, so monotonous and mediocre it crushed me, even though my revenge was minimal and harmless, no big revolutionary plan, just a surprise needle prick in the back of a pug or a Boston terrier while I styled their hair or rubbed their skin with a sponge, fuck this shitty dog, I thought, laughing at my sad consolation, definitely a pathetic, weak response to a system that I nevertheless participated in. I'm pretty sure that's what I was thinking about when I was finishing my second mojito and this guy dressed as Rocky came through the door, who didn't ask me the typical questions, where I'm from in Peru or how long I've been here or what I do, as if he were one of the few to understand the triviality of these facts, their absolute insignificance and irrelevance and, worst of all, their undeniable substrate of melancholy. Maybe that's why he made a good impression, the Balboa getup seemed to highlight his detachment from the country, and I liked that, an emotional distance which didn't mean things were going well for me here, actually things were going very badly, I'm fed up with the United States, there's no American dream, no nightmare, I just don't give a shit. But that doesn't mean I'm thinking of moving, people in Peru don't understand, they think if things go wrong, it's normal for you to want to go back. But nothing could be further from my plans, I'm not going back even if deported, and if ICE grabs me and pushes me onto a plane, I'll jump out mid-flight, they'll never see me there again, that's one of the few things of which I'm convinced, I no longer belong to that country, I won't ever return, and it seemed Rocky felt the same way, and based on that simple coincidence, we could see eye to eye. No other reason justified the unhealthy pleasure of getting together with other Peruvians, not to get drunk and sing the national anthem, nor to shake my body to an Afro-Peruvian *festejo* or an Andean *huayno,* not even to watch the national team matches together, but to reiterate that we'll never go back, that even if things go to hell around here we'll never return to the country where things went so badly for us, the same as here, it's true, but there it would've been different. I was thinking about all that, ready to shoot my unpatriotic venom, when Rocky started talking about his dream of appearing on Peruvian television. A Sunday variety show, he specified, those programs are very popular, that's how my friends from Pueblo Libre will see me, folks who haven't heard from me for years since I left Miami and came to Philadelphia chasing Shawna, a voluptuous, neurotic and loudmouth black woman who had a tremendous ass and worked as a dancer at the Pink Pussycat, near the airport, on 36th Street next to the Palmetto Bridge. I used to work at the airport basically illegally, I washed taxis with a Uruguayan who aspired to become an airline pilot so he went to the airport every day, as if convinced his simple presence near the counters or runways would lead him to being hired by American or United even though he'd never even practiced in a simulator. We washed taxis from eleven in the morning until five in the afternoon, and at the end of the day we went for a beer at the Pink Pussycat, and that's how I met Shawna when her name wasn't Shawna yet but Destiny, bad name, I should've predicted it, meeting her screwed up my life, although actually, I was already screwed up, washing taxis at the Miami airport at twenty-eight was not exactly the image of the successful Peruvian migrant. The thing is, Rocky said after a brief silence, at the Pink Pussycat she got used to my lack of funds and to seeing me show up hoping to be granted a free grope in the slowest hours, when hardly any clients were there, we'd go to a corner and she'd let me touch her tits and bite her nipples, which looked like a couple of prunes, black and fleshy, sometimes she'd let me touch her down there, put my finger in her and shake it for thirty seconds that seemed like an eternity, glorious fingers that I'd then press against my nose so their smell would explode in my brain and then I'd carry them to my mouth to lick them furiously, my tongue like a whip, eyes closed, I'd lick like a desperate man, I don't think I'd ever been so proud of a part of my body as I was of my index and middle fingers every time I'd pull them out of Destiny's mysterious depths. She quickly realized I admired her, her panther move-ments, her thighs and buttocks, her dancing moves, I admired her as one admired a singer or an actress full of talent and fame, not a Pink Pussycat dancer, and then when she got tired of Miami and decided to go back to her hometown, I came following her and that's how I ended up with her in Philly, living at 53rd and Osage in early 2001. Rocky picked up his bottle of Budweiser, took a long drink, and then kept talking. Of course she'd never taken me seriously, she put me up in her apartment, but deep down she always saw me as a loser, it wasn't worth making plans with me, I can't blame her, I'd just been a random client who'd become infatuated with her, not one who wants to bite her clitoris or tear her ass up, nor one who falls in love and proposes to her, but a client who admired her, idolized her, deified her, my goddess of ebony and oil, black hole of the universe with whom I shared a bed for a couple of sensational weeks, going from the majestic eternity of the kingdom of heaven to plunging all the way down into the last ring of hell, until one day Shawna got bored of me and kicked me out of the apartment without much preamble or drama. Depressed, no money, no place to go, I rented a miserable studio on 57th Street, north of Market, rough zone, bullets whizzed in the dark, but I had nothing to lose either, if one of those nights the drug dealers hit me in the forehead it would've been a glorious end for me, which is ultimately what it's all about, not a good life but a glorious end, don't you think?, Rocky asked me, the empty bottle spinning between his fingers. And then a couple of weeks after Shawna kicked me out of her house, while I was walking around West Philly, dejected, reflective, downcast, afraid of possibly ending up like one of those beggars who finish the day playing chess in Malcolm X Park under the glow of streetlights, I decided I needed to get back on my feet. And for some reason I remembered that as a boy I'd seen *Rocky* in the filthy Ídolo movie theater in Pueblo Libre, and the inspiration I needed exploded in my brain. I went to the Clark Park flea market to spend my last dime on a good hat and black jacket, I knew what I was doing, a symbolic act to end my failure, and once I put on my new wardrobe and looked in the mirror, I felt very Rocky Balboa, ready to punch life and knock it out, Rocky said, looking at me askance, as if debating whether that last metaphor had exceeded the limit of obviousness. But I didn't say a thing, I finished drinking the nasty Budweiser without looking him in the eye, and then heard him say that one afternoon, dressed in his new outfit, he walked from 57th Street to the Museum of Art. It was

November or December, Rocky said, cold, but not snowing like in the movie, and I was moving toward the museum at a good pace, feeling a definitive transformation was beginning to happen inside me. I was to climb the steps of the museum without stopping, which wasn't difficult, Miami had prepared me for physical work, Shawna too, those mattress workouts ended up being much more intense than the hard hours washing taxis, much more exhausting and overwhelming, so I began to climb the steps listening to the melody of the song in my head, *trying hard now, it's so hard now,* and then I reached the top and raised my arms like Rocky, feeling like a winner, a competent, successful guy, a guy who knows how to overcome adversity, a better guy than me with whom I was suddenly merging. I turned around, ready to give the city a defiant look from above, just as Rocky had done in the movie, happy, satisfied, improved, when I realized that a small group of Japanese tourists were staring at me, amused, and they called me over to take some pictures with me. And in a second I recognized the signs of destiny, I immediately understood the paths my transformation was taking me along, and so I responded with a boxer's speed and said "five dollars," still jumping, warming up my body, shaking my arms, and then my confidence grew before the Asians' hesitant silence and I added "five dollars each," with a certain affectation that I thought sounded just like Stallone's. They looked at me, murmured indecipherable words, impenetrable oriental wisdom, and I, afraid of their refusal, interrupted them and said, *Rocky is your friend. Ten dollars for all.* And they immediately seemed convinced and took out their big cameras to photograph themselves with me. I raised my arm in triumph, I showed my right bicep, well protected by the jacket so its scrawniness would go unnoticed, and then I squared my shoulders in a fighting position, and in the last photo I pretended to jab one of the Japanese tourists's cheekbone, when ordinarily, I'd have really given it to him, under his slanted eye, but I held back because these were no longer times of resentment, the worst was behind me, my new life was beginning, Rocky said, and sipped his Budweiser, said his new life had given him greater satisfaction than he could've ever imagined. No other activity in my life, not in Lima or in Miami or in Philadelphia, not the goals I scored as a child in Candamo Park, not even the glorious lovemaking I nobly engaged in with Shawna, will ever be able to compete with that feeling of immortality buoying me up every morning as I put on my Rocky outfit and jogged off to the Museum of Art to wait for tourists to come take pictures with me, Rocky said and paused before continuing. I took advantage of the silence to head over to the bar, ordered two more beers, returned to the table in the back and prepared to keep on listening. They'd just inaugurated the Rocky sculpture at the museum entrance, he continued, raising the second bottle of beer, the mayor unveiled it, quite an event, as if the city had been waiting for this tribute to its favorite son, which was not Benjamin Franklin or Bill Cosby, not even Grace Kelly, but the underdog fighter who emerged from the tough Philadelphia streets and rose to the top of the world. And then, when the stone figure began to appear in iconic photographs of the city, next to the LOVE sculpture and the Liberty Bell, the flow of tourists grew dizzying, and with it my popularity spread through travel forums. In the sections devoted to Philadelphia, comments like *don't miss Rocky!* or *take a picture with Rocky Balboa!* began to appear, and when my photo was posted by some random person, I felt really happy and proud, as if it were me who had gained fame and glory, the boy from Pueblo Libre who played ball in Candamo Park achieved international celebrity status in his late twenties posing for pictures with tourists, his fists raised, his firm thighs climbing the steps, his triumphant smile, and so I became more and more well-known, and began to earn more money, I charged five dollars a photo, I could easily take home a hundred bucks a day, everyone wanted a photo with Rocky Balboa, and if I were lucky I could make a hundred and fifty or even two hundred bucks because some fans were willing to pay an additional fee to get Rocky's preferential treatment, a pat on the shoulder, a firm hug, and for the girls, a little kiss on the cheek, one of my fans even offered me five hundred dollars to let him suck me off behind the museum, next to the Schuylkill River, camouflaged between the trees. Five hundred dollars wasn't bad, so I accepted on the condition it be a short blowjob, the guy had a certain resemblance to Rocky, though not as much as me, he was the son of Italian immigrants who saw in Balboa what he would've wanted to be but never was, the same old story, nothing out of the ordinary, a fan who dreamed of sucking Rocky off and nobody better than yours truly to fulfill his fantasy. I'd only been working outside the museum for four or five weeks, I thought the future would offer multiple opportunities like that one, but if I hesitated, I wasn't going to get anywhere. I needed more money, I was becoming a star, I had to get a nice car and a dozen fancy suits for my nights out on the town, money was my main concern, so I accepted the offer, and without making a big deal, we left our spot next to the idol's statue, one after the other and headed out behind the museum, he left first, and I caught up with him five minutes later, five hundred dollars, he told me, close your eyes for a while and think about something else, like, remember the night you knocked out that black guy Mr. T, you saw the sweat on his bald head and hit him with such a blow that to this day he still regrets squaring up against you, I dropped my pants, the guy knelt in front of me, mouth open, rubbing his hands together, the sound of water from the Schuylkill running through my ears, the image of Mr. T didn't materialize, from the beginning something was not working, surely that shitty Italian thought he'd find himself someone more endowed than what I could modestly offer him, I hadn't anticipated his expectations were going to be that high, but the guy didn't give up so easily before the obvious discrepancy between fantasy and reality, and he began to suck me off skillfully and with a sense of urgency, even desperation, and as a result of such painstaking labor, to my surprise, and also annoyance, my mighty member grew to its maximum size, which wasn't entirely negligible but not enough to satisfy the expectations of my greedy client, who looked at me, resentful, sad, disappointed, he'd been about to reach for glory and his dreams collapsed, and so he pulled my cock from his mouth and said *fuck you, man!,* he looked at me with rage, yelling *you aren't Rocky! Fuck you!,* he repeated, on the verge of tears, motioning to my dick with his chin, as if the missing inches were conclusive proof of my falsehood, and as if the sudden revelation had instantly annihilated his life's dream of giving Rocky Balboa a blowjob. And so I quickly pulled up my pants, my erection remained, which made it difficult for me to adjust, convinced he was going to understand me, I said *my five hundred bucks, asshole* in Spanish, but the poor guy didn't look at me, he was tearing up, uneasy, he looked so disappointed I almost succumbed to a paternal impulse of tenderness, I almost went to hug him, which would've been awkward considering I still had a hard-on, but suddenly, as he got up from the grass, the fucking pussy unexpectedly brought out a crushing fist that slammed right into my chin. I should've predicted that a true Rocky fan knew how to box, that fist left me knocked out on the grass with my dick in the air and dreaming of my childhood in Pueblo Libre, and I stayed like that for a long time until my gallant erection had definitely subsided and my penis was more shrunken than ever. But that smallness didn't lower my morale, it empowered me to keep fighting. I put my elbows on the grass with much effort, Schuylkill's running waters lent a strange feeling of unreality, and I made my way under the shadows of the trees, dizzy, bruised, humiliated, but always fighting, I returned to my job and continued taking photos with tourists, Rocky concluded, in a slightly different tone of voice, perhaps a tinge of bitterness when pronouncing those last phrases.

And then he grew serious, a certain unconcealed disappointment emerged from his whole body. Things were apparently going really well, he said, lowering his voice, I was earning money and feeling valued, which is ultimately what we all want, isn't it?, he asked without waiting for an answer. I'd gotten that recognition from the first time I dressed up as Rocky, he told me, and that's why I didn't realize that behind that armor, my real self was becoming more and more unprotected. I noticed the first sign of catastrophe one morning when another guy dressed as Rocky showed up at the museum intent on competing with me for the tourists' business. I won't ever be able to describe the feeling that hit me when I laid eyes on my enemy, arms raised, hat hiding locks of blond hair, surrounded by a group of tourists who'd never know the magnitude of the invisible disaster unfolding before their eyes. I'll never come close to describing the feeling of collapse, of absolute pain that I experienced in that moment. It wasn't simply a money problem, or even a question of what's usually called dignity. It wasn't about fighting for my job or showing that I had the nerve to defend my territory with a knife. It was something else, Rocky said, jaw trembling in the yellow light of Pasqually's, something much deeper, related to an ancient sense of being invisible, spectral, an interchangeable body, a tool for work and exploitation, and just when you think you've overcome that dark stage, reality soon shows you your mistake and puts you right back at your point of origin. That happened to me when they left me without my Rocky outfit, and I became a nobody again. I became, if anything, what I never ceased to be other than in appearance, he said, serious, not looking at me, and then he remained silent and motionless, in a state usually defined as profound silence, I could almost hear it, almost hear the silence even though all around us other drunks were laughing out loud and the television was blaring with the baseball announcer's voice. And then I looked at Rocky, attentive, careful, diligent, and my eyes came upon a huge scar that crossed his throat from one side to the other. And he, who seemed to be waiting for me to discover the mark inscribed on his skin, fixed his gaze on me with an intensity that gave me chills, and without moving a single muscle in his face, without allowing himself the slightest gesture, raised his right index finger, started at one end of his throat and slowly ran his fingertip along the scar, fingertip against skin as if to confirm its path, pretending to slit the skin's surface once more. And when he'd finished the short route, he traced the same path, but this time much faster, less than a second from one side to the other, as if he wanted to remember the wild impulse of slitting someone's throat. He began to speak again, but his voice sounded cloudy and gloomy, a voice that hides more than it reveals, or maybe that's how it seemed to me because I didn't want to know the details of what he'd called his catastrophe, ruin, the end of a wasted life, a guy from Pueblo Libre who works dressed up as Rocky at the entrance to the Philadelphia Museum of Art, why did he end up there, how many things happen for a person to end up locked in a space he never wanted to reach, I wondered, disoriented, in that interval of absolute silence, the ominous scar reflected in the center of my pupils. But after that ephemeral interval, Rocky kept talking, my fleeting distraction hadn't disrupted the flow of his story, he said he was still the tourists' favorite, perhaps because they recognized my photos from the tourist guides, and despite the fact that two other Rockys roamed the area, each backed by their own crew of photographers and vendors selling t-shirts, keychains, postcards and other souvenirs, I saw them working as a team, with that corporate and entrepreneurial spirit, so different from mine, less interested in money than in reaffirming I was indeed who I appeared to be, the two groups were working in harmony, they must've reached an agreement or perhaps they were a single group pretending to be two in order to monopolize the market more efficiently, the same company that sells two products pretending to compete with each other, the possibility made me panic, Rocky said, confirmation that everything was going to hell, which is why I began to suffer from insomnia, fear didn't let me sleep, there's nothing more terrible than fear when it's experienced in its pure state, when it's felt inside, impregnating organ tissue, a paralyzing, unbearable feeling, not the consequence of reasoning or any mental process, but the pure feeling of panic, those were the worst days of my life, the prelude to a catastrophe is often worse than the catastrophe itself, the impossibility of avoiding what hasn't happened yet increases the anguish, I knew something was going to happen, time was ringing in my ears, there was nothing I could do but let it pass while waiting for my destruction, Rocky said, the scar on his throat, the smell of grease wafting from the oven where they reheated pizza slices, a slight unease that threatened to turn into something serious, I felt nauseous, scared, disgusted, but Rocky kept talking and said that one sleepless night he decided he needed a gun. I had to resort to the black market, he indicated, we immigrants, especially the illegal ones, don't have the right to bear arms, the black market was the only alternative, I thought the phrase had multiple meanings, an illegal weapon not to defend myself but to precipitate an outcome that was unavoidable anyway. A surprise attack, I'd kill two or three, then I'd shoot myself in the chest, a single shot in the heart, Rocky's costume stained with blood, it was an extraordinary end, I don't know how I didn't think of it before, I was trembling with emotion, a dignified, heroic death, it'd be headline news, dying in Rocky's skin, don't you think it's an unbeatable ending?, he asked me without waiting for an answer. They told me I'd meet the seller on a Friday, he continued, they were going to give me an address in Point Breeze. I waited for confirmation of the exact time I was supposed to show up, but the day before something very strange happened. It couldn't be a coincidence, those things are by no means a coincidence, Rocky said, serious and concentrating, as if calculating the slim possibility that chance had indeed intervened. The day before, just one day before acquiring the gun, the other two Rockys and their crews started to leave their sites earlier than usual, a bad sign, something was going to happen, but I didn't want to stop it. At that time of year, I worked until six, when darkness finally prevailed, but that afternoon the last people vanished from around the museum before five. My heart was pounding in my chest, I knew that my only alternative was to disappear before the shadows finished merging. But I stuck to my spot, Rocky said, staying near the museum entrance even though the cold had chased away the last remaining patrons. I started to warm up my body, uppercut the cold air as if in a fight, looked at the time now and then, five thirty, cold and dark, I wouldn't move until six o'clock, if it struck six I could go home and consider myself saved, that's what I thought, punching the air to combat the cold but above all the fear, five forty, I climbed the steps, it might be the last time but I didn't feel any emotion, I was surprised by the detachment with which I faced my end, I raised my arms as I'd done thousands of times in the last few years, but it did nothing for me, five fifty, I started to slowly go down the steps, waving my arms to keep warm, when I saw them coming toward me. There were three of them, holding baseball bats, Rocky said, they were crossing the avenue with an air of seriousness that terrified me. They didn't seem especially geared up to fight, they just approached me with bats in their hands. They'd reach me in two minutes, I could already feel my fractured bones, the excruciating pain of the multiple breaks inside my body, they pushed me out behind the museum, I think they were surprised by my lack of response, we stepped into the woods, the Schuylkill slithered whispering in the dark, I was thrown onto the grass and my clothes were forcibly removed. They ripped off my vest and hat and pants, and left me naked, Rocky said, bitterness gleaming in his pupils. And then they tore everything with their hands, my clothes reduced to shreds disappeared among the plants, a savagery that left me paralyzed, I endured the scene with dignity and resignation, I didn't escape, I was no coward, I faced each blow with integrity despite the pain and infinite sadness it caused me to recognize the sound of my own bones breaking after the violence of each strike. They didn't hit my skull, they took care to carry out the massacre slowly, they were just beginning, I hadn't received more than six or seven blows but I already felt my broken ribs, and then one of them, I don't know why, maybe because he couldn't stand the cruelty of the punishment they were subjecting me to, dropped the bat on the underbrush, and from his jacket pulled a knife and held it to my throat. A show of humanity is how I understood it, being slaughtered in those circumstances was a sign of infinite mercy. But immediately, one of his accomplices, noticing his partner's unexpected movements, hit him hard with the bat just when the knife began to perforate my throat. I thought the blow had saved me, that nothing had happened to me, the pain in my bones was excessive and unbearable, preventing me from noticing the magnitude of the cut along my throat, everything happened so quickly, intense cold seeping through the cracks of broken bones, I didn't realize that blood was spurting on my bare chest, I heard a gunshot, the shot rang out in the dark and chaos broke out, the sound of patrol cars and then ambulances, reality blurred, I lost consciousness before they put me on the stretcher, I woke up in the hospital, the doctors were surprised I'd survived, several fractured bones, my throat wrapped in gauze, I had to protect it from infection, I knew the mark would stay with me forever, but I didn't care, I didn't care about the mark itself but what was written on it. I cared about its meaning, Rocky said, I could read it even if it had no words, I was an impostor and that was how my falsehood was certified, he repeated, taking a Budweiser with a concentrated gesture, those April days when they started to rob cafés in the area.

Three assaults in less than ten days and they were unable to capture the criminal, even though he operated in the university area, guarded twenty-four hours a day by the police so thousands of rich students could enjoy the fantasy of invulnerability. The assailant always used the same method, he showed up shortly before closing time, approached the cashier at a slow, calm, serene pace, as if he were going to order a cappuccino or latte, moved his hands in his jacket and pulled out a gun, he'd receive the bills, put them in his pants pocket, turn around and walk out unhurriedly, as if floating on his feet, witnesses said, and when he stepped onto the street he'd take off and quickly disappear into the darkness. Not a trace despite the multitude of police officers in the surrounding area, it made no sense, it must've been a provocation or a secret message, when I left work, I'd walk around the neighborhood and stare at the security guards, six foot tall fat men standing on street corners, green vests, guns on their belts, focused, furious, vigilant, I'd walk around the area thinking about what decisions I'd make if I were the criminal facing those repressive forces. But no alternative seemed viable, there was no chance of success, none at all, the police were everywhere, surely the assailant strolled around just like me, observing, calculating, formulating, perhaps I'd come across him during my walks, it'd be difficult to recognize him, he wasn't a lunatic or drug addict but an extremely lucid guy who processed in an insurmountable way the continuous flow of information, invisible to most, but offered up by the streets, I thought one afternoon, on one of my walks, when suddenly I passed Rocky on the corner of Walnut and 38th. He was walking with his hat, black jacket, dressed in the same outfit as always, greeted me naturally but didn't stop, didn't ask me how I was or mention that we should meet for a couple of Budweisers, he greeted me and walked on with ease, but at a brisk pace, and when I turned my head, I saw him disappear like a snake down the street, making his way through the crowd with unusual agility, and an idea exploded in my head: I was looking at the perpetrator of the robberies. I thought his clothing was the perfect disguise to avoid suspicion, not a thief who hides to commit his crimes but who is noticed, shows himself as he is, so as not to be recognized, and then, when the fourth robbery happened, one night when Rocky didn't stop by the bar, I pondered how to let him know I'd found out his secret and was going to keep it, not so much out of loyalty but out of admiration, not just anyone can commit crimes in that area, feeling like his accomplice would help me cope with the monotony of my job at the pet grooming salon. I also imagined the story in the national press, two Peruvians causing an area full of rich students in a North American city to go on alert, transferring the national nightmare, carrying it in the belly and depositing it in a distant land, the idea began to seduce me, but I didn't have time to confess that I'd discovered his clandestine activities, much less to propose any form of participation because the end came sooner than expected.

It happened one seemingly typical morning, I was sitting behind the groomer's counter, my newspaper open, when a tall, thin girl appeared, wearing sunglasses, her short, generous blue skirt made her look elegant, with a white bulldog on a leash, breathing heavy, jaw large and slimy. The girl greeted me with a smile, as if she found my presence especially pleasing, even sexually pleasing, but I had no illusions, I know that people with money can make everyone feel they're special, it was clear this girl wasn't even talking to me when she explained how she wanted her animal groomed, she didn't even notice me even though she was talking to me, I'm just a pet washer, not a human being but a specific function, and that's why I decided to retaliate with a few needle pricks in the bulldog's back as soon as the refined client had left and I'd begin the process of scrubbing her obese pet's fur. The girl walked out the door and let herself be enveloped in the midday light, I stared at her through the window, her little blue skirt moved in the wind, but not as much as I'd have liked, everything went on as normal, just a strange sense of danger as I pulled on the leash and guided the bulldog to the back of the place, the poor unhappy animal calmly followed me, moving slowly, clumsily, obediently, never imagining what was about to happen to him, when I heard the buzz of notifications on my cellphone. The phone rang near the counter, I hurried to chain the bulldog and went to look for the device, finding a message from the local police, of course, nobody writes me messages or calls me on the phone, but lately I received them from the police, I'd subscribed to the alert system to follow the news of the armed robberies, if ten blocks away an old lady's wallet had been ripped off, a text message immediately informed me of the crime and suggested I avoid the area. This time, however, the news did not prove to be irrelevant, I read it carefully and nervously, my heart was pounding in my chest with energy, my intuition apparently confirmed when I read that another café in the area had been robbed, in broad daylight day, and that the suspect was shot dead by police while trying to escape. I put the bulldog in a cage, closed the shop and headed out at full speed, the café was a few blocks away, I had to hurry even if it was too late, maybe I could've prevented his death, I should've warned Rocky that I was going to give him up if he didn't stop. But he wouldn't have listened to me, I'm sure of that, Rocky was consciously rushing toward his own end, he sought it with some desperation, there's no way to save someone when all he wants is to destroy himself, I quicken my pace, I think I've started to run, I turn the corner and approach the place where the incident occurred, it's surrounded by yellow tape and police cars, I try to make my way through the crowd and say that I'm a friend of the deceased. But no one pays any attention to me, the policemen don't listen to me, the body is lying on the sidewalk, a few yards from me, I want to get closer to look at it, but they won't let me, it's partially covered by a blanket, however, I manage to make out a black hat and pants that look like Rocky's, the evidence confuses me, maybe it was a mistake, it doesn't make sense he would have used his Rocky outfit this time, it doesn't make sense unless he allowed himself to be killed to appear as Balboa in his final photographs, I try to push the policemen who block my way, I insult them in Spanish but they don't pay any attention to me, they don't even seem interested in listening to me. *I am Peruvian like him*, I shout out loud, several times, *Peruvian like him*, fists clenched, I know him, I exclaim, out of my mind, but nobody pays any attention, and then everything loses coherence and in my head I start to hear his voice, the day I met him, when he told me that he was going to be on a Peruvian television show. I'll stare straight into the camera, Rocky said that afternoon at Pasqually's, his voice reverberated in my head as I unsuccessfully struggled to get past the police, I'll stare into the camera as if it were possible to communicate with Peru, as if the country were a person I must make peace with or whose approval I still need. And I'm going to look it in the eye, Rocky said with emphasis, I'll look Peru in the face and tell it that since I left the country my life has been a simulation, an echo, an imitation, not only because I've spent years pretending to be someone I never really was, but because leaving pushed me into a kind of double life, neither of which was really complete. As if I'd existed here as a faint projection of what I could've been had I stayed in Peru. That's why I'm going to take off my hat and my vest, and drop Rocky's hoarse, slurred speech, and say once more, as if to leave no doubt, that ever since I left the country I've been nothing but a caricature. And not because my intention was to return, but because I never stopped feeling that nothing made sense if news of my successes and of my failures didn't reach there. That's what I'll tell Peru, it'll be my farewell before waving goodbye to conclude the program. That'll be my final farewell, Rocky said, because I'm not even interested in having my body shipped for burial in Peru. I just need to say goodbye, do you understand me?, he asked me the afternoon I met him at Pasqually's. I need to say goodbye. I don't know why, but I need it, he repeated, his voice on the verge of breaking, the afternoon I met him at Pasqually's, and at that moment I heard my own voice begging to be let in to see my dead friend. *I'm Peruvian like him*, I said once more, stupidly, not understanding the meaning of the phrase myself, when I felt a hand rest on my shoulder. I turned to see who was touching me, but it took me a moment to recognize him. It was Rocky, my friend Rocky, without his hat, without his characteristic projected attitude. It was my friend Rocky who smiled at me and looked at me kindly, as if he knew the reasons that explained my presence there. And then, suddenly emotional, I went over to him to give him a hug. I don't know why, but I really needed to give him a hug, as if I could finally get close to him, the true exiled Peruvian, and through him to a part of myself that I now understood I'd lost too. But Rocky threw his body back to avoid contact. And then, loose, relaxed, unsentimental, he stretched out his index finger, brought it to his throat, and ran it across the scar, back and forth, just as he had the day I met him. And without another word, without saying goodbye or adding a single gesture that would help me wake up from my shock, he turned around and disappeared forever into the crowd. And at that moment, perhaps for the first time since I left, I began to think of Peru with infinite sadness.

Those Waves

By Claudia Salazar

> *The rawness of the world was peaceful. The murder was deep. And death was not what one had imagined.*
>
> Clarice Lispector

His eyelids feel like two lemon peels, coarse. He opens his eyes. He stretches his arm down to his waist and then, with some trepidation, below it. A steppe, vast, so vast, a void. Shit, it wasn't supposed to be like this. He waves his right hand. He scratches, rubs the white sheet. Shit, he thinks. Shit, he says. They cut off the one they shouldn't have. Only bed linen where a leg should have been. His leg. He struggles with the stiffness of the two lemon peels—those eyes just don't want to open—and all of a sudden his daughter appears. Yes, Papá, she tells him, yes, they cut off the wrong one. Those lemons are going to turn to lemonade. He wants to cry, but stops himself, he shouldn't do it. Shit, the wrong one... *He dives in again, shakes the water from his head and calls to you. Come here, hijita, let's go into the sea. You are so small and tremble at the thought of going there, into that cold water, with those waves that leave white foam and sweep away everything in their path. Those massive waves could swallow you whole. We'd better not, Papi, maybe later. You get the feeling you won't be able to escape this time. Only up to the shoreline so you can dip your feet in, he says, let's go. There he is, standing, smiling at you, and it is only thanks to that smile that you drop the red pail and yellow shovel in the sand...*

How could they be so stupid? My God, how could they be so incompetent? He composes himself, bites his lip, can't look her directly in the eyes like this, so diminished, broken, incomplete. He in the hospital bed with her by his side, staring at him from above. A nurse arrives, at last. They talk, argue, the nurse tries to feign shame. The doctor is coming soon, she says and leaves. Let's wait, my little girl. She remains calm, clutches his hand and tells him that she'll take care of this, that they'll pay for their mistake. They'll pay, this is not over. The nearest bed is empty—the public hospital blue mattress that has endured so many bodies, moods, secretions. How many have they really cured? she thinks while caressing her father's face and wrapping her hands around his; they are bony and slightly bruised due to the IV drips. *He takes you by the hand, and you feel the scorching sand, which makes you jump up and down. The sand burns, Papi! He picks you up in his arms, your body looks like a green bean. Up you go, little grasshopper! You arrive at the water's edge after a short trek, the water chilly; you smile, and he splashes seawater, it splatters on your face. He lifts you up to the sky. An enormous jump. Again, again, you say to him. Papi could do this a thousand times without getting the least bit tired…*

The doctors arrive, talk, it was not a mistake, we need to amputate the other leg right away, the diseased one, or rather, the other one as well, because really, both of them were infected. But doctor, we came here for the sick leg and not for you to cut off the healthy one. Señor, Señorita, please understand, both legs were in bad shape, your father has diabetes, and because of the signs on the other leg, sooner or later, we'd have to remove it too, you know that diabetes… One word after another, and they continue to string together reasons, explanations, complications. Something about the good one, the bad one, that both were diseased. We are practically doing you a favor… *This time you're the first one to run to the ocean as soon as you arrive at the beach. Jumping in the waves, that's all you want to do. Papi runs behind you and scoops you up like a seaplane and he lets you fall down as if you had made the jump yourself. The other kids are playing in the sand, digging boring wells or building deformed castles. They don't know what they're missing. Maybe their dads are a bunch of weaklings and that's why they don't dare get in the water. Nobody is as strong as my papá. And now you prefer to jump over the foam that touches the shore, even though sometimes pieces of shell and sand crabs hurt your feet...*

The gangrene on his right heel is purple, almost black, and is motionless, patiently waiting for its moment to reach the shore. They need to operate on it that very night. No way, she says, he is too weak. We can't wait much longer, there are risks. There are always risks, just let him recover. The doctors confer amongst themselves. It will have to be today, that leg is not doing well. Of course, that's why we brought him here. One of them fills out a few forms, new medication is prescribed, lists and more lists. They never hear apologies, just a decision. Rest, Papá, tomorrow they're going to operate on you... *The sun. Everything is bright. Papi's shadow blocks the rays from hitting you directly on the face. Up again, jump! And he picks you up by the arms, up, up and dunk! The water gets in your eyes and they sting, but you don't care. In the distance you see a fishing boat, over where the waves appear to emerge. On the beach, Mamá rests and reads a magazine. Hopefully she doesn't get bored and realize that it's almost lunchtime.*

When he opens his eyes again, he is but a half. A mere half. He doesn't want to say anything, avoids his daughter's gaze. They both remain silent. How can one say anything without it sounding shameful, sorrowful? The doctors arrive and announce that the procedure was a success. He looks at them and finally opens his mouth: It was the only option you had! Animals! he yells. He squeezes the sheets with his fists, full of rage, a vein jumps across his right temple and another grows on one side of his neck. Animals! You abuse me because you think I look old, this is not over. Don't get upset, Señor. The main doctor, unperturbed—it is impossible for the patient to get up and hit him — reiterates the success of the operation and that they expect a quick recovery, although some of the test results deserve special consideration, but we will discuss this later on. They leave... *The water now reaches your waist, the sea stirring up sand between your legs. Stand like this, to the side, keep your legs firm, he says while showing you the Colossus of Rhodes pose. Solid and safe. Papi is very big. You also put your hands on your waist. The tide pulls the water, pebbles and sand under your feet, circling about, as if they are letting you float above the shore. Let's turn back...*

He is now a mere half. How can they just leave me like this, all cut up, hijita? I've been left with only half a body. She asks him to contain himself, to not insult or yell at the doctors since his life depends on them. Let's avoid getting them mad at you, let's do everything for you to leave this place as quickly as possible. Calm down, Papá, I know you're full of anger, but try to contain yourself... *Farther, Papi, take me farther. No more jumping, no more resisting the tide or the breaking waves, now you want to get closer to the fishing boat, closer to the pelicans and seagulls who swoop down. Farther, you tell him. Are you sure? And he takes you in his arms. You cling to him and see how the waves lift and then lower the fishermen. They rise once more. Three seagulls grow tired of swooping down and now allow themselves to get caught up in the swaying. Papi smiles at you and keeps going.*

So many weeks in hospital. Winter has arrived. Recovery is slow. Days and nights of nurses, check-ups, capsules, tasteless foods, pills, syringes, IVs, tests. First a spasm, then chest and back pains. He eats less and less every day, hardly talks even though she tries to cheer him up, sharing about her day, her work, her new boyfriend, he might be the one, they might get married and grandchildren would come. He'll be so happy when she has kids to teach them how to swim, to face the waves. *When you see that wave develop and grow in front of you, you get scared, bury your face in his chest and sense how they rise and fall like a swing. That was a wave, see how you have nothing to worry about? You won't drown when you're with me. You remove your hands from your face and turn to watch how that wave breaks on the shore. Again. And again. How strange that foam is, no longer white but rather yellowish. He plunged his head under the water and emerged again. You wiped the water from his eyes. The sun shone down brightly on the two of you. In the distance, the people grew smaller and smaller. You were now in the area for those who knew how to swim...*

He doesn't want to talk about anything, he hasn't even put in his dentures. It is cold on this winter evening. More weeks pass, new tests. Parades of nurses and receptacles full of blood. They give it a name, a diagnosis, a decree: hospital-acquired pneumonia. A gift courtesy of the hospital, in exchange for his legs. The gray sky invites you to hide, cry, not think, remain motionless, curl up under the blankets and squash yourself against the mattress. Procedures that take weeks and doctors who continue slicing off healthy and unhealthy parts. Waves in the lungs, the alarm goes off and nurses come running. Señorita, you need to leave the room. Tubes and syringes, a ventilator, the unmistakable sound... *You know that he'll never let go when he says you've gone so far that it's best to return. And he smiles with his perfect teeth. His smile is an invitation. No, Papi, there's still a lot more to go, we're going to leave everyone behind, we're going to keep going until we reach the fishermen. He keeps hold of you, and the two of you continue until you cross the line where the first row of waves emerges. Everything is calmer there. You climb up on his shoulders, and behind you, toward the beach, the rising wave stretches out like a blue rug. Nobody has gone this deep, Papi, we are the ones who have made it the farthest! You both smile victorious. Yes, mi hijita, no one can beat us, look how close we are to the fishermen. They greet you. Let's go back to the beach and tell mamá how far we got...*

The machine keeps beeping with that melodious rhythm, which rolls and unrolls the breaths of life. The water reaches his neck, filling his lungs. What is that strange smell? They left the door to the room open, and his daughter can see him. The room seems to be tinged with a yellow sheen like the foam from those waves. He feels the air escape, reduced to a mere half and without legs. He is going under. Now water is coming in where it shouldn't. He wants to breathe, but there is too much water. A death rattle. Papá! That yellowish wave does not return.

Homeowner's Association Meeting

By Gustavo Rodríguez

Every three months it's the same thing, that damn memo printed on copy paper slides under the front door. I was the one who spotted it last time when I got out of the shower, the towel still wrapped around my waist. My impatience gushed forth like water until I bent down and could see it up close. And then I felt relief: there was no red seal on the notice. You checked it properly? Maybe it's on the other side. My wife is meticulous and even more so with a seal of that nature, but yes, my love, I checked it closely. I'll attend because tomorrow's my day off.

The meeting was to be at five thirty, punctuality kindly requested, and I thought that, as dramatic and dreaded as these gatherings could be, they were a necessary evil in a building like ours. The chaos was predictable from the first time we visited the building. CLASSIFIED ADS. GORGEOUS CONDO FOR SALE, 6TH FLOOR, LAS FLORES RESIDENCES, ASK FOR SEÑORA CARMEN. That Saturday morning, upon getting out of the car, we liked the location a lot more than the actual highrise. Built in the sixties, I assumed, everything was so rigid and the aluminum windows outdated. A quick peek and you could see the plants in the window boxes were all dried up. A few more steps and there were clearly more cars than parking spaces. Many were double or even triple parked; the process to get them out had to be precise and perfectly timed so as not to block those farthest from the exit.

Nevertheless, the location was incredible. The building rested on one side of broad Avenida San Felipe, ten minutes from my work. The neighborhood's well connected, check it out, honey, six bus routes pass by here, plus a Supergangas discount grocery store and the Lux movie theatre are just around the corner. Point one for Señora Carmen. She turned out to be rather short and plump. She looks like a giant empanada, I whispered to my wife. Shut up, she'll hear you and goodbye apartment. The living/dining room was big enough for us, each wall painted a strong, dazzling color, hard to categorize at a glance, but that formed striking, multifaceted patterns wherever they met at certain angles. At our feet, gleaming hardwood floors reflected our increasingly appreciative faces, especially when we saw the charming bathroom: the majolica tiles are Italian and the faucets are imported because the earlier ones were a disaster. Here you have a bidet, something you'll never find in new apartments because it's always the first to go on blueprints to save space. I had this giant mirror hung to enlarge the space; it looks nice, doesn't it? The tiles in the kitchen aren't Italian, but they *are* from the United States. Follow me so I can show you. As you'll notice, the kitchen is a decent size and well lit. The pantry is made of Chilean pine, just like the breakfast nook table, conveniently located next to the fridge. Speaking of which, I haven't offered you anything; I'd starve to death as a salesperson…would you care for a refreshment?

Señora Carmen had earned another hundred points even before offering us orange juice. Although she'd deny it, she was an excellent salesperson, or perhaps the product was so good you couldn't help but believe her. I particularly liked how she didn't go overboard showing us the apartment's features. She let us discover the benefits on our own, and would take pleasure whenever we nodded approvingly upon noting a lovely detail, like the one in the master bedroom: the carpet is hypoallergenic; my nose can't take even the slightest dust particle floating in the air, and it goes well with the curtains, which will stay if you buy the apartment. A bronze bed works best in this room. An interior decorator friend of mine agreed when I showed her the apartment just after I moved in. You might already have a bedroom set, but if you want, I can sell you the bed and nightstands at a special price. I like you two. If Señora Carmen wasn't an expert salesperson, we weren't exactly expert buyers either. We didn't measure our praise: the apartment is totally unexpected in a building this old, señora. To be honest, we love it, though I imagine the price could be a dealbreaker. Let's sit in the living room and talk about that, she said. Proud of her good taste, she smiled in thanks when my wife said the apartment was surely the best in the building, right before we negotiated the sale. My wife was a terrible strategist, but what can you do? After a bashful nod, Señora Carmen stared at us intently, unblinking, before enunciating each of the five figures in dollars.

The price wasn't excessive considering the finishes. Nor was it a sum two middle-class newlyweds could afford, in the middle of an economic crisis and in the middle of a living room that was bidding us goodbye. Sadly, our savings barely come to 70 percent of that amount, señora. But I can assure you that if we had the money, we'd pay without hesitation. What a shame, right, my love? In that instant, a poorly disguised look of fear passed over señora Carmen's face, a startle in her gaze for a fraction of a second, incomprehensible to anyone who didn't already live there. The you're-not-going-to-get-off-so-easily face I seemed to detect was a far cry from the friendly woman who minutes earlier had shown us majolica tiles and curtains with cheerful indifference. In the blink of an eye, she had reverted back to her usual self. As I said, I like you two. You're a lovely couple and this apartment suits your personality. You mentioned 70 percent, is that right? Well, you're in luck today. I don't need the remaining 30 percent right away; you can pay me in reasonable installments. I felt my wife's hand squeeze my fingers tighter. I let myself get swept away by those polished floors, and that stylishly-carved front door devoid of excessive chiseling, by the view of San Isidro's impressive buildings in the distance, and the treetops, where swallows undoubtedly sang early in the morning, by the masterfully-chosen wall colors, until a momentary slap of reason hit me, striking my most impulsive side: I'm sorry, señora, but my monthly budget is calculated to the last cent, so I don't think I can pay the outstanding balance no matter how low the payments. That's the bad thing about being employed, one has to live within one's means, you know. My wife let go of my hand, and Señora Carmen grimaced briefly without meaning to, no doubt fearing the red seal. She got up from the sofa, smiling again—we didn't notice her effort to appear calm—and distractedly walked to the window, lost in thought. You've been very kind, señora, we apologize for taking so much of your morning; and this time her words sounded like a last chance as she asked if the Beetle was ours. Yes, we answered. She asked about the year. It's a 1974. German. Then say no more. You give me the Volkswagen instead of the remaining 30 percent, and we've got a deal. We can finalize the transaction right now. My wife and I looked at each other, perplexed; obviously this woman was no salesperson, much less a negotiator. We gladly accepted. That fifteen-year-old car was worth less than a closet in this apartment. Overcome by enthusiasm, not until I said goodbye did a suspicious feeling creep into my thoughts. There must be something wrong with the condo for her to close the sale so quickly and so generously. Though she mentioned having to travel as soon as possible, she'd have received a more reasonable offer if she waited a couple of days. By the looks of it, everything seemed in order. The possibility of fraud faded when she showed me the legal title to the property: thankfully you're a lawyer and understand these documents, young man. We can go to the notary public of your choosing to finalize the sale as quickly and transparently as possible.

Once I had rejected the idea of a scam, I recalled childish fantasies of houses possessed by frightening spirits who pull at bedsheets and turn off lights, causing residents to flee the way Señora Carmen literally appeared to be doing. What nonsense you come up with, man; you're about to lose an incredible deal because of a ghost story. Still, a third possibility existed. I wondered if the neighbors might be so annoying they'd cause one to run away as if from the plague at the height of the Middle Ages. Only insufferable, unhinged, incendiary and dangerous neighbors could make someone sell a property so hastily, for less than its real value. My question was direct, point-blank, calibrated to gauge reactions and prevent any attempt at concealment. Do you get along with the neighbors? Her response was frank, without a second thought, without that hint of fear I thought I saw earlier. We have the greatest respect for one another, she answered, and went on to say that her neighbors were the best, they would all sacrifice anything to maintain order. I get the feeling you two are the same and will adapt better than I did to the discipline in the building. That bit about discipline didn't sound great, reminding us of a school principal's speech, but maybe it was just a matter of vocabulary in the absence of a more appropriate term.

We moved in two days later—so young and already homeowners—with utter pride and shoes ready to walk for lack of a car. The president of the Homeowner's Association welcomed us, spoke in generalizations we didn't quite understand about cooperation, discipline, yet more discipline, and the sacrifices that Señora Carmen must have already mentioned with regard to living together in harmony and integrity. When we replied that Señora Carmen had never spoken of sacrifices, we noticed a slight annoyance in his brow, which, after the initial surprise, relaxed at the same time as his lips. *Sacrifice* is a harsh word, perhaps misused. You'll soon learn our good neighbor policy when you attend the quarterly meeting today. You'll be able to soak it all in, and while we're at it, we can discuss what to do with that parking space you're not going to use. You'll meet a number of neighbors who'll want to rent it and you can pick the highest bidder.

An exceedingly friendly smile preceded his departure, leaving us with a strange taste in the mouth: that man's a bit off, he reminds me of one of those Nazis in the movies. I reassured my wife, saying nonsense, that's nonsense, the thing is, to manage a building this big, you have to be firm. After attending that first meeting—and as the days went by—I confirmed that, to some extent, my theories about being firm had solid foundations, cemented on the serious problems caused by overcrowding on each floor. The building where we fought to live is fifteen stories high, not counting the wooden penthouse that crowns the concrete. Seen from above, the complex is shaped like a capital L. My apartment belongs to the short side of the letter, while the longest segment contains much larger condos partitioned into smaller ones over the years and sold by the original owners. As my wife says, in real estate, three small apartments are worth more than one big one. So, if there were thirty apartments in total when the building was first occupied, by the time I moved in that had already doubled. And resources to properly maintain the common areas were similarly divided.

The day I sweated with pleasure while situating our recently-moved belongings, I went into the first bathroom I had ever owned, ready to sing, to generously lather myself with soap and be rinsed by the caress of that imported showerhead Señora Carmen had installed, what a good-natured lady, *la donna e mòbile qual piuma al vento*. Then soap got in my eyes, the stinging exasperated my hands, which tried to turn the tap more, with the same useless result: the spray had ceased, gone until the next day. We soon learned that the ongoing lack of water in the building's tank due to excessive demand was not the only thing to dampen our spirits. All it took was Gene Hackman, dying from three bullet wounds, about to confess the names that would unravel the unfathomable mystery we'd been glued to for the last two hours with a bowl of popcorn, for the television to suddenly show its dark side thanks to an ill-timed power outage. Damn it, fuck, bring the candles I left in the kitchen. The building's scorched main circuit breaker tripped frequently, overloaded by sixty televisions turned on and as many dinners cooking in electric ovens at the same time. Many of the condo's inconveniences occurred in the elevator, due to overweight neighbors who, attempting to be considerate, wound up being the opposite. Most endeavored to get down early in the morning to move their cars so as not to block their neighbor's vehicle, filling the elevator with good mornings, many pounds over the limit, and then curses, as they had to wait huddled and suffocating for the time it took to fix it.

This detail mattered the least to my wife and I. We opted to pretend that we simply lived in a building without an elevator. Plus, going up and down six flights was healthy for the heart. You're lucky you're young, the elderly couple from 201 told us, and we're lucky we live on the second floor. It used to be worse, the doorman once confessed, when he said the elevator wasn't working that day, this time due to a power outage. Things have been improving since they created the Homeowner's Association, slowly but surely. As I was about to ask for more information, the little man went to open a car door, but not before saying, in a conspiratorial tone, every cloud has a silver lining.

Nevertheless, as the months went by, the chain of shortcomings plus the proliferation of rats and other vermin due to the ever-increasing accumulation of garbage became part of our life without even noticing, as if humans really were creatures of habit. That is, until the sight of the fat woman in the parking lot caused me to react: maybe the Homeowner's Association and the red seal had a reason to exist after all. That morning the parking lot packed with cars spread out before my eyes, the sun glaring off a colorful mosaic of metal roofs. Suddenly, I noticed the fat lady from 802 squeezing between the cars, trying to reach her little green one to go to the beach. She carefully opened the door, trying not to scratch the neighboring car, and settled into the seat. She sat still, undecided about turning the ignition. She must have forgotten something, I thought, and is debating whether to go up and get it. That's it. Now she's opening the door to head back. How odd. She opened the door, but stayed there, crouched next to the chassis. It then occurred to me she might have dropped the key under the car and was looking for it, but seconds passed, and the poor lady was still squatting, covered by the open car door, until the brownish puddle slowly trickling along the pavement explained it all.

A broken elevator is disastrous for fat people, I thought, dumbfounded; and that poor, desperate lady preferred to go right there rather than walk up eight floors and risk leaving that semi-solid glop on a step in the staircase. I tried to justify the poor woman's actions to my wife: her toilet must be full of shit, like ours, and what difference does it make to go there when we have no water in the bathroom anyhow. But she was absolutely right, I can bear the lack of electricity, water, elevators, but that filthy diarrhea is too much; it's time to leave, and all the better if it's before the next meeting, because you never know.

The last meeting I attended before selling the apartment was held on a day my office had closed for inventory, which meant I had plenty of time in the afternoon to try and relax by reading a book. At 5:25 pm, I went to the living room window to smoke a cigarette and admire the scenery. The silhouettes of buildings in San Isidro awaited sunset, buses began to fill with employees returning from work, and a pair of buzzards circled in the distance, high in the dome of sky. I watched their flight, imagining what it must feel like to master air that way, how lucky it must be to observe the city as if a scale model, until I saw some faces now appearing in other windows. The diarrheic lady from 802 was already upstairs, greeting me courteously. Above her appeared the face of the gentleman from 902, waving as always, but without a hint of a smile. He's awfully polite for being rude, I thought. I lowered my gaze to see who was joining from the lower floors, and right under my nose caught sight of the perfectly-polished bald head of Dr. Flores in 401 greeting the old man from 201.

Every time I looked up to count who else had joined from the highest windows, I realized the time chosen for these sessions was perfect. You could address the opinions of your upstairs neighbors without the sun punishing from on high. Meeting in the middle of the afternoon, for example, would have been an ordeal for the eyes, and very early in the morning would have been impolite for those with jobs.

At five thirty on the dot, in each segment of the L, every window displayed its duly-framed representative. The president of the association appeared between the curtains of 903, offered welcoming remarks and then announced the agenda items to be discussed that afternoon. The same things were almost always discussed. When talking about the water problem, you had to remember that, due to the surplus of inhabitants, a much larger reservoir had to be built, but unfortunately couldn't be put on the roof because the structure was not planned to support such additional weight, and besides which, said construction would involve demolishing the legitimately-built penthouse.

The problem of blackouts led to the same issues as always, and the most practical solution was to further ration power in each unit. The excess garbage problem, on the other hand, appeared to have a brilliant solution proposed by Dr. Flores, two windows below mine. He suggested hiring a private company that charges a modest fee for daily pickup, we would just have to increase the maintenance fee for each apartment by a small percentage, and problem solved. What do you think? All hands went up in approval at each of the windows except in 902. That man was always so serious, and nothing seemed to interest him, except the knot of his tie, which he constantly adjusted like some sort of nervous tic. Having gone through the day's agenda, the quarterly sweat broke out on my hands, alerting me that my heart would soon accelerate, just as must be happening to everyone in the other windows. We all remained silent, the angel who steals voices passing over the building at this point in the meeting as always. Dr. Flores began smoking to calm his nerves, while the fat lady was already praying Hail Marys two floors above my head. The president of the association cleared his throat impatiently, slyly glancing at all the windows, trying to guess, like the rest of us, who had been chosen by chance, who would set the example of respect for the by-laws and love of thy neighbor, the quarterly hero of the most severe form of population control. Then before my eyes I saw a shape fall, screaming in vain for his life, and I felt my insides twitch at the horrible sound of skull slamming against pavement. Now I understood the serious face, the stern expression, the abstention from voting and the nervous tic displayed by Mr. 902. Poor man, we all thought; I might be next. The windows were closed one by one, hiding the unpleasant shock that we should already be accustomed to, and a respectful silence seized the building until the following day. The heavy atmosphere that night contrasted with my wife's good mood when she arrived home from work: I got a good raise and soon we'll be able to leave this place, if we trick someone like we were tricked. Noticing my mood, she grew serious, suddenly remembering there'd been a meeting that afternoon. Who got it this time? she asked. The serious guy, the one on the ninth floor. She kissed my cheek and went to the bathroom to see if she was lucky enough to have water for a shower. Let's see who gets his parking space, I heard her say from behind the door.

Chocolate

By Katya Adaui

We used to collect the wrappers from impossibly imported chocolates, licking the remains without being seen, flattening them out and showing them off in an album, as if they were family.

I had two albums and took care of them, flipping the pages and sniffing. During recess, we'd exchange them, the aromas passed from hand to hand.

When I was eight years old, I experienced my first ambush.

Patricia came over and hugged me from behind: I traded you for a chocolate, they asked me to stop being your friend.

I returned home and mom:

Not even your friends like you.

My godfather had gone on a trip, he brought me a new chocolate. Raisins, walnuts, almonds.

I gave it away.

It weighed on me, as if I had stolen the chocolate.

Enjoyment is learned.

If you want to stop eating all the time, smell a chocolate, take a deep whiff, they told me, it'll disgust you, then go to the bathroom and brush your teeth, you'll lose your appetite.

Patricia, I remember your name.

You're a singer in a rock band and in your lyrics you love everyone's bodies.

If you're still the same person, I become nauseated, I hold back the vomit.

Antonio's Skin

By Julia Wong

I don't know how many times the old chino had crossed the Pacific from Lima to Hong Kong to find the cure for his son's skin disease. Some say seven, others eight. Some believe he went to Hong Kong to get silk. Perhaps he was seeking to restore the skin of his only heir to the texture of silk or velvet.

All of the dividends he had legally earned from his expert investments in mining bonds went toward that unhealthy search. Antonio, his only child, suffered from excruciating eczema and itchiness. Nothing is more important to a Chinese man than his only son. And Antonio, though handsome and healthy, suffered from terrible skin breakouts and erosions. Until one day he met that Venezuelan girl and fell in love, almost believing she'd heal him from such a terrible affliction.

It was just a fling, according to the old chino. It was true love, according to Antonio. Whatever you want to call it, his skin became worse after those two years of many nights in bed spent furiously kissing, the mattress the only witness to the delirious passion of two young bodies devoted only to themselves.

Ysmeri did achieve one thing with Antonio's skin that no woman, whether Chinese or Peruvian, black or mixed with the sun or moon, ever could or wanted to do. She licked Antonio's raw flesh, the sore, diseased skin that was peeling off. Day after day while she was with him, she licked his arms, his face, the back of his hands, and yes, the skin on his feet as well.

When Ysmeri told Antonio she had two little children in Caracas and would die of grief if she didn't see them, Antonio let her go.

That night Antonio went to the shore and bathed in the Pacific Ocean off the Costa Verde. When he came out, his skin was no longer red but green. He thought that when love ends, you're never the same person again.

The night before, the old Chinese man, who'd heard the Venezuelan would be returning to her country, made an ancient chicken soup with many dried lotus seeds he bought on Calle Capón.

Maybe she'll come back, he thought. Maybe she likes my soup. Deep down, he wanted the girl to let Antonio get her pregnant. But even deeper down, the old man didn't want his son to be cured because that way Ysmeri would continue to visit them, out of pity or necessity. The reason didn't matter.

That last night, neither she nor Antonio were in the mood for soup, nor for their bodies or their tongues. Instead, she vowed to return if he would wait for her and if he were faithful to her. He said yes, but thought he couldn't bear to say goodbye or live apart from her. He felt for the first time what they call goosebumps.

Ysmeri confessed that their relationship was forged in soul and skin, that she'd never felt the same for another man, not even in her own country or in all of Lima. And he'd come to know that for sure because if Antonio's skin spoke during her absence, it would prove their love was greater than the thousands of miles separating them. Antonio didn't understand how his skin would "speak." He often thought Ysmeri believed too much in supernatural nonsense. Maybe in Venezuela people are used to believing in magic formulas and melodramas about love with so many black people there, he thought. The Chinese were also superstitious, but not as much. At least neither he nor his father believed in those things. His mother half believed in other-worldly phenomena. The late Señora Chong always cleaned the house according to feng shui, hanging red pendants and charms to avoid bad vibes.

Every time they made love, Antonio would shed his skin and Ysmeri would get an inexplicable itch, but only for a few seconds. Afterward, Antonio would console her saying he wasn't contagious, and Ysmeri would look at her forearms and notice her skin was smoother than before, that she hadn't contracted any rare disease. She'd then remain calm and think those seconds only amounted to a temporary change in the environment.

But despite all the cleaning and artifacts for luck, the good Señora Chong passed away one moonlit night when the old chino, her husband, was talking with his small yellow bird locked in a cage. She always felt she got in the way of the old Chinese man and her son, that life in that house only belonged to her elderly husband and her little Antonio. Although the good Señora Chong loved them both dearly and in her own way, she also sensed they had karma she didn't share.

She felt as though her role was to clean the shop, prepare rice with Chinese sausage, which they call Lap cheong, and put up charms to ward off bad luck.

The old chino said nothing when his wife died. But Antonio was extremely sad, inconsolable. He realized his mother was the kindest being in Lima or Peru for that matter, and the poor thing hadn't been able to stand her husband's cold disinterest. The old Chinese man then looked for a woman for Antonio. He put a sign on the door that read "Girl needed to help with bookkeeping work." It was a trap; if he said he wanted a woman who'd act as a mother and as a lover for Antonio, or someone who'd bring a little feminine energy and help around the house, no one would accept the job even if the old chino paid a lot. With the death of the good Señora Chong, Antonio's illness arrived. Out of nowhere, his skin turned red and every morning he'd peel it until it bled. At first Ysmeri was reluctant to help wash the Chinese man's son. She herself didn't know if it was disgust or prudishness, but then she let herself be guided by the pleasure and pain Antonio caused her.

During those two years, the old Chinese man went to Hong Kong seven times, acquiring a number of concoctions and potions for his son's illness. He knew that in his absence they'd love one another more tenderly, and Ysmeri would certainly give him a grandson. But the medicine from far-off China never had an effect on his skin. After the last trip, the old chino acknowledged that all the money had been spent in vain; Antonio's skin was not going to heal with exotic remedies. The only one who seemed capable of easing the pain of his changing skin was the faithful Venezuelan.

When Ysmeri confessed she had two children in Caracas and would return for them, the old Chinese man didn't like the idea that a *veneca* would come into the house with children of her own and no longer exclusively take care of his only son with his skin problems.

Antonio didn't cry his eyes out, but the first month of Ysmeri's absence, his skin fell off like dried fish scales. The floor of his room nearly filled with dry skin, and the strange thing was that another layer grew, only to fall off again the next day. He swept it silently, and the old Chinese man began to grow impatient.

"Why you so sick?" he berated his son.

"Why you not normal?"

"Why you not make baby with chola or Venezuelan or normal woman?"

Antonio remained silent and swept his skin off the floor. With damp towels, he carefully moistened his reddened skin which scabbed up overnight and fell off again the next day.

Antonio remembered that during the pleasurable act of lovemaking, his skin would greatly improve and almost return to normal. But whenever she showed indifference or didn't fulfill his desires, the cutaneous rash would flare up again.

"You miss your mother," Ysmeri sometimes murmured with compassion, after waking up to find pieces of smooth skin lodged in the sheets like foam on hot milk.

"I don't know," Antonio whispered. "I don't know how to talk about feelings," he said. He didn't cry, didn't demand, didn't get annoyed by his father, didn't complain; he just accepted everything as it came.

But his skin would continue to shed and grow, peel and redden, or he'd scratch until it burned.

Ysmeri came to take pleasure in the ritual of finding the flakes of skin and plucking them with her fingertips off the sheets to place them on the nightstand. Before throwing the pieces away, she examined them and felt part of her beloved's daily metamorphosis.

"If your skin changes every day, that means every day you're no longer the same Antonio," she said.

And Antonio, looking at her with a puzzled expression, as if he didn't know her, was at a loss to respond.

Trash

By Romina Paredes

In 1983, during President Fernando Belaúnde Terry's second term in office, the district of San Borja was created. Two years later, my father bought my family's apartment. Most of the adjoining lots were empty and belonged to Fortunato Brescia, the head of one of the most powerful families in Peru.

In the nineties, only the prominent districts in Lima hired private household waste management companies. In the others, that responsibility fell to the municipalities. Unlike developed countries, which rely on immigrants for garbage collection, the municipalities faced a shortage of public employees because not only was it an unattractive and poorly paid job, but it also involved high occupational risks: cut hands due to damaged garbage cans and handling unsegregated waste, lumbar injuries from poor posture when lifting up to thirteen-gallon receptacles, traffic accidents caused by reckless drivers or because trucks slid into sinkholes brought on by broken water pipes, and constant exposure to respiratory, gastrointestinal and dermatological infections that the uniform—overalls and safety gloves—didn't prevent. What's more, the garbage collectors would bring their work home at the end of the day. Before long, their coexistence with trash meant their skin was blackened by the filth.

Nowadays, in San Borja refuse is temporarily stored in underground dumpsters sorted according to organic waste, paper, and plastic. These are then transported to the outskirts of Lima for final disposal in landfills. In the early nineties, household waste was collected at noon on the first few blocks of Calle

Federico Chopin. Because of union strikes, the sanitation truck wouldn't always pass by every day, and trash would overflow. Some bins were rusty or full of holes, and trash was strewn on the sidewalk. From time to time, neighbors would solve the problem by forming mounds of debris they then burned on the vacant lot adjacent to the police station.

With garbage always available on the sidewalks, a mafia of informal scavengers or *cachineros* emerged. At first, they took the trash bags. This was a relief to the neighbors, who even appreciated the gesture. The *cachineros* rummaged through the bags in search of items to resell. They'd come by on tricycles and enter houses to steal seemingly insignificant objects, such as door handles, faucets, or even lightbulbs. These items would be hidden among the stuff they took from the trash, and their crimes went unnoticed by police.

Most of the municipal garbage trucks were open-topped. They would announce their arrival a couple of blocks before with the tinkling of a percussion triangle, and the characteristic stench emanating from the overflowing hopper. The truck operators also engaged in informal recycling. They rifled through the trash looking for things that could be sold to the *cachineros* at the end of the day. Municipal security guards would often have to intervene in brawls between both sides. More sophisticated collection vehicles passed through on weekends because of the higher volume of waste. These had a cab for the driver, a compactor for the waste, and a rear door the operators used to manually load and unload the trash.

Garbage trucks sometimes replaced car bombs during the years of political violence. They were filled with explosives or set on fire. Other times the vehicles were used as mobile morgues. Most perpetrators of femicide and rape in Peru used them as secondary crime scenes. That's where they'd leave dismembered corpses inside black plastic bags. Like any other household waste.

* * *

I would always visit my neighbor Mari on Sundays after eight o'clock mass. Despite being one of the first buildings in San Borja, her house was the only one left unfinished. On the first floor was the garage for her father's cargo taxi and a small bodega, which her grandparents built thanks to the Agrarian Reform. They only sold salt, sugar, bread, powdered milk and, at night, cans of gasoline to truck drivers heading to the Panamericana Sur highway. Her family lived on the second floor.

That Sunday, her two older brothers were helping their father wash the Datsun truck they used to transport construction debris. Mari ran out, but her father grabbed her by the arm and put a red rag in her hands. She gave the truck bed a quick once over so her dad would let her go out and play.

"How was mass?" Mari asked me. She carried a bucket with water and two bamboo skewers tied together with cotton yarn, forming a circle.

"Bad. God doesn't listen to me. I always ask for my dad to come back."

"Don't worry. He'll come," she said, pulling her straight hair up into a ponytail. Her hair was as black as a Friesian mane but appeared blue out in the sun.

I put detergent in the bucket, shook the container hard until it foamed, and then soaked the sticks to blow bubbles.

"Nothing! It doesn't work! Can't you get someone to redeem points at the supermarket and get the bubble wand?"

"No. My mom says it's a lot of money."

"This crap!" Mari shouted and threw away the sticks.

* * *

I invited my friend over for lunch because Mom wasn't home. Mari finished the mondonguito tripe stew in five minutes and my grandmother packed two tuppers for her brothers.

My grandmother turned the television knob. The news featured a story about "trash monsters." There was signal interference. Mari said it looked like thousands of ants in a race and didn't mind watching it. My grandmother turned the volume down and kept changing channels, but all of them featured the same trucks, black bags, and people crying. She turned off the TV, grabbed the newspaper and sat in her usual chair. She'd spend all day there, looking out the window to see what the neighbors were doing, reading the paper, watching television, or she'd go for a walk around the block and pour rat poison along the perimeter of the building.

"Señito, what's all that about 'trash monsters'?"

My grandmother folded the paper and put it in her apron pocket.

"They are monsters who take spoiled little girls," she said, gesturing at me to finish my mondonguito.

"You're ten already. Eat it all, don't be such a baby," Mari snarled because I left the peas and carrots along the edge of my plate.

"They don't exist, Señito. You can't trick me. I'm already twelve."

My grandmother got up from the table, making a great effort to move her skeletal body, and opened the door to the garbage chute.

"Oh, is that so? Come here and listen."

We put our heads together and peered down the trash chute. The smell of vomit and vinegar hit our faces, but neither of us flinched. We wanted to know what was in that hole, so dark and deep it might reach the center of the earth.

"Do you hear the screaming? Do you hear it?"

I nodded. It sounded like someone was trapped at the bottom of a cavern. Then I heard pleas reverberating with a guttural echo. I started to shake. Mari scowled at me and poked her head deeper into the trash chute.

"It's the gate to hell!" my grandmother said in a sinister voice and laughed.

Mari startled and slammed the garbage chute door.

"That's so silly! Don't believe her," she said, trying to compose herself. "Besides, at my house, we don't have a door like that to get rid of the trash, so I'm safe."

* * *

In the nineties, the news was a symphony of rape and femicide that accompanied my family's breakfasts on a daily basis. The case I remember the most is that of Nicolás Gutiérrez Mendoza, because his victims were my age. From 1995 to 1996, the Monster of Parcona raped and murdered six girls in the districts of Villa María del Triunfo and Villa El Salvador. His mother covered up his escape when police began looking for him. In Ica, the city of eternal sunshine, he murdered five more girls. Gutiérrez confessed to first suffocating the girls because they screamed so much when he penetrated them. He didn't want them to suffer, that's what he said, so he raped their corpses and threw them into a pit or a sandy area in a black bag. The press followed the case in morbid detail. The newspaper headlines seemed like they were ripped from a comedy-horror film. My grandmother used to compare these cases with that of Jorge Villanueva Torres, the Monster of Armendáriz, one of the criminals sentenced to death in Peru back in 1957. "The press only reports what's convenient. The Monster of Armendáriz was a poor black man who was in the wrong place at the wrong time, and they shot him. I don't believe a word of it anymore, hijita. Only God knows if this is the Monster of Parcona or if the real one is still out on the streets raping little girls," she said.

A monster is a frightening, fantastical being. The media labels rape cases using a catchy marketing formula. They start with the noun "monsters," followed by their area of operation, so almost every province and district in the country was represented. Over time, the style of attack was added as a prefix: the Bicycle Monster (a man who ran over girls, offered to help and then raped them), the Cudgel Monster (a pedicab driver who clubbed drunken passengers to death), the Hammer Monster (a medical student with disproportionate strength and a marked weakness for masonry tools), and the Apostle of Death (a self-confessed homophobe who abandoned the corpses of transsexuals and prostitutes on the side of southern highways). The digital age brought the Social Media Monster, a rapist who lured five- to twelve-year-old girls through Facebook accounts. Only one type of rapist escapes being called a monster: men who are high-ranking members of the church or the government. The press calls them "alleged rapists."

Only one out of four monsters is ever reported or attracts any media attention. The press, however, only sells monsters from the outskirts of the city or rural areas, the "second-class citizens," as one president referred to them. What about the other monsters? What about the lawyers, entrepreneurs, teachers and artists? Where are the middle-class stepfathers, uncles and grandfathers? Those who negotiate silence and buy memories. Those who smile in family portraits, at board meetings and shareholder gatherings. That kind of trash is not taken into the street. It's hidden at home and rots families from within. Or it evolves into fictional characters in books.

* * *

After lunch on Sunday, Mari didn't want to make giant bubbles or play in the park. I was surprised because she knew it was the only day I was allowed to play outside. She got it into her head to look for the end of the trash chute in my building. I explained that everything fell into a little room on the first floor that smelled awful and was full of cockroaches."Why? How do you know?"

"Because I do. All the trash goes there."

"You repeat everything people tell you. I want to see where the screams come from."

"Liar! See, you did hear the screams!" I said accusingly.

We went into the main trash room and retched so violently our eyes watered.

"Cover your nose and breathe through your mouth."

"No way! That's like eating trash."

I reached for the light switch, running my hand across the grease-covered walls. The sticky texture disgusted me, but fear activated my adrenaline. I just wanted to know where the chute ended and get out of there. Mari walked up to the rusty duct that emptied into a large dumpster. It was the only illuminated area.

"I can't hear a thing, how weird," she said, walking around the container.

"Let's go now, Mari. It smells gross."

"Wait. Go up to your apartment and tell me if you hear anything. If you don't, where are the screams coming from?"

"What are you doing?" my grandmother asked when she saw me with my head in the garbage chute.

"We're looking for the trash monsters. Can you hear them?"

"Who's screaming?! What's going on?!"

We flew down the stairs. Mari's screams led us out into

the street. We saw her struggle against two men who threw her in the back of a truck.

* * *

I slept by the window all week waiting for Mari to come back. My grandmother woke me for breakfast, but I didn't want to move. I kept a close eye on the spot where they took her. My grandmother changed my clothes and, as she mopped the urine on the floor, she assured me that she'd go to the police station and city hall to find out what happened, but every time a car passed, my heart stopped.

At eleven o'clock on Monday morning, screams on the street led me to Mari. She dragged her feet in a funeral march, bare thighs exposed and blood running from her belly to her calves.

My grandmother didn't let me visit her. She said Mari was going to be fine, but was sick, and we had to pray a lot for her recovery. After dinner, while my grandmother kept my mom company as she waited for my dad to come home, I hid behind the living room door when they sent me to bed.

"Well, Mamá, that brat didn't act her age."

"What do you mean?"

"She was a bit of a tease. I'd sometimes see her giggling with the garbagemen when she'd take out the trash, exhibiting herself as if she were in a shop window. She provoked them," my mom said while sipping her Amaretto coffee.

"You sound just like her stupid mother. She doesn't even want to take the girl to the clinic!" my grandma said, crossing herself.

"What does the father say?"

"The father and brothers don't even know! The mother is more concerned about the family's reputation and what people

128

might say, stuff like that. She even had the nerve to threaten me!"

My grandmother grabbed her rosary but couldn't concentrate.

* * *

Two weeks passed and I still wasn't allowed to visit her. I stopped eating until my family grew scared. My grandmother made me pray with her every afternoon. We prayed for Mari's speedy recovery, until one day I got fed up and threw the Sacred Heart prayer card down the trash chute.

My mom didn't know what to do, so she redeemed points at the supermarket to get the bubble wand. The first thing I did was ask if I could show it to Mari. My mother and grandmother argued a little, but eventually said yes, and I ran to her house. We stood in the doorway until, half an hour later, Mari's mother finally let us in.

My friend was sitting on her bed. Her face was pale, her head shaved, and a plastic bucket sat beside her. The room reeked of spoiled milk. I wanted to hug her, but thought I might hurt her if I touched her. I went over to show her my new bubble wand and realized there was vomit in the bucket.

We didn't talk. I did my best to make perfect bubbles with my new wand. I wanted to make a huge one, one big enough to encompass us both and strong enough to take us away from there. Mari stared at them in silence, as if an invisible cloak squeezed her so tightly she couldn't react.

When we left, my grandmother explained that Mari was sick, and we had better let her rest. At home, she served patita, a cow's feet stew with peanuts and sat next to me to pray the rosary. Seeing I hadn't eaten, not even the potatoes, she scolded me mid-yawn.

"Hijita, eat all the—"

"Abuela, even if I eat all my food and say all my prayers, the garbagemen will still take me away."

A Random Hack Writer

By Hemil García Linares

I know you won't believe what I'm about to say, but I don't give a shit what you think (apologies for the informality). If you're reading this, you know it contains some truth. It didn't get published for no reason. Well, listen to me or don't; that's your problem.

I know you're young and want to be a writer. Deep down, all of us who read want to be one. I was once your age too and though I am still young, I'm not eighteen anymore.

Just like you, I went crazy thinking about what it would take to see my work in a bookstore; how they, the ones who publish, do it. So, one day I discovered the secret of that trickery called literature and since I've got nothing to lose, I'm going to tell you.

I participated in quite a few short story and poetry contests in Peru without any success. I was never a finalist, or even received a modest honorable mention to post on Facebook as they do these days. Without a doubt, my writing was a disaster, and the only thing I excelled at was getting plastered in some seedy bar in Barranco or a dive in downtown Lima. Early Friday morning, I'd zigzag my way home, dodging shadows and insulting imaginary literary enemies. Still drunk, I had trouble getting to sleep, and would look over my manuscripts, enduring testaments to my failure that I'd bequeath to my future children. Assuming the latter would exist, if by some miracle someone might see poor me as a potential suitor.

In the short story workshop I took with Prof. Santos, I received a course packet containing an interview with Faulkner and several of his stories. I think one of them was "A Rose for Emily." I tried to read it but fell asleep while Santos droned on about symbolism and allegory.

The interview, however, piqued my interest. From what I read, when Faulkner was young, he showed a manuscript to a published author, who promised to speak to his editor as long as they didn't discuss the topic again. What's more, the published novelist was shocked to learn that Faulkner wanted to be a writer, as if literature were not a beautiful muse but a horrifying witch dressed in catfish skin. The author did as promised, and Faulkner was published. No one knows if they discussed the manuscript again.

I was fascinated by the interview, where Faulkner said he didn't give a shit about criticism, that his best job had been as a manager at a brothel, and that an author didn't need financial independence. Was all this true?

While my friends would keel over analyzing symbolism and necrophilia in Faulkner's famous piece, "A Rose for Emily," I'd think to myself: Who the hell do I ask to publish me? My workshop instructor? But that poor man published with fifth-tier publishing houses! The pages of his poorly-edited books fell like hair from a balding man. Yeah, that's how bald I'd end up if I did the same.

I didn't want to keep being just a random hack writer; I wanted to be known. In college, I befriended Josué, another young guy like me; he claimed to be a poet and wore his hair long. We started hanging out, got ourselves some black jackets and called ourselves the Protons (because we carried the positive charge of pure poetry). In Jirón Quilca, we bought books by Baudelaire and Rimbaud. We found photocopied poems by the Comte de Lautréamont, and an almost handcrafted book on literary trends.

And just like that, we memorized some verses. I began to participate a little more in our literature class and quoted phrases from the book on literary movements. We'd declare that authenticity could perhaps reside in symbolism or surrealism, but never in Dadaism. What the hell could you unpack from a concept like Dadaism, whose very name didn't mean anything?

I think the literature professor took a liking to us, and that semester Josué and I earned the highest grades. The second semester, we were now four hack writers in black jackets; two were a year behind us, and since Josué and I had founded the Protons, they accepted us as their gurus. Then two girls joined. One of them, Astrid, forcefully caught my attention. She had long black hair and very light brown eyes, almost the color of honey when it absorbs the sun's rays. She had a leopard's gaze, and sometimes her eyes seemed to be searching the void, a place I feared because of its depth, because to fall in there was to be trapped, and to try to get out of that infinite black forest, I'd have to slash through the thickness of ether.

Astrid and I soon hit it off and became friends. She wanted to be a painter or a poet, but didn't know where to start. "Bretón was a writer who inspired the surrealist painters. He's the father of surrealism," I proclaimed. "Really?" she said, looking at me, pleased and maybe with a little admiration.

To be honest, Astrid was beautiful, but a bit on the dumb side, and I didn't think she'd ever be a poet. But apparently her family had money.

I continued to "discover" secrets hidden in other secrets: I didn't read authors' stories, but rather what they said about them. I looked at their photos, imitated their gestures: I put my hand on my chin à la Vallejo and bought a hat like Neruda's. In downtown Lima, I bought a used brown overcoat in good condition. In the mirror I'd practice what Neruda might say: Surrealism is this and Realism is that.

In Vargas Llosa's novel *La ciudad y los perros*, I found a "confession" in which the author says his friend Claude Couffon recommended the manuscript to the publishing house Seix Barral. Its director, Carlos Barral, later awarded the book a prize.

Then, like an epiphany, the whole mystery of literature began to reveal itself: Jaime Bayly declared in the press that *No se lo digas a nadie* was published in Spain on the recommendation of Vargas Llosa. And it didn't stop there: on his television show, Bayly recommended that viewers buy his new wife's book. So everything happened through a chain of discipular succession.

I made the rounds to numerous bookstores and that's when I noticed how big publishers were churning out books by cumbia singers, journalists and even actresses. One had published a collection of children's stories that would've made Hans Christian Andersen, who as we all know wrote *The Ugly Duckling* and *The Steadfast Tin Soldier*, sick to his stomach.

I enjoyed poetry, but to be fair, I wasn't exactly adept at writing verse or very knowledgeable about meter. It was obvious a sestina contained six verses, but I couldn't describe epanadiplosis, archilochian strophe, antithesis or synesthesia. I memorized the characteristics, but quickly forgot them. In our story workshop, Professor Santos would recite "verde que te quiero verde," and explain that this summed up the simplicity and beauty of García Lorca; I understood that, but still couldn't remember that it was an example of epanadiplosis.

Professor Santos took pity on me and suggested I write short stories because they were easier, following the Aristotelian structure of beginning, middle and end. He recommended some by Monterroso, Cortázar, Bierce, and told me a little about Poe's "unity of effect."

I ended up learning a few things about short stories. In college, I'd open my mouth and seem to know what I was talking about. My lit prof encouraged me to submit to the upcoming campus writing contest. He offered to read my piece and give me feedback. He wasn't on the jury, just to be clear, so the haters can't claim anyone could win that way.

Yes, ladies and gentlemen, I sent in my story (after correcting a few mistakes) and wound up winning the university's inaugural story contest. With that award under my belt, I kept writing and was even selected as a finalist in other competitions in Lima.

Besides being a writer, I also wanted to learn French. That's why I was attracted to Astrid. She had studied at the Colegio Franco-Peruano. Her great-grandfather had been French, so it was a family tradition to speak the language of Rousseau. Thanks to her, I learned trivial phrases like *je ne sais quoi* and *c'est la vie*. Or even a little line out of a Baudelaire poem taken from a pirated, dog-eared copy of *Les Fleurs du mal*. And I could rattle off basic greetings. I must confess, the first times I jerked off were to that delicious soap opera: Naná. Years later, I learned the voluptuous, rosy-cheeked *Naná* was a character created by Émile Zola.

Astrid belonged to the upper-middle class and, well, I think you've already surmised that I was lower-middle class, also known as half-scraping by, half-going to shit. At college, I had a partial scholarship for being an orphan (my poor old man, a member of the Civil Guard, was shot in Ayacucho during the years of terrorism). To keep the scholarship, I was required to maintain good grades no matter what. I wasn't lazy, but still, I didn't like to study. No, I wanted to be a poet or a writer, be irresponsible and drink like Bukowski.

One day we were at Astrid's house and she introduced me to her father, who asked if it was true that I liked French, and I nodded nervously. Don Jacques sounded like a native Frenchman. After hearing my rudimentary French, he said nothing more than hmm. (Astrid later told me that her father had compared my pronunciation to that of an aphonic rooster with a scratchy throat suffering an asthma attack. All at the same time.)

Don Jacques showed me his library and said he wanted to speak with me alone. Astrid excused herself, saying she had to call her friend Silvina, and headed to the second floor. Astrid's father asked me to grow a pair and be honest. He no longer used French, but spoke to me in Peruvian. In *limeño*:

"Bullshit aside, young man. You have no idea what my *petite* princess means to me. Tell the truth. You like my daughter, right? Are you going to behave yourself with her? I wasn't born yesterday and I've noticed my daughter is fond of you. She's always talking about you, she says you're a nice guy, and well—between you and me—she feels bad that you don't have, um… resources. It saddens her a bit. You seem like a good kid. My Astrid told me about your father; I am so sorry. If you treat my daughter well, I'll be your best friend, and if you don't, I'll be worse than Napoleon. And look, I'm not short. What are your intentions with my daughter?"

So I told him the truth: to me, his daughter was the most beautiful girl on Earth; I wanted to be her boyfriend; I'd never do anything to hurt her; and I was someone who had dreams; I wanted to be a writer. That's how we had met in college. Don Jacques signaled for me to wait as he left his library full of classics. There was a large worktable, like the kind used by engineers or draftsmen. According to Astrid, her father was an engineer and worked for a transnational company.

I was alone for a few minutes, wondering if I should head out, imagining it was all a trick and that Don Jacques would soon appear with a stick to break my ribs. When he returned to the library, he gave me two telephone numbers, explaining that one belonged to the director of the French Language Institute and the other to a publisher. "The first is Astrid's godfather and the second is a half-insane cousin who studied literature in France and England. He was kind of lazy and crazy, and his parents decided to help him start his own publishing house. I myself have helped my cousin Jean a couple of times."

Later I found out that it was through this Tío Jean that Astrid became interested in literature, but for her it was nothing serious. Astrid's uncle was a publisher! Wow, Astrid wasn't serious about writing at all! She hadn't even mentioned her uncle, the publisher. And here I was bleeding out trying to be a writer, skinning my fingers writing insignificant stories that only won shitty prizes!

Astrid's Tío Jean met with me and I showed him what I'd written. He looked over the pages. Maybe half an hour passed, while I poked around his large bookshelves. He told me that out of the eight stories I had, he was going to keep six to carefully read them. The beginnings were solid, he told me. When a story is good, he said, you sense it from the start. If it's good shit, as soon as you start reading, the text flows. Write four more. Lift something from Maupassant or Boccaccio, but don't be blatant or foolish, copying them exactly. Write pieces like "Boule de Suif" or a tale from *The Decameron*. When you're done writing those stories, I'll edit and publish them. The advance I'm going to pay you isn't much...

The Director of the French Language Institute, Don Jacobo, interviewed me for about an hour and offered a full scholarship if I committed to learning French in a year. I was about to achieve every apprentice writer's pipe dream: to be a young, published author who speaks French.

I kept my promise to everyone: I wrote, studied and behaved like a gentleman with Astrid; I respected her. Her hazel eyes were all I needed to forget about the hardships at home, my mother working as a cashier at the mall and coming home with swollen feet.

A year passed and much happened, great events that left an indelible mark, I'd say: I learned French; I became a man (with Astrid, my young Gallic goddess who hadn't yet become a woman either until she met me). I presented my first book of short stories at the French Language Institute to an almost full house, since many friends from university and my French class attended.

During the book presentation, my editor said I could be considered an emerging voice in Peruvian literature, judging by the garbage being released by other national publishers. I had the mettle, presence, seminal force (actually, he used the term "balls") and came from the working class. I suffered and understood what was happening in the streets, where true and transcendent things occurred.

After the wine, photographers, including one from a century-old newspaper, took many pictures of me, and I gave an interview on a state-run television channel for a cultural program that nobody watched. It was hosted by a bigwig writer, but that day they sent over a young reporter.

My "Tío" Jean promised to introduce me to Bryce Echenique when the cultured writer returned from Europe (provided he was sober enough to meet with us, he said). The future, without a doubt, seemed promising and fruitful in every way.

Thanks to my dedication, the French Language Institute awarded me a yearlong scholarship to continue my studies in France, with travel and lodging paid. It was only eight hundred euros a month, but I could get by on that. When I shared the good news with the deans of my university, they offered me a full scholarship upon my return (I had two semesters left). They assured me I'd have a job teaching French or as assistant academic coordinator. They described me as a fortunate, young go-getter, a good match for the daughter of the engineer Don Jacques Bartres who, coincidentally, happened to be a close friend of the university's. His company had donated computers and books to the library.

At Astrid's house, Don Jacques congratulated me because I'd achieved everything by putting in the effort. He told Astrid, whose eyes sparkled like shooting stars when she looked at me, that he wanted to speak to me alone. I was about to tell him that I loved him like a father, but he beat me to it: son, I see you've done it. You're going to France, to Paris, for God's sake, *la ville lumière*. You'll be gone for a year. Astrid will miss you terribly, but you can't miss this great opportunity. I don't want you two to split up. Besides, women over there are more liberated, not like Astrid. You're a good-looking kid. I'd have no problem if she were to go with you and study too. I can make that work and put you guys in a bigger apartment. But don't think, by any means, that my daughter's just going to take off after you like some hippie. She loves you; you love her. I know you're young and should enjoy this beautiful chapter in your lives, but still, I'm not stupid, much less an irresponsible father. So I thought maybe it'd be better for you to get engaged and then travel to Europe as a married couple. Astrid can study whatever there, graphic design or who knows, and then help Jeancito. I can send you to Barcelona for a one-week honeymoon. From there, you just head to France. You can take some classes in European literature that I will pay for.

I watched Don Jacques standing in front of me, with open arms. And I began to think about the scholarship, my secure job at the university, meeting Bryce Echenique. I was too young to get married, too young. Then I pictured myself in rags, my mother and her swollen feet, as big as rolled-up carpets, my mother hunched over, working as a cashier until she was sixty-five, if she didn't die first.

Then I hugged Don Jacques and said: "*Merci beaucoup, Papá.*" "Astrid," he yelled, and she nearly flew down the stairs and kissed me right away, wrapping those freckled arms around me, those delicate, bewitching arms.

And so it was consummated: my writing career and my marriage. I'm not in love, or maybe I am, but I'm very young. I'd have liked to explore and experience more, but I think my life is better now than before, because I'm a writer. I've been invited to the Buenos Aires Book Fair and will be included in an anthology of young authors. I live in Paris. Ah, the City of Lights is so radiant at night! It's so electrifying that Astrid and I live intensely every day, although for a week or so she has been feeling unwell and dizzy.

I plan to return to Peru and teach French or literature. I live and will live surrounded by the right people, that's the right thing, and what I should continue to do. You should do that too so you're not a random hack writer.

Man in the Mirror

By Alexis Iparraguirre

To Marco García Falcón

Mónica wakes up late, after midday. She sits on the bed, kicks off the sheets with her sockless foot and yawns. The room smells of aged wood and coats that had been stored in the closet with mothballs. She looks at herself in the mirror on the dresser: pale skin, small eyes, a face with chiseled cheekbones. Arranging her hair with a comb by reflex, she decides that she will do something today. *I'll do whatever*, she thinks, boldly. *I'm eighteen now*.

Then she sees the man. Standing still among the clothes in the wardrobe. He has a wide forehead, dark skin and eyes ready to scrutinize every movement. He's dressed in a long overcoat, full-length. Mónica throws down the comb and overcomes her first instincts: to scream for help.

She knows all too well that no one can enter her room. She doesn't even bother to turn around.

"You don't exist," she says to the mirror.

She blinks. *He'll disappear.* And with eyes violently open, she stares at him again. *Not interested!*

He acquiesces unexpectedly and disappears.

* * *

As she makes her way downstairs to have breakfast, she notices he's following her: he walks right beside her. She spies him through the expansive balustrade that flanks the staircase. Mónica picks up her pace, jumps from step to step. On the landing, he is infinitely reflected in the oblong and opposing mirrors. The man hangs back a few yards. Silent. Mónica pretends to ignore him. She leafs through some forgotten newspapers on the living room sofa and adjusts two miniature centerpiece decorations. She wants to smell the fresh air coming from the garden; the only thing capable of cheering her up. But she only feels stifled.

* * *

She sits at the head of the table in the dining room in front of the three-way mirror. Once more, the man shoots her an inquisitive glance, like a nightmarish emanation; he hovers behind her, his long, perfect fingers atop the carved back of her chair.

"What are you?" Mónica asks.

The man stays silent. He only stares at her, attentive.

"Where do you come from?" Mónica insists, her voice wavering.

The man speaks in a clatter that sounds like glass breaking:

"From the other side."

She trembles at the sound of his shrill voice, but decides to make a comment so as not to faint:

142

"You look like someone straight out of a children's story."

The man doesn't respond. When Mónica's mother brings the food, he stays motionless. As expected, her mother doesn't see him. She takes spoonfuls of soup while the man continues behind her, rooted to the back of the chair.

* * *

Mónica slips into the abandoned attic where her mother stores antiques. It is the dusty center of the house. *It's not here,* she frets. Right next to a plaster statue of the Virgin Mary, she finds a dirty mirror. Mónica cleans it with her hands. She makes out her profile. And sees the man watching her.

She doesn't resist. She feels her breath quicken.

"Why don't you leave?" she shouts, choking with emotion.

Her breathing distorts the reflection. The man only shrugs.

Mónica contains a scream. She's worn out. She clasps the mirror, hoping to shatter it to pieces with the pressure of her fingers, but can't and bangs it against the corner of a glass cabinet. Then, she begins to cry. She collapses against the cabinet, all the while feeling stifled. That's when she senses she's being watched. She opens her eyes.

Incredulous, she observes the man as he steadies himself, completely free of the boundary of the glass, silent, on the ceiling rafters, hanging upside-down, completely free of body weight.

Mónica is unable to shout. The terror freezes her.

* * *

She escapes from him or at least tries to. In the labyrinth of options, she feels the need to leave her house. She heads out into the open like an animal expelled from her cave. She bounces among the garden hawthorns: they seem like scrawls that could entangle you with ease. *The boulevard doesn't have walls*, she thinks. She finds the path almost without looking. It's an endless route, gray, lined with solemn, dying trees, squeezed into streets that slope toward the sea. She jumps, as usual, down the stairs. She hopes the physical exertion will prevent her from noticing her thoughts.

* * *

The man in the mirror follows her, walking on the houses and balconies perfectly parallel to the ground.

Mónica gives up. She leans against a tree. She doesn't know what to say.

She speaks to him:

"I come with Ton in the winter."

She knows she won't get rid of him.

"I'm with Ton," she continues, grasping at straws.

He follows at her pace. Mónica knows that she's not going further, that she's not going anywhere.

She speaks aimlessly, babbling:

"Ton…is a nickname, you know? His name is Washington."

She looks at the man who stopped as she did, his appearance unchanging. She tries to smile, though she feels like crying. Or calling for help.

"Doesn't it sound awful…Washington?" Mónica says.

He nods.

"It's horrible."

Mónica sighs, looks at the houses, shakes her head.

"What did you used to do?" he asks.

"We'd run," she remembers. "We'd go from here all the way to the beach."

"Let's run," he proposes.

He surprises her as always. She doesn't expect a defiant response from that creature. She agrees, without giving it much thought.

"OK, then," she laughs. "Go!"

She starts down the boulevard as fast as her legs will take her. The man takes long strides along the walls, doors and windowsills. Mónica begins to laugh, as is her custom, at her own excitement.

She looks to her side: all she distinguishes is the overcoat transformed in a billowy patch of cloth pierced by twilight beams, just behind her. And without reaching her. She sees how the man leaps, how he reels, and the desperate gesture, mouth wide open, of someone who realizes, without warning, that the ground ends, that the houses and the walls don't go all the way to the beach, and he falls flat on his face. The strange man can only cling in agony to a post, impotent, so as not to injure himself. He looks at her, tidies his suit and shrugs, visibly uncomfortable.

Mónica doesn't know what to do. *How lovely*, she squeals on the inside, sticks out her tongue. She approaches him, still panting, at the edge of the boulevard.

"I beat you," she says, without thinking whether all of this was sensible or appropriate.

He shrugs. She smiles:

"I think I'll be able to get rid of you."

"How?"

"I don't know."

Now Mónica waivers. She adjusts her hair. She looks the other way.

"But you do make me laugh. That's the first step."

He shakes his head, indecisive.

"The first step is for you to no longer feel any fear. That won't be long now."

* * *

"Ton goes to his parents' beach house in the summer," Mónica says. "He hangs out with the twins and Gabo's group."

In silence, they had walked along the waterfront. Mónica has gone inside one of those empty stately mansions in ruins that extend along the promenade. They move in the dark through what was once a bedroom. The light from outside barely penetrates with slashing, dusty beams.

"Why didn't you go with your friends?"

"I don't know."

She feels awkward. *How should I know, damn it? What does it matter? Who cares?*

"Maybe it's my personality."

She realizes the man has once again adopted an air of absence.

"You don't know it, but a wind is coming," he says, after a long pause, the first that Mónica does not interpret as hostile. "You await it, but don't know that yet."

"There are no winds here." She looks at him, somewhat uneasy. "There's not even a breeze."

"A wind will come."

Mónica blinks, not understanding what he's saying, but a shiver runs down her spine:

"I'm only waiting for Ton."

146

"It's too late," he says, raising his shoulders in disdain. "You're already gone."

"I'm here!" she protests, exasperated.

The man only adds:

"You were a long way away. That's why you found me."

She falls quiet, afraid.

* * *

Some afternoons they run again. He jokes that he'll show her how to walk like him. Even though the man extends his hand, encouraging her to climb up to the ceiling, he doesn't make the slightest attempt to come down. And Mónica grows scared imagining what balance must be like when one is upside down. Besides, she can't put her sneakers on the wallpaper. She knows she'd stain it, and her mother would complain. Every now and then, the arguments between her and the man turn boisterous. When her mother hears it, she doesn't understand why all the racket. Mónica has nothing to do, and friends don't visit her. But when her mother pops her head into the room, she is surprised to see her on the bed alone talking to the mirror or the ceiling. She prefers not to meddle because young people have their issues.

That midday in summer, the air warms up, Mónica's room is a pit of heat; she draws back the warm sheets with her body. She immediately looks at the mirror.

"Ton arrives today," she tells him, sleepy, and smiles. "There'll be a get-together at the twins' house."

The man changes his expression:

"Your face looks hopeful."

"How's that?"

Mónica has gotten used to his comments, to his insinuations that lead to a thousand put-downs, or to a primal fear she detests.

"It's a smiling face," he declares. "You're wasting your hope and you're going to need it."

A shiver shakes her to the core. Mónica hugs the pillow. She doesn't reply. She wonders why he seems to enjoy making those remarks, and why she, stupid, tolerates them. But isn't she complicit in her own annoyance? She doesn't do what she thinks. *If he bothers me, I should get rid of him.*

Instead, she asks, with tears in her eyes:

"Are you my friend?"

He doesn't answer the question.

Mónica becomes infuriated. Stupid. His company is a farce. Actually, he doesn't exist: he's a piece of glass. So then, why not act sensibly? Why not reject this hallucination that bothers and torments her?

But she can only manage to mumble, distraught:

"If you're my friend, you shouldn't be so cruel."

The man just gazes at her slowly:

"If I weren't cruel, I'd be lying."

She stays quiet. She tries to utter a few words, but only wants to cry. Before she does anything, he speaks up:

"Are you going to invite me to the party?"

Then, she kicks her feet as laughter gets the better of her and she feels like jumping up to hug him.

* * *

The couples dance slowly. The air reeks of cigarettes and liquor. The piano keys strike against the silence with a dim melody. There are synthesized shouts of human voices, a muted trumpet. Los Fabulosos Cadillacs' jazz plays in the twins' pickup. Mónica feels the effects of the alcohol, the melody, the reverberations of soft music.

She falls in sync with Ton's elastic movement. They twirl imperceptibly in the shadows. A double bass blends notes that flow in no apparent direction. *I dream my death is coming,* Vicentico sings, *I dream I see my fate.* The snare drum accentuates the lyrics. The cowbell trembles as if it were blacking out. *They hang string lights at dusk and party in streets.* Mónica dances. *I bid my farewell, death is coming for me… they embrace me and wish me luck.*

Without warning, the double bass drum and the sound mixer start blaring, like thousands of war drums. Then, a tide of bodies dashes into the shadows and they begin to spin and collide into one another. A distorted voice howls from all directions: *The saint dreamed of wounds, of wounds. Far from the flesh, the tortured one cried…her ominous dream!*

Mónica momentarily evades the swarm of arms and legs. But then she, too, jumps in with the others, quickly charting her own collision course. She loses her footing in the absolute confusion of the dark. The space is a mosh pit of jumping and blind encounters.

* * *

Mónica pulls Ton aside during a pause. They chat enveloped by the diffuse music and the rest of the group immersed in lax contemplation of the smoke.

"You're acting weird," she says to him. She stares at him with sad eyes, she passes him a drink.

"You're the weird one," Ton replies. "But we'll deal with that later."

He smiles. The atmosphere wears Mónica out. It wraps like a rubber band around her mouth.

* * *

When the uproar and smoke subside, she notices the oval mirror. She examines herself seated on an armchair against the wall, face gaunt, knees touching her chin. For a few moments, the blurry bodies of the dancers block her view. And then the man appears there.

With a stony expression, he sets his eyes on her:

"Do you see anything new?"

Mónica takes her time to respond since she understands how the game of senses is played.

"You." Nevertheless, she suspects that's not the only possible answer. She doesn't want to think anymore.

She prefers to distance herself from the question with some pretext, and it occurs to her to signal to the man with an elaborate gesture and begin a dance, like in a period film. He looks at her, skeptical, even though it's clear he's somewhat content. Suddenly, the glass trembles, as his hand reaches through it to take Mónica's fingers. His hand is warm and trembling.

"Why don't you walk on the ceiling?" Mónica asks to avoid feeling the way she does.

He doesn't answer.

Yes, you can, she thinks, entertained. *But if you walked like everyone else, you'd be at my level.*

She spins to his rhythm, as he leads her by the hand. Many laugh at the sight of their dance moves awkwardly out of step with the music.

"As always, she's had a bit too much to drink," Ton laughs.

Mónica dances with her eyes closed. When she opens them, she discovers, horrified, the spectacle offered up by the twins: Pedro and Manuel imitate each other dancing. They are watched by a small group of rowdy drunks looking for spoofs. The twins synchronize their slightest movements: the flex of neck muscles, the lateral movement of a pupil, the distance a foot slides. Mónica gazes at the man. *The same thing happens to me*, she thinks. *It's only me.* She frowns and strains her eyes. She can't see him. She wants to cry for no reason. Ton stops her in the midst of the out-of-control spinning of a demented dance.

Mónica and Ton stumble, at daybreak, along the seashore. The shore is still a foamy mirror of a black sky. With arms around each other, they walk amidst the crashing waves. They jostle one another. Ton nibbles on her neck. She thinks about mirror games. *Silliness*, she calms herself, lies down, buries her feet in wet sand. Finally, she gives in. Ton caresses her little by little. Mónica senses the moans coming from his body, which throbs and smells.

When Ton possesses her in a shuddering movement, her legs in the air, Mónica fixates on the image of her face in his mirror-coated sunglasses.

The man scintillates in the glass reflection. She looks at him without curiosity, or a way out. She can't continue. She abandons her body and her motions under Ton's weight, who thrusts into her. She imagines that everything stinks, including herself. She sinks, cries, moaning in silence.

* * *

She stops in front of the mirror in the room. She sobs:
"I don't understand a thing…"
The man in the mirror attends to her without becoming perturbed, in the middle of the darkness, in the quiet room. She can't make out his features, but, as if in a dream, she knows he's moving his lips.

"A wind is coming."
Mónica becomes flustered.
"I don't feel any wind."
She wants to smash and kick the mirror.
"I only feel disgust! Disgust with everything!"
She whimpers and, for no reason, begins to turn pale.

* * *

"A nervous breakdown, it's perfectly understandable," the family physician explains. "With Mónica's history, this is completely normal." Mónica hears a mixture of voices after waking up.

"It's been three days now, doctor," her mother complains, and she hears her sobs. "She gets up, she screams."

* * *

The mild winter cold on the promenade dissolves like a vapor cloud. Daylight fades into a humid curtain of dew. When she least expects it, at last, a bright afternoon in the midst of that haze of gloomy fog. Mónica remains still, staring at the ceiling. Nothing prompts her to move. She is constrained by a nameless peace.

Ton comes over, as he's been doing, ever since she went on bed rest.

"I'm a little better now," she whispers, her expression recovered. "Let's go for a walk."

152

* * *

Among the trees on the boulevard, the cold grows, swells, begins to feel almost solid. She extends a hand and the cold cuts her like crepe paper. She shatters it with a sudden movement of her arm, and it rebuilds in an instant, as if she'd never touched it. She blinks. This is not her world, not the one from before. Mónica has the impression she's entering an artificial realm, a stage decorated by images as thin as prop houses and trees on a movie set.

"The air feels like wool," she whispers.

Ton smiles at her. He doesn't understand.

There's a difference between us, Mónica thinks, as her words become surprisingly revelatory. *Now everything is a symbol of what is not present.*

She's overcome by melancholy at this realization. *He doesn't know.*

Ton begins to cuddle her with loving whispers the moment he sees her become engrossed in thought. Mónica returns his caresses because the sensation lets her be totally absorbed in herself. She feels his hands running over her breasts, intensifying her sensitivity by instinct.

He lifts her off the floor and kisses her. He massages her sides. She notices his excitement. As always happens when he doesn't know how to express that juvenile arousal, he wraps one arm around her waist and with the other grabs her legs, raising them horizontally. But this time Mónica doesn't understand what is happening until he lets go of her waist and suddenly hoists her up by the ankles. Sensing the ground so close to her eyes makes her bristle and choke.

"Let me down, let me down!" she howls, her heart in her mouth, shaking her head from to side to side.

Disconcerted, Ton puts her back down on the floor, as fast as he can.

Mónica gasps time and time again, hunching over herself. She sits downs slowly. The houses and trees spin around her.

Ton embraces her tightly. Only after a minute does Mónica understand, her eyes wide open.

* * *

"I know," she confronts the man. "You want to hurt me. You want everything to stink!"

The man becomes evasive:

"I'm not doing anything."

"I don't have that pestilence in me!" Monica says. "You're manipulating me so that I see the way you do!"

"How do I see things?" he counters. He appears on the ceiling, upside down, and advances through the room without moving.

"You see ruin and rot. I know it."

The man stays in front of her. Mónica feels an unease that weakens her. How frightening. It's a nuance she can't quite identify, but which troubles her and makes her feel stupid.

"Space changes appearance," he says. "It's a sign. The wool in the air is the skein of a thousand strands that no one sees."

Mónica thinks of the objects scattered in the darkness of the room. The cloud of wool fibers all around her. It resembled crepe paper, but now she feels the strands. If one were to follow one piece, it would go on infinitely. Ever since summer she has kept all of them inside, like breath. Those strands exasperate her. They stitch across her mind, her feelings, her multilateral reflection in the mirror. *It's the abyss of worldly things.* They're thick, tangled weaves, and bruised, pale corpses swing from the knots. She glanced quickly behind her and it's the breath of her past: a personal labyrinth of her suffocating on the way back home.

"I can't take it anymore!" she stammers. She turns her head, gasps, her eyes pulse about to burst. "I see it…everyone is dead! Ton, the strands!"

With her back to the man, she can't see him extend a hand with a distraught expression. Nonetheless, she continues to screech, vitreous.

"Yes, they're dead. Now and when the wind comes. Not even I know when it'll occur. But I know what I see, I know it's soon. The houses will levitate in the air, the sea will be the deluge that everyone has seen in dreams. It'll be an autumn morning; at first, there'll be dozens of corpses. Don't hope. Ton will be among them. Pay attention to the strand in the mirror…"

The puff of air cools and reveals a port scene. Thin characters made of tinsel dance in the wind. The figure with Ton's profile gets lost among the others moving to and fro out in the open. But it's him, eviscerated, among a row of dead people, naked. Half his skull is missing, his stomach open, and the threads of his exposed intestines are tiny, restless, white worms. She smells the decomposition.

"You see the wind," the man explains.

Mónica's eyes are wild.

"I don't want to see you!" she mutters, gasps. "Get out of here!…You hear me?…No more!…"

The man obeys. He dissolves into the mirror through a duplicate room that isn't Mónica's, even though she knows it's one and the same.

* * *

After midnight, she's still awake in the dark. She studies herself in the mirror.

"Are you there?"

She leans forward to touch the glass. She confirms there's nobody inside.

"Good."

* * *

Dawn breaks in the room. She hasn't slept. She tries to breathe easy. The man only brought problems. The objects aren't the ends of strands that lead to corpses. But the illness and the visions continue. And now she has elaborate dreams of him. She goes on walks with Ton, but the strolls only bring the consolation of ice to fever. She thinks: *This is a placebo.*

"Where is there peace?" she whispers. The days pass. Confusedly, she knows her problem is not a solution. She perceives that inside of her is a jungle of objects that constitutes the limit of a question. She doesn't know the question, but senses the density of fibers and strands, starving.

The days go on; her breathing agitated. She goes in and out of the house, always wearing a dressing gown or barely dressed. Standing, on the doorstep at the entrance, she looks at herself in the side table mirror in the foyer.

"What's your name?" she asks. She asks for him. Her own anxiety answers back.

She then delves slowly into her own features. She discovers in her eyes impatience, alarm.

He's not there.

The thought saddens her, but then she immediately gets annoyed. She goes up to her bedroom. The sun rises countless times. She doesn't dream of rows of dead people. She dreams of him in enormous rooms, smudged, where they talk without pause about the fabric of the world that is quickly becoming thin. He tells her: "Loneliness isn't being away from everyone, but rather just one person."

* * *

Night comes and she dreams again. Once more it's a scene in a room of her empty house. It contains the highlights of the twins' party: the mosh pit, the jumping, the shouting, the tangled mess of hair and clothes. Mónica walks among them with the same ease as if she were awake. He should be there. But the violence intensifies with every turn, incessant: faces beaten into deformity, terrified masses trying to flee, gunshots to heads with terrified faces. She receives a blow to the head. They take her down and she yells. Blood drips down her cheek. She whimpers. She tries to stop the blood with her hand, but they're strands from the weft.

I must get to him, she repeats to herself. This time she'll get to him. She must speak to him. And then the dancers start to stampede. But they don't touch her. Not even the air touches her. The world hangs by a thread. The man waits for her in the middle. Motionless. Mónica catches up to him.

* * *

I love you. It is said without words.

"Who are you?" she asks. "They call me Michael," he replies. "I'm the angel that comes before the end of the world."

"Who am I?" Mónica asks, not understanding.

He responds without hesitation:

"You're the woman they talk about in the song."

She listens, the distorted voice leads the commotion, as it makes way through the dream:

The saint dreamed of wounds, of wounds. Far from the flesh, the tortured one cried…her ominous dream!

Then she looks at her hands. Massive wounds. Everything makes sense: the disgust, the premonitions, that dream.

The man cleans her face, arranges the strands of hair with his fingers. She draws herself closer. They kiss.

There's a silence that shatters, like a scream, like thousands of screams.

She opens her eyes. Only the empty mirror, the darkened room.

* * *

"How is she doing?" the doctor asks.

"Much better," her mom answers.

"That's normal," he says. "These cases tend to stabilize."

They move down the hall. The doctor lightly knocks on the door. They don't wait for a response. When they see her, Mónica has one foot on the wall. Mouths agape, they watch as she lifts her other foot. Perfectly perpendicular, she takes agile

158

step after step, up the wallpaper until she's standing upside down on the ceiling.

She observes the sea through the window, like one looking for boats.

"A wind is coming," she declares.

At that point neither her mom nor the doctor dare deny it.

Glowworms

By María del Río

To Blanca Varela

A series of precise words insists on taking up nearly all of the space on my desk, demanding figures, logical phrases, heroic histories of exemplary women, bravery and battles. There's another list of minor words, which are harder to identify, as if disguising themselves in a foreign or nonexistent language, to be read aloud (and cause laughter, evoke curiosity or give goosebumps to those who attempt to employ them) but not necessarily understood. At the same time, capital letters are wanting to be placed, or not, like on a crown, a decision made for aesthetic reasons rather than as a solemn investiture.

The first ones are necessary in a world in which we must show good sense and competency. To win a race whose prize is another race. To win.

The second ones only appear like glowworms, unaware of their mission, not knowing whether they shine to attract predators and serve as instant food, or to intimidate their admirers/adversaries with the light produced upon contact with something else. Or with themselves. On second thought, they're not scared of being devoured, since that would also give their life meaning, since that would also give, since that would also.

Loss of Appetite

By Juan Manuel Robles

Andrea would always say she dreamed of crossing the pond. Europe was a series of museums and squares floating around in her romantic aspirations. It's easy for me to close my eyes and remember us together, losing ourselves in literature in my room; her, lying down on the bed with a black laptop while I offered dazzling, yet stolen metaphors. Andrea wanted to learn how to write so her visits had something to do with that, I suppose. But distractions won out. We'd stare at the red wall hung with an enormous picture, among many others, of me when I was three years old (a sweet anachronism for all eternity). You *were* a cute little boy, she said the third or fourth time she came to my house, her gaze openly oscillating between that two-dimensional past and the corpulent present full of craters. I think it was the emphatic tenderness in how she highlighted this contrast that made me fall in love with her. It was on a Friday. We had just finished the usual pollo a la brasa we'd always order when our stomachs growled. Andrea was praising my gigantic eyes —the ones in the picture—when she detected, in the black pupils of my childhood, a tiny, duplicated reflection: Look, the umbrella lights the photographer used over twenty years ago, how crazy is that! Her observation amazed me (even glancing at a picture she was baroque). At that point, I'd say I was melting. I noticed her thick platform sneakers, my eyes then rose to the cherry-colored pants that hugged her thighs, and I stopped at her neckline, a deep neckline condemned to a life of perennial instability. I prepared to touch her, my hands in hers, but she looked at the time, said a hasty goodbye with a lukewarm kiss on the cheek and headed to the door with a silver purse tucked under her arm. She said she'd come back the next day. She never did.

What happened the night of the party when I finally got to see her again is pretty obvious. Offering details would be a vain exercise in verbal pyrotechnics, a schmaltzy theatrical reconstruction and an insufferable display of bad literature. Certain clichéd scenes everyone can imagine: to wit, an idiot gets drunk at a social feast, which the woman he secretly loves attends; aided by the evening's colorful concoctions, he decides to approach her; he nervously smiles and, after a cheap prelude, manages to say, I'm in love with you. Well, Andrea replied, she was very flattered that I felt *that* for her, César, but you have to understand, you don't choose who you fall in love with. I sighed. As of then, the tape is erased. A few days later, they told me I wound up sprawled out leaning against a column in the living room, stripped of any vestige of psychomotor dignity, moaning that my life was a misery.

After some time, I called her on the phone. I vaguely apologized for the scene and offered to explain everything over an order of green tamales, my treat, but she didn't want to see me: listen, César, it's going to be awkward. Silence ensued. I wrote some things for you, I insisted, right when the last-ditch effort of a drowning man resembles a poetry recital. For me?! Hmmm, look, to be honest, I don't know what you could've written about me, I don't know, I still think this is awkward, but since you insist, go to Café Italia tomorrow around eleven and you can give me what it is you have for me…I'll just say one thing: if I'm not there, don't wait … She hung up. Outside, a rat gray bird became a colorful harbinger of blind optimism. In a torrent of amorous fervor, I compiled all of the documents I had written about her. It turns out I wasn't terribly imaginative: andrea1.doc, andrea2.doc, andrea3.doc… I stayed up until the wee hours correcting typos, inflating metaphors, tempering hyperboles and censoring lubricated verbal secretions—and erections. I noticed there weren't enough decent poems, so I included short stories and imaginative passages from unfinished novels in the packet in an attempt to show how *she* had also inspired these literary artifacts. I woke up early the next day and grabbed a yellow envelope. I then headed for the café. Andrea never showed up that morning, and the tamale orders followed one after the other until I was stuffed. A sunny day is the cruelest of scenes for a man to wander with the weight of sadness on his back, I wrote in my diary that night (at that age, you value paradoxes way too much).

When the final violins played in that lonely scene, and I was about to split, shall we say, to the soul's dressing room (urgently, to the café bathroom), I ran into Ángel, an effeminate aspiring photographer, a mutual friend of mine and Andrea's, who also happened to be, among other things, the artist behind the image of a legless dancer that perpetually balanced on the wall in my room. After asking without much interest why the long face, he said he'd offered a personal photo shoot to Andrea: a cheap lie to take advantage of darling's vanity. Since he was going to see her, I asked him to give her the envelope (I squeezed it tightly with my right hand as if it were a heart). He replied, with an air of annoyance, that I shouldn't involve him in *my* issues. But after I treated him to a couple of butifarra country ham sandwiches, he decided to accept my request. I told him I'd better drop off my collection later: I wanted to add a few last-minute poems, and final palpitations.

I took him the envelope the next day. I went to his house with my boxer (Andrea had petted him effusively the last time she visited me, transforming the poor animal into a symbol). Don't read what's in there, I told Ángel. He feigned serious outrage and asked, what do you take me for? It was obvious Ángel was going to read each and every page. Just ask yourself the question: what would you do? But dignity is the fraction of the hypothalamus that melts before everything else when a woman floods your gray matter with color. Everything else is inconsequential. He let me know that he'd be seeing Andrea the following Tuesday: he was doing the photo shoot that day. Don't worry about it, *bróder*, I'll give her the envelope. The wind rocked the branches on the tree at the entrance to his house, and my dog, tongue out, appeared to join the festive literary moment by showering the trunk with saliva while birds sang and cars seemed to get along well with the asphalt. Hope is a white elixir that intoxicates the soul and makes us profoundly pretentious and tacky.

* * *

When I was writing my first short stories, someone suggested that, right after I met a girl I liked, I should draft a brief description of her features: this would, in turn, serve to create a sort of Profile Database for use in future literary efforts. If films utilize real people, why would you go around inventing combinations of eyes, noses, necks, eyelids and cheeks? Anyway, the description I wrote of Andrea in my diary contained the following: She has generous breasts and always wears light tank tops, her expression is tender, she has a very wide forehead and speaks as if she were deflating. Her make-up artist was wise to sharpen her eyebrows, giving her a pinch of character and a certain feminine power of intimidation, which creates a truly unsettling contrast if you catch her smiling: a smile activated by the same facial muscle movements that insinuate shyness. But careful, that's not to say she's shy: *that* is the point. The general puerility of her expression is diminished by the way she frowns: a rough phenomenon, tremendous, universal, capable of attracting American independent film producers or, at the very least,

French auteurs. Andrea owns purses in metallic tones, a large private collection. When she wears one on her arm, you're tempted to watch her from the second floor of a building, small, walking down a random street: her purse swinging as if created for the sole purpose of being *there*. I was thinking of that naïve text-icle—the words that passed through the cranial cavity like those neon signs with flashing letters—when Ángel phoned to tell me he had enlarged the photos of Andrea. You have to come check them out, he said. The prints were still wet when I arrived.

It turned out to be an insufferably immense assortment of poses. Andrea sitting on the edge of her bed subjected to the harsh backlight, forcing the observer to undertake a lovely exercise in anatomical memory just to discern her features in that thick blackness. Andrea, barefoot, hugging her knees, ephemerally timid, hair deliberately disheveled. Andrea picking something up, adorned by the slightest trace of a light-colored bra. And check this one out, he said. A close-up of Andrea looking down with a tender gesture so natural it appeared staged. I got closer. Dutifully, Ángel handed me a magnifying glass. The ghostly reflection of a written page appeared in her intensely-focused pupils: Andrea reading a poem by a man she wasn't all that interested in. I caught her in the exact moment she was reading your work, Ángel pointed out. He smiled. Never had a friend ever done anything so beautifully mean-spirited to me.

Summer vacation began, and I decided to look for a job. Andrea and I had studied Humanities, but what we both wanted was to write. We dreamed of having a full-page column in a bourgeois newspaper where we could discuss, for example, art and culture, while we quietly—at night, perhaps—became writers. But reality tends to arrive as a slap in the face: I was hired as an intern for a website. I drafted pieces for the entertainment section. Intrigue, gossip, unconfirmed love affairs, confirmed love affairs, love affairs destroyed. I think I sank to protozoa status. I sought profundity and found it, ha! I'd go to breakfast with a trendy singer, lunch with a trendy conductor, dinner with a trendy dancer. After a while, my boss told me they needed to hire another person. I thought of Andrea. But if she couldn't stand to grab tamales with me, she'd be less inclined to stand the idea of sharing an office. I thought then of Paolo, her best friend and a law student with journalistic interests. A week later, Paolo was working by my side. Every now and then, during our lunch hour, I'd ask him about Andrea. He'd respond with flippant trivialities, which I'd mentally equate with the poses from that awful photo shoot. One day, while we were out, he told me he was having a birthday party on Saturday. You should come.

I went. I arrived with Ángel, who was wearing a gay t-shirt that was appallingly tight in the waist. I shall reserve the description of my clothing, leave it to the sensible capriciousness of the reader's imagination. I gave Paolo a hug. I offered a sweeping, open-handed wave to his inebriated friends. At one end of the garden, I caught a glimpse of Andrea. I'd decided not to drink any alcohol, even if that meant suppressing the production of experiential literature that evening. So I ate. There were hors d'oeuvres to snack on: *papa a la huancaína*, skewers, breads, *anticucho* grilled beef heart kebabs. All of a sudden, she approached with nocturnal calm. Nervous, I bit into a crusty piece of bread, and the sight of Andrea walking toward me caused my jaw to tremble in a lithe quake.

"So, César, how are you?"

"Hi. Good. Just hanging out…"

"Hey…I wanted to tell you…I don't really know how to say it…I loved what you wrote. I really liked it, for real. It was amazing."

"Oh, yeah? How cool."

"…"

"…"

"I loved it. You know what?…I think you could actually make a living doing that."

It was one of those sentences that seemed to be uttered before it was articulated, and even after it was uttered, carried on in a sharp, unbearable echo. I couldn't help myself, I began to laugh. That's the benefit of seeing yourself as a character: tragedies lose their weight. But the anemic glow of a nearby lantern had haughty, dramatic aspirations. I was growing sad. Andrea grabbed a potato, dunked it in the creamy sauce and placed it in the smooth curl of her divine tongue. I wanted to turn into a potato. Forced by the sudden silence, she told me about a long trip she was planning to Amsterdam. This left me speechless. The partygoers laughed in their small groups. Ángel smiled mockingly from a distance: it was sweet to imagine him with a dagger stuck in the middle of his heart. That's what I wanted to tell you, she repeated and headed back to her corner of the party. A curtain of people began to close in around her again. The lantern finally achieved its melodramatic effect (and was included in my corresponding diary entry). Once Andrea left the get-together, I started drinking. The next day, Paolo found the name ANDREA, lovingly carved by a key or other sharp object, on the bathroom wall, written in a sliding scale, in which the first A was twice the size of the last. Everything pointed to me.

* * *

Months later we ran into each other at a current affairs magazine. I live in a very small city, where folks tend to cross paths. I'd left the entertainment section to become a rookie beat reporter, or something like that, and my work now consisted of writing urban stories: circus tamers overwhelmed by loneliness without their animals, television dwarves, children who crushed gravel to survive, true stories of people stuck in jail. I specialized in social dramas. She, in turn, had a position in the culinary section. She'd interview chefs and transcribe recipes. They'd invite her to fancy restaurants. She gained weight. To me, she looked prettier than ever: her new pace of life had padded certain previously imperceptible protuberances. I tried to get close to her a few other times; I sent emails full of generous invitations to enjoy the sunset with a ceviche overlooking the sea. But one night followed another, and the only thing she'd talk to me about— the few times she talked to me—was her impending trip to Amsterdam. And her new boyfriend, who apparently had a lot to do with the matter. Whenever she'd bring him up, I'd remember that photo where her bra was showing (sometimes I'm a linear thinker).

A year or so had passed since the embarrassing declaration of love when I found out, through Paolo, that Andrea had a departure date for Holland. She'd be going with her boyfriend who, according to several vague descriptions from friends, was an athletic guy with black curly hair, bushy eyebrows and happy, royal blue eyes. They also said Andrea had won his heart by cooking those *Novoandina* recipes she'd learned at work. But at the time, I found myself at the other end of reality, knee-deep in an investigative report on drug mules incarcerated in the women's penitentiary: beautiful girls, both Peruvians and foreigners who had lost their freedom for the possibility of getting their hands on three or four thousand dollars. Every Saturday, I'd go to the prison disguised as a regular civilian. I became especially friendly with Karen, a nineteen-year-old from Seville who had hidden three kilos of cocaine in her vagina, and who's duck walk alerted airport security. Each week, I'd bring her rotisserie chicken and the daily papers. We'd eat. We'd laugh. It took me six Saturdays to realize Karen, seated with her back to the sea in the distance, around two thirty in the afternoon, would be enveloped in a light that softened her cheeks, smoothed her eyelids, and defined her lips. By chance, this same light struck directly at my hypothalamus.

One day, as I was returning home, Ángel stopped me half a block from my house (with such surprising apparitions, he lived up to his name in an astonishing way) and told me Andrea had organized a farewell party. What? She didn't invite you? The streetlight appeared divine as it suddenly collapsed and split the nape of his neck. He said he was on his way there. I kept quiet and then half-heartedly said goodbye. I decided to stay in with my dog that night. I watched Nickelodeon on cable. A lightbulb suddenly burned out and lent the red room the necessary desolation to provoke a few tears. I remembered her right there, writing on her jet-black laptop, exploring twist endings in stories featuring well-mannered fishermen who possessed an enviable lexical richness. I didn't leave my room.

On the Friday morning Andrea was leaving—Paolo had confirmed the date—I decided to call her one last time. When she answered, distant nasal voices reciting numbers told me she was at the airport. The casual precision of my call felt so cinematic…I became inspired.

"Before you go, I wanted to tell you…"

"…"

"Nothing, just…that I'll be waiting for you…"

"I don't think it's a good idea for you to call me right now. I have to hang up. Bye."

It's incredible how telephones can shine when the woman you love hangs up on the other end of the line. I spent the rest of the day in pajamas. When night fell, I decided to put a porno in the VHS, which prompted a faltering erection and subsequent premature ejaculation. I slept. On Saturday, I headed early to the prison. I bought the usual half chicken. Karen asked me why I was so sad. I figured it would border on the height of imbecility if I were to bring up my miniscule miseries in front of someone who had lost their freedom. I responded that nothing was up, it was just her impression. Look, I brought you the paper. I set it on the table. On the front page, the president was offering condolences to the families of the 112 victims of the *Paraíso* supermarket flooding; on the right, the national soccer team showed off bronze medals won in the recent Paralympic Games; and, at the very bottom, the photo of a woman who, if she hadn't been handcuffed and surrounded by agents, could've been Andrea: wide forehead, pronounced furrowed brow, and large breasts that could still be seen despite her struggling attempt to keep her head down and conceal her identity from the cameras. The chicken wafted its habitual steam. Those at neighboring tables envied us.

"She'll be brought here in a couple of weeks," Karen said.

Only then did I look back at the photograph and begin to read the news report:

Last Friday, the Anti-Drug Unit of the National Police detained a young woman who was attempting to smuggle almost eight kilos of high-grade cocaine into Holland. Andrea Rivera Ruiz (22) was waiting at the Dutch airline KLM's gate for the boarding of its flight bound for Amsterdam. She appeared nervous. A sudden call to her cellphone alerted international airport police (according to the phone intercept carried out by the intelligence division, an unidentified subject said, "I'll be waiting for you"). Upon her arrest, public safety officials confirmed their suspicions: the thorough search performed by agents and a representative from the Public Prosecutor's Office revealed 912 grams of cocaine hydrochloride hidden in her platform sneakers. After being transferred to a nearby office, police examined her luggage and found an additional seven kilos concealed in the bottom of her backpack, wrapped in the banana leaves used for tamales to throw off canine detectors. Rivera, a Peruvian citizen, was immediately placed, according to the law, in the custody of the National Anti-Drug Directorate, which will be in charge of the investigation.

"Of course, and according to the law, they'll investigate her, they'll strip her, they'll grope her and, after fifteen days, they'll bring her here in a van."

I compulsively ate a chicken leg. Karen began to once again recall her time at the police station, the cell she'd been in before they brought her to the prison. She'd already told me the story when we met. It was the first thing I had asked her with the feigned tenderness my job demands: she spoke of bad cops who fondled the women and asked them for money while threatening to aggravate their charges. I already had everything written down and couldn't imagine any additional detail that could intensify the dramatic quality of her tale. On that occasion—months earlier—she had cried. Now, her voice began to crack. I had no intention of listening to her account again. So, sad and defenseless, her lips assumed intolerable creases. It wasn't even two thirty in the afternoon yet. I gave her a kiss on the cheek. Once I was outside, I thought how Karen would smell of chicken for quite some time. Life in prison is hard.

* * *

It took me two hours to convince the agents that I had nothing to do with the matter. My phone number had been stored in Andrea's cell and, without the boyfriend—who had since vanished—they came to my house while I was at the penitentiary with Karen. To be honest, apart from a bit of damage to my lock and the fact that they knocked out my boxer, the officers were extremely cordial. I told them everything. I think I bored them a bit: they asked how it was relevant that Andrea had noticed that the photographer's umbrella lights could be seen in my eyes on the print from twenty years earlier. I told them I didn't know: I'm just sharing details because I know you all work with details. Nor were they interested in the fact that, in the very room they had just destroyed, the two of us used to eat rotisserie chicken legs. They took the photo of her reading my work to analyze it in their investigation. They had already confiscated my writings. How? Andrea had kept them in the same backpack where she hid the other disastrous package. I smiled when I learned she'd planned to take them with her. The lead agent stated: We've carefully read the material. I'd like to enlist your services in the future. You see, there's someone I'd like to write things to, you know, a lady friend. You know what, man? I think you could actually make a living doing that. I discreetly grimaced, with the timid scowl of one who shows tepid indignation before an armed authority figure. He seemed to understand and, in a more serious tone, added:

"Thanks all the same. Without your call, I don't know if we'd have risked taking action."

I thought the universe had exceeded its powers in settling scores. I behaved pathetically right until the end. But what happened when I went to the prison to visit Karen and, in addition, ran into Andrea? Well, that, too, would be a vain exercise in verbal pyrotechnics, a schmaltzy theatrical reconstruction and an insufferable display of bad literature. The clichéd scene gushes freely from any sensitive imagination: the beautiful girl, fallen from grace, realizes that the idiot who desperately loved her is actually a good guy and his love should be reciprocated, but the man who would once have given his life for her, discovers that the colorful spirits that flooded his gray matter have disappeared. Of course, a third element completes the story, the long take that slowly expands like at the end of a bad film: Karen will be out on parole in three weeks. For the time being, I like to see her on Saturdays between two and four in the afternoon, to touch her long, white hands, while in her pupils is reflected, in duplicate, a tiny, hot, dead rotisserie chicken. Twenty days is nothing. Ángel has offered to take photos of us. Holding one another tightly. With our hands all over each other.

The Nesting Phase

By Nataly Villena Vega

The manuscript had been sitting in a drawer for over five years. One day Tiziana asked me to empty the two large shelves in the basement where she had saved old contracts and long-abandoned projects. I carried up stacks of paper and organized them on a table in the courtyard set up for that purpose since my tiny office could barely hold the essentials to handle the paperwork at La Tempête, the publishing house where I worked. It was May, I remember it well because a radiant sun shone despite the chill gusts of wind that flowed along the Rue de Seine and entered through a crack under the door. I had been filling a black trash bag with what I determined to be truly useless—uncorrected proofs, advance copies, galleys—when all of a sudden, I found a manuscript with a French title, *Diamants et silex.*

The first paragraph didn't remind me of anything, but after reading the second one, I realized it was a translation of José María Arguedas: *«Ses yeux étaient petits, son front bas, ses pommettes brillantes; il était râblé, de courte taille. Son pantalon était retenu par un chumpi, une ceinture ornée de canards et de taureaux».* The manuscript was old, the paper had taken on the characteristic yellow of failed endeavors. I found this discovery both odd and fascinating, a symbolic welcome to the heart and soul of La Tempête, and when Tiziana arrived at the office that afternoon, I asked if she'd absolutely given up on the idea of publishing Arguedas. "Nothing would've pleased me more," she responded, "but it became complicated back then," she added without offering any more details before answering the phone, which rang incessantly when she was present. We didn't broach the subject again, and I continued with my tasks after jotting a note in my to-do list and putting the text in a safe place. The rest of the papers went in the dumpster that same weekend.

That whole month and most of June, I had ample time to meticulously review our catalog and lose myself in the forthcoming titles. Those were intense weeks in my personal life. Andreas asked me to move in, and I left the room I'd rented at Emilie's for the last two years. It wasn't a drastic change, we already spent most of our time together, but moving my things into his apartment, depriving myself of my own personal space, put me in a vulnerable situation. We were forced to get along.

Finding a place in Paris requires a lot of time, money and luck, and up until then, I'd had it. One afternoon in the metro, squashed by the rush hour crowd, I ran into a Peruvian girl from one of my French classes. "I know of a room," she said before getting off the train, "I'll text you the information." Soon after, I met Emilie, a Frenchwoman whose father was from Pucallpa and who welcomed me into her home with her lovely Amazonian accent. And just like that, a twenty-four-month period of rebuilding began. I had left behind a post-war Peru and almost anywhere else seemed much more hospitable, much safer to me.

But that hadn't been my first move. I was first dumped out of the nest fifteen years earlier after an explosion, a deafening noise that rocked my adolescence. One of the many bombs that shook Huanta that August shattered the roof of our small store one Saturday morning. Early Sunday, we climbed onto a packed bus with whatever we could carry and, stunned by fear, sped from the city in the dark that precedes dawn, not knowing it would be forever.

Whenever we arrive in a new place to settle down, the city sparkles, and discovering it all makes life far from our loved ones appear more like an exciting adventure. In Lima that excitement dissipated in just a few months and we had to keep on moving.

Fifteen years later, coming to Paris meant coming out of the dark, understanding that the sum of daily activities could be so much more than survival, pure and simple. Still, once the initial euphoria fades, starting a new life abroad is always a challenging proposition, taking on odd jobs just to make ends meet, to pay for a small room, a monthly metro pass and a couple of tickets to the movies.

That's how things were going when I found work at an architecture firm, and where I met Andreas.

We started dating, and once I finished my editing course and thought I'd return home, Andreas encouraged me to quickly find a job, not knowing it was one of the hardest industries to break into in France. I sent out countless applications, was contacted by a handful of places, got very few interviews, and passed through Odéon and Sèvres-Babylone so often I came to know the tiny map of Parisian publishing houses like the back of my hand. Men and women with pompous surnames welcomed me, praised my work ethic, but in the end kindly, yet firmly rejected my candidacy.

For the first time I began to sense the invisible barrier that stretches beyond effort, beyond language, and which I'd never seen or wanted to see in myself. I felt as though I'd stepped into the shoes of those young people from the Peruvian highlands who arrive in the big city to earn a living and quickly understand there is no space for them in that world. I was overcome by rage and hopelessness. I seriously considered going back to Peru, visualizing my defeat, and deciding to tell no one. My hesitation lasted almost six months, and just when I was about to throw in the towel, La Tempête called.

That's how I stepped through the door at 18 Rue de Seine for the first time and began work at one of the most unique independent publishers in the French intellectual world.

La Tempête was founded in the 1960s and passed down from hand to hand until it fell under the direction of Tiziana's father, a Romanian intellectual who had arrived in France after the Second World War. When he died, Tiziana took the reins and continued to engage in the political incorrectness that Mihail had vigorously followed; like him, she managed the business with the same fiery character and financial impulsiveness. When I started at La Tempête, the company was on the verge of bankruptcy for the umpteenth time.

It was an agonizing period we emerged from unscathed thanks to a sympathetic benefactor, and week after week, we anxiously watched the situation slowly improve. March arrived and suddenly, we entered an exciting quarter of new titles and satisfactory sales figures. The latest releases from our *Dossiers* collection appeared in the pages of *Figaro Littéraire*, *Libération*, *L'Express*, *Le Monde*; our authors visited us, pleased and intrigued by the work that a publishing house so small and independent could accomplish. Feeling confident thanks to the small victories I'd contributed my grain of sand to, I set a personal goal to publish at least one Peruvian writer during my tenure at La Tempête. Shortly afterwards, I found the manuscript.

* * *

At the end of June, Andreas suggested we buy an apartment together. I'd never thought about it before. That would mean putting down roots, if not permanently, at least for many years. Without giving ourselves much time to reflect, and despite my initial reservations, we set out on an intense search. Summer had begun. We devoted the little energy we had after work and visited all kinds of properties, most of them puny and not in the best neighborhoods. Andreas didn't have high expectations and his pragmatism led him to reduce his wish list to the bare minimum. I, on the other hand, projected all manner of hope onto this future home. "You like the old France," he said one day, appalled. "I prefer to design my own habitat; all I need are four good walls."

The weeks passed, and as the days went by, our enthusiasm gave way to impatience. Andreas spent his evenings checking the classifieds. I devoted a large part of my mornings doing the same, in the midst of budgets and distributor contracts, discreetly neglecting the upcoming publications. It took all my attention until one morning, Geneviève, the editor at La Tempête, received a visit.

I wasn't surprised. Our offices were near the Académie Française, and authors would stop by spur of the moment, say hello, grab a coffee and browse our most recent titles. Her visitor was Claude Fell, a Latin Americanist and translator, and Geneviève called me over to introduce us. I knew him, having attended one of his lectures during my Master's, and had the utmost respect and admiration for him. He obviously didn't remember me, but seeing my enthusiasm, tactfully pretended to recognize me. Geneviève said she'd been thinking about publishing a series to celebrate the "Year of Mexico" in France, and Fell presented a list of authors that deserved to be translated. As I listened to him, I thought it was the perfect time to mention Arguedas. We wrapped up our discussion, and I told him about *Diamonds and Flint*. Fell smiled. He knew the translation quite well: his wife had done it.

They tried to find an editor for a few years before abandoning the idea. He was surprised to learn we had the manuscript in our archives. "Arguedas is a unique case," he told Geneviève, "a writer who wore his heart on his sleeve, torn between two languages, the product of two cultures that have always been in conflict. He's a very special writer. Deep down, he's an outlier who managed to create a hybrid language. In literature, I'd call him a *rara avis*," he emphasized, adding that for a translator, the novel was both a joy and a challenge despite its brevity, and precisely because of it. It was powerful and delicate at the same time, structured like a Greek tragedy. Geneviève, who had never heard of him, was immediately interested and took notes. The two of them carried on talking about the Mexican series, and I said goodbye feeling satisfied. After walking him to the door, Geneviève stopped by my office to say she found the idea compelling, but knew Tiziana would reject it. I promised to do whatever it took to convince her.

Just as Geneviève thought, Tiziana was skeptical of Fell's proposal. "It'll be the 'Year of Mexico,' but Latin American literature has fallen out of favor," she said. We highlighted the government's planned activities and the available funding. She didn't seem convinced and her face betrayed mild annoyance. "Latin America's time has passed. It's the East, the Orient, that is all the rage now," she declared cuttingly.

I thought it best to leave Peru out of the discussion and raise the topic on another occasion, plus the phone rang and I left to answer it. While I dealt with the phone request, I could hear Geneviève mention Arguedas. Tiziana shot me a look, sighed and gestured in annoyance, then stood and told us we'd be better off finding her a Turkish or Syrian author, for example, because that's what was hot today. She entered her office and slammed the door.

Geneviève beckoned me over, and I followed her out to the courtyard. Smoking a cigarette, she gently told me it didn't look good for the Mexican project, at least not how she'd envisioned it, but I should insist on Peru. I was filled with enthusiasm. I imagined the printed pages, the cover. I waited a couple of days and quietly began making initial inquiries. It was 2010, and the crisis hadn't yet decimated resources. With a few phone calls and emails, I was certain I could come up with the funds for the translation. I told myself that Geneviève, and the keen instinct she was known for, had picked up on the originality of an author this seminal to someone like me, and so far-removed from a world like this. "If we don't jump on it soon, someone else will," she warned me days later.

That same afternoon the *Livres Hebdo* magazine arrived at the office announcing the upcoming book releases and I found what felt like a sign in the name of another Peruvian soon to be published by Gallimard. As soon as I could, I logged onto the Edistat portal, searched every project related to Arguedas, and noticed that Métailié had registered *El Sexto* some time ago. I was going over my plan all afternoon while attending a talk when I remembered that the 100th anniversary of Arguedas's birth fell precisely in 2011, a major oversight on my part that had caused me to lose valuable weeks. That evening, I returned to La Tempête determined to extract a yes from Tiziana and contact the translator right away.

I found her in the office accompanied by a writer we'd been having issues with so I didn't dare interrupt her. Still, I began making inquiries and after a call to Claude Fell I had obtained the address for the person who'd have to approve the project. It was Sybila Arredondo, Arguedas's widow, who coincidentally lived in France. Fell suggested I write her a letter.

That simple, yet essential, part of my day-to-day activities, hadn't dawned on me: I would have to contact Sybila Arredondo to secure rights for the translation into French.

The mere thought of having to do that made me stop. In my mind, and in my heart, Arguedas represented the possibility of finding salvation through art from a painful and fractured reality, while the figure of Sybila, as I remembered her, evoked the destruction of dreams, insanity, fury, the death of ideals, hate. Doubt and profound discomfort plagued me. I couldn't write that letter. However, I couldn't give up on the idea of seeing that very book published under our imprint. I went to find Tiziana, to lay out the situation, express a sense of urgency and my inner conflict, but she had already left.

That night Andreas returned to the apartment in high spirits. He had just visited a house on the outskirts, a fifteen-minute train ride away, and was positive he had finally found our future home. He showed me the pictures he'd taken and asked me to go see it in two days.

Tiziana arrived early the next morning, and I took advantage of the reigning tranquility. I reiterated the idea of publishing Arguedas. Her reluctance was obvious. I told her about the conversation with Fell, the 100th anniversary, the novel. She listened until I finished speaking. "You know I love Peru," she said, "but I don't think this book works, and as you know, we're in no position to experiment. One mistake could be fatal." I detailed the sales potential, saying he was fundamental to understanding Latin America, and this opportunity was a stroke of rare luck. She smiled and sat down beside me. "Here in France, we were interested in Peru in the 1980s when your president said he was inspired by Mitterrand. Interest grew when the massacres and bombings began. That whole situation was unbelievable to us. I went there on vacation with my husband and kids," she laughed. "I don't know why none of the warnings were enough for us, and I have to say, we spent several happy days there. When it calmed down a bit in the 1990s, we stopped hearing how things were going, and years later people couldn't even find your country on a map. Back then, I rented my attic to a family, and we got along so well that the father took care of my twins for their first few years. The family was from Piura." She became quiet for a moment, considering the matter. "Look, if you can get the funds for the translation and printing, we'll do it," she finally conceded with a sigh. I thanked her and felt ecstatic, envisioning a possible launch at the Maison de l'Amérique Latine, a roundtable discussion.

"No so fast," she stopped me. "Let's first acquire the rights. It won't be easy; as a matter of fact, I was in touch with the widow back in the 1990s." I remained quiet. "Don't tell me you hadn't thought about the rights," she continued. And then I asked her to do it. She looked at me in surprise. "Please, that's your job," she replied, still puzzled. Then, in a liberating instant, like removing a thorn from my side that finally let everything flow, I revealed what I'd never shared with anyone since arriving in France, because remaking yourself in a different place is also an opportunity to embellish your past, I shared the reason behind my two long trips, the one I took to reach Lima at fifteen and the one at thirty to get out of there. And when I finished my story, I continued with what I knew about Sybila Arredondo and Shining Path. After a long silence, Tiziana said, "What you're going through is just a phase. Look, let me tell you my own anecdote. You wouldn't know this, but in the 1970s, Ceaușescu ordered residents from downtown Bucharest to abandon their homes and move into new buildings. That's how things worked there," she said, snapping her fingers. "The families went, leaving behind their dogs, and those strays proliferated to such an extent that people ended up slaughtering them in the streets, with rifles or sticks. You cannot imagine it. I witnessed horrific scenes that I'll never forget. It was the worst possible metaphor for everything happening at the time." She stood from her chair and went to the window. "I hear what you're saying," she continued, gazing outside. "The first time I read about Shining Path in the press, it was a story about dogs hanging from lampposts, equally cruel and awful." She sighed. "But you know what? We've got to have more faith in literature. Draft a letter, in Spanish and under your name," she calmly concluded, and I felt that this was now our project.

Two weeks later, Andreas got the green light from the bank and a series of events were set in motion. He contacted an insurance company, completed the documentation the agency requested and sent our offer to the owner. The house would be empty in two months. If everything worked out, the agent said, we could make arrangements to take possession by the end of September. It was around then we also found out we were expecting a son in February.

* * *

The response came in a handwritten letter. Arguedas's widow addressed me with courtesy and gratitude. "It's a marvelous idea," she wrote. "I know the translator and have every confidence in her." She gave me her number to discuss the formalities, but we had her support and approval for the future book. That same morning, Geneviève and I ran the numbers, estimating the size of the print run and price point, and calculated the bid to procure the rights. Tiziana gave her consent.

Despite my misgivings, the negotiation was surprisingly simple. On the phone, Arredondo's voice sounded warm and close, even friendly. I presented our proposal, she thought for a moment, and made a counteroffer, which I took to Tiziana. We confirmed and settled the matter.

That month, I prepared the contracts, we submitted the book to our distributors and officially got the ball rolling so that copies would be in shop windows come January. Geneviève took the baton and began the editing, which we calculated would take roughly ten weeks. The project was underway.

Only then did I begin to look at the new publications and realize the unstoppable passing of time. It was already July, Paris had begun to empty out and calm settled over our daily lives. Andreas called one morning to let me know the owner had accepted our offer and we had an appointment at the agency that afternoon. We read the documents, confirmed the assessments and signed the purchase agreement. After leaving, we sat at an outdoor café and watched people amble past. With both feet now on solid ground, our future lives heralded something serious, complex, permanent. Farewell to any doubts and to the many different paths. Farewell to the possibility of going back. I couldn't sleep that night, or the next, replaying in my mind, like a disjointed montage, ludicrous scenes from here and there until morning came.

In October, I received a message from Arguedas's widow that she'd be in Paris soon and wanted to visit us. It rained hard that day, almost an Andean downpour, raucous and powerful. I awaited her arrival with a mixture of anxiety and fear. She came into the bookstore completely soaked and I immediately recognized her. In the 80s, she was featured in countless articles in the papers and appeared numerous times on TV, looking fierce and with a fist raised in the air. I was surprised by her mild manners and the simplicity of her gray hair in a thick braid. She had come alone. Taking off her raincoat and smiling, she remarked that I must be the architect of this adventure and gave me a hug.

I couldn't help myself. We chatted for minutes on end like old friends. She was, without a doubt, an interesting woman. I felt as if I were talking to one of those French grandmothers who had experienced the fervor of May 1968. She was like those women who, having seen the world both in theory and praxis, serenely embrace old age, knowing themselves to be, if not ultimately insignificant, at least innocuous. But France was never Peru of the 1980s.

"You've got a project on the way," she noted, staring at my belly before saying goodbye. Watching her leave, I couldn't help but think of the extraordinary circumstances that might lead someone to choose pure and simple insanity. And the terrible irony of having to go through Sybila to translate Arguedas.

* * *

Before Christmas, I announced that I'd be taking maternity leave right after the holidays. I wouldn't be there to handle the final phase of *Diamants et silex*. I organized the activities, left some instructions for the launch and calmly moved away from the whirlwind of books, from that electrifying, fast-paced pleasure, to devote myself at last to my new home. We painted the walls, cut the grass, added some plants, put furniture together, and each one of those peaceful days was a settling in, deepening roots, writing a new chapter. And in some way accepting that, even though I might be there for a long time, in no way would I renounce my country or my past.

The period right before birth is called the nesting phase. Piece by piece, the bird constructs a fragile space in a distinct, inaccessible location where an array of factors allow it, with any luck, to give birth. My nest was ready. All that remained was to wait.

Birthday

By Katya Adaui

For my sixth birthday,
which still falls in summer,
my brother drew and cut out,
as a last gesture of an older brother,
cardboard figures of my favorite cartoon character, Woody
Woodpecker,
he pasted them on the walls in vibrant colors,
and crowned the cake with a small marzipan log.
But it was summer, and no kids showed up.
We had no phone, they had received a tiny piece of paper with
the invitation on the last day of school, two months earlier.
I myself would've forgotten.
I don't know if they'd have even come in April.
Then my mother knocked on the neighbors' doors, the kids I'd
have been prohibited from playing with any other day.
Still suspicious, they crossed the road,
they didn't even ring the doorbell, my mother waiting for them
like a god at the back of a church.
We are unsure, silent,
taking possession of our fear,
me in a yellow dress, or maybe red,
air writing with my finger the number
six.

That same summer, during carnival,
they let me be them,
we hid
behind the wall of our house and we counted the seconds and we counted,
and when my mother finally emerged, out of reach
to survey her borderless kingdom,
her life again,
we threw a water balloon with salt at her and laughed until our stomachs hurt,
then we separated, neighbors and opposites.

The Final Judgment

By Oswaldo Estrada

It was unbelievable to see him like that, wispy and defeated, lacking the will to insist on his innocence. After denying two massacres, the kidnapping of senior officials and the torture of young people and children no more than eight or nine years old, the aging dictator silently listened to his crimes as if he were out of time. Almost smiling and with a slightly contemptuous gesture, he let the accusations slide down his tiny nose like the metal glasses that had always looked enormous on him.

The life sentence struck him in his rocking chair as if he were the one who would have to serve the time. And even more so as he gazed at him with his unkempt hair and the bewildered demeanor of a patient recently admitted to a psychiatric center. He no longer cared about making a good impression on those who had taken to the streets to protest for him. When he finally managed to get up, he realized he was living on borrowed time. He shaved by touch and reluctantly put on his clothes from the day before.

As he went out for bread, he confirmed with the neighbors the spectacle he'd just seen on television.

"How can they sentence him after he restored peace? If it weren't for him, we'd be living hand to mouth, worrying that a bomb could explode anytime, anywhere."

Gathered in front of a convenience store, the elderly residents lamented what had just happened.

"People are very ungrateful, *vecina*. They don't remember how things were before."

With their bags and coin purses in hand or with newspapers and alfalfa bunches under their arms, they argued heatedly.

"I guarantee you that now the terrorists are celebrating all of this."

"The terrorists? More like the government. The judges, the prosecutors. They're all bought off."

"What about human rights?"

"And the others didn't kill?"

"What rights are you talking about? Get outta here! Wouldn't you say, don Casimiro?"

Leaning on his cane, the old man couldn't hide his discomfort. His face looked unsettled, as if the dictator they had just sentenced were a close relative. Poor guy, he said, wondering what his own life would be like if at this point in the game he were condemned to spend his last days in a cell. He wasn't the dictator's son or grandson. He hadn't even seen him from afar. But in his seventies, still walking upright and without any help, he'd been excited to see such a trustworthy candidate, devoid of the malice of other corrupt politicians.

Unlike his presidential opponent who jogged along the Barranco boardwalk, El Chino rode on tractors wearing ponchos and Andean chullos, talked about reforming the entire country, building schools and roads, ending the violence, creating more jobs. He promised what everyone promises. Nevertheless, his newcomer's aura and the foreign cadences of his accent effectively captivated the masses. He traveled to the most inhospitable parts of the country, went to the slums and played soccer with children. When news reporters asked him to show his muscles to see if they were as defined as those of his opponent, instead of shrinking, El Chino displayed his fifty-something belly without shame, pretending to be strong and raising his arms like Tarzan.

For all that folksy cleverness, don Casimiro loved him as if they had been friends forever. He imagined that one day

El Chino would pass through the neighborhood and honor him for his vociferous support to gain the presidency. When they said in the newspapers that El Chino had been born abroad, don Casimiro flatly rejected the idea. I've been asked my whole life if I'm from China or Calle Capón, and I'm more northern than our chicha de jora. My mother was from Monsefú and up there all the peasants, he laughed amusedly, are half Chinese and half cholos. Our last names are Huamanchumo and Chamochumbi. And we dance barefoot *Chiclayanita, dame tu amor*. I assure you they wouldn't give the poor guy so much grief if blue blood ran through his veins.

On election day, he woke his wife up before the first rooster calls. Hurry up, Paula, the polls open any moment. Hurry up, he told her, as she put on her regular clothes. She'd never liked being rushed, but this time the old man was right. They gulped their coffee with milk and walked together to the voting precinct they'd been assigned. As if they'd been paid a commission to campaign for the party, don Casimiro and his wife asked everyone they crossed paths with to vote for El Chino.

With that same joy, they celebrated the day the President dissolved Congress. Well done, she noted. It's what was needed, he applauded in front of the TV. Someone with the guts to send home a group of useless individuals, all the congressmen who feed off the people and live like royalty. They didn't give a damn that his actions were unconstitutional. Like many from the provinces, they were glad it was him, that little man without a commanding voice and no other credentials than his university degree, who promised on camera to rebuild the government. Now they're screwed, Mamá, he celebrated happily, clicking his tongue, humming a *marinera*. Screw them, she retorted, laughing. Withered on the outside but clinging tooth and nail to the memory of their best years, they felt happy to be part of a change, even if it came to them in their twilight years.

He would've loved to be more like him. At seventeen, he wanted to go to the war with Colombia. But they dismissed him in two seconds at the sight of his skeletal physique and the scars of orphanhood in his pupils. Go home and eat, boy, the frightened recruiting officer insisted. The way you are, you'll die at the drop of a hat. He knew it but wanted to die like a hero. He wanted a plaque with his name on it in the Plaza de Armas for having defended the homeland, not for dying like his mother and brothers. Of tuberculosis.

He'd been lucky enough to get a position at the Lambeyeque Steam Navigation Company, where he was given the job of pinchasapos, which meant he'd run errands, sweep or mop, carry packages to the dock, deliver messages in sealed envelopes to the captain of some ship. From Japan, Chile, the United States.

"Wouldn't you say, don Casimiro?"

The easy thing would be to agree with the neighbors. El Chino had done a lot for them and now they were all ganging up on him. Who knows what he used to capture the leader of the opposition and all the heads of a movement that wanted to cleanse corruption through bloodshed? How many, like him, didn't applaud when the rebel leader was publicly displayed in a cage, wearing a striped suit to feed the people's morbid curiosity? But the deaths didn't lie.

He had supported the Aprista Party until he could no longer bear it, when the country went to hell with the currency devaluation, and he found himself endlessly waiting in line to get ten bags of powdered milk. Hard to believe this was the same country that only a few decades earlier exported raw materials to Europe. Coffee, cocoa, molasses, premium quality rice, sugar and the highly valued Pomalca rum, when the northern haciendas were experiencing their best period, and he went from being a pinchasapos to executive director of the same steam company at the Port of Pimentel.

At ninety-four,he felt useless when questioned by the elderly who had been his neighborhood companions ever since he left his small hometown to settle in the capital, after the agrarian reform distributed lands belonging to the old haciendas, dividing them into cooperatives and agricultural enterprises. He was tired of living, of going from one government to the next and realizing that politics is shit. According to his calculations, he'd lived through between four and six military coups and a string of pseudo-democratic governments, witnessed at least three institutional takeovers, one self-coup and countless electoral frauds.

He no longer wanted to start over as he'd done before, as he did during one of the last crises, when he grabbed his yellow Volkswagen and began driving taxi. Don't go out, Papá, his daughter would tell him. Your car has already been stolen twice and you insist on going out there on the streets. With what I earn at school, we can cover our monthly expenses. Don't run the risk of getting killed one of these days. But the old man couldn't stop working. I'm ashamed, *hija*. He didn't mind charging a pittance for racing from one end of town to the other. Or that his glasses were stolen at a stoplight. He did it with the same pride with which he once swept the company's warehouses, where after years of paying for algebra and trigonometry classes and taking correspondence courses, he obtained his Commercial Accountant degree.

What would his Paula say if she were with them, if she knew what they had discovered? What if one of those missing was my child? Of course, a major crisis had to be stopped. But like this? Premeditated murder because the others had done the same thing? And wouldn't I have followed the dissidents if they had knocked on my door when I didn't have a cent in my pocket? He was tired of living, and even more so of thinking that he'd made a mistake. That while he celebrated El Chino's achievements, summary executions, corruption offences, spying on journalists and politicians, embezzlement, and the forced sterilization of thousands of women who underwent surgery without anesthesia just for a little bit of food were being carried out behind closed doors.

He said goodbye with a distant gesture, waving the bag of bread. He went his usual way and turned right onto Calle de Las Perdices until he reached number 427. He wanted to cry, but that too seemed pointless to him.

He would've loved to see the sea again. Run along the beach in Pimentel and feel the salt on his feet, destroyed by all his wandering. Or climb the mango tree with his brother Miguel. But he ran out of time. The bread rolled on the ground. Embracing his mother's grave in the Tumán cemetery, he was ten years old again and felt a light caress on his forehead. The smell of alfeñique old-fashioned stick candy. Champú corn and fruit drink sweetened with cane molasses and marraqueta crispy buns fresh from the oven.

Because he hadn't spoken since his last stroke, no one was surprised he didn't answer. Nor that he didn't insist on his innocence on the day of final judgment.

Story of My Life

By María del Río

I'm on one of the loveliest trips of my life, in a place too wonderful to be mine, too good to be true. The trip has just begun; I know nothing bad can happen to me. I'm happy, safe, amazed by what I see. And yet, something deep inside won't stop reminding me that in a week I'll have to return home, in unsuitable clothing and claustrophobic, disembarking from a plane that's way too impersonal, even though I get on one every month. The sliding doors of Lima's Jorge Chávez Airport will open, and I'll be in a taxi with my eyes closed so I don't have to see Avenida Faucett, ugly, ugly as can be, ugly as if condemned to be ugly, and sad. And then I'll remember that I can turn on my cellphone again, but I won't, because I don't want to connect with the world that awaits me. I hardly have ten words for everything I refused to say last night, when so much beauty hurt me.

White Christmas

By Luis Hernán Castañeda

I remember him saying he was friends with Santa Claus and that he'd bring him home for Christmas. A girl doesn't grow up by choice, but back then I was silly and naïve, running every night to excitedly look through the peephole in the alley that peered into his bedroom, the same hiding place where I'd once seen Señor Agustín trying on an old red coat and making faces in the mirror to show off his white hermit's beard.

Shortly after my thirteenth birthday, I was picked up from that alley, which until then had been like my home, by a smiling old man who suddenly approached, stating he'd known me since I was little:

"Indeed," said Señor Agustín in his elegant voice. "All these years, while you'd come here to sell your delicious candies, I'd spy on you through the hole in my room. Today I've decided that you're ready, so if you'd like, you can come and live with me in the big house."

I thanked him and felt happy, but was also very afraid that this good man, who looked like an old prince, might've seen me with the other bad men who'd offer me a few coins to take me to a hotel. Fortunately, I never agreed to go with them.

Señor Agustín and I never did anything bad; we did fun, exciting things. Every morning, instead of going to school or work like normal people, we put on our bathing suits and stretched out on our towels like two ordinary sunbathers, but we weren't at the beach; we were in a huge garden that seemed like a forest of bluebells, blueberry bushes and trees that provided shade, so green, so big, so beautiful, although now it was empty and sad since his only son, Señor Gonzalo, had grown up and left home without ever seeing my beautiful red bikini with yellow sunflowers. Señor Agustín's bathing suit was black, tiny like a professional swimmer's Speedos, and which he took off when it was very hot. He was always reading some impossible-to-understand books while I, excited to be able to hang out with him, jumped from the swings to the trampoline, screeching like a squirrel, until his migraine would hit. Then I'd stop the racket and pass the time playing quietly with my dolls.

"Shall we go chat with Sigmund?" Señor Agustín would ask at noon, and I'd burst with happiness because I love Sigmund.

If I were in my room right now, all I'd have to do is look out the window to see Sigmund's pool, a pond with greenish water, a little dirty and covered in mist like a wild swamp, which Señor Agustín dug to please his late wife. Like me, she used to enjoy sinking her feet into the soft moss on the shore and staring at the little goldfish, orange, purple, black. Too bad there are fewer and fewer of them now because they devour one another like barbarians. They're not civilized like the dolphin that lives in the pond and whose name I want to change. Sigmund is a terrible name for a dolphin, and I always tell Señor Agustín. He says he agrees with me, but there is nothing he can do, Sigmund's his name and that's that. The dolphin has never complained about his name and wouldn't welcome such a sudden change. Well, Néstor, because that's what I nicknamed him, Néstor like my little brother, was our friend and as soon as he heard our footsteps, he began to fan his fins and crow like a rooster, it's hard to believe, but that's how it was. He's always been a docile dolphin, friendly and talkative with people, and even lets his head be stroked, that's why it makes me very sad to watch him swim; he has a hard time splashing in the shallow waters, dragging himself like a fat old man and half of his body is floating while his fins, stranded, churn up mud from the bottom.

I'm sure that in the past, when he still lived in the sea, Néstor was capable of the most incredible pirouettes: they'd throw a ball at him and he'd fetch it; they'd raise an arm and he'd do a somersault; everyone would applaud him, but not anymore, those days were gone. He was so sad, his back had faded and, hardly moving, he floated like a drowned man in the putrid water. Señor Agustín tries to cheer him up with his fireworks, setting them off very close to his ears, maybe too close, but they never work. Néstor squeaks in pain and begs us to leave him alone.

"You don't deserve it," said Señor Agustín. "Do you ever leave us alone?"

After lunch, Señor Agustín would devote himself to his studies. Our garden outings had to come to an end because, and I was forced to accept this, Señor Agustín couldn't dedicate all his time to me; he had other obligations, tasks impossible to carry out in the presence of a girl. When I asked him what his tasks were, while putting my hands on my waist, he tenderly patted my head, saying there'd be no point in explaining anything to me, and closed the door to his office, a small room where he locked himself up with his studies for hours at a time. If I'm not mistaken, he used the same word, "studies," which, as I found out later, had something to do with manufacturing products such as jam, mosquito repellent ointment, tomato sauce and cream sauce, all types of creamy substances, some edible and others not so much. To find that out, I had to break the rules: just like before, when I sneaked into other people's houses. Always at night, when nobody would see me.

This time I waited until Señor Agustín had gone to bed so I could steal the keys from his pants and quietly slip into his tiny secret room. It was a small, narrow space with a high ceiling and no windows, no pictures, no decorations. There were two pieces of furniture: a purple recliner and a long metal table. On the table I noticed many small glass jars, I estimated more than a hundred. They all contained fine miniature figurines, statuettes of women molded out of a white substance, a type of mayonnaise. But it didn't taste like mayonnaise, and I had to spit it out. I took a jar and went back to my room to study the little figurine. I had no idea what that cream could be. After several hours of thinking and thinking, I let out a little cry of joy and immediately covered my mouth. I didn't want to wake Señor Agustin or let him know that I'd already guessed, and that he wouldn't have to keep hiding his suntan lotion business. Suntan lotions for the beach, suntan lotion figurines in the shape of a woman, for the beach! The next morning I showed up with my face smeared in white, and when I tried to put some suntan lotion on poor Néstor, who's constantly exposed to the sun, Señor Agustín snatched the bottle from me, calling me a bad girl, rude, a thief and other cruel insults that made me cry. Then he begged my forgiveness, but I hold grudges and, from then on, every time I'd ask him why he had been like that, why he had gotten so angry, Señor Agustín would send me to my room, shouting and then giving me the silent treatment for days. Later he'd regret it, hug me and mutter strange words:

"In the shadows, child, in the shadows," he said.

To draw my attention to what he said were "more interesting" topics, he promised to tell me all about his real studies, totally different from the sale of suntan lotion and more complicated to understand, so complicated that at first, I thought it was just nonsense he'd made up to play with me and keep me entertained. It was one of two things: either Señor Agustín was pulling my leg or he'd lost his mind.

"Do you know why dolphins smile?" he asked me once. "You must have noticed it in Sigmund. His lips are shaped like a beautiful smile, and the sounds he makes, his characteristic clucking, has a happy ring to it as if he were laughing. Well, that impression is accurate. Sigmund laughs and his laughter is sarcastic. He mocks us because he understands our language perfectly and patiently waits for us, mere humans, to learn the language of dolphins at our own pace."

When Señor Agustín spoke to me for the first time about dolphins, we were both sitting on my bed. I was licking a strawberry ice cream while he watched me, asking from time to time, always so attentive, if I felt comfortable, if I needed anything, if I liked my ice cream, if I could offer him a lick.

"I'm keenly interested in these creatures. You've seen how brilliant, how extraordinary they are. Their brain size far exceeds that of humans; with such incredible neuronal capacity, what's incomprehensible would be to discover they couldn't think like us, or even better than us. With a mathematician's precision. What's more, I'd go so far as to say that the species has reached the highest degree of evolutionary sophistication to be found on our planet."

He asked me if I understood, and I told him truthfully, no, but seeing that my answer disappointed him, I said wait, wait a minute, do you mean that Néstor is very intelligent, like when he splashes droplets of water at us with his fins to put out the fireworks?

"It's an example, but it doesn't fully illustrate my point. Look, right now my main interest is in translation. I'm undertaking a linguistic and scientific project with infinite repercussions that will result in ideal communication between man and beast."

He asked me again if I understood, and this time I was so confused I didn't even manage to reward him with a lie.

"Yes," he scratched his head, "that's understandable. It just occurred to me. How about if I tell you a story? An entertaining one, of course. It has to be, if Plautus is involved. More than twenty centuries ago, I mean a long, long time ago, a gentleman named Plautus correctly stated that Nature endowed the dolphin with superior virtue, which even philosophers aspired to: the ability to develop sacred friendships. María, you and I are friends, right? Naturally yes, but we don't have a sacred friendship. We love each other in a different way."

Señor Agustín was cultured, I'd say very cultured. He always had to use a different word, or tell a weird story that happened many years ago. I used to half-understand him, after much effort, until one day his wisdom bored me, and I took the risk of telling him what I thought:

"You're crazy," I said, "and crazy people live in a mental hospital."

He looked at me with "irony": I learned that word from him. And then his laugh became a violent guffaw.

"Of course I'm crazy," he answered. "If I wasn't, you'd still be on the street."

"And that's why you hit Néstor?"

"I assume you mean Sigmund, because Néstor is a lousy name for a beast. Okay, I'll tell you about it. Have you ever had a chance to see Sigmund...naked? I mean, when he's frolicking in the shallow end, spinning like a barrel, exposing his private parts. If you haven't seen the show, I assure you that I'm right. Also, Sigmund is a horrible name for a damsel. Our dolphin is female. Thanks to her, my studies will bear fruit. The darkest day of the year is approaching for virgins, aren't you worried?"

It was around then that Señor Agustín's son, Señor Gonzalo, paid us a visit. He came to spend time with his dad. I'd been living in the house for a few months and was beginning to feel a little sharper, strangely enough. At first, I'd have to rack my brains trying to understand Señor Agustín's stories, but by that time I felt as though I were already a scientist. I'd listen to his mysterious speeches from beginning to end and, on some occasions, just to annoy him, I even took the liberty of disputing certain things, for example, that bit about a dolphin's smile had to be fake. It was a heated discussion; Señor Agustín refused to concede, and I was also stubborn, but in the end, I gave up because otherwise he'd have punished me. He had begun to sweat with rage, his eyes seethed and his lips trembled a little. Besides, it's not right to contradict our elders.

"Whatever," I backed down. "Dolphins are people like us, and we're animals like dolphins."

Señor Gonzalo left his cup of coffee on the dining room table and looked at me in shock. He was a young man, but his skin was dark. He wore a black overcoat that looked like a cassock. He seemed upset even though there was no reason to be. Livid, he asked his father what we were talking about, what the deal was with the dolphins he'd heard us mention so often throughout the afternoon, starting when we went to meet him at the airport. I braced myself for the long sermon I'd heard on several occasions. While Señor Agustín talked about his secret studies, the dolphins and their language and fables like that, Señor Gonzalo looked at me strangely: aggressive, disgusted, I'd almost say hateful. That look of rejection brought back bad memories; it was the same look fancy ladies used to throw at me in the street when they saw me chatting with men.

"You're not crazy, you're sick," Señor Gonzalo concluded and got up from the table, spilling his coffee.

That night I couldn't sleep. A bad air wafted through the house, something given off by Señor Gonzalo's body. Around three in the morning, I was startled by a knock on my door. When I got up, the sheets felt wet. I thought it might be rain, but it wasn't: I had wet the bed.

"Did I wake you up?" Señor Agustín asked delicately.

He was wearing yellow striped pajamas and his eyes were bloodshot, as if he'd been drinking liquor.

"Gonzalo is mortified. He says my studies are unacceptable. We had an argument, and he threatened to take Sigmund away first thing in the morning."

It was time to act. I threw a blanket over myself, handed another one to Señor Agustín, and together we went out into the flooded garden. The downpour had started in the afternoon and late that night it fell like a waterfall. We took refuge under the umbrella mounted near the swings, watching how the drops made the water in the pool boil, like shots from God. There was a thunderstorm on the horizon, and every flash of lightning turned the trees purple. In that broken darkness, Néstor's cry reached us like a sad whistle as his shadow swayed. Señor Agustín ran toward him, or her, becoming a ghost, nothing more than a ghost squatting by the water. In the lightning flashes I could make out the shape of his back and his white hair. Suddenly, a piercing bellow rang out, a single one, similar to a human scream. I went over and put a hand on Señor Agustín's shoulder, but immediately withdrew it, fearful, protecting it under my arm. He clutched a kitchen knife. The wound in Néstor's belly was bleeding profusely, staining the pool red. His little black eyes had closed, and his fins were still moving, first one and then the other, making furrows in the mud. He clicked very softly, as if calling out to us or asking what we'd done to him.

"Please don't be alarmed," Señor Agustín stammered. "You need to understand. Sigmund's death is necessary. I must examine her vocal cords up close to determine if she's capable of articulating human language. Besides, my son would have inflicted worse brutalities on her; you should be happy."

But I didn't care about Señor Gonzalo, or the projects, or the studies, or anything more than my friend's death. For the first time since I had arrived at that house, I went back to my room without saying good night to Señor Agustín. Maybe I should've been more understanding, but at that moment I wanted to hate him. I cried until the next morning, the last one I spent in that house. They knocked on my door early again, but this time the knocks were more insistent, brutal, destructive, and I kept hearing the pounding as I rode in a taxi with Señor Gonzalo. I imagined them busting my face the way the coin Señor Gonzalo mockingly threw at me shattered my heart when he abandoned me, a twenty-five cent coin like the ones Señor Agustín would give me with the promise that we'd travel together to a beautiful country that summer, or the next, or maybe in the fall, another one of many promises that will never be fulfilled.

Entire weeks passed. If I was in many different neighborhoods, I don't remember, even though it seemed that way, because my feet had been walking a lot every day. I watched them move forward, surprised by their speed, and allowed myself to be led as far as they wanted to go. None of the streets mattered to me because they led me to other similar ones. Like before, as always, I slept in the street, I ate in the street, I begged in the street, I sold candy in the street, I stole in the street, I peed in the street, I crapped in the street, I got drunk in the street, I took drugs in the street, I vomited in the street, and something I'd never done before, not once, I accepted bills from a filthy old man who didn't trim his beard like Señor Agustín, who didn't put cologne on his face like Señor Agustín, who didn't wear elegant clothes like Señor Agustín, and who'd pissed in his underpants. This man knew many things Señor Agustín never taught me. Most of all, he knew how to tell the difference between things. From him I learned the difference between suntan lotion and the liquid I'd found in the bottles, and I also learned the similarity between how dirty some men are and the immaculate appearance others want to show.

I'm not saying I didn't want to go back. The door to the house, which more than ever seemed like a palace to me, was always closed. No one could be seen through the windows, no matter how many hours I waited. It was as if they'd all died overnight, just like Néstor. I tried to spy through the little hole in the alley in case someone, some shadow, happened to pass by, hoping that a car, even if Señor Gonzalo were in it, would stop, dreaming that Señor Agustín had taken his pills and fallen asleep, and that's why he wouldn't open the door for me. At any moment he'd wake up and I could reclaim my room, my swings, my dolls, and Néstor, who was actually female, maybe she'd been saved, maybe there hadn't been that much blood and she was cackling with joy at that very moment, how happy she'd be to see me after all this time. Maybe, I imagined, we could even take her back home to the beach; I'd heard that in this huge country there were many beaches, and we could take her there.

It happened on the night of December twenty-fourth; I remember it clearly. It must've been late when the car parked in front of the house and turned off its lights. I'd hidden in a little garden on the other side of the street, and lying on the grass, parting the leaves on a bush, I saw a man get out of the car and enter the house. A few minutes later, I heard a cry from inside, a sound muffled by the thick walls. The same man, I'd recognized him by now, came out again, got into the car and skidded off. I took advantage and entered through the door Señor Gonzalo had forgotten to close. I went through all the rooms as if dancing, believing I'd been saved, calling out to Señor Agustín in a very low voice because I was sure he was close by. The rooms were the same, the living room with its antique furniture, the kitchen with its window onto the garden, the dining room with its golden chandelier and my perfect room, as if it had been cleaned that same afternoon. On the nightstand, on my nightstand, was a tiny tree with white stars, as dazzling white as the moon's heart. It was the only Christmas decoration in the whole house.

I found the office closed, but not Señor Agustín's bedroom. The light was on, an old radio screeched like the offspring of some unknown animal and the window let in a cold wind, a wintry wind that made the half-open bathroom door shake. I pushed it, tiptoed in and saw the puddle on the tiles, the red waters overflowing from the bathtub and the body that floated face up in that sludge. Her mouth was half-open in a permanent smile showing little yellow teeth, as if filed down to inflict pain. Her skin, partially covered under a towel, was dry and wrinkled, and her two fins stuck out stiffly. The scar on her belly had been stitched up, but her vagina had been mutilated. It was just a torn hole, plugged with a bottle from which a white cream flowed, sliding like streaks of pus over her belly.

I backed up, stumbled. I noticed, almost fainting, that they'd left a piece of paper on the bed. I skimmed it, a letter with my name as addressee. Most of it was written using complicated words I couldn't understand, but the end was a very simple declaration of love that seemed to be written by someone my age. As I was trying in vain to figure out what all this was about, I heard a noise in the hallway. Señor Agustín came into the bedroom and froze when he saw me. His face looked haggard, as if years had passed. Though I wanted to tear him apart with insults, I spoke with chilling serenity.

"Me too," I said quietly. "I also loved dolphins. Why did we have to kill them?"

I rushed toward Señor Agustín, collapsed at his feet and my hands pulled down his pants without him putting up any resistance. A ridiculous pink penis jutted out and my mouth opened to receive it. So simple, so vulgar. I raised my tear-filled eyes to his and saw that he was covering his face with one hand. I didn't close my eyes, not until the end of the story.

The Old Woman and the Fisherman

By Gimena Vartu

"That was me, always pleased to see that my presence in their lives lit up those smiles. I didn't know whether to let them do what they wanted with me. But just being together… I was happy."

That's how the old woman spoke as she suddenly sat down next to him. The fisherman had finished his day, resting while stretched out on the beach next to his wooden boat, under the full midday sun, and eating some sweet rolls.

"Well, *vieja*, it seems to me you've lived a good life. I feel the same about the fish to avoid feeling bad. I think they're even grateful."

"I've seen something in those rat eyes of yours. I saw the yellow yolk."

The fisherman let out his first laugh.

"Oh, *vieja*, your head's a stew; must be the sun."

The old woman wore a straw hat that seldom allowed her wizened, gloomy, dark face to be seen in all its magnificence. Her lightning gaze, however, illuminated strong qualities, and fixed on the young man's juicy body with the astonishment of rediscovery, his lightly bronzed chest, calloused yet beautiful hands, the coolness of the beach.

As she circled the boat, dragging her feet through the sand, she discovered it had no name.

"Your boat doesn't have a name, son."

"I want to name it after my wife, but I don't have a wife yet."

"What about that girl who's looking at you?"

He turned to where the old woman's gesture led him. Sure enough, a young woman, almost a girl, had just stopped on the path to look at the boat and take in the scene.

"Wonder who that is. I don't know her. I'm new here."

"I'm also new here."

The old woman had sat down again and become a kind of living stone in which neither legs nor arms could be distinguished, only a hat, under the hat a head and under the head a lump. Her diaphanous skirts in opaque colors were abundant.

"I don't know what I'm going to do the rest of the day, *vieja*, before I get sleepy."

"We have returned, we are back where we started, here. We're fine; there's fresh air, sun, little things, nothing stinks."

"Is that why you came? Maybe that's why I came here too, but I'm a fisherman and you're an old lady," he said and roared with laughter.

"You can have a wife, little girl who stares at you, son. I no longer can."

"But you've already lived… You look like you've raised many dogs, cats."

"I only raised you." And she hid her eyes under the straw hat.

"*Vieja*… If you were many years younger, maybe…"

Time was the winner on the beach, it subtly slipped through all the blue and copper, every second was every grain of sand and standing still was the same as moving. They both felt it on their hot, bare feet.

He finished the sweet rolls. He hadn't offered the old woman a single crumb, but she didn't complain; on the contrary, she smiled realizing that at no point had they imagined this was the reason she had approached him.

"It's burning hot, how nice."

"It's the sun I told you about, in your eyes, in the sky." And with shyness, almost to herself, she whispered, "Love, boy."

The fisherman didn't respond; he preferred to let the seagulls fill the silence with their squawks, or the noise of the crashing waves or the whistle of the wind. His thoughts were lost along the horizontal line in the distance that joined the sky to the sea. A sigh made him take a deep breath.

"What period of your life would you like to be in right now?"

"Just here. I'm not moving from here. I just wake up hoping to be here. Now you, later."

"I like being here too. I don't know if I'll be here sooner or later, but I am." And again, that spontaneous laughter.

"A smile, see? Me and your smile."

"Yes, thanks for joining me. Starting tomorrow, I'll give you fish to eat."

"Do you already have a house?"

"I sleep on the boat sometimes to get up early, or at a friend's house."

"I can give you my house. I can give you the girl who looks at you."

"You look lonely, *vieja*."

"I've always been alone, like you."

"So who had you before?"

"Had, well said. But only with you have I been, am."

"Ah, ungrateful people. I'll go to your house, *vieja*; it'll be enough for both of us. I can help you clean."

"I already cleaned; I already made the food."

"Great. And…"

"You'll have a girl, you'll see; she took a good look at you. If I hadn't come early, I would've been the one on the path."

"You're early and I'm late." He laughed once more. "But next time we'll agree to be on time. You'll see. I promise."

When Did the Beat of a Butterfly's Wings Distract You From the World?

By Pedro Novoa

Out there where this passion demands a master in its own image,
Submitting its life to another life,
With no more horizon than a face with other eyes.
Luis Cernuda

In the first place you should know
that everything with a manifest face
also possesses a hidden one.
Georges Bataille

The curtain will be drawn back, Juanjo, and it'll be a large eyelid opening to the world. You'll finally see the winning billboard after a humiliating wait. You'll sigh before it, motionless from the waist up even though your legs tremble, you feel short of breath while desperately smoking as you're doing right now. You'll look on in disbelief like a first-time voyeur who doubts and downplays the merits of another's achievement. Nevertheless, after a few seconds, you'll absorb it: subterranean, submissive, you'll suck up to it. You pant, slow and exhausted. The cold wind licks the street, benches, and hardened architecture of your face. How will the photograph look? What will be the slogan? What will be the design that'll grab hold of your eyes and those of the rest of the onlookers crowded around in the presence of its inclemency.

In the meantime, you examine the shiny satin texture of the drape covering the winning advertisement. Would the photograph embody artistic spirit, spanning it from side to side, or would it be a mere artifice of light and color? In a few minutes you'll find out. You take a long drag off your ninth cigarette of the morning. The tobacco smoke envelopes your tongue with a thick and bitter taste. You lose patience, you feel out of place, an extra: as if you didn't belong to time or that time, suddenly, didn't belong to you. Although the outcome is apparent and almost shocking, you don't fully understand it, or perhaps you simply don't want to.

You close your eyes and try not think about the Browning 9mm nestled in one of the pockets of your overcoat. On the other side of your eyelids, the world passes by, ordinary and monotonous. It's Monday, almost seven in the morning in Lima. The roar of the street violently unstitches the silence of its asphalt skin. The traffic acts selfishly at its most crawling hour: vehicles cut each other off, scrape against one another, and encroach on different lanes. If they had serrated snouts, they'd open them wide and viciously bite down on everything in their paths. The pedestrians, for their part, continue past, heads in the sand, overtaking others at full stride. They fear being delayed and getting lost amid the crowd of urban ruffians that they themselves drive to despair.

You are unfazed, still hoping the enormous billboard has artistic flair. Enough, at least, that it would leave no doubt in any remote corner of the universe. You are even seduced by the idea of succumbing to its charm. Like one who covets his neighbor's wife, you want to sin with the other photographer's work and abandon yourself to its prohibited seduction. You sigh, Juanjo, toss the cigarette butt on the ground and squeeze your eyes ever so tightly. A question remains floating in the air: when did the beat of a butterfly's wings distract you from the world?

It all began when you set out to win the Cannes Lions prize for culinary advertising. This year the organizers had gathered a number of companies in the food industry to treat the lucky winners. The award categories included best design, best creative concept, and best photograph. In addition, the Publicis Groupe, one of the most important French agencies in the field, offered the opportunity of a lifetime: the winning team would sign a spectacular one-year contract with a trip to Paris and per diem included. And you, Juanjo, well past fifty, couldn't afford to waste any time, much less these kinds of opportunities. So you immediately considered submitting a proposal to Burger King or McDonald's, the two companies with the best chance of winning. You decided on the latter because the McDonald's marketing team had devised a campaign compatible with your convictions: associating food with pleasure. For this, they needed a photograph as shocking and suggestive as possible. Something playful and risky that stimulates gluttony, makes you salivate and excites you. All at once.

The strategy was both aggressive and invasive as it should be in these cases. The billboards announcing an alluring, unbeatable offer would be placed quite close to the competing establishments. People would be given a special combo if they were new customers; two if they brought a guest. The hook was the usual one: upon scanning the QR code, a user's mobile device would be breached since they'd have to accept terms and conditions before claiming the offer. The rest would be done by a robotic algorithm more insistent than an insurance salesman.

The day you were selected as the photographer for Team McDonald's, your wife came over and congratulated you, fluttering the butterfly wings of her eyelashes, and joked, "Honey, they picked you only because I didn't enter." Complicit giggles ensued since you both recognized it wasn't far from the truth. In her early twenties, Malú was a consummate professional in culinary photography. You smile, and the wind numbs your happy gesture. You remember when the two of you met a few years ago. A restaurant chain had hired you both for an advertising campaign.

Memory offers you the key moment, that proverbial firing pin that ignited it all at a work meeting. The boss was breaking his own personal record for the most asinine comments in the shortest amount of time. And no one answered back, until you lost your patience. The beast raging inside you entered the ring. Furious, you showed off all your credentials as a rebel without a muzzle. You cut the boss down to size with a couple of technical explanations and then threw your years of experience in his face. That's how you impressed the then photographer trainee. Puffing out your chest and stiffening your brow, you refused to take pictures of dishes without people, declaring that to do so would alter the essence of your camera lens. Advertising food meant eating it or watching how someone ate it, not passively gazing at it on a plate. That boundary must be transcended: snapping shots of pleasure-seekers to capture pleasure, you argued, flushed and yelling at the top of your lungs. You looked at Malú and added, "It's like having a naked woman and not making love to her." By the end of that day, Malú allowed herself to be swept away by your lens and captured by it.

Years passed by and now you were presented with the great opportunity to reach the climax of your convictions. In your philosophy of art, eating was the closest experience to having sex. Because of that you acquired the peculiar custom of photographing couples eating and then making love. You had found close to thirty matching characteristics between the two activities (and which according to your logic were interchangeable).

You used to say that only humans ate or had sex for sheer pleasure. That's why there were so many food-related expressions in our colloquial speech. We talk about sexual "appetite," and say things like "I want to eat you up," "you make my mouth water every time I see you," "you're my sweet thing," "I want to butter your biscuit," and things of that nature. That's why a lover wants to "swallow you whole" and the other lets him or herself "be swallowed." You claimed that would explain expressions like "I want to be inside you," "I carry you inside me." Idiosyncrasies that labelled a hypersexual individual as "voracious" or "insatiable," a sex addict as "predatory," someone lacking sex as "unsatisfied" or "abstaining." And that's why we tend to use an abundancy of food terms to refer to sexual organs like "sausage," "bearded clam," "muffin," "salami," "pink taco," "nuts," "banana," "candy cane," and others. It was because of this that it occurred to you to connect the exact moment of orgasm with the pleasure of taste and interchange them. You'd photograph a woman climaxing and superimpose that image in front of a plate of food.

With feverish intensity, you plotted the insane task of having intimate relations with at least twenty women in a month. You would capture each of them at the peak moment of sexual satisfaction. And that's how it went. You kept gaining experience as diverse as it was intense, while your personal collection of prints continued to acquire more variation and precision in details. You and your professional camera. You and the light. You and your eye because a true photographer is not merely a replicator of reality. He is a chaser of moments, a person talented enough to catch what the naked eye can't see, misses or simply takes for granted. You perfected the chase, making sure to take pictures during the day with the sunlight traversing the room from left to right, downing three or four glasses of white wine while rose petals slipped off the edge of your bed. And there you were, concentrating, astride your lunacy, and pressing the camera shutter like a sniper who shoots to kill.

As the deadline was fast approaching, you felt particularly overwhelmed. All of the hundred-odd photos you had fell short. They were, of course, all quite good and displayed a certain charm. But art is not found in what's lovely or charming, art resides in that liminal zone where what's ordinary becomes unique; what makes you stray allows you to find yourself at the same time; what's ambiguous is spot on, and what's distant is inside of you. That border zone where everything and nothing is generated, horror and love, absolute trust and betrayal. That photograph, dear Juanjo, that damn photo, you didn't have it.

That's when you returned to Malú's arms. You had neglected her the whole time you spent on this frustrated search. And all of a sudden, you stumbled on exactly what you were looking for. Juanjo Fernández, advertising photographer, 54 years old, more than three decades in the trade, you took your pro Canon camera out and captured Malú's orgasm on your USB memory stick. The next day, you confessed to your deranged actions and apologized a thousand times. You told her she was the inspiration not only for your art, but also your life, and if there was any artistic quality to that photograph, it emanated from her eyes. Malú stared at you closely, taking your face in her hands and fluttering those butterfly eyelashes of hers, and forgave you. There was no need for more drama, as a photographer herself, she was in tune with your art and your madness. You sealed your reconciliation as it should be: in bed, in the light of day, and yes, with many photographs. She also became inspired to fulfill one of her elusive fantasies. She dressed you up as a priest, with a cassock and crucifix, and photographed you levitating above her.

At breakfast, Malú asked how your proposal for the contest turned out. You explained that the photograph of her you chose was perfect, not bordering on the obscene, but possessing the required boldness and intensity. You revealed that the billboard slogan would be: "If you want pleasure like hers…" And the line below: "McDonald's will keep your secret." On the side, the QR code would have the following instructions: "Scan the code and claim your offer at the restaurant that appears on your cellphone." Malú nodded, finding it interesting, though she would've added something else to the advertisement, but decided against it to avoid ruining the moment.

Now all that remained was to wait for the winners to be proclaimed. And, of course, the organization in charge couldn't think of anything better than to postpone the decision on three separate occasions. With a touch of sadism, they decided that the announcement would be streamed live on their website. In addition, prints of the winning proposal would be revealed in Tokyo, New York, Barcelona and another hundred cities around the world. Due to the time difference, it would be seven in the morning on a Monday, right smack in the middle of Lima's civic center.

As the days passed, you kept convincing yourself you hadn't won. You felt engulfed by a black aura. Your attitude had become unbearable; your wife left you and took a trip. You assumed it was to her hometown of Trujillo, but had become so intractable that you actually couldn't have cared less if she'd gone to China. Nothing mattered to you, only your imminent failure.

With one day left before the announcement, you got a hold of a Browning pistol. An absurd suspicion began lurking in your head. Depressed, the night before the big reveal you couldn't get to sleep, not even with pills. Thanks to the time difference, the unveiling of the award wouldn't coincide with the official one in Cannes. By now, you assumed the winning team would already be in that city living it up. You drank a coffee, chain-smoked almost an entire pack of cigarettes and headed over to the civic center to see the copy of the winning project.

Your anxiety led you to arrive two hours early. Despite this, you weren't the only disheartened photographer there. A group of grayish characters congregated in a kind of tacit solidarity. They stopped in front of the wall and stared at you as if saying: let's tear off the curtain and see who the hell won. You ignored them, breaking their gaze. You closed your eyes for a few minutes to try and balance your outer and inner worlds. But you were unsuccessful. You flung the ninth cigarette of the day on the pavement and mechanically lit the tenth one. You felt numb with the acrid taste of defeat in your mouth and waited for the end.

At seven o'clock on the dot, a representative from the prize committee arrived with a notary public and two bleary-eyed members of the press. After yawning, stretching and wiping the sleep from their eyes, one of them began filming the other, who in a matter of seconds, transformed into a charismatic reporter. He smiled and began to explain the importance of the prize and how difficult it had been for the jury to select a winner (as is usually the case). All at once, the synchronization signal came and the representative announced the title of the winning proposal and the sponsoring company: "We invite you to sin for the first time" from Burger King's marketing team. He mentioned the sum awarded and declared that in a few minutes they'd transmit the winners' acceptance speeches live. Without further ado, the representative pulled back the curtain.

You read the slogan: "If you want to sin like him…your first time is on Burger King. Scan your QR code and go to the restaurant listed to claim your offer."

In the photograph, you discover a priest in ecstasy in front of an enormous triple burger (the kind that requires two hands). The clergyman is in his fifties, wearing a cassock and a golden crucifix. You recognized your own face, with a look as engrossed and pleasurable as if contemplating the flutter of a butterfly's wings. The gesture was both tender and disturbing at the same time. With profound fervor, you envied the poetry of this art. The only thing that differentiated you from the image was that Browning 9mm, which you took out of your overcoat, emotionless, to balance the outer world with the one collapsing inside you."

Fish Bring Bad Luck

By Katya Adaui

Choose the ones you want, my father said, and I grabbed two bags with orange-colored fishes that hung transparent, a Chinese man sold them at the market, we got home, we admired them in a glass, my milk glass, they swam in circles, a kaleidoscope or washing machine, my mother arrived, she saw us happy, why did you bring them?, they're bad luck, and in front of me told my father, unclog the drain, and from the same place our shit left, so too the fishes, floating in an orange-colored instant. They disappeared. My father's consolation: all of the pipes from the house, from the neighborhood, from the city are connected, with any luck they'll reach the sea.

Domestic Animals

By Miluska Benavides

The tree grew without warning. At first, it was a stem mistaken for one of the weeds that used to accumulate around the tomatoes, detritus unfit for consumption. The old man tugged on a dry branch he believed to be the natural trellis of a tomato plant, but unlike other times, the stem resisted, simulating the roughness of old skin. The plant had climbed so high that after two attempts to get rid of it, the old man's palm turned red. He crouched with difficulty to get a better look at the undergrowth and separated the remaining shoots from the growing stem. He noticed it wasn't bare. It harbored small buds on its sides, a crystalline green indicating recent growth. He decided to wait two days to see what resulted from the sprouts, to determine if by some stroke of luck it was a plant he could harvest or one he'd eventually have to throw away.

He told his wife a peppertree had germinated in the garden, but she insisted that species didn't grow in the ravine. He chose not to contradict her, knowing the terrain of Santa Lucía, although close to a river, was never ideal for large trees. Accustomed to their absence, they kept a garden behind the house so as not to lose the habit of making use of what they sowed: aromatic and digestive herbs, plants that had accidentally germinated but matured and they burned in the fireplace, as well as white and yellow flowers with which they decorated the dining room.

In the following weeks, the stalk began to make a place for itself and, little by little, the weeds and all the plants in the flower bed began to disappear, as if the new stem forced the other crops to die. A few chamomile and other sprouts for his wife's personal consumption were the reason she insisted on getting rid of the plant every time they sat in the dining room and had to look out at the back garden. The tree couldn't grow in such a narrow piece of land. In the beginning, he'd say that he wasn't taking care of it; it had to be feeding itself through some underground water source, and for over fifty years it must've been bustling underneath and drawing nourishment from the ravine. He took care of the fruit-bearing shrubs planted along the back fence that delineated the arable area. He wasn't going to confess to her that he still hadn't gotten rid of the sprout.

Over the next three months, the grayish bark of the new stem gradually became wood and acquired a thin, calloused thickness. Seeing this transformation, he felt encouraged to routinely water it from the meager water supply the town rationed, even going so far as to deny the other plants irrigation. By the time summer arrived, when the sun cracked the garden and the house's surroundings, there was only a medium-sized stem, almost bare, and a handful of medicinal plants that sprung up haphazardly. The stem didn't look healthy, didn't appear to have put down thick roots, and even seemed to lean to one side. He fastened it to a stake he inserted at its base, trying to straighten and domesticate the tree.

By the time his birthday came in December, his wife had resigned herself to its presence, even complaining to her sons when they visited that the only interesting thing their father had to share was the existence of a deformed tree. And when they were about to leave, after the birthday dinner and hugs, the children commented among themselves that although they didn't believe their father had descended into eccentric behaviors, they worried how he'd not only aged so much since the last time they saw him, but how he couldn't speak well anymore. "He's half gone," they agreed. They argued about what exactly he had said at dinner before opening his presents. The sons asked him to offer a few words for the occasion, but he, who had previously given long, emotional speeches about his past and recounted his efforts to provide for his family, offered only a hasty thank you. He just expressed the joy he had felt in seeing all his children together.

In February, the most prominent neighbors commissioned the felling of trees for carnival. Over the last few weekends, he saw healthy specimens tied to the beds of pickup trucks. Only then did he accept the abnormality of his tree. It grew without resembling its peers: the eucalyptus or peppertrees that scarcely populated the surrounding area. Even neighbors his age were surprised. Never had a tree like this one been seen in the ravine. It had grown almost three feet and its brittle branches were beginning to invade the horizon of the garden like a mist. Noticing the growing shadow cast by the tree in the chilly afternoons of that false summer, he'd pull out a chair and read the newspaper: he'd found a place just for himself, and perhaps because of this he came to believe it a blessing.

By the end of March, the tree suddenly announced its growth. He and his wife woke up in the early morning to a damp, cold feeling, only to find their house flooded. All the objects they'd left on the floor the night before floated leisurely in the great pond the house had become. The tree roots had split part of the underground pipes that ran through the town to a canal that emptied into a river. Their shoes were ruined, the wooden bases of several pieces of furniture, the bottom of the curtains and some rugs received as gifts grew moldy. The granite floor became porous due to the accumulated water over the seven hours it took him and the neighbors to dry out the house. With their pants rolled to their knees, they lined up to scoop up the water with buckets, hoses and pots. Stagnant water damaged the medium-sized bushes and lemon verbena, and drowned the tomatoes, an essential ingredient at dinner. But what it didn't destroy were the tree branches, the only thing left alive in the seven square meters of mud left behind by the subterranean leak.

His version that the pipeline collapsed due to its age was only half believed. In afternoon social gatherings, people wouldn't dare tell him the tree roots might've damaged the pipes. Some women suggested to his wife that the tree might become so large it'd quietly dismantle the house. After the flood, the systematic harassment began at mealtimes, but he didn't listen. Their sons broached the subject, and he avoided answering how and when he'd get rid of the tree. He waited for the sludge from the flood to dry before he tucked the chair back into the shade of the orchard to enjoy the dry spring air.

One afternoon, he stumbled upon some brown, oval shapes, some sort of small, dried, cracked pine cones. The tree had begun to shed its fruits, which brought insects. It didn't take long for mosquitoes to lay eggs upon leaves at the base of the tree. A swarm of bees had also colonized its tiny orange flowers, so he could no longer spend the afternoons there like he'd grown accustomed to. Friends would hardly ever come by because they couldn't spend more than five minutes without being pestered by the insects, which had also invaded the house. His wife took advantage of his self-absorption and stopped talking to him. She went to see her kids, to take a break from what she called his "obsessions." And then one day, right before bed, the old man realized he had spent days without speaking to anyone.

Some time later, while cleaning the garden, he discovered footprints had damaged some violet flowers along the back fence. Their rhomboid petals were caked in the mud of a recently watered patch of dirt and their gray stems had snapped as if a body had been on top of them. The tracks were shallow, divided into four uneven sections. He thought a dog might've entered through a hole. He reinforced the wooden fence surrounding the garden, securing the multiple entrances. After-ward, feeling dissatisfied, he hired two workers to renovate the fence, and once it was completely repaired, he was finally able to sleep well, convinced that his house and tree were protected.

Soon after, an unpleasant odor poured into his house. He couldn't locate it along the usual path from the back door to the yard. He scanned with his eyes and saw nothing. Over the following days, the smell grew, mixing with that of the moist dirt. It was a strange scent, a mixture of urine and an acidic odor. One day it became unbearable, and he carefully searched for the source. He went through the house and garden inch by inch until he found, under a thick, almost dry bush, a large ocher stain mixed with crushed plants, the remains of what might be a dead animal. They were just rotten old tomatoes, he realized. For some reason, an explanation as simple as that didn't satisfy him. Bending down, he picked up the dry, caked leaves. He discovered a tunnel hidden under freshly-disturbed black soil, extending less than a meter from where he stood to under the fence, leading out of the yard. In the coming days, he went around the house and scrawled on paper, as if to make a plan to prevent that animal from entering again. From then on, the garden began to smell strongly of urine and feces, and he told himself that nauseating nature, with a pasty and stinking quality, couldn't be that of a domestic animal but definitely one accustomed to feeding on scraps.

Although he filled the critical parts of the fence with cement, that impenetrability lasted only a few days. One morning he stopped at another hole in the corner of the yard. He began tracking footprints through the garden, in search of the smallest organic residue of its presence. He put his body into the hole, trying to reconstruct the animal's entrance. He removed the headless flowers, the lemon verbena broken in two and the disturbed soil from the corners of the fence. What began as a hunt became a conviction to exterminate whatever was trying to enter the garden every night. All efforts to block the viable entrances seemed impossible, the ground had a sandy texture, easy to undo with even the most delicate tool.

Although the cold was becoming intense and could lead to pneumonia, he decided to stand guard at night. He always took a heavy blanket and flashlight to await the arrival of the intruder, which had already begun to attack the base of the tree. He'd stick the chair in the garden soil, by the door, and sit with the flashlight and a wooden stick in his hand. He once fell asleep and couldn't tell if the animal had appeared or not. He would wake himself up snoring or with his body suspended, saved by some mysterious mechanism that prevented him from falling. Obsessed with catching it, he neglected the plants in the vegetable patch, and even the tree itself. He realized too late that the trunk's base had been scratched; the bark was opening little by little, and you could see green and yellow filaments, the transparent layers of the plant. The bark had been attacked several times and the core of the tree had been exposed, along with roots that contoured on the surface.

He feared the unknown animal's obsession would end up destroying the tree and tearing its roots. His wife stopped calling so as not to feel guilty for being far away, while he remained attentive to every movement in the garden in case the animal—taking advantage of the fact that he fell asleep—circumvented the barrier he was trying to impose. The usual fruits had ceased to sprout from the tree and its branches were fading: it looked like a withered plant. It was hard to know if this appearance of dying was due to the animal's presence, or was a natural part of its cycle.

Around that time, he told his wife he had spotted the animal.

"I was returning home," he tells her, "down the cobbled street, the oldest one, and stepped off the corner onto the unpaved part, the vacant lot, because I'd gone the wrong way. I'd thought the cobbled street ended at the square, not the one that leads to San Mateo. There I saw the San Mateo bus fare collectors luring passengers by yelling out routes and realized I'd strayed. I thought about taking a shortcut home by crossing Salazar field. There's a path up that hill with the eucalyptus trees, remember? I saw a dog head up, and ran after it, only it didn't turn out to be a dog. It was walking crouched over and carried something in its mouth. I ran but the animal kept going and fled behind the trees. It was gray and reddish in color, with a showy tail and a streak of white on its back. Then I headed toward the trees and realized it wasn't a dog. The animal turned and stared at me for a while: I think it was a fox that had a live animal in its snout, writhing with its little head drooping, bloodstained. I pursued it, going up the path with the trees ahead, but it'd already reached the base of the mountain.

She interrupted him:

"Without a doubt, you were walking around drunk."

* * *

Some nights, when exhaustion got the better of him, he'd go to bed early. When he'd fall asleep, he'd hear a song that sounded like a lament. He'd hurry out to see if the animal had entered the yard and was performing some silent ritual, crushing the plants or urinating on the bottom of the fence. It was always the same result. He approached the orchard and heard the echoes of a high-pitched howl, but when he'd open the door from the hall into the garden, the sound disappeared, leaving only the crackle of leaves and revealing an extinct presence. He tried to convince himself that perhaps it wasn't an animal but a person who had decided to harass him for some past offense. He sat for long hours, remembering past conflicts with neighbors, the times he'd argued with a close friend, but couldn't come to a definitive conclusion. And the damage continued in different ways. And like that, little by little, the garden began to lose the old splendor of its halcyon days.

One night, shortly before his wife's return, he was awakened by a crackle interrupting his sleep; a bitter smell filled his lungs. His room was submerged in a dense mist that stopped him from breathing, forced him to leave his room. Desperate, he thought of all possible sources for the smoke as he made his way out. He hurried to the kitchen, but the oven was off, the elements were cold. The smoke had grown thinner and his breathing improved. In his room, he felt the heat of the fire most intensely. He went through the living room and through the biggest window that faced the backyard, he noticed a large fire in the garden. Waving flames billowed from the branches of the only tree. It burned without scorching, and the dry branches were illuminated by a golden fire that radiated heat felt from afar. Standing in the doorway, he watched the fire crackle and listened to the whisper the fibers of the burning tree made: little sparkles that spattered the ground. In the dark of that starless night, the tree offered a vision of the cycle of fire, small flashes that concealed the limits of its birth and extinction.

He wanted to move but stayed there, watching.

He snapped out of his thoughts when he felt the fire near his face, threatening to reach the house. He dumped dirt in a bucket to calm the fire. The burning branches scared him away, as if repelled by tentacles or arms. After several minutes of battling the fire that consumed the tree, the intensity diminished, and he was able to return to his room, resigned by fatigue. He opened the windows and tried to fall back asleep in the midst of a darkness that was gradually dissipating with the early morning air.

The next day he woke up with an intense scratchiness in his throat. He looked sideways and up, wondering if it had been a dream. He then opened the palm of his right hand, burnished with soot. He stood and headed into the garden. It hadn't been a hallucination or a dream. In the middle of it all, surrounded by dry branches and black ashes sprinkled with white, he found a black stick scorched by fire. In the coming days, he tried to fix the scene of the accident. Neighbors said nothing about the smoke, as if the tree had been consumed by obvious, spontaneous combustion. He never mentioned the possibility his neighbors might be responsible for the arson nor did he suspect them. "Maybe," he told his wife on the phone, "they didn't even notice the fire." "Maybe," she replied.

Over the next few days, he let the black stick be, even pouring water on it a couple of times in the hope a bud might revive, but the tree showed no signs of life. It stood inert amid the gray ash that covered what was once dark and fertile land. Two weeks later, after trying unsuccessfully with compost and new soil, he pulled out a hoe and drew a circle around the stick. He dug hard for two hours, until he saw thick roots coming to the surface; then he chopped them up with his pick, little by little destroying its foundation. Slowly, the tree fell, and he left it there.

* * *

Whenever he leaves his house, Don Manuel always wears a light gray suit when it is sunny, and a dark one when it is cloudy. Summer afternoons in Santa Lucía are bright, especially when snow has accumulated in the mountains the preceding season and its sparkle reflects throughout the city. After lunch, he sits on one of the wooden benches in the square and watches the passersby. He carefully observes those who gather around the fountain: children in shorts who play with objects invisible to him or throw little stones at one another, small groups of women his age who whisper among themselves. He becomes so engrossed in the scene that he even notices the bright afternoon dust the small crowd kicks up like invisible waves. His hat barely covers his face but, despite the heat, he doesn't take it off. Two young men pass behind his bench and greet him. They are the workers who helped him repair his fence. They approach and greet him with a slap on the back.

"How are you, Don Manuel? It's been ages since we've seen you at the square."

"I'm well, just here, soaking up the sun. Taking advantage of the fact that it hasn't rained for days and it's hot out." His voice is muffled, perhaps because he's not used to chatting. They come closer; he understands the gesture and makes space for them on the bench.

"And how's it going, Don Manuel? What's new?"

"Fine. Not much going on. My wife just returned from seeing our children. I left the house for a bit to get some air, take advantage of the sun. I unwind by watching people go by. And what are you guys doing here so early?"

"We've also come out because of the heat inside. We worked up there in San Damiano all morning while it rained, and came down here because we're done. If you have any work that needs doing at your house, let us know. It's better to be down here than to have to head up into the hills."

"Oh, that's right," he says. "I remember I called you to fix my garden a long time ago. But that was a while ago. Just so you know, I've since gotten rid of my garden."

"What? You got rid of it?"

"Yes, recently. At first, it was because my wife got annoyed at how much water we wasted, and the plants had begun to die from the heat. I was constantly watering and watering."

"But Don Manuel, that's a quick fix. In three, four days, it's back to normal. One day to remove all the depleted dirt and then bring in new soil from San Damiano. It'll only take three days."

"No, you don't understand. Two days, three days, and how much does it cost me? How much have I spent on the garden fence, which serves no purpose now? All the effort so that in the end it catches fire because of some cables that had been stripped near the water intake. One of those guys I called to help me left me in the lurch."

"Did it burn down? Your home too?"

"No, my house didn't burn down. A piece of wood near the exposed cables flared up a bit. Thank goodness the smoke woke me in the night, and I was able to put it out quickly."

They keep asking questions, but he barely hears: "What had you done before that? Had you moved the power lines or something? Don Manuel, you must have moved something in your garden..." The two young men speak, raise their voices, gesticulate. But he seems not to hear. He stares at his fist resting on his wooden cane, and thinks it's pleasant to be relaxing in the sun, as if time has stood still in order to forget what will happen next. His limbs surrender themselves to the relaxation of the heat, when all of a sudden, a memory leaves him puzzled. He feels a strange tingling in his feet, as if he's just solved a riddle or found a long-lost object. The murmur of the young men's conversation becomes more and more distant. He remembers the violence of the fire crackling that night and wonders exactly when it started. A kind of certainty comes to him, but he doesn't know if it's a revelation or an invention. He wonders if he wasn't saved by the tree on that night of no witnesses: if that fire, however it may have started, had perhaps been looking out for him. It doesn't matter if this thought doesn't approach the truth. He slowly closes his eyes and, with inner serenity, tunes out the noise of the nearby conversation.

Research

By Bethsabé Huamán Andía

It was a fact. She was pregnant and didn't know who the father was. Actually, those were two facts. One, the pregnancy. Two, the unknown paternity.

She had no idea how it even happened. She'd used a condom. Always. She herself had put it on, often with her mouth, following the instructions from a blog or video promoting responsible sexual behavior. It was useful and helped turn up the heat during intercourse. Each time she had ensured it was put on correctly and that the condom wasn't broken or ripped. She had kept her panties in place, employing an almost violent stubbornness to avoid genital contact without protection. She was certain no spies had escaped. (And by spy, she meant sperm, in affectionate language.) At least, she believed in that certainty especially given the fact that she was sleeping with numerous men. Yes, she was a researcher.

Choosing the right man required arduous, meticulous research. The selection criteria were divided into three categories: 1. Sexual Performance; 2. Social Position; 3. Future Potential.

1. Sexual Performance

Regarding this first aspect, empirical evidence suggested that in her case, historically, sexual attraction was linked to lower social position and nonexistent future potential. That's why her previous relationships ended in failure, sentimental disasters and appointments with psychoanalysts. She had emotionally and financially supported her partners, but even so, they'd all left her. Therefore, sexual attraction could not be considered a reliable measure for this study; however, a component related to sex had to be included, and Sexual Performance seemed consistent with the pursuit of pleasure, one of the main objectives of the study. Its weight was 30%.

The criteria to determine whether sexual performance was average, good or excellent turned out to be difficult to establish since it was intimately linked to sexual attraction. And this created an *a priori* predisposition to rating someone higher based on desirability. Additionally, it conflicted with something even more complicated and dangerous: love. For that reason, love had been ruled out as a factor, or even as a hypothesis, and had become a secondary objective or random variable in the study as a whole.

At the same time, sexual performance was defined by different variables. First, knowledge (whether intellectual or empirical) of successful sexual techniques. Of these, oral sex that was done well earned a high point value even though most men were quite inept at it. Caresses and stimulation of body parts, the farther away from the sexual organ the better, were extremely appreciated. This meant the feet and head tended to receive the most points. These two body parts weren't generally stimulated, and for her, they represented the shortest and most memorable paths to orgasm. Knowledge of the G-spot's exact location, regardless of position, was desirable.

Second, initiative. This was an important part of sexual performance. She didn't care for men who had to be convinced to make love, as if it were a mortgage application process. She liked to be surprised by a gaze, a caress, a hand under the table, a burning phone call at midnight. By the same token, she couldn't stand men who disregarded initiative, in this case, hers. She also enjoyed surprising men with her already wet crotch, in the middle of the hallway, on the way to the bathroom, in the car.

She'd slide her hand into a man's pants and stroke his member while they made small talk about the weather. Respect for her initiative was essential. At the first sign of rejection, annoyance or disinterest, the subject could be expelled from the study. Initiative didn't solely pertain to the sex act; it also referred, of course, to variety (of positions and places) and to surprise, and spontaneity mainly through new items or aspects of the sexual relationship (words, toys, drinks, clothes, dances).

The third element had to do with affection. She liked men who could be masculine, but also loving, who'd tickle her bellybutton, delicately run fingers along her skin, kiss her as if that were the endgame for them both. Affection was taken into consideration before, during and after. If he brought flowers, he'd receive the maximum number of points (before, during and after). If he thought of a good place for breakfast, woke her up with a kiss, whispered goodnight in her ear or tucked her in at midnight. All of these gestures mattered, a lot. Their opposite, any violent or aggressive action, was grounds for expulsion from the study.

In summary, the first set of criteria is outlined as follows:

Primary Objective: To Seek Pleasure
Secondary Objective: Love
Research Criteria:
1. Sexual Performance
    1.1 Knowledge of Sexual Techniques
        1.1.1   Oral sex
        1.1.2   Stimulation
        1.1.3   Location of G-Spot
    1.2 Initiative
        1.2.1   Initiating sex act
        1.2.2   Variety
        1.2.3   Surprise
        1.2.4   Respecting initiative
    1.3 Affection

2.   Social Position

The second criteria, Social Position, was important even though that bothered her, not only due to her negative previous experience, but also because it was related to Future Potential (the third criteria), and because it determined what could and could not be done in the relationship. It was impossible to conduct research with a subject who had no work-life balance and worked 24/7. Impossible with a subject who made minimum wage. Impossible if he didn't live in her district or in one of the ten neighborhoods closest to hers. Impossible if he didn't know who Kusturica was, if he didn't like Padura, if he didn't read *La República*. She didn't want to place too much importance on it, but she did, so it also counted for 30%.

What had failed before wasn't that the men didn't move in those circles (intellectual, financial or political), but that they had other priorities: not interested in springing for a hotel but wanting to sleep with her; not paying for tickets but wanting to go to the movies with her; not giving her gifts but spending their entire salary on alcohol. In this case, therefore, social position wasn't a unit of measurement in and of itself, but rather its application to the relationship. The number of hours they were available to see one another. The time devoted to the relationship per week or per month. Shared cultural, political or social affinities.

Primary Objective: To Allow for Future Potential
Secondary Objective: To Have Fun
2. Social Position

      2.1   Number of hours available for the relationship each month

      2.2   Amount of time devoted to the relationship each month

      2.3   Shared cultural, social, political affinities

3. Future Potential

The third factor represented the core of the study since the research aspired to produce long-term results, and of course, with outcomes that could be replicated, reproduced, cited and celebrated the world over. All of that would be based on the continuity of the results over time. This component carried the most weight (40%) and, in a way, was related to the previous elements, but also somewhat more subjective: picturing them together ten years later, in a comfortable situation, with the possibility of creating a home, with the security and trust to be able to give a part of her life to that person. Here the variables were the most complicated to measure and evaluate.

Primary Objective: To Last
Secondary Objective: Happiness
3. Future Potential
 3.1 Long-term possibilities
 3.2 Possibility of replication
 3.3 Future visualization
 3.4 Trust in the other

All of this had been ruined by the pregnancy. It was true this could've been regarded as a possible secondary objective, but a much later one, and certainly not anything to be seriously considered before the studies had concluded. If the research led to choosing which would have the most longevity, perhaps a force of nature, by choice or chance, would have appeared, a variable in the study she hadn't contemplated or had believed was under control but turned out to be invasive.

Abortion was always a way out. This wasn't an easy option since it involved a clandestine practice, an expenditure, risks, guilt and a feeling of failure. Nevertheless, it was much less traumatic than to be a mother without wanting to, without being ready to handle it. And that was the worst thing, because in that moment she not only felt ready but happy to be pregnant, even though the circumstances were complicated and confusing. That research outcome was much more interesting: the possibility of having a child. In other words, a total future potential, with all of the study subjects at the same time. Maybe that is what made her research even more revolutionary. But society wasn't ready for it.

I Could Never Bring Myself to Hate Her

By Diego Trelles Paz

Back then, I was fifteen and I was crazy. I know this unsettling line belongs to someone else, but I had no way to start this story and when that happens to me, I steal. Apologies if you think it's unethical. If you find it to be lowly, pathetic or rude. I don't believe it's harmful. Or cynical. Or taking advantage. I like those verses, I like the author of those verses and for that reason alone, I steal them from him. And I feel from the bottom of my heart that I'm doing good work. Why didn't I know how to start this story if I supposedly write and people pay me to do it? I think it's because of her, because I should've written about her that summer of '93 when the last thing I wanted to do was write, and I was fifteen, and I was crazy.

Don't get your hopes up, the "her" in question wasn't the most beautiful girl on the beach nor was I the most imbecile and docile of her suitors, although my story does take place on a beach south of Lima when Lima was a shithole a little less crowded than today. Why did I think I was crazy? Perhaps because of the analgesic effects the drugs had on me. I liked marijuana and I liked cocaine, but what brought me to my knees was mixing weed and freebase into a white blunt, long and slender like a modest woman's finger (which is what we in Peru call "un rico mixto"). I wouldn't say I was a drug addict because drugs and I have always had this senseless concubine relationship, intense at times, but never fully a commitment. Even today, when it occurs to me to call Sherwood, I feel as though the guy looks at me suspiciously, as if he hates dealing with a stingy foreigner who buys a few grams of coke only when depressed or when the snow melts on the Brooklyn sidewalks.

Worst of all, Sherwood is right. I like to do lines while watching this city melt and that doesn't happen often. There's something raw and charming about feeling clumsy and elated as the snow ceases to soak into surfaces and the whiteness fades. The pathetic thing is that I'm aware of my writerly affectations and idiosyncrasies—a nauseating individual in every sense of the word — and I've done nothing to remedy them. Of course, it wasn't like that back then. Back then, I was a slightly more stupid human being but much more sincere: I took drugs to ride waves and after that, I ate and then went to sleep thinking how nice it'd be to wake up and smoke up again. My life was simple: I read for pleasure and acted out of instinct. I lost my virginity like an animal at the age of thirteen. It was me on top of Mercedes, shaking my pelvis at her for three frantic minutes. The idea had been hers but later, in front of my parents, she denied it. When my folks would leave the house, my cousin would come to my room and we'd have a pillow fight until the pillows fell to the ground on purpose, and by then we were screwing with the ferocity of beasts, clumsily imitating positions from the porn movies Mercedes stole from my Tío Memo.

Mercedes was a slut and that's why I loved her, even though I saw her as voluptuous more than pretty. She is not, however, the woman I'm writing about now: Mercedes inspires characters but can't be considered a muse. Perhaps it's fair to say that it all began with Abraham. The beginning of this saga has three well-defined parts I'll summarize to make a long story short: 1) Abraham and I meet at the small pier on one of the unnamed beaches that make the south bank of San Bartolo anchovy-shaped. The seaside town is twenty-five miles from Lima, and my parents have the typical middle-class house. Although I'd been going every summer since I was eleven, I didn't have any friends and just spent my time smoking and riding waves and having sex with Mercedes when my parents weren't around. Abraham has a beaver face, a short military-style haircut and is always smiling. He asks if I can dive from the highest rock at the pier and I say I don't know. He then calls me a pussy, even though he doesn't want to jump into the sea either. 2) Penélope is Abraham's best friend and is always making fun of him. Penélope fell for Abraham when she was thirteen; without thinking about it, almost happily, she said yes to him, although five days later, after three French kisses and innocent dry humping by the campfire, she told him she was no longer interested. Abraham stopped talking to her for a month. Penélope called him an immature brat and an idiot, letting him know she'd only speak to him again if he apologized. Abraham met Mariana and, two days later, apologized to Penélope. Mariana broke up with Abraham after two months, when he was already courting another girl. When Abraham and I become friends, a girl from his school has just dumped him and he asks me if Mercedes, the girl he always sees sunbathing on my terrace, is my girlfriend. 3) Penélope is a year younger than me: when I meet her, the first thing she asks me is whether I'm a little less of a jackass than Abraham. Stoned and half understanding the question, I respond vaguely: I don't know, maybe. I'm attracted to Penélope from the start, but I don't really know why. I'm kind of a slacker, a crazy kid and I don't ask myself those kinds of questions.

Every time I think of Penélope—and that has happened often since I came to New York—I see her on the beach again, young and flirtatious and full of life; she's frozen in time and that's why I still remember her as the girl with long brown curly hair who went around barefoot. That's the image I keep of her because that's how I knew her. She was a skinny, freckled young woman who told dirty jokes and never lost her tan; she looked like a rebellious surfer even though she had no interest in catching waves and said she was a little turned off by the laid-back surfer slang. She also had large brown eyes, almost round, and the inquisitive gaze of a teenager who knows she is growing up fast.

The first time we kissed (she kissed me), we were sitting on the dock waiting for sunset. She didn't say anything, just put her hand in my hair and gently pulled me to her mouth. Marijuana had made us relaxed and a little euphoric. Kissing, in those circumstances, seemed as natural as falling asleep or throwing ourselves into the sea. That was also the first time she mentioned her father. She said he didn't talk much, which gave him an air of arrogance but that he was a good man. She asked me if I'd ever seen him on the beach and then, without waiting for my answer, turned her face in his direction. When the man in uniform, who was waiting on the balcony, raised his hand to say goodbye, I realized that no, I'd never seen him before. She blew him a kiss as his car with tinted windows pulled away, followed by a truck full of young, hulking bodyguards in sunglasses. She didn't mention him much, although later I noticed the gentleman appeared in San Bartolo twice a week with the same enigmatic men who stood waiting for him on the sidewalk smoking, opening their blazers to dissipate a little summer sweat, listening to Peruvian soccer league matches on the radio.

The bodyguards were tall and boisterous and only took off their glasses to play a pick-up game of soccer with Penélope's cousins and uncles. Inside the house, on the other hand, they were very reserved: unless the General asked them something specific, they answered with a smile or polite monosyllables. If they were invited to eat with the family, they'd sit in a small corner of the terrace and acknowledge the hospitality with a respectful nod. They called General Valdivieso "my General," his wife "Doña Jimena" and Penélope "Señorita Penélope." The female household staff—the cook, the maid and the youngest child's nanny—were the only ones called by their names. They never got a chance to give me a name, but I quickly knew from their looks that they realized I was high most of the time and pretended to ignore it. It was clear to me that if they knew, the General knew. Nevertheless, Penélope's father, and the discreet acquiescence with which he approved of my turning up at his house, measured and prudent in the face of the natural passage of time and the sudden maturity of his only daughter, never stopped being kind to me. He was tight-lipped, no doubt, but he had the elegant reticence of those who seem to listen to everything with attention and respect. The most intriguing thing was that this man and his honest demeanor dismantled my preconceived notions of how a military officer in the Fujimori era looked and spoke (actually, I don't remember what my ideas were at the time; it's likely I was confused and mimicked my father, his fury and frustration). I didn't detect, therefore, the slightest sign in this soft-eyed gentleman of that cold and sinister cynicism with which the military expressed itself the night Congress was dissolved. It's also very likely that, given my absent-minded state, I didn't know how to perceive that. General Valdivieso was shy and a model for children, guests and maids, and had a special talent for reinventing himself during the few days he spent in the beach town: quietly hiding the other, the transfigured face of the other, one who physically resembled the same man with white hair and firm waist but who was, however, his corroded and shady double, already completely stripped of the affectionate image he'd patiently built among the still-innocent people around him.

I write and read the word "innocent" and think of us and our Edenic adolescence of '93, when we seemed immune to what was happening outside the beach. We were far away. We were enjoying the summer. We ate ice cream, drank beer, grilled chorizos and meat on the terrace on Sundays while watching soccer on TV. My father would organize those family get-togethers with Charito and Mercedes, and Tío Memo and Tía Yolanda, and he'd laugh and get drunk and gently caress our hair and celebrate Universitario's goals, shouting like a man possessed. He was also the only one who talked to me about those things. Students are disappearing, he told me, young guys, not much older than you. They're taken at night by the military, and they don't come back. Don't tell your brother, he's still too young to understand it, and he gave me a kiss, I love you very much, little dude, he whispered, already drunk, I'm not going to let anything happen to you. And I really trusted what he promised, grateful that the good-natured man with a bulging belly and thick mustache was my father, although, deep down, I didn't really understand what could happen to us. I didn't place much importance on it either, I must confess. Drugs made me a little more dim-witted and cretinous than I would've liked. Sometimes I thought of the disappeared and felt a motionless sorrow that only made me want to light another blunt and hit the sack. I remember telling Abraham about it one day and being surprised by his response. "They take them because they're terrorists," he said convinced, without much desire to argue; when I tried to get him to explain what he'd said, he replied he wasn't interested and abruptly changed the subject, demanding I put in a good word for him with Mercedes, that it was no big deal for me, damn it; that I should stop screwing around and being so jealous and stingy with my cousin.

The truth is I didn't care if Mercedes hooked up with him. I even wanted it to happen so Abraham would leave me alone. It didn't happen. She didn't want to and was quite polite in telling him she wasn't interested. Although my cousin knew Penélope was my girlfriend, there was never the slightest reproach on her part. She continued to sunbathe on the terrace, I continued to ride waves and take drugs, and the two of us would eat lunch together with my parents and my brother, and it was— my mother joked— as if Mercedes were the sister we never had. On days when my family went out for a walk along the boardwalk or out to eat, Mercedes would call me up to my room, and I'd obediently go. Walking in and seeing her naked on the bed was so natural for both of us that there was never a need for words. We savagely fucked, surrendering to our instincts like symbionts, and with the crazy fervor of occasional lovers impatiently awaiting a new encounter.

I never told Penélope. I don't know if she knew or suspected. I'm guessing she didn't. I also don't know what I could've said to her because I didn't feel guilty or immoral passively obeying my impulses. I knew that, yes, what I felt for Penélope was nothing like what drove me to sleep with Mercedes without the slightest reluctance. I'm sure, however, that if someone had asked me how I felt about Penélope, I would've kept quiet or said something random just so I wouldn't have to think about it. Luckily, Penélope never asked me those kinds of questions. We spent most of that summer together, laughing at our craziness whenever we'd smoked more than three blunts, drinking until dawn with friends from the southern boardwalk who used to play guitar and hang out at El Huayco, a nightclub full of surfers where pills and coke were plentiful.

Life, of course, couldn't be so harmonious no matter how sedentary and relaxed we were while living it. The invisible bubble of ignorance our parents had built to protect us was suddenly broken by the immanent violence floating in the country's fired-up atmosphere, a climate of dormant horror that we experienced in the worst way one night that should've been like all the others, but something changed. There we were, smoking and getting plastered and going to the disco almost hand in hand, happily marching drunk through the streets of San Bartolo until we reached the crowded door of El Huayco, taking the last hits from the blunt, kissing Penélope behind the cars while Abraham called to us, you'll have to stay outside if you don't hurry, he yelled, with his back to the green 4x4 emerging from the shadows like a war tank. It wasn't hard to recognize ourselves in those grungy teenagers who were traveling in the bed of the truck and quickly jumped out to confront us. There we were, in the middle of that blond, long-haired mob who lived on the other shore of the beach, also brutalized by boredom and ready to let ourselves go even if chance and circumstances had made us the victims that night.

Abraham realized what was going to happen and ran off screaming "please, no!" as if the caravan of death had come to take us away. I stayed still and silent, not because I wanted to play the tough guy, but because right then I didn't understand that the night's entertainment consisted of beating me up for no reason, in emptying out the pent-up anger all of us carried inside. The beach was theirs, they said, why the fuck are you looking at me, idiot, they broke down the door, pounded the shit out of them, took them with hoods over their heads and they never came back, dude, they put them in single file, looking down at the floor, don't look up, you piece of shit, and the bullet went straight to the head: for being terrorists, Abraham said, convinced although he was no longer there. I don't really know how many guys beat me up or for how long. When they left, I was on the floor curled up like a fetus, bleeding from my head and nose. I would've done the impossible to light up a joint at that moment. Penélope, next to me, was crying scared.

A week after the incident, General Valdivieso's bodyguards came out to meet me on the boardwalk. I was coming back from surfing and had just smoked a joint. I hadn't seen Penélope since the day of the beating. After going to the clinic in San Bartolo, I told my father I'd gotten into a fight. "Let's go for a walk," said the guard who seemed to be the leader, in the friendly yet dutiful voice of a man trained to give orders. I got in the back of the car and didn't say a thing. They knew what had happened at the nightclub, muttered the one who spoke first, there are abusive people who find it funny to punch folks just for the hell of it, that's not good, because, what kind of country is this? He paused to take a long drag of his cigarette; the General is very upset, he told me to talk to you, said you're an honest young man from a good family; he threw his cigarette out the window and didn't say anything until we reached the other pier; let's head over there, okay? Slowly, don't worry they can't see you; you tell me which one and we'll leave, there's always one who's the biggest son of a bitch, right? Point him out to me and that's it, we'll take care of talking to him and then I'll drop you off at home and you forget about this forever, what do you think?

I pointed and said thank you, and when the bodyguards left me at my house, I went down the stairs and began to cry.

This is the moment when the memory of those years becomes painful. The one who came to tell me was Abraham. His name's Rafael but they call him Burnout, he said while devouring an ice cream, he has long blond hair but don't fall for it, of course, he's blond like that thanks to his dough because he's the only one from the north shore who's half cholo. He lived in San José —the town next to the summer homes and that extended up into the hills, inhabited by the workers who took care of the beach houses in winter—they called him Burnout because he smoked and when he was high he liked to pick fights or did cruel, stupid things to please others, the ones who drove the SUVs and had houses with balconies facing the sea and never called him if they were in Lima and called him a bleached Indian behind his back. Burnout was the one who kicked you while you were on the ground, but don't worry, they messed him up, Abraham added, putting his hand under the ice cream so as not to drip on the floor, the gorillas who guard Penélope's old man (don't say anything because nobody knows, but I do), he gave a satisfied smirk, they grabbed him by the hair and threw him in a car and knocked him around, two days and nothing, his dad even filed a complaint and everything, but nobody knew exactly what was happening. They said it was a gang of drug traffickers from Punta Hermosa and then, on the third day, as if nothing had happened, Burnout walks down to the beach with his board and says he'd gone to Lima for a while, that it was all a misunderstanding but things have been resolved, but he's kind of like chump now, whisper the people who don't believe a damn thing he says, and when he crosses paths with Abraham or Penélope he lowers his head or discreetly crosses the street so as not to face them.

The day I came face to face with Burnout, and he lowered his head submissively, I didn't recognize him. Abraham found it funny to see him docile, he was grateful to the General's thugs, he spoke of divine justice, but was surprised and annoyed by my silent indifference. Although we both knew it, neither Penélope nor I ever discussed the intervention by her father's bodyguards. We tried our best to carry on the same routine as before, but we couldn't: something vague and elusive had come between us, something that even now I consider unspeakable because it couldn't be defined in words, even though it was so palpable and caustic. Sometimes I think I should've told her and maybe, if we agreed, we could've fixed things between us. I didn't really understand why the action and its consequences made me so angry (Burnout's submissive attitude in the face of who knows what they had done to intimidate him), but I knew for sure that my apathy was a product of my indignation, seeing him in the street and knowing the guards hadn't kidnapped the person I had pointed out but the weakest and most defenseless, the only one of the surfers who couldn't have done anything to denounce them because he was poor and lived in San José and was condemned to act and present himself as someone different in order to be accepted on the beach.

What followed our bewilderment was all too predictable and remained that way until the Fujimori regime fell and General Valdivieso and his family fled the country. Summer was ending, families were beginning to pack up and put locks and bars on the doors, and promises to see one another in Lima faded with the days and classes at school and new friends who went out to Barranco on Saturday nights or to quinceañeras at the Country Club, and soon the prep academies, missing summer vacation to get into college, the Pontificia Universidad Católica del Perú for her, Universidad de Lima for me, growing long hair and a bushy beard until the first-year hazing resulted in them being shaved off. You were happy and drunk, soaked in beer when you started reading seriously, you liked short stories by Cortázar and Rulfo and Onetti, and you were already marching in the streets against the government with Jimena and then hugging Carola, and then you were alone until the following summer when you saw Penélope and said hello to her and she squeezed you hard, my friend, how have you been, she so grown up, so unharmed and sheltered, holding hands with the one you hadn't been able to forget, the same one who drove the green 4x4 and had kicked you on the ground the night she cried for you.

* * *

From dusk until dawn, with the heat on because it's snowing outside and Brooklyn is being filled with the thick, white, evil foam that grows and multiplies until it's buried, with the empty bags of cocaine next to the keyboard and the growing impulse to call Sherwood again, I think of Penélope and life after Penélope and the melancholy dries my mouth and silences me. I write drugged and drugged, I think I understand that it's from here, from this oscillating present, that the act of remembering can become hostile and deceitful. Sometimes, for example, I have this slightly ridiculous fantasy of running into Penélope on the streets of New York, she's the one who's distracted walking down Fifth Avenue and hasn't seen me yet, and I'm afraid she won't recognize me but, yes, her surprised look and the same mischievous smile from our afternoons on the San Bartolo pier, how could I forget you, I thought about you too, Diego; I'd asked Abraham and he only knew you'd left the country, tell me about yourself, she said, and I invited her to have a coffee and asked her about the guy in the 4x4 who'd gotten lost or died, she didn't know, she was alone, alone and sad, as sad as Mercedes

251

when she broke the spell and her tears brought me back to our little apartment in Brooklyn, threatening to leave me, to take the boys away if I didn't change my behavior once and for all and go back to being myself, the boy from the beach house, the man she'd waited so long for.

Sierra Norte

By Yeniva Fernández

When the bus crossed the bridge, she was awakened by the attendant's voice announcing their arrival and wishing the passengers a pleasant stay in "beautiful Sierra Norte." She looked out the window. The street seemed like a succession of traditional folkloric paintings, barely tinged by a few cars and passers-by in jeans. "Yes, it's beautiful," she said aloud, feeling a brief shiver. She'd wanted this vacation so much and it was the first time she'd traveled alone.

A taxi took her to the only hotel in town, an old mansion with an interior patio and a fountain in the middle. Her hands were cold, but she was still happy. She was right to have chosen a province and not the state capital, noisier and more polluted compared to this peaceful place where all the people wore hats. Plus, it was so close to the ski camp. She was about to share those thoughts with the guy at the front desk, but he turned up the volume on his radio and handed her the registration form almost without looking at her. She picked up the pen, the page was blank and for an instant, which she thought would last forever, she forgot what her name was, but then wrote with certainty, Rocío Pérez, and signed.

Once in her room, the first thing she did was look inside the suitcase and take out a picture frame that she placed on the nightstand. In it was a photo of a young man sitting on a bench, petting a huge German shepherd's head. She looked at it and ran her right index finger across the man's face. She liked to see him like that, dressed in jeans and the beige leather jacket she'd given him, his eyes somewhat shy and his long fingers tangled in the fur of his faithful puppy, since he still called him that. An eight-year-old puppy; he was so silly, she thought. She walked to the window. The day hadn't warmed up yet, and in the distance, you could see the mountains with their white plumes like girls who'd just woken and stretched their arms to the sun, she thought and automatically stretched her arms, feeling like a girl with no past to remember. But she had to call him, tell him about the landscape, tell him she'd arrived safely and that from her hotel she could make out the mountain ranges that appeared in the catalogs they'd looked at so often together. She picked up the phone, and soon tired of waiting for someone to answer. Surely, he would've already left for the office. She'd try his cellphone later.

She decided to have breakfast and then go for a short walk. The hotel was near downtown and through a narrow street she quickly reached the square. As she walked, she noticed some people looking at her and bowing their heads to greet her. She found the town charming and stopped for a moment to observe a few old men sitting on benches in the square. There were three of them who must have been over eighty years old, but they looked healthy, talked in a distracted way, laughed from time to time. Behind them, a thick-trunked palm tree completed the group of octogenarians. She smiled; how could they have got it to grow at over six thousand feet above sea level? With time, she said to herself, because time was plentiful there. And she wondered what it'd be like to always stay in the same place, without moving or taking vacations. Maybe it wasn't all bad, she thought.

                                * * *

She walked into a restaurant across from the church. It was small and cozy, only eight tables and the walls decorated with local crafts. A woman with a round face and black braids came out to greet her.

"Señorita Beatriz, what a surprise! When did you arrive?" The woman hugged her.

"No, umm... I think..."

"No, no, please señorita! Don't say a thing, tell me later. Right now, I'll bring you a green soup, with plenty of cheese just the way you like it. I'll be right back, right back," she said and disappeared behind the counter.

She felt like leaving, but was also curious about this woman so she took a seat. The woman returned a few minutes later.

"Here you are, señorita, to start the day off strong." She placed the bowl in front of her.

"Thanks, but I think you're confusing me with someone else."

"How...?"

"Yes, I just got here. I'm from the east."

"You're not Señorita Beatriz Morales?"

"No. My name is Rocío Pérez. I came here to ski."

"You're not?" The woman put her hand to her mouth, then burst out laughing. "You're so funny! Now, tell me how you've been. It's been a long time!"

"It's not a joke; it's true."

The woman blushed.

"I'm sorry, it's just you look so similar..."

"Don't feel bad. But now I'm intrigued. Who is this Beatriz?"

"She's a young lady who lived in town years ago. Her mother died and she married an engineer who came to survey the new highway. She left with him and hasn't come back. That was over ten years ago."

"Was she your friend?"

"Yes, she was very kind. She always came here to have her green soup. She liked the one I made. She taught here, but only preschool. She was my Liliu's teacher... Forgive me! You really look a lot like her... Do you want me to change your soup?"

"No, its fine. Don't worry."

Liliu, the name kept spinning around in her head; it seemed like the name of a bunny not a person, just as sweet as the German shepherd whose name was... She couldn't remember, yet it was on the tip of her tongue. She shrugged. She tasted the broth, didn't like it, but still took a few spoonfuls. Then she paid and headed to the hotel. On her way back, she felt as though someone were following her, and turning her head, saw a green-eyed man who immediately crossed to the other sidewalk. It must've been her imagination; she was exhausted from the trip.

She woke up at three in the afternoon, amazed at how much she'd slept. She realized it had been a long time since she took a nap at that time of day and on a Monday. At her office, she barely had forty minutes for lunch, which flew by while she ate with the girls, each one talking about their marriages or work. They were so funny. Especially the chubby one, who constantly showed them the latest miniskirts her husband gave her, the perverted midget, as she called him. She smiled. Ah the girls, she kind of missed them already. But she'd buy them all souvenirs; in fact, she even had a list with their special requests. She rummaged through her suitcase but couldn't find it. She must've forgotten it since she left in such a hurry. Well, she did remember a few things anyway. She called the front desk, asked if they had room service, and ordered a steak and fries. After eating, she went out to sign up for a tour to the ski area the next day. The salesman asked if she was interested in skiing, why didn't she stay at the hotel on the mountain like the other skiers. She didn't know how to answer, only saying that she liked the town.

Back in her room she remembered she hadn't been in touch with him all day and dialed his number. The answering machine picked up, but she didn't want to leave a message. Knowing how distracted he was, it didn't seem strange he'd left his cellphone turned off. At five in the morning the following day, the bus picked her up to take her to the mountains. They were a small group of about ten people, mostly English and Italian. The guide began explaining the geography in both languages, and when he switched to Spanish, she preferred to concentrate on the music the driver had just put on and take in the view. The melody was typical of the region, with upbeat arrangements that appeared to say, "we've been waiting for you," and the valley of wheat fields extended like an open hand inviting her to stay. But the idea frightened her, and she closed the window curtain.

In the mountains, while the Europeans were already enjoying themselves sliding down small slopes, she was still struggling to stay on her feet. The instructor said that she was doing pretty well for her first time on skis, but she felt ridiculous. What had led her to take a ski vacation when as a girl she had never even learned to skate? Maybe that wasn't exactly what she came looking for. Maybe she just wanted to see that white expanse where time froze, was canceled. She spent the rest of the afternoon in the camp cafeteria, watching the skiers come and go, chatting with an Italian lady who didn't dare ski either and who was waiting for her husband. That brought his image back to mind, but the memory faded easily into the snow.

The bus returned to town with only her. The road zigzagged, and the driver looked at her from time to time until he finally said:

"Señorita, excuse me, but aren't you a relative of Beatriz Morales, the teacher?"

"No, I don't know her."

"Ah...well, I thought you must be related."

"I don't know her, but someone else already told me I look a lot like her."

"Yes, very much so. Aren't you from here?"

"I'm from the east."

"This lady I mentioned, I think she also had relatives there. She left town a long time ago."

"Umm, and what was she like?"

"Good person. I used to bring her canvases and little bottles of paint from San Bartolo. Before, I had a big truck and brought things to sell. Before, the town was different; there weren't many of us and everyone knew each other. Now with the new highway there are a lot of outsiders here."

"And...she painted?"

"Yes, and very pretty. When she left, she gave away her paintings and sold her other things."

"Her house too?"

"No, her house has been shuttered, and now it's falling apart. You seriously are the spitting image of her, although when I look at you more closely, I can see the differences. Well, what do you think of the town...

* * *

In the morning, she decided not to return to the mountains and went out early to contemplate the streets. She walked further and further away from the square, appreciating the houses' rose gardens, the contrast of reds and pinks against the white walls, until she stopped in front of one of them. The door was boarded up, a few roof tiles scattered on the ground the only sign of color among the weeds. Seeing it, she felt pity; she thought of a woman sitting on an empty path and looking down at the ground. Maybe if she stayed a while and, even though she knew nothing about gardening, she could help out by weeding the entrance and picking up the broken tiles. The fence wasn't high, and she decided to jump over it; however, as she was about to, a man came out of a neighboring house, and seeing she'd been discovered, she headed in the opposite direction. As she walked away, the image of the crumbling house began to overlap with that of her apartment in the city.

She found an open Internet café in the square, reserved a machine and opened her email. Her friends had written to her, but no messages from him. She answered succinctly, without carefully reading the message contents; everything is fine, the place is really nice and I miss and love you all very much. She would've especially liked to tell him that last thing. But he hadn't dropped her a single line. She was furious, but decided that if he hadn't communicated, it was probably because she hadn't either; he was that childish. Besides, he didn't even know where she was staying to be able to call her. She ended up writing to him, noting the hotel phone number, and told him about the town, about the incidents with the woman from the restaurant and the driver, and asked him for his pet's name. I'm a bit out of it and don't remember, and also he shouldn't forget to water the plants on the terrace, although she mentioned this without much conviction, because now she couldn't hold onto the exact memory of her apartment terrace. But she didn't reveal this; she preferred to fill the screen with the conviction of her feelings for him.

At the hotel, she waited for his call until lunchtime. Then she left, her feet leading her to the restaurant owned by the woman with braids.

"Hello."

"Señorita, how are you? Come in, sit down."

"Thanks. I like your restaurant. It's lovely."

"Señorita Beatriz helped me decorate it. She chose these baskets to hang on the wall and those vases over there in the corner. And it turned out pretty, right? I was planning to put colored tablecloths and that's it because I said the most important thing in a restaurant is the food, but she advised me to... I'm sorry, I think I talk too much."

"No. I'm interested in listening... I think I saw her house today."

"Whose?"

"Beatriz's. I was walking and found an abandoned house behind the church."

"It used to have the most beautiful garden in town, and Señorita Beatriz and her mother painted the exterior every year. Now it's sad to see it so neglected. I'd like to go one day and fix it up a little."

"Why don't we go this afternoon? I'll help you."

* * *

They met at five. She carried a plastic bag for garbage and the woman with braids, a couple of brooms and dustpans. One by one they diligently picked up the broken roof tiles and the garbage that people had chucked over the fence. They swept the stone path leading to the porch and cleared the railing of cobwebs. Then they sat down and began to talk about the town; later, the woman described her family and children. She listened; she liked the woman's voice, her use of diminutives and her brown hands. Suddenly, she looked up; behind the woman, green eyes were watching her. She stood up right away. However, the man immediately turned and left, pulling a girl by the hand.

"Who is that?"

"That's Guillermo. He was Señorita Beatriz's boyfriend. She left him to get married."

* * *

The man's hardened face lingered in her mind as she pressed the keys on the phone. She'd been back at the hotel for an hour and had tried several times to reach him. Still, a busy tone invariably sounded on the other end of the line. She decided to wait a half hour to call back. She felt restless. That man, Guillermo, was the same one who'd followed her the day she arrived in town. And now, like last time, he didn't say a word. Though it was clear his silence constituted a reproach, it was also obvious it wasn't directed at her, but at this Beatriz with whom he'd surely confused her. A misunderstanding between two strangers, something that was easy to resolve just by telling him her name was Rocío Pérez, that she was someone else. Even so, she couldn't stop thinking about his gaze and the dark emptiness that love leaves behind when it's gone. She wanted to talk to him, but why? She wasn't Beatriz. She took the picture frame from her nightstand, put it on her lap and picked up the phone again.

The next day she went for breakfast with the woman with braids. It was early, customers hadn't arrived yet, so they sat down to talk for a while. The woman told her about her life, how difficult it had been to start the business as a widow and how little by little she acquired everything in her establishment, from the freezer to the paintings. She looked at the paintings, most of them mountainous landscapes, except for one depicting a lone boat sailing on a calm ocean.

"And what about that painting over there?"

"That was a present. Señorita Beatriz gave it to me. She painted it herself; she always drew the sea. She wanted so badly to go there. She went to live on the coast, you know... I'd like to see her now and ask if the sea is what she imagined it to be like."

A silence came over them and she wanted to take the woman's hand. But by then people had begun to arrive at the restaurant and the woman ran to serve them. She stared at the painting again and told herself the sea was painted an exaggerated shade of blue, that just like expectations when contrasted with reality, its true color was more of a dull green, closer to gray.

The next few days she spent in the garden at the abandoned house. She didn't know how to handle a hoe and pulling weeds required a great deal of effort. The yard was small, but she needed almost a week before she finally planted roses. That afternoon, she couldn't resist approaching Guillermo. She'd seen him spying on her ever since she undertook this task, always at a distance, always just an instant before disappearing. And there he was again. But this time her boldness won out.

"Hey! Hey, wait! I know you're confusing me with someone else. But my name is–"

"Yes, I know," he said somewhat nervously and nodded at the woman with braids who was approaching, carrying a piñata. "I was looking at the house. They say houses preserve something of the people who lived in them... In any case, I like to believe that... Well, I should be leaving. Nice to meet you. Oh! I forgot, I also wanted to give you this because of what you've done to it." He pointed to the house.

He put the package in her hands before she was able to thank him.

"Señorita! Señorita!"

She turned to find the woman with braids almost by her side.

"I'm glad I caught you." She took a breath and set the piñata on the ground. "Tomorrow is the feast of San Blas, the patron saint of the town. There'll be bamboo castles for fireworks, piñatas, dancing and food. It's a wonderful party; stay until tomorrow night at least."

"What do you mean?"

"Yes, I know your ticket is for early tomorrow morning. But busses leave at night too. I'll arrange it. Come on, stay, even if it's just to try my stews."

"My ticket?"

"Yes, you told me your departure was tomorrow."

"Oh that." She didn't remember seeing the date on her ticket, much less mentioning it.

"Well, are you staying?"

"Yes," she said, amazed how quickly she made the decision.

* * *

Arriving at the hotel, she took a quick bath and immediately looked for her return ticket. She didn't find it, but that didn't disappoint her at all. She sat placidly on the bed and began to look at the package Guillermo had given her. She opened it slowly. It was a large pad of paper and a box of colored pencils. She took one of the pencils and began to draw until the notebook was almost full. Then she slept soundly, a white dream, flowing and without memory. But when she opened her eyes in the morning, the first thing she saw was the portrait on the chest of drawers and she shuddered. She hadn't heard back from him, hadn't communicated with him since she arrived in Sierra Norte. She picked up the phone and dialed his number over and over without getting an answer.

The square was lined with stalls offering everything from fabrics, to balloons, to pork rinds. She was on her way to the Internet café, but stopped first to look at the stalls. She knew her friends had asked for certain items. But what? She felt uncomfortable. Not only because of her forgetfulness, but because the very image of her friends began to blur at the edges in the colorful landscape surrounding her. Despite this feeling, she stayed to watch as they assembled, one by one, the seven stories of the fireworks display instead of continuing on her way. She remained seated on a bench until the procession with the saint mounted on a frame left the church. The entire town participated in the ritual, and she let herself be carried along by that mass of humanity in which individual identity dissolved. Then came the troupes with their sparkling costumes and their joy. The woman with braids handed her a large bowl of green soup, and it tasted delicious. It was as if nothing had existed before that moment.

The end of the castle burning marked the beginning of the dance. First as a group and then in pairs. As she followed the beat of the music, she noticed Guillermo standing on a corner. They'd already seen each other during the procession and even greeted one another. But now his gaze was different. She tried to ignore it and concentrated on the piñatas that were being opened one by one, releasing their treats and toys. She forgot about him until he suddenly reached out and took her arm.

"I want you to tell me why!"

"I don't know what you're talking about. Let go of me!"

"Just tell me why!"

She managed to get away. He tried to follow her, but the people held him back. Excuse him, I think he's drunk, the woman with braids told her. But she wasn't convinced of his drunkenness.

She got back to her room. The man's question still rang in her mind. Why? Why was she there? Why had she come to Sierra Norte? Why did people confuse her with someone else? She grabbed the picture frame. Why hadn't he gotten in touch even once? Why were her memories getting hazier? She took the photograph from the frame, and now the image was foreign to her. She looked at the back; the date didn't tell her anything either. She took the pad and wanted to copy the figure from the photograph, but only managed to draw the frozen, deserted silhouette of the mountain. Desperate, she tried to go back in her memory and saw herself boarding the bus that brought her to town, and before that, sitting on the plane listening to the loud engine, which didn't let her think; and before that, running down a street without noticing anything around her. The last thing she remembered was a door closing and someone crying with long, choked sobs, but she couldn't recognize who that was either.

Crystal City

By Carlos Yushimito

1

Jacobina's paws appear to mess with her own balance. Long and skinny, they still manage to move forward, intertwining in the air, and with seeming ease, make short work of the entire street to search for the boy again. The boy has followed her this time, even though his steps are slow and half-hearted. He pats the furry, dancing head that crosses his path; and the dog, acknowledged by her master, snorts cheerfully, as if in that involuntary stroke she sensed a reward full of meaning that transcends the mechanical prowess of a body superior to hers.

The boy's Christian name is Pedro. Alternatively, in the language of his ancestors, he would've gone by Hideo, the name his mother imagined on the day he was born, the name that belonged to his grandfather, Hideo Komatsu, before borders were opened to boats and exiles. Today, however, he's called Pedro, just like his father began to call himself the moment he disembarked from the ship that took him away from Hokkaido. To him it's just a name, not a connection to an uprooting and a passenger manifest full of smudges imposing a new self: Hideo or Pedro, what's a name, after all, but an identity that gets lost in the sounds people barely recognize.

"Jacooooo!" the boy shouts.

After reaching the empty lot, Jacobina wags her tail and sniffs the emptiness that exists at the end of the backstreet. Her barking fades down it, lost in a desiccated darkness where not even echoes can take shape. Hideo Komatsu takes it all in as well. Not today, he secretly says to himself, and before going straight past and leaving the lot behind, he clinks Nazareno's coins in his hands and before long the hole is filled with adobe and tall doors and wooden windows and a corner plastered with posters.

"Spiders are nocturnal," Tsuchigumo had said, adjusting his glasses behind the counter. "If you're looking for one, best to try at night."

That night Hideo dreamt of an enormous spider with six black eyes, compact and shiny like tiny crystal balls that seemed to not penetrate anything. Also in his dream, Tsuchigumo had asked him to return, and he had.

"If you don't have a good spider, you're going to keep on losing," the bodega owner, who was from Kajiki, insisted. "Listen to me, go to the market at night and have her sniff around for a while," he said, gesturing at Jacobina. "She's sure to find one."

The boy remembers it now: the dog was panting with muffled growls, and her barking was rapid and loud, yet hoarse and truncated. She had chased the little shadow into a cluttered pile of crates and her own disoriented stride ended up trapping it. He pushed Jacobina aside with a rotted board and upon finally seeing it, crouching next to the packaging lumber, he slid the jar over with his foot and it entered. It's still there. The spider obeys with caution, resigned and sad. And, as if guarding her eight exhausted feet, she folds up on herself.

But Hideo Komatsu had kept the secret: not even Señor Tsuchigumo would understand; not him, not Abuela, not Sayoko, not anybody who hadn't seen Nazareno feeding his spider with the other jumpers could understand. No one who had coins bulging in their hands could understand, that's what he wanted to say, but he didn't. How, at his age? Not even in his dreams does Señor Tsuchigumo seem to understand.

In the meantime, the old man said, "Some arrive from Brazil, camouflaged by the fruit...

"They frequently end up squashed by a street vendor's *llanque* sandals or the hard soles of a dockworker's boots. Some go out and hunt for rodents," Tsuchigumo says nonchalantly. He had seen them bind and drag their prey to a cave formed by the market stall frames. He had seen them, *sí, señor*; he took his time now to choose the sweets and wrap the pastries, but he'd seen them and his serious face lit up when he began to speak again.

"Like this," he stretched his fingers, "the size of my own hand."

On the other side of the street, the trolley leaves a trail of dust in its wake, as if it were a calming low tide that disappears along with its weakening sound: like a loose kite string that then floats away. And when the noise of the metal clattering stops, following its own tail, Tsuchigumo is waiting for him with the package ready to go, and returns to the old habit of adjusting his glasses.

"How's your *obachan*?"

"Fine," the boy replies.

"And Sayoko?"

"With Nazareno."

"Tell her not to forget about the mass for Ryo," Tsuchigumo says, hesitating. "Nara said something about next month...right? Not sure if that's accurate..."

"Three weeks, *ojisan*."

"Ah," he says. "And school?"

The boy blushes.

"We're almost done with the book."

Hideo Komatsu stares at the old man's enormous drooping ears and the sight repulses him; he's happy to be young, and feels (even though he doesn't quite understand this yet) that at seven years of age he doesn't ever want to get old. Tsuchigumo takes out a pack of dark tobacco cigarettes, tapping the box until one of the thin tubes pops up. He grabs it with his mouth and looks for the matches: Hideo looks at the sticks inside the matchbox, the man's rough, yellowish fingers fumbling, and hears the scrape and then a blue light that quickly extinguishes.

"Any news of the old man?" he asks a while later.

The old man is his father: Pedro Komatsu, Hideo Senior. That's how they differentiate between the two. Ever since they took him to the Crystal City camps, no one has heard anything from him, except for the note a neighbor from Manco Capac was able to catch in the air when the truck packed with Japanese folks drove off, invisible, to the port. Nazareno opens and closes the shop now, life goes on, but regarding his father, all anyone knows is that he threw a note so people would realize he hadn't disappeared of his own volition. That they were taking him because of a war he didn't fight, but apparently had lost. And that he was a good man who hadn't abandoned his children.

"My *obachan* says nothing's been on the radio," he replies.

"And I still call myself Minoru Tsuchigumo and I still have a store," the old man shakes his head. "I still call myself Minoru Tsuchigumo and I still have a store."

The ashes fall to the floor and, with them, a blackened, bent matchstick.

2

"It's dead," Pedro said.

Nazareno found his near Jirón Sáenz Peña, between the adobe dislodged by a tremor and a patch of stucco that had fallen under its own weight. He saw the web, reflecting a strip of light that shone like a thin tear that had been stretched too far, and went after it. It was a large spider, the largest he'd ever seen in the area, Nazareno later told everyone. He carried it in a jam jar and he himself had said, look, *chino*, do you want to see it? And Pedro Komatsu had observed the size of the monster's claws, its quiet balance like a timeless carousel.

"It's dead."

Nazareno clicked his tongue and shook his head. It was the same expression he made whenever he'd go into Pedro's sister's room. Nazareno would wink at him so Pedro would leave them alone for a few hours. He'd then put some coins in the boy's hand, the same coins he'd put in Abuela's hands at the end of each month, and he'd click his tongue, like that.

"It's resting, *chino*. Wait for it to come out."

He was right because a short while later, the spider slowly crawled out. Until then they'd poke them with chopsticks for the *gohan* and an old clothespin Abuela no longer cared about, like she no longer cared about being alone, stuck in her own silence. They'd lower them into an arena dug in the ground at the park, and the spiders would fight until one bit the other or escaped or simply died. The jumpers are black and proud, spread their legs and wait before attacking. This time, Pedro knew it was useless to hope for a different outcome and there was no need to fire the spiders up by sprinkling grains of sand on them; the tarantula is carnivorous by nature and it was just a matter of time before that soft coppery mass would lay its little challenger to rest, as if it were a human finger. It took very little time for it to wrap the opponent in a sticky web of silk. And when at last it was snug, and the tarantula began to suffocate the other spider, it injected its venom.

"It's dead, dead," the boy says.

And feeling afraid, he begins to toss sand on it.

3

Abuela had grown tired of crocheting on the sofa, and the afternoon light, a golden color, began to permeate the open window. The wooden ceiling is high, and the sunlight appears lazy, as if inundating the room without enough energy to fill it right up to the cornices. It's the only light outside, but at least there's light. It's like being alive, the boy thinks (but he doesn't fully grasp this); otherwise, he wouldn't see her. Abuela is tiny and her face is sinking into her cheeks, like when spiders are injected with a venom that numbs, and their legs are sucked into their bodies, they become tiny too, until they're nothing. Abuela hardly speaks anymore. She just pretends to be listening, but can't hear a thing. She falls asleep in the afternoon, sitting on the sofa, listening to the radio she can't hear.

The boy watches her from the table. Stuck in a jar, the spider doesn't move, as if it senses that someone is also watching it. It would be like a giant eye looking in at it through the glass, Abuela said before falling asleep. Don't scare it. That'll be the image it remembers you by. An enormous eye, expanding in the light of its iris, as if an eclipse had blocked out the sky. The spider is as big as a peach pit. It's the color of dirt, with a coarse hairiness that extends to its feet, long, thick feet that grip the soil and make it a part of them.

"I wonder how much a bite hurts?" Tsuchigumo had asked, faking a gesture of pain and closing his hand.

Hideo draped the blanket over his Abuela and listened to her warm, steady breathing as he moved the crochet hook and the wool next to the sofa. The old woman moistened her dry lips and opened her eyes.

"I fell asleep," she said.

But it was clear she hadn't woken up.

"Do you want to eat?" she asked in her nasal voice.

"No, *obachan*."

"Good," she responded without hearing him and closed her eyes.

Nazareno also sleeps bundled in thick cotton muslin. Sleep has enveloped him, and when the boy appears, his body is already nothing but a pure, snug shadow that expands and contracts with untroubled breath. Pedro doesn't rattle the door, which opens slightly, like a drowsy eyelid; he won't wake up this time, he had told Tsuchigumo in the dream. He opens the jam jar lid. Yes, he opens it completely. And then he gently shakes the container so the spider, awakened from its timeless captivity, spills into the room with the hunger of an entire day. The chirps of a handful of crickets that no longer make sounds with their violin legs have turned into a silent, sticky net that fills the glass shelter. But the spider marches, slow and proud, as if it has already forgotten them. Its shadow taps the ground, and it feels its way, getting lost in the clutter under the bed. It'll stay there until something takes it out, the boy thinks. Or it'll find a shoe, or a chink in the wood, or Nazareno's sharp breathing will remind it of a familiar sound it'll soon climb out to meet. All the better. Because maybe, when it gets there, the spider will see his enormous open eye and have a reason to hate him.

Martín

By María José Caro

Martín played bass. He lived real close to my school and on Fridays he'd come get me. He used to wait on the corner, leaning against a grayish pickup truck with flat tires. The second he'd spot me, he'd raise his hand and we'd walk one behind the other until we reached the avenue. Ever since Claudia Gómez's pregnancy, the school's guard wouldn't let a boy come near the entrance when classes were let out. "Young man, you can't be here," he'd say, brandishing his baton and putting on a show for Sister Trinidad, who spied from one of the windows of her perch. Martín and I dated for a month. We'd kiss while lying on his twin bed listening to Pearl Jam. From time to time, I'd open my eyes and gaze at the posters in his room. Eddie Vedder's face in black and white accompanied by an inscription that read, *"Yeah oh, I am still alive, Yeah oh, I am still alive."* We'd stay there until Martín's mom got back from the office; my visits never lasted more than two hours. The gate to his building had a bell that would shrill every time a car entered. As soon as we'd hear it, we'd run to the living room sofa. Martín would tune his bass while I'd request a song. When he played, he pressed his lips together accentuating the cleft in his chin. That used to be my favorite moment. We'd talk and laugh. Martín knew the most obscure details about any band. He'd talk to me about producers and how boy bands were formed through casting calls, like for models. Then we'd walk over to Romina's house. He'd leave me there and go rehearse. Once, a few blocks from my friend's place, he took the instrument from his shoulder and pushed me against the rugged wall around a vacant lot. "Someone's going to see us," I said, taking his hands off my hips. "I know," he responded with bloodshot eyes and sweaty palms. Martín dumped me in that exact same spot. Without changing his tone and staring at the tip of his shoes. "I think we're better off as friends," he uttered while picking up his pace. I told Romina about it that same afternoon. "He'll regret it," she said taking a long sip of her soda. "No idea," I replied and took out one of the magazines she kept in the drawer of her nightstand. We weren't interested in the bands or the teenage actors that paraded on the covers; we'd immediately jump to the *Love and Sexuality* section and, in between jokes, we'd devour that half page on a pink background titled "The Confessional." I opened the magazine and began to read, surrendering to the healing power of other people's tragedies. Still, the one question that bothered me spun in my head like a tornado out of control.

What's wrong with me? (Macarena, 15)

Martín showed up at my school festival a few weeks after our breakup. He crossed the basketball court looking at the floor; he had very short hair and wore a flannel shirt. He stopped beside me and asked about the end of the year concert. Romina explained that ever since Claudia Gómez's pregnancy, Sister Trinidad had gone crazy and decided to cancel it. It wasn't enough to turn teachers into guards with fluorescent vests ready to jot down in a red notebook the names of any students who kissed their boyfriends. "What a drag. Don't you feel like doing something else? Braulio's at the gate." We didn't think twice, and in a matter of minutes, found ourselves at the park. Martín and I spread out on the grass despite the smell of pesticide that drove children and adults away, while Romina and Braulio rocked on a pair of rusted swings. That evening we didn't kiss, we simply drank the cheap vodka that Martín had poured into a water bottle. "I downloaded a bootleg of the Pearl Jam concert in

Barcelona. It took, like, three days. We can listen to it on Friday," he said, taking me by the hand. I happily nodded, not understanding what he was talking about. I closed my eyes and let myself get carried away by the feel of his thumb strumming against my palm. I didn't need any more proof.

After she was expelled, the only time I saw Claudia Gómez was while I was walking to meet up with Martín. I saw her climbing into the backseat of a green car parked a few yards from school. She looked different, her eyes wide open and her face contorted with fear. I felt as though something were choking me on the inside, seeing her squirming to hide from me. Her pregnancy had made her toxic, only to be gossiped about in small groups at school. According to my friends, they'd give the baby up for adoption, but that didn't happen in Lima; in the best case, the child would be raised as a sibling. Martín raised his eyebrows as I passed Claudia's car. He was waiting for me leaning against the grayish pickup truck, and on his shoulders, the backpack covered in rock pins that made him sound like a human tambourine. Once we were far enough from school, he carried my bag and put his arm around my waist. Martín never looked me in the eyes when I told him stories about my family or school. His gaze would only light up when we talked about music; we were two kids worshipping the same god of chords and lyrics. The magic wasn't in me. Even when he kissed me, the magic was somewhere else.

Martín closed the door to his room and turned on the computer. He had speakers, a woofer and his own modem. He'd download music without any parental restrictions even if it took days. At my house, the computer was in our family room and at around eight o'clock my mom would make me shut it down. When I'd get home from school, I'd sit in front of the screen and read a website that posted the scripts from Roswell episodes until I'd gotten my fix. I'd recreate those scenes that would only be released in Peru several months later. Afterward, I'd print them out and keep them in a drawer in my dresser. The scripts for the first and second seasons remained safely in there. My drawer served as an analog bunker in case the web page disappeared from the Internet. A refuge established a couple of years back to protect myself from the supposed Y2K computer glitch that threatened to shut down all computers with the arrival of the year 2000. "My mom is running late tonight," Martín said, adjusting the speaker volume. He then took me to his bed. The concert began with Eddie Vedder's voice welcoming the audience in rudimentary Spanish. We kissed as soon as the first song played. After a few minutes, he was on top, pressing down on me with his body, kissing my neck and caressing me under my blouse. We rolled to the edge of his bed next to the wall. My back hit the cold cement and I froze. When I opened my eyes, I discovered my rapid breath, my exposed abdomen, my deep navel, the faint stretch marks beginning to show on my hips. I thought about frail Claudia Gómez in that green car. Then I imagined her as the protagonist of all the gossip that had spread around our class. Her, naked, inside a translucent tent that exposed her body and allowed a group of teenagers to watch her from the beach as she had sex with her boyfriend. Her, on the sofa at someone else's house, her blouse open and plaid skirt raised. I envied Claudia for a second. Taking your clothes off in front of someone required a confidence I didn't possess. I remembered the teen chatrooms I'd visited that summer. I had cyber boyfriends from Mexico, Argentina and Honduras. I'd send them pictures of my brother Sergio's female friends. Our conversations revolved around how much they wanted me and what we'd do if I were in front of them. This never bothered me; it was all make believe, where no one touched me, where no one could see me. I did it for fun, to try to understand what the fuss around sex was all about. Suddenly, a moan escaped from Martín's insides. He kissed me with his eyelids pressed shut so tightly a vein popped on his forehead. Everything seemed different without his mother's usual lifesaving arrival. I didn't close my eyes again. I concentrated on his computer screensaver, which, across the room, displayed a pair of dolphins following a cruise ship. "It's late," I said, straightening my clothes. "Wait, what do you have to do? When? Can't you stay a bit longer?" I freed myself from Martín's swarm of questions by slamming the door. That was the last afternoon I visited his house. I waited a few minutes outside his building, but Martín never came to find me. I jumped in the first dilapidated taxi that came down the street. I didn't even pay attention to the driver's face. According to Romina, the safest taxis were driven by old men or had a rosary hanging from the rearview mirror.

As soon as I got home, I locked myself in the family room and turned on the computer. I put the music on full blast, though I could still hear Ruth talking to my mom in the distance. "Yes, yes. She says Romina's mom dropped her off." Claudia was logged on to Messenger under the alias she always used. Her name in a mixture of upper and lowercase letters flanked by two butterflies frozen in the time when she was still a girl. I tried to contact her and immediately regretted it; I'd just be another reminder of her misfortune. When I was about to log off, Martín's words appeared on the screen: "*Sorry,*" and a long pause that hit me in the gut. "*This was a mistake.*" Then I remembered him before he was my boyfriend. It was summer, and he was wearing skater shorts. He was waiting outside the box office at a movie theater with his ex. Martín smiled, looked straight into her eyes, ran his fingers through her hair, and every now and then, kissed her cheek. One look was all it took to know she was music to him. I was merely the gap between songs. "*It's all good,*" I typed and became filled with an unknown rage. I opened the pictures folder intent on erasing him from my computer. The first image that appeared was my brother with his arm around a girl's waist. They were at a party and she was smiling, holding a beer between two fingers. A picture of Martín followed; he was in his school auditorium, attached to his bass with eyes completely closed. I couldn't delete it; it was the only thing I had left. After that came an image of a naked woman. Sergio had downloaded it from the Internet. He had loads of them in the folder where he kept his university documents. Women without clothes, with big tits and false eyelashes. Women with no shame, proud of their bodies. Martín wasn't to blame. I would never be like them. My anger grew, and right away, I realized it'd only stop by attacking the problem. *What's wrong with me? (Macarena, 15) What's wrong with me? (Macarena, 15) What's wrong with me? (Macarena, 15)*. Without thinking about it, I punched my leg. A shooting pain radiated through my thigh. I repeated the blows until my knuckles grew numb and my muscles wouldn't stop contracting. Afterward, I began to cry.

Taxi Driver, Without Robert De Niro

By Fernando Ampuero

That night, the windshield wiper motor was hardly working and the blades could barely get rid of the mist. But I managed to see, or maybe just imagine. The same story that I knew so well repeated itself. Indifferent to the passing traffic, the two drunks had stopped in the middle of the street. Effusive hugs, stumbling, and at times heads locked, suggesting two bulls preparing for combat. However, instead of fighting, these poor guys—with the stylish look of office workers, perhaps bank employees—simply laughed loudly and gestured like opera singers.

Meanwhile, having parked the car on one side of the street, I waited in silence. The lights were off, my hand on the key. It was hard to decide whether or not I should continue with this ugly situation.

Recent experiences hadn't been what you could call good; they were lucrative, yes, but definitely not good. And that's where my conflict lay. I needed to earn much more money. My youngest son, Raulito, had been born with one of those rare diseases found in one out of every hundred thousand—a weakening of the neck muscles that prevented him from keeping his head up— that required physical therapy and medicine. If I'd been at the law firm, like last year, I wouldn't have had so many problems. Working as a legal assistant provided income. But I no longer have that job: the shysters in labor relations had lost their clientele because the new government could care less about strikes and employment stability. And so, for some time now, I've been working hard as a taxi driver, and on the weekends I had to deal with drunks.

First, it was just a matter of course, because I owned an old Pontiac and didn't have anything else to do. I worked twelve-hour shifts, as if I were renting a car. Second, those drunks revealed just one more crazy aspect of this deranged city and, in time, became a temptation. Raimundo, an Afro-Peruvian taxi driver, showed me the ropes.

"It's all about robbing and selling drunks," he affirmed. "A blessing from God! You'll earn in one night what it takes others to earn in a week. You up for it?"

I laughed and laughed. I could understand robbing a drunk, but it was the first time I'd ever heard you could sell a drunk.

"Are you serious?" I asked.

"Of course!" Raimundo was a new friend, but he inspired confidence. "You frisk him first, take his money and then sell the rest. This is the best way to take everything he has, without getting involved or leaving a trace. He's unlikely to remember you after a few days, but if you were to keep his gold lighter or expensive watch, they'll send you to jail. So, the best thing to do is sell the drunk."

"And who do you sell him to?"

"Many junkies and delinquents buy them. You can earn between fifteen and eighteen soles, depending on what you offer them. A drunk is good for his clothes, shoes, jewelry, and if he's solvent, his credit cards."

When I saw he wasn't joking, I grew concerned.

"Still, it seems dangerous," I said.

"It is, but not too bad. The biggest risk is you have to drive around a lot before the drunk goes to sleep in your taxi."

"I'm not sure I see it."

"I'm telling you it's as easy as that."

"And what happens if the guy wakes up while you're emptying his wallet?"

"Nothing. Don't forget the dude is drunk, and you have a good excuse. You could say you were trying to find something with his address. You could also act mad and accuse him of falling asleep, wasting your time or dirtying your seats."

Raimundo knew everything. He'd been at it for a year and, without going into details, he was obsessed with security. The first thing, he said, is to recognize any bulges under their clothes, given that these days lots of people carry pistols in their belts.

"And what do you do in those cases?"

"Some steal the pistol and continue with the plan. Not me. I prefer to wake the drunk up and ask him to get out. You don't play with guns."

Methodical, meticulous to a fault, Raimundo had been in the civil service. He was one of thousands who, having quit his job in exchange for an economic incentive (in accordance with the program to reduce bureaucracy), he invested his money in a taxi. He owned a 1987 Toyota Corolla, which was in great shape, and his spiel seemed all the more convincing. As a friend, Raimundo was only interested in me becoming his colleague, in the fullest sense of the word.

For three good weeks I pondered the advantages and disadvantages of his proposal.

During that time, aware that something in me was changing, I made the typical rounds. But I wasn't the same anymore. As the days passed, I felt different: I didn't talk with the passengers anymore, I didn't listen to the news on the radio, I didn't complain about my bad luck. The whole business of the drunks spun around in my head. The idea was like a splinter lodged in a delicate nerve.

Until one cold Friday night in August, that is, when I became determined to follow Raimundo's instructions and picked up my first drunk.

It happened in Breña. I had just dropped off a passenger and as I turned onto a wide, deserted street in search of a direct route downtown, I saw him on a corner. He was one of those specimens who looked like the perfect "candidate." He was staggering down the street with an idiotic smile on his face. And as soon as he saw me, he raised a hand as if attempting to grab a bird in flight.

I stopped. The drunk came over to the window on the right side.

"Evening," I said.

Slurring, he said the same. "To Chacarilla. How mush?"

"Eight soles."

"Eight sholesh?" he grunted, blurry-eyed. "You outta your mind?"

It was ironic this moron said that to me, but I was ready to put up with anything.

"After midnight, there's a fifty percent surcharge," I argued. "And, there's the distance."

"I'll pay you six," he said.

"No, it's not worth it."

"Seven."

"No, sir. Eight. You want a ride or stay here?"

Squinting, the guy just stared at me. Having defended my fare, as well as refusing to barter, must have made him think hard; a robber wouldn't go to such lengths to lose a catch. He got in.

"Let's take the Primavera bridge," he said, getting situated in the back seat. "When we arrive, I'll . . . I'll guide you. You got any music."

"Of course," I said, tuning into a station playing boleros.

Within five minutes, having just passed Lince, the guy was out like a light and sleeping like an angel. But me, damn it, I was suffering the curse of Cain. I was sweating, the steering wheel slipping in my hands. I was scared I might see a police car or one of those Serenazgo security units. Despite it all, I drove him to Campo de Marte, turned onto a dark street, and after lightly joggling him to make sure he was in a deep sleep, I pilfered his wallet. He had ten US dollars and 250 soles. It wasn't a fortune, but the money would come in handy.

It was an easy score, right off the bat. I looked for a park bench, slowly hauled the drunk out and, taking him by the arm—the poor guy was as limp as a drugged blindman—I sat him down so he wouldn't fall over. How long would he last like that? Not long, I imagined, and before I left, I saw some bushes in the park moving suspiciously.

Still, for good or bad, it worked. And it stimulated my desires to take this on fair and square.

Generous and talkative, Raimundo was the ultimate teacher. The next Saturday, he spent over an hour of his night shift to show me, beyond the basic procedures, a couple of naked guys sleeping it off on the street ("That's how our clients end up," he indicated), and, of course, several places to sell the drunks in La Victoria.

"First rule: never pick up two drunks at the same time," he said. "Take only one. I've heard about several ambitious types who can't tell the tale after they got punched in the face . . . Ah, and one more thing to help you save time: study human behavior and train your eye. Not all drunks look like they're about to fall over; don't dismiss the ones who are standing straight, who might not look drunk. You'll see how their drunkenness concentrates behind their knees and suddenly they double over. I call them the air drunks."

"Air drunks?"

"Yes, air, because the air knocks them flat. They spend their time drinking inside a bar and then walk outside. They feel a little rough, they resist, but in no time they're leaning against a wall, opening and closing their eyes, as if seeing double. You'll find lots of these standing at the doors outside of clubs downtown and salsa dance halls, and it's just a matter of waiting. All you have to do is slowly drive by and they'll hail you down."

"But do they fall asleep quickly?"

"In a flash. Of course, there'll be the stubborn ones who don't give in easily, but there are more of the opposite."

"I lulled my drunk to sleep with boleros."

"Good idea," Raimundo smiled, eyeing his glove compartment. "But I'm going to recommend something better." He pulled out a cassette. "Chopin. Sonatas, piano music, all winners. You can buy pirated copies on the street."

With Chopin, a diverse circuit of bars, clubs, regional music venues and salsa dance halls, and with all the courage I could muster, I set out to cut a new path. And in two months, I'd batted a record of sixteen drunks, averaging 250 soles each, not including selling them to the druggies at fifteen to twenty soles each.

Plus, during that time, I discovered lots of new things. Those making the purchases valued not only the drunks' clothing, glasses and other personal effects, but also the depth of their sleep. If they were light sleepers, they were worth less. On the other hand, if the drunk was jostled a couple of times and continued to sleep like a log, they paid handsomely. The buyers wanted to avoid force, blows or the threat of a scandal.

I also found out there were five other taxi drivers involved in this business, who little by little I'd get to know. And even though we didn't necessarily sell to the same junkies, following Raimundo's advice, at least three of us made good use of Chopin. One time, the five of us got together at a bar to celebrate Raimundo's birthday and we all got drunk. And then for a good while we stood on the sidewalk watching other taxis go by. It gave me the shivers.

Now then, I don't want to insinuate that our business is a piece of cake. It has its advantages, true; driving at night is a pleasure, the streets are empty and the motor doesn't overheat, but unexpectedly, we can become the target of predators: robbers, from whom some escaped by brandishing a tire iron—each taxi driver in our group had experienced two or three assaults, minimum—and the police, who are much more difficult to deal with, are experts in getting their way.

As for the drunks, in the end, you win some and you lose some, but mostly you win, and this demands a good measure of "criteria," as Raimundo says, now that, besides enhancing my finances (which has been and continues to be the reason I'm in this dance), my view of the world has changed. Now, it's a "view directly from the rearview mirror." There, in that small rectangular mirror, the world passes by and acquires form. Sometimes it's a smile and at other times a threat. I see faces passing by, dozens of faces: timid adolescents; buskers from the provinces; noisy men; silent men; sad old people; indecipherable beings; battered women; and even riffraff, oh my gosh, who don't want to pay.

And in terms of experiences, I've had my share . . .

After midnight a few days ago, I picked up a woman in Quilca who silently watched two individuals beat up on each other. The chick sat up front— smelling of perfume and liquor— and blurted out an address in Jesús María. To prevent her aggressive friends from getting in the car, I got out of there honking the horn. She seemed like a decent girl. I looked at her out the corner of my eye, twice. Thirty-five, well-dressed, dignified attitude and, although she was getting plump, good-looking. She only looked straight ahead. A block before reaching her address, she turned to me: "Stop here, please. I don't have any money, but I can do this for you." Completely surprised, I didn't say anything. And an instant later she unzipped my pants, and with alarming determination, buried her face in my crotch. Her wet mouth, the sweep of her hair . . . I couldn't stop her. Afterward, I just sat exhausted in my seat, my head tossed back, breathless.

The woman got out of the car without a word, while I sat there feeling strange. And it wasn't because I thought about the wasted gasoline, or the loss of money, or the medicine that Raulito needed, or any other concrete thing. I think I was feeling something like anxiety, some type of painful relief, even though it didn't have much to do with that either.

Another drunk, who I still remember often, was a fat guy who for the life of him couldn't take two steps without tripping. He hailed me down, crawled into the back seat, muttering something about his mother's old age ("She's getting old, getting old," he said) and within ten blocks started snoring. While I searched for a dark street, I looked at him more closely. He was just a run-of-the-mill guy, a bit ridiculous looking, but not much different from any other drunk. When I removed his wallet, which only contained 300 soles, I felt something fall on the floor. I turned on the interior light and discovered it was a laminated picture with a dedication: "To my only son, with all my love."

I turned off the light and he half woke up. "What's going on? What's going on?" he asked in a weak voice. He made an almost infantile gesture, disconcerted, and before I could say anything, he fell back asleep, so I headed straight to one of my druggie hideouts. On the way, however, he woke up three more times. I could see his head bobbing in the rearview mirror and, in that same weak voice, repeated: "What's going on? What's going on?" I thought at the time that if he asked that question once more, I was going to explode. And when he did, I stopped the car, grabbed his wallet, put the money back, and woke him up with a couple of slaps.

"Where do you live?" I said flat out, furious.

The fat guy just looked at me, frightened.

"On Arenales," he said. "32nd block."

I stepped on the gas and ten minutes later he entered a downtrodden three-story building. I still don't know why that poor devil got on my nerves.

If that was it, then no harm, no foul. Unfortunately, it wasn't: something even worse happened. That's what I was thinking, whether I should continue with this business or not, as I said, when out of the blue, Raimundo appeared and parked in front of me. He got out of his car and into mine, seeing that I was sizing up the two drunks who were screaming like opera singers.

"Are you waiting for them to each go their own way?"

"Yes," I replied. "Although it make take a while."

"When that happens, they likely live in different places."

"..."

"Best case, we'll each take one."

"Maybe," I answered.

A certain despondency, a certain dullness must have come through in my voice because Raimundo looked at me, concerned.

"Something wrong?"

I might have smiled or told him no, of course not, but I was hopping mad. And right there I told him everything.

"It's about something that happened last night," I said without losing sight of my target. "I picked up a drunk who was wearing dirty clothes, looking like he had fallen down or leaned against a wall. He was one of those guys who gets tongue-tied when he speaks, and frankly, didn't look too promising."

"And it turned sour?"

"No. Just the opposite: he was carrying 1500 soles?"

"Fifteen hundred?" he almost shouted, captivated. "Who was he? A kingpin?"

"He looked like he was from Lima. Heavyset, broad shoulders, face like an indifferent son of a bitch. He fell asleep, leaning sideways until he fell out of view in the rearview mirror. He must have been a money changer, or a street seller of electronic devices, someone who makes good money. I don't have a clue. But he was wearing a heavy gold bracelet on his right wrist, a really sweet piece of jewelry."

Thinking I had taken the bracelet from the drunk, Raimundo bristled. I told him that wasn't what happened.

"Then, what?" he asked, impatient.

"My problem involves something else, brother. . . The guy went limp."

"Limp?" Raimundo repeated, astonished. "Are you saying he died?"

"Yes."

"But how? When you were patting him down? Don't tell me you hit him with something!"

"No. The guy just up and died. I don't know why. It must have been a massive heart attack because once he fell asleep, he never moved again. What really bothers me is that I didn't even realize! The druggies on Jirón Iquitos, which was the closest place to drop him off, would be the lucky ones. 'Hey, man, this guy's stone cold,' said the one who assesses the loot. It was the puny dude, the one with spikes on his arms. I thought he was being smart, but when I looked in the back seat, I saw the drunk sprawled face up, eyes open, and saliva dribbling down his chin."

"Damn!" Raimundo exclaimed. "What did you do then?"

"That's what messed me up: what I did next... I looked out at the street, pretending to be calm and in control. I looked all around, smiling, scratching my head as if nothing abnormal had happened, while the dude moved around in the back, evaluating the drunk's bracelet, clothes, shoes, identification, and exchanging looks with his two associates. 'Yeah, man, your drunk is totally cold,' he repeated. With my hands on the steering wheel, I answered, 'Well, it'll cost you then, another five bills. I want twenty-five.' The kid looked surprised, which quickly turned into a grimace, but I wasn't scared: 'The dead don't kick or wake up,' I snapped. 'This is going to be easy for you.' He just stood there thinking... He looked at the bracelet again, nodded twice and, finally, he stuck his hand into a pocket."

Leaning against the car door, stiff, Raimundo appeared stupefied:

"I can't believe it!" he mumbled. "Wow, I can't believe it!" He was silent for a few seconds, but then, as if animated by a magic wand, complete, happy, he broke out laughing uncontrollably. He was truly excited and feverishly drummed the fingers of both hands on the dashboard. "Very good, buddy! Very good indeed!" he added. "You were amazing! This means you've sold your first stiff!" And continuing to laugh, he added, "Now you're in the lead!"

He didn't give me time to react.

I felt, I think, that he was essentially proud of me, that he sincerely admired me, and that he had even put me on a pedestal as a model for emulation.

And, afterward, when I once again turned to talking about my doubts and anxieties, the opera singers caught our attention.

"Look," Raimundo said, looking alarmed. "Those two guys have started to walk off in different directions. They've said their goodbyes."

We saw the drunkest one stop under the red glow of a traffic light.

"He's mine," I said.

And then everything changed, everything came over us, everything was channeled into a single fixed idea: a common fixed idea.

Raimundo got out of my car and crept over to his. Meanwhile,—filing the corpse from my story as something acceptable, metabolized—I turned the key and started my car. A docile spluttering broke the silence, like domesticated thunder. A short ways away, Raimundo's taxi thundered in a similar fashion, although the sound of his motor suggested a less powerful vehicle. And then, simultaneously, as if we had agreed, we turned on our headlights. The street lit up. Blinded, one of the drunks covered his eyes with his arm; the other one, staggering, raised a floppy hand into the air.

A Day Out

By Jennifer Thorndike

1

Today is Friday, my day out. I get up, change, wash my face and put my hair in a ponytail. I then leave my room. She's waiting for me with the shopping list, cellphone, keys and exact change. She knows how much we spend each week on groceries, no extra money is needed. She removes the three padlocks that secure the door before opening it. They're not the only ones: every door and window is reinforced to avoid the possibility that an intruder, knowing there were two women living alone, might enter and rob us. Her fear is unhealthy, like everything else about her. Now she comes closer to say goodbye and bless me, but I instinctively reject her.

"Don't take too long."

I won't take too long, I can't. She controls the amount of time I can be out. Between an hour and a half and two, no more. If the minutes begin to stretch, she'll start to call nonstop. I can't stand the vibrating cellphone or her usual questions: *Where are you? Why are you taking so long? Don't you think it's bad to leave me alone for so long?* I leave.

Every Friday, once she closes the door and I breathe the outside air for the first time in seven days, I entertain the idea of not returning. It'd be easy for anyone else to steal the weekly money, cellphone and just run away. But for me, it's not that simple: as I continue walking along, I feel her presence overwhelm and haunt me, no matter how far I am from home.

293

Then I imagine my escape: I'd start running, desperately trying to lose myself before she can track me down. But I know it's impossible: she is able to invade every city space where I could possibly be. Turn around and start over, walk unsettled, hiding, nervous, counting the bills, unable to bear her watchful gaze and her voice repeating *you're a wretched, terrible daughter, leaving your mother by herself and without food, knowing she's a sick woman, a terrible daughter,* on an interminable loop that would make me feel guilty and end up tearing my body to pieces, which she would then pick up and reassemble as she pleased, under the protection of another padlock in the ultrasafe home that only opens its doors when her will deems it necessary.

I abandon the idea of escaping and enter the supermarket. I begin to get the groceries while keeping an eye on my watch, walk down the aisle of cleaning supplies, constantly checking the cellphone screen (heaven forbid I miss a call from her), and then stop at the alcohol section, calculate to see if this week I can buy a bottle of her favorite wine just to be annoying, and so that she can feel, as I do, the weight of the ton of anxiety pills she takes and that don't allow her to drink alcohol. But I stop, take the wine to the register and pay. I'm not going to receive any money back.

"Would you like to donate the coins?"

"No."

No, leave me the few coins so that I can feel as if I have money and that it's enough to flee, change cities, my identity, and prevent her from finding me. The stress of facing that other unknown side increases. I count: one, two, three, four, five, six… six cents. I'll save them in my little can. It would've been great if they'd invented those tiny coins twenty-five years ago when all of this began. Perhaps by now I would've had enough. I put them in my pocket and return home, pulling the trolley with the bags. I want the trip to take longer so that I never arrive, but my feet pick up the pace because they know the cellphone could soon start to vibrate. She's waiting for me: her eyes glued to the window, phone in hand. I open the door, unload the bags. She slips the padlocks back through their latches. She grabs the key from me, and I go up to my room. I close the door to not hear her complaints. The last thing I make out is the word *ungrateful,* which stands out each time she says my name.

2

I tried to remove the mirror from my room, but she wouldn't allow it. I gave her my reasons, but she refused to listen to me, so I decided to break it. Her desperation led to another one of her typical meltdowns. For the first time, however, she kicked the door and began fumbling through her bunch of keys, attempting to find one that could pick my lock. But she knew it was in vain, that I had managed to take the only copy of the room key the day I decided to seek refuge in it. It was for the best: shutting myself in the room to see her as little as possible.

The door didn't seem like it could handle any more blows. I pulled the dresser over and blocked the entrance. I then looked at myself in one of the mirror pieces and rediscovered the changes my body had suffered. I was tired of seeing the wrinkles that ran across my face, the sagging skin, the gray hairs that increasingly appeared, the fuzz on my upper lip, the mannish eyebrows. My reasons were valid, I repeated to her until reaching the point of exhaustion. I pulled the dresser again, opened the door and threw the shards of shattered mirror at her feet.

"Go away."

"But *hijita*..."

I locked myself in again. Through the door, she began to speak in a conciliatory tone. Lately, she hadn't done so because she knew I wasn't going to respond. Over the years, I developed the ability to pay no attention to her. Nevertheless, with her ever-active mind looking for the perfect way to hurt me, she had devised a system of torturing me even in the one space where I could avoid her. Every day she'd slip tiny pieces of paper to communicate what I didn't want to hear. They all ended the same way:

Let God soften your heart, hijita, so you leave that room and return to your mother's side. You know you're all I have, that you are my only family. You can't leave me alone because something might happen to me, I could die. I know you're not bad like your brother, I know you won't do what he did. Don't treat me this way, find some compassion for your mother. I'm dying to hug you and for you to hug me. I need it, mi hijita. I can't be alone. I beg God to soften your heart. I love you very much.

I had to read every tiny piece of paper she slid under my door because I feared she might actually do something, that one would be a farewell note and I'd end up bearing the guilt. She wasn't a normal person. She had always had trouble calming her nerves. That's why my father and her other child had left. I would've done the same, but couldn't. She restricted my outings and made all of the decisions about my future. She made me feel guilty for her mistakes, and ultimately forced me to stay by her side to take care of her, saying I owed it to her for the sacrifices she had made. Moreover, she began to act like an invalid starting when she was still young, always using her anxiety as an excuse. She'd acquire prescriptions for tranquilizers and antidepressants, pills for neurological disorders, all to convince me she was ill and couldn't take care of herself. She succeeded, and that's why I'm still here. But I don't plan on leaving my room. Hugging her would fill me with repulsion, hate. Hate is the only emotion I can feel with clarity.

The glass in the window of my room is broken. Just like the mirror, I smashed it in one of those moments of distress I frequently have. The night I broke the glass, for example, was the first time I experienced my now recurring nightmare: I see her jumping out of the window and slamming into the ground. Then the image of her shattered body appears, and I can even perceive the stench of her flesh rotting. Yet when I get closer and pause to observe the expression on her face, I notice a smile of satisfaction staring back at me.

"I've ruined your life a little more."

I woke up. At first, I felt a bit off, mildly in pain. I looked at the ceiling unable to move. Overwhelmed by a suffocating angst, I tried to get some air, but the window was locked. I began punching it until I managed to break the glass. Some air came through, but not enough for me. I started to inhale deeply as if gasping for air through a ventilator. It worked. After I finally calmed down, I felt grateful for the nightmare. I now had that ventilator (which I covered with clear plastic) any time I needed it, especially on Sundays when she'd once again slip the same note attached to the housing classifieds:

Look how expensive apartments are, mi hijita. It would be impossible for you to go and live somewhere else considering how expensive even the utilities have gotten. Electricity is the worst, you know. I've marked off a few to convince you. I love you, hope you come out soon.

Highlighted in yellow, the list of apartments that weren't accessible to me, the confirmation that I'd be tied to this room, to this house, to her, for the rest of my life. And in that moment, I looked for my ventilator, removed its plastic cover and stuck my nose out. I felt relieved. But then I opened my eyes and hated that source of air, the entire window, because it was limiting not enlarging the space. The window provided the perfect representation of my confinement, and that's why the ventilator was not enough. And the dizziness, once again, led me to collapse on the bed next to the newspaper, my lungs completely empty.

4

I'm sitting against the door to my room. She bangs and yells. I realize she has broken the bottle of wine I brought her because a red liquid begins to leak under the door. I distract myself by forming figures with the puddles of wine on the parquet.

"Wretch, everything I sacrificed for all of you was in vain. When I die, you're going to realize how badly you treated your mother."

I touch the wine puddles and stretch them out with my fingers. The liquid is absorbed by the wood while I endure her shouting, her insults, her threats. And the little puddles extend, surrounding and protecting me, because as I concentrate on them, I don't hear, feel, see anything but their redness on the parquet. I look at the figure twisting and mutating, and I ask her to calm down because if she does something, I'll be responsible and the responsibility will take care of erasing all the stains that now distract me.

"Terrible daughter."

She stops banging on the door. I then hear her lock herself in her room, next to mine. Her presence so close it overwhelms me.

I get up and head to the window. The plastic falls off and a rush of frigid air enters the room. It's never enough for me, but I don't complain. At the ventilator, a thought pops into my head and I begin to count. How old is she? How many years does she have left? I'm 50…51…52…55? So she must be 83. How many more years do I have to wait? Ever since she turned 80, I count and count, not knowing when I'll be able to stop because time continues to stretch, my wait is prolonged and there's nothing to indicate it'll end any time soon. The ventilator ceases to fulfill its function, and I feel suffocated, and I admit you're right about me being a wretched, terrible daughter, that I don't care about you at all, because every day, I hope *the* moment arrives, and I go back to counting and I'm exhausted and I can't breathe and the window with the broken glass is of no use to me.

In that instant, I decide to go through the drawer where I file the little notes you slip under the door. And I take one out that I keep in a special place, protected, isolated, marked up, one that could give me a future despite my 56 years (is that right?), which I feel more and more unbearable every day:

Mi hijita, I wanted to talk to you, but you won't open the door for me. I spoke to a lawyer and he said that the rest of my inheritance would probably remain tied up in legal proceedings and your grandfather's debts. It appears unlikely that neither I, nor you or your brother will get to enjoy that money. In the end, we have what we need for now, but I imagine that the day I die, you might be left out on street since you didn't bother to finish the degree I chose for you and that cost me so much sacrifice. Because I worry about you, even if you don't deserve it, I've decided to list you as the beneficiary on my life insurance. With that money, you'll be able to do something when your mother is gone. I've left the papers in the white briefcase where I keep important documents. I hope that God, the Virgin Mary and her little angels protect you always. I continue to beg Him to soften your heart and that you'll come out to see your mother, who is alone in this world and only has you.

The tiny piece of paper and I momentarily come to life, we get our hopes up: it has promise, I have faith. All of a sudden, we hear her leave her room and begin banging on the door again. The paper slips out of my hands, landing on top of the puddle of wine at my feet. It drowns.

"Come out here and clean. You don't expect an old lady like me to break her back doing it, do you?"

I open my door and grab the rag she's holding. I get on my knees and pick up all the glass. She supervises, indicating what I should do, making me obey her orders. I clean, wax, polish while I continue to count, count, and count…

5

Two days without slipping any notes under my door was uncharacteristic for her. That's why I came out, still taking precautions. She could be planning something to force me out of my room, thus leaving me vulnerable in her presence without the door, the ventilator or the tiny pieces of paper between us. Nevertheless, I couldn't hear a thing, the house seemed empty. I looked for her on the top floor, but she wasn't there. I walked down the stairs and found her in the living room rocking chair, motionless. I got closer. She still had a pencil in her hand. On the coffee table was a note that she hadn't finished writing:

Mi hijita, these past few days I haven't been feeling well. I didn't tell you before because I didn't want to worry you, although if you weren't the way you are and if you did what you were supposed to, you would've noticed. If this discomfort doesn't go away tomorrow, I'll call the doctor. I hope you're here when he comes because that is your duty. I know you won't leave me alone, that you love me despite your difficult nature. I don't know what I've done for you to behave this way with me. In any case, if I did do something to you, please know that I always did what I thought was best for you and for that reason, I know I haven't done you wrong and I don't regret…

The note ended there and, even if she had written more, I wouldn't have continued reading. I took the paper and shoved it in my pocket so I could store it in my drawer. Then I took her pulse and couldn't feel anything. She wasn't breathing either. The pencil fell from her hand to confirm what I already knew. The time had come to stop counting, to leave, to forget. I noticed the bunch of keys hanging from her waist. I struggled to move her and get them. Rigor mortis was continuing the mission she'd planned for me since I was conceived. And I fought, becoming a vulture who needed her remains to survive. She finally gave way, and I began to suffocate again, as I tried different keys on the three padlocks on the door. And these too, conspiring, slipping, getting stuck, not fitting, until at last, I bested them and broke the locks with my reddened hands, with my cracked nails.

I left. I took a deep breath and let the memories flood in to let them go. And once they were gone, I realized that they were all I had left, that erasing them meant being left empty. I looked around and didn't know what to do, or where to go, or where to begin. Then I remembered how she'd always repeat that I shouldn't concern myself with whatever happened outside of the house. And I, when still young, I'd get indignant and want to hit her, to silence her and to sew her mouth shut so she wouldn't repeat it anymore. As the years passed, that comment, which once stung, stopped hurting, stopped bothering, stopped being felt. Now, I finally realize why.

Graveyard

By Richard Parra

You have to leave now, and never come back here.
Have you ever heard of insect politics? Neither have I.
Insects…don't have politics. They're very…brutal.
No compassion, no compromise. We can't trust the insect.
I'd like to become the first…insect politician.
Y'see, I'd like to, but…I'm afraid…
The Fly (1986)

I

Once Susana was pregnant with me, she and Ciro moved to a squatter settlement in a sandy area of Tablada de Lurín. There they paid a few land traffickers for a tiny lot in a disputed section. Shortly after, and with help from some of Ciro's fellow Cajamarquinos, they built a shack out of wood, straw mats and corrugated metal.

Susana told me that at first the area scared her. She was afraid of the thieves, the subversives and the recurring plagues that devastated the settlement. She also told me it was a time of need. Food, drinking water and employment were scarce.

Soon, Ciro got a job as a roofer at a construction site in Atocongo. Susana, for her part, partnered up with two women and began to sell ceviche out of a pot and breaded smelt sandwiches at the Ciudad de Dios market.

* * *

Two years later, Susana found out a fruit seller was pregnant with Ciro's child. The neighbors gossiped, telling her the woman came to our house one afternoon when Susana took Lucero and me to a clinic to deal with our diarrhea and dehydration.

That same night, Susana laid into Ciro when he got home from work. He denied everything and, after an argument, ended up hitting Susana. And then, he went to a bar to continue getting drunk on sugar cane yonque.

Susana packed a few things and took Lucero and me to our Tía Lourdes's house in San Juan de Lurigancho. A few days later, Ciro arrived with two maniacs who almost broke down the door. He yelled at Susana to go back with him to the squatter shack in the sand. Since she didn't come out, Ciro and his friends broke the windows and peed in the water tank.

When Tío Bruno, an Army veteran friend of Tía Lourdes's, found out, he looked for Ciro in the neighborhood's seedy dives and messed him the hell up.

* * *

Susana got a job as a cook at a folkloric bar in La Victoria called El Curruñao and we moved to a rundown house on Jirón Abtao. I remember we shared the space with one of her co-workers, a single mother, and her son, a little idiot who never learned to speak.

Shortly after, at a barbecue chicken fundraiser organized to help a neighbor who had cirrhosis, Susana met the man who is now my stepfather and who I call Papá Ernesto, a man devoid of vices thanks to his evangelical faith (a belief involving the idea that sinners don't go to hell, but after death end up totally obliterated). Within a few months, Susana changed her religion. She was baptized in a ceramic tile pool and married in a mass wedding.

Papá Ernesto worked as an electrician at a mine in Matucana and earned a decent salary, so soon my family moved to a duplex in Lince near Calle Risso. The next year, my half-sister Valeria was born, who was and still is Susana and Papá Ernesto's clear favorite.

* * *

I have two scars on my face. I guess that's why some used to think I was a criminal or something like that. One time, I was arrested because a cop suspected me of collaborating with some thieves. A security guard thought I was the lookout.

One of the scars cuts across my forehead. The other, my cheek. I got them when I was little, playing near some barbed wire Ciro had left out while drinking cañazo cane liquor and emoliente barley water with his friends.

I don't remember how it happened, but I do keep a photo taken from before. This picture is of special value to me since it's the only image where I appear without the marks. It's of my sister Lucero and me sitting at the table next to a cake with two lit candles and some Casper the Friendly Ghost glasses. Lucero's hair is up with a tie and she has buttercream icing on her lips. My hair is done in traditional Andean braids.

What I don't like about the photo is that in the background you can see a cupboard with bottles of vegetable oil and jugs of cheap pisco. You can also see the unstable straw mats that doubled as a wall, a Castrol calendar featuring a woman with her tits bared and my father's hand grasping a tumbler of pisco.

That picture makes me cringe, which is why, recently, with the help of Photoshop, I removed everything I didn't like about it and threw the original in the trash.

* * *

I barely remember Ciro's wake. I have vague images of a coffin on top of metal supports. According to Susana, Ciro caught tuberculosis by drinking alcohol from the same glass as some cocaine paste addicts.

But the TB didn't kill him. It was his weakened state during a big brawl. On that day, the so-called owners of the usurped lands, the Benavides Baca family, hired thugs from Callao to evict the squatters.

Due to his poor health, Ciro couldn't escape the hoodlums chasing him all over the settlement, and they stabbed him with butcher knives.

* * *

Susana told me that, before I turned fifteen, she'd pay for plastic surgery. She even took me to several medical centers on Avenida Alfonso Ugarte to get quotes for the procedures. But she broke her word. She preferred to spend money on my stepsister Valeria, enrolling her in a private evangelical school.

That afternoon, Pablo and I ran from campus, fleeing tear gas and the confrontation with riot police. Since I had just gotten paid, I thought it'd be good idea to invite him to have a few beers at La Ramadita on Avenida Venezuela. A few hours later, we left the bar hammered and ended up fucking without a condom in a hostel room with a shared bathroom.

Every two weeks or so, we would go to the same flophouse, El Cisne—which I paid for because Pablo didn't work. The rest of the time, we'd fuck on the field at San Marcos stadium. Or in a bathroom. Or in Parque Castilla, with the whores and working boys who prostituted themselves there.

Only once did we have a problem: some glue-addict street kids attacked us while we were screwing on top of cardboard inside an abandoned house on Jirón Camaná.

* * *

Pablo slept with my cousin Gisela, who seduced him in my own house. That hurt, not so much because of him, I was already getting tired of his freeloading laziness, but because he made a fool out of me.

Since Gisela had a Pekingese named Chacho that she adored, I bought poison at a hardware store on Jirón Zela, mixed it with a chicharrón pork rind and threw the morsel onto the roof where the dog slept.

As for Pablo, I showed him how quickly he could be replaced. I let him know about a few of my hookups. He found out, for example, that I had sex with a metalhead he hated, a dude they called Pazuzu, in an Internet booth on Avenida Uruguay while watching a porno starring Rocco Siffredi.

II

When I was nine, I traveled to the Andes with Susana. We'd spend the last two weeks of December with my Abuela Flora. Even though my mother had abandoned Catholicism, she still felt indebted to the patron saint of her town, the Divine Child, for a certain miracle granted, which is why she'd organize a mass.

The trip there took more than twenty hours. I remember I got altitude sickness and my ears plugged. I also suffered chills, a pounding headache and threw up the sheep's head soup. Plus, I had to put up with an annoying passenger who got on the bus with a ram and sat down next to me.

Abuela's house was located on the edge of a gully. From her door, climbing a hill, you could see a building in ruins, which she said the terrorists had blown up during the war: an aguardiente factory the peasant patrols used as a refuge.

My abuela's house had one story, a pitched roof, small windows. It was surrounded by trees and corrals. There was no bathroom or drinking water, which is why we had to bring water from a well and head over to the outhouse.

The afternoon we arrived, a kettle was boiling in the tiny kitchen. The pots, cups and coffee strainer hung on nails. The knives looked worn, wide at the handle, thin at the tip. Under a makeshift adobe table, Abuela raised guinea pigs. From a distance, all you could see was a dark hole, but as I got closer, I could hear the rodents squeaking.

The next morning, Abuela woke up furious because during the night, a huayhuash had come into the kitchen and killed two pups. The weasel bit their necks and sucked their blood. The babies were left lying next to a chicha gourd.

For Christmas, Abuela announced she'd prepare deep-fried guinea pig. I remember she reached into that hole and pulled out two guinea pigs. Then she told me I should learn how to kill them.

The first one, Abuela took by the neck and slit its throat. To slaughter the second, she held the rodent so I could cut off its head. But as I cowered, Abuela grabbed me hard by the hand and I felt, through the handle of the knife, how the blade broke the little animal's neck.

* * *

In Lima, my Abuela spent a couple of weeks at the Hospital Neoplásicas, but they released her, saying she was going to die and another patient needed the bed.

Susana moved her into the bedroom I shared with Lucero on the roof. Because of that, the next few days, my sister and I had to spend the night in the living room, taking turns on the sofa or a tiger blanket.

I was the only one who helped Susana with Abuela. We gave her her medicine, read her the New Testament and helped with her grooming and necessities.

One night, arriving home from work, I noticed the house smelled like incense. Susana and my sisters were gathered around my grandmother's bed. Papá Ernesto was praying. Abuela had just passed away. Her body was still warm. She was wearing a robe and no socks. They told me she died screaming like a beast.

There were some problems at her wake the next day. It infuriated me that some of her children — especially from her first husband— remembered her as a tough woman.

How, in front of strangers, could they say Abuela forced them to drink piss from the chicha gourd when they misbehaved?

Why did they have to mention she'd burn their hands with cigarettes if she caught them stealing?

I had no choice but to raise my voice.

Later, there was another incident, and I ended up in a hair-pulling fight with Tía Lourdes. She was drunk and began arguing with Susana about who would get Abuela's house, and she crossed a line.

* * *

Susana began to attend her church more often. She also went to the El Ángel cemetery every weekend. I remember the dark circles under her eyes were more pronounced and she lost weight. And since she hardly slept, she was moody. On top of that, her finances dwindled. She had paid for Abuela's medications and hospitalization. Her shameless sisters hardly contributed.

To make matters worse, Papá Ernesto was fired, so he and Susana fell behind on their rent. The landlord even made a big deal out of it. To help fix the situation, my mother demanded that Lucero and I give her all our wages.

For a while, Lucero and I didn't go to a single party. Susana wouldn't let us go out. And this posed a problem for Lucero. She hadn't had a boyfriend for over a year and was dying to meet a guy. Lucero was shy and didn't take advantage of her qualities. I suggested she be more provocative. Show those boobs more. Take the initiative. I told her men are easy. But for some reason she could never let herself go.

$$* * *$$

One Saturday, Susana ordered us to help her slaughter ten guinea pigs. I'd slit their throats. Lucero and Susana would plunge them into a pot of boiling water to then skin and gut them.

That day we worked all morning. I ended up with scratches. Susana, with some burns, from splashes of hot water.

Once finished, Susana allowed us to keep some money. The first thing we did was go to the market to buy new underwear. For Lucero, a thong, and for me, a G-string. We even convinced my mother to let us go out, but we had to be home before one in the morning. To persuade her, we told her we'd go out with some girls from the neighborhood who, in Susana's eyes, had an impeccable reputation because of their Christian faith.

What my mother didn't know was that those girls, secretly, led a libertine life.

$$* * *$$

Once we left home, we hid behind some bushes in Parque Castilla and put on low-cut black T-shirts. Further on, under a light post, we put on makeup: thick lines around our eyes, black nails and slicked-back hair. We did this on the down low because Susana would never have allowed us to leave the house dressed like that.

The Karloff nightclub was located on the third floor of an old building in Plaza San Martín. It was a bit of a sketchy place. I once witnessed a knife fight. Another time, I saw some peperas drugging their unlucky victims.

Arriving at Karloff, Lucero, I, and our "Christian" friends bought Pilsen beers and menthol cigarettes and eyed a group of guys. We agreed who'd go with whom. I picked the one wearing a Chicago Bulls cap. I smiled at him a couple of times, and he at me. Just then Lucero said:

"Chola, that boy can't stop staring at you."

"Which one?"

"Turn around."

When I turned, another guy toasted me with his glass of beer from the bar and I responded with mine. The dude then came up to me. His name was Leonardo.

* * *

As Human League's "Don't You Want Me" played, someone grabbed my hand. It was the guy in the Chicago Bulls hat. The asshole was trying to hook up with me. I no longer wanted anything to do with him and resisted. Leonardo, who was coming back from the bathroom, noticed and intervened.

People formed a circle around them. The guy in the cap broke a bottle and cut Leonardo's arm. Luckily, the fat security guys showed up and the instigator ran away. I told Leonardo we should go to a clinic.

"It's nothing," he said and bandaged the wound with a bandana.

I had never been the cause of a fight between men. I thought it was typical of tacky people, lowlifes. But I'm not going to deny I liked seeing two guys fight over me.

.

* * *

Leonardo and I left the club and took the stairs up a couple of floors.

Trash was scattered around and it smelled like piss. On the landing, Leonardo took out his dick and I sucked it. Then I lowered my pants and he got behind me.

While he put it in without a rubber, I realized a guard was taking pictures of us with his cellphone.

* * *

Since Lucero had a habit of sleeping without underwear, she threw her thong beside the bed and, when Susana came into our bedroom, she noticed the panties.

"What's this?" she asked raising her voice.

She pulled the covers off me and discovered my G-string.

"Shameless whore," she yelled. "Where did you get this crap from?"

Susana forced me to remove my G-string and cut it with the knife she used to kill guinea pigs. Then she sent us to clean the shit in the cages.

Lucero hated guinea pigs and got angry. When Susana saw her pouting, she slapped her.

"Don't sulk, goddamn it," Susana said.

"You clean it up, you shitty Indian," Lucero replied. "That's what you are: an uneducated chola, half-breed. A disgusting peasant."

Susana dragged Lucero by the hair into the shower. There she turned on the cold water and gave her a terrible beating.

That's how Susana disciplined us. I remember once she punished me horribly when I went without permission to the Servando and Florentino concert at the Feria del Hogar. That night, nothing happened to me, but a friend from Colegio Fanning was suffocated by the crowd during the human stampede.

There was a time when my sister and I accepted the punishment without questioning it. Who knows? Without it, maybe now I'd be just some random girl or a criminal. But that last beating in the shower humiliated Lucero and hurt her female pride.

III

Leonardo told me his father died fighting insurgents. About his mother Natalia, he told me she had lung problems and went to an Alcoholics Anonymous group near Óvalo Gutiérrez. What happened was that after becoming a widow, the woman turned to drink, cigarettes and gambling.

I remember being surprised when I found out this formal, elegant lady was a drunk and a gambler who'd stay up all night. Natalia even served a brief stint in the Santa Mónica Women's Prison for hitting a street food vendor while driving drunk.

For Natalia's birthday, Leonardo invited me to have dinner with them. They prepared roasted pork leg with green rice seasoned with coriander and opened a bottle of Ballentine's. Already a little drunk, we danced to rancheras, mambos and Peruvian folkloric music, several tunes by Polo Campos. It was fun at first, but then some things happened. I threw up and clogged the sink. And then I noticed Leonardo was a bit handsy with his mother, embracing her and even gave her little kisses on the lips.

* * *

If I went out with Leonardo, I'd come home after midnight. And this pissed off my old lady. One morning, she insulted me after I said, "And what the fuck do you care what I do with my life?"

When I told Leonardo about the fights with Susana, he got horribly upset.

"Why don't you tell your ratchet mother to go to hell?" he said. "I'm not trying to be a dick, but your mom is a piece of shit."

To avoid problems with Susana, I told Leonardo that maybe it'd be a good idea to introduce him as my boyfriend. He agreed.

So one day, Leonardo came over. We all sat down in the dining room: him, my family, all except Lucero, who decided not to come downstairs, feigning cramps, and me.

Papá Ernesto took a liking to Leonardo. He congratulated him for graduating as a journalist from the PUCP. Plus, both were rabid fans of the soccer club "la U", Maradona and Rubén Blades.

Susana used to be rude to every boy I brought home, but Leonardo knew how to win her over. He praised her culinary talents. And that day Susana had prepared a carapulcra stew with basil pasta that turned out really well. Afterward, they spent the night talking about Novoandino cuisine, about Cucho La Rosa and Don Pedrito. Leonardo knew something about the topic because he'd interviewed several famous chefs for a weekly newspaper. Susana liked Leonardo so much she offered to prepare spicy guinea pig for him the next time.

The only bad thing happened when Leonardo asked me where the bathroom was. I showed him, opened the door and noticed someone had left the toilet shit stained. The person responsible was my stepsister Valeria, who never deigned to clean anything.

I hated the spoiled way they'd been raising her. So when Leonardo left, I gave that filthy bitch a good talking to.

* * *

If there was no one in our living room, we took advantage. Since we couldn't undress (in case someone showed up), I'd just lift my skirt. I'd lean against the door leading to the stairs and he'd do me from behind. Other times, I'd get on the couch on all fours and he'd mount me without taking off his pants.

Leonardo didn't explicitly ask for my ass. But, because he'd rimmed me and put on anal porn, I started saying: "I want you to pierce my ass," or "Baby, make me bleed," or "Leave me wide open." That kind of stupidity turned him on.

Leonardo got over his disgust at getting dirty when I bled. In his bedroom, red marks were left on the walls: my handprint, for example. In my living room, there's still a stain on the sofa. To hide it, Leonardo deliberately spilled burgundy wine on top, faking an accident.

* * *

One night, returning from Santa Rosa de Quives, Leonardo was driving his Volvo and inadvertently cut off another vehicle, which ended up crashing into a rock formation. Since Leonardo was drunk, he tried to run away, but I convinced him to stop.

I got out of the car. The driver of the other vehicle had his head smashed. The woman with him had been thrown through the windshield and ended up on the highway.

316

"Let's go," Leonardo said. "I don't have a license. If the pigs get here, I'm fucked."

Before we left, Leonardo, covering his hand with a rag, rifled through the woman's wallet and took her money.

* * *

For an article he planned to submit to a contest organized by an NGO financed by the German government, Leonardo wanted to write about a massacre perpetrated by the Peruvian Army in a town called Pariamarca.

He didn't agree with what the Truth and Reconciliation Commission had reported on the matter. What's more, since his father was involved in that story, personal interest motivated his investigation.

Leonardo interviewed some military men. He researched newspaper archives and those of the Commission itself. When he learned of the existence of a survivor of the massacre who was still living in Pariamarca, Leonardo asked me to go with him to interview her. Since I wanted to spend more time away from home, away from the annoying Susana and my sisters, I said yes.

But things started off badly. To begin with, Leonardo's car broke down, forcing us to go by bus. I suggested we postpone, but he wanted to do the interview right away.

So we left early one Saturday from a bus station at the UNI Engineering campus. Arriving in Canta, the town before Pariamarca, we had cheese sandwiches and coffee with milk for breakfast at the market. Then we looked for a taxi to our destination, but the cab drivers told us they didn't go up to Pariamarca at that time of day. Those trips were only in the afternoon, when residents returned to home after the fair. Fortunately, a teenage girl driving a mototaxi agreed to take us.

The girl claimed to be thirteen, but looked older. She said her name was Roxana and she was a shepherdess, but because some dogs had attacked her father a few days earlier, as the oldest daughter, it fell on her to be in charge of the mototaxi.

Leonardo asked Roxana if she knew Señora Juana Requena, the survivor.

"She lives behind the church," Roxana said, "in a tiny room. She lives with her daughter Adelaida, who was left a bit demented after the head injury."

* * *

Leonardo got a colleague of his from the PUCP to lend him a house in Pariamarca. The place was a mess, with dust and cobwebs everywhere. We had to assemble the bed, not with screws, but a few loose nails. The mattress had urine stains. The house was near the plaza, which was nothing more than a dilapidated cement slab with a pole in the middle. We walked to the back wall. Even after all those years, we could still make out the bullet holes from the executions.

Back at the house, I unzipped Leonardo's pants and sucked him off. As I was, I sensed a presence. I turned without taking his prick from my mouth and saw Roxana spying on us through the window. As our eyes met, I stopped for a few seconds, then continued until Leonardo came on my face.

* * *

In Pariamarca, Leonardo and I greeted passersby, appearing like friendly tourists, but they were indifferent to us.

"Why don't we go back to Canta for the night?" I asked Leonardo. "There's a hostel there. There's nothing here, just that filthy bed. Also, people keep giving us the stink eye."

Leonardo refused. The next day he wanted to go up to the lake where the army killed several peasants. Leonardo wanted to walk the same path the victims took before they were killed.

"I'd like to capture something of what those people felt for my article," he said.

I called his idea naive. What's more, I pointed out that I thought it was morbid.

"What right do you have to mess with the suffering of others?" I asked.

Leonardo gave me his reasons. But since I didn't want drama, I didn't contradict him. I was there to relax, not to fight over nonsense.

* * *

We entered Juana Requena's house. On a table was an altar with flowers, saints and a crucifix. There were jars with a greasy liquid and some knives. I also made out a few family portraits. I recognized the old woman with a few children. Juana Requena was a head taller than me. She wore a long dress and a scarf.

"What do you want to know?" she asked Leonardo.

"Did you know Major Adolfo Carrasco?" he asked.

"Are you related to him? You look like him."

"I'm his son."

"You have the same jaw line. The same forehead. I hope you're not as stupid."

"Do you know how my father died?"

Juana told Leonardo his father had a dispute with the colonel in charge of the detachment in Canta. She said he was furious when soldiers, including the colonel himself, kidnapped her and other women. By then, Juana and Leonardo's dad were already lovers. To top it off: she was expecting his daughter. So, to get revenge, Leonardo's father passed information to the insurgents, the senderistas. Those Shining Path militants then ambushed the colonel and his men.

Shortly after, the senderistas betrayed Leonardo's father, who was later found dead. On his body, they'd placed a communist flag. The official report blamed the terrorists.

At a certain point, Juana's daughter came into the room. She and Leonardo looked alike. He noticed this and was convinced the woman had been honest when she said she'd given birth to his father's daughter. The girl could barely articulate words. She was wearing a young child's dress and rubber sandals. Suddenly, the girl violently lunged at Leonardo, and I had to push her away.

* * *

I left Leonardo talking to the lady about the massacre at the lake. Outside, I walked around the square. I found some children playing ball, including Roxana. I took out Leonardo's Kodak camera to photograph them. But the children stopped playing and one approached me to ask for payment for the photo. I refused and the boy said, "Get the hell out of my town, you ugly piece of shit."

I stayed on the sidewalk. After a while, the ball shot out and hit me in the head. The kids laughed. In response, I kicked the ball right back at them. It hit a little boy in the face. The children then ordered the old woman's dog to attack me. I grabbed a stick to defend myself. Luckily, Juana and Leonardo showed up, and seeing her, the children left.

"Come, Nino," the old woman said to the dog and pet him.

Leonardo then said:

"Juana doesn't want to go to the lake with us. No matter how much I offer to pay her."

"The woman limps. What were you thinking?"

"Well," he said, "we'll have to find someone to guide us."

On a corner, we found Roxana in her mototaxi with another child. Actually, this kid looked more like a big-headed dwarf. Since we caught them making out, they were a bit short with us. Even so, Leonardo convinced Roxana to guide us to the lake for a good price.

We returned to the old house, turned off the lamp and tried to sleep. But the noise of the rain hitting the corrugated metal bothered us. We heard a thud in the attic and a sound like a small steel ball falling down a ladder.

* * *

We climbed up a steep trail. Roxana moved at a fast pace. For our part, we'd stop every now and then to give ourselves a break.

When we reached the top, we noticed a few ruins, pre-Columbian burial towers. Further out, the landscape opened up into a gully. That was the famous lake, now dry. A mine had drained it. On one side was a cross marking the site of the massacre.

Leonardo took photos from various angles. Roxana sat down on a rock, and I moved next to her. Face to face, I criticized her behavior, how she spied on us the night before. But the little bitch acted as if it had been no big deal.

As we began descending to Pariamarca, the fog thickened. We could barely see a few feet ahead. There were mounds, crevasses, and sudden drops. We wanted to wait for it to clear up, but Roxana said, "I know the path by heart." Leonardo took me by the hand. Roxana walked two or three steps ahead. I could barely make out her silhouette. Suddenly, I don't know how, she disappeared, leaving Leonardo and I sitting there on the hill for hours.

IV

Leonardo didn't tell his mother what Juana had shared. Nor did he finish his article on the Pariamarca massacre. His excuse: he said he couldn't find the right style. He didn't want to repeat the same old clichés from journalists who dealt with the topic. I told him to just write. I didn't know why he had to complicate things.

Leonardo also wasn't able to progress with his article because he began to party way too much. He'd started drinking with some downtown punks to the point of blacking out. Before I met him, I'd never been so drunk I passed out, but to keep him company, I went to extremes. Once I became violent and got into a fight with a whore from Quilca who was giving it to him for free.

He also got hooked on coke like never before. All over his apartment were compact discs and small mirrors covered with white spots next to cut-up straws. When I brought it up, he justified himself by arguing that coke helped him stay sober and got him out of depression.

His coke connection was a young girl with thick black hair, known in the downtown streets as La Leona, and who worked as a delivery girl for some drug traffickers in Barrios Altos.

* * *

I heard that, during a fight, Leonardo was thrown into a huge mirror at the Karloff nightclub and was covered in cuts. I immediately called his house.

"I haven't seen him in days," his mother told me. "He left with the bandages on. And I believe he's with that little whore, with that Leona."

I asked around the bars and got La Leona's phone number. I called her and we met at a restaurant on Jirón Puno. She arrived late that day: disheveled, skinny to the bone, wearing a Mötley Crüe *Shout at the Devil* T-shirt. She told me that three days ago, she and Leonardo had bought a bag of coke in La Victoria and then went to a hotel on Avenida La Marina. According to her, she only stayed with Leonardo until about eleven that night. She hadn't seen him since.

I went to the hotel to find out more and was told that on the fourth day of his stay, all of sudden Leonardo started throwing hotel furniture out the window. And then he stood naked by the window yelling at passersby. The hotel staff kicked him out on the street without any clothes. Outside, Leonardo began to run between the cars, and the cops captured him.

I didn't happen to catch it, but they told me Leonardo appeared on TV. Firemen had to go down a slope of the Magdalena cliff to rescue him. A police officer said that Leonardo had thrown himself from the back of the police van in motion.

This incident caused Leonardo serious problems: he was fired from the newspaper where he worked. His landlord, for his part, evicted him after verifying he stored drugs in the apartment and the place was in complete disarray.

* * *

About a month later, Leonardo told me in an email that he'd ditched his Volvo at a body shop after crashing it while driving drunk and that he was desperate because he couldn't get a job.

He told me he was currently at home, living off his mother's widow's pension. In the message he also asked me to bring him two bottles of pisco. He claimed to suffer from anxiety thanks to his drinking. He wrote:

"I'll pay you at the end of the month, Romi. Or if not, you can take what you want from my house in exchange."

I brought Leonardo the alcohol. I remember he welcomed me in his underpants. He had trouble moving. His skin looked yellow and parched, covered in sores and pimples. His house was neglected. In the kitchen, dishes and pots piled up in the sink. I even saw rat shit.

When we went into his bedroom, I noticed his mother was passed out drunk. On the nightstand, I saw bottles of booze and pills.

"What's your old lady doing here?" I asked.

"I sold the other TV and she wanted to watch a James Dean movie but fell asleep. I'll take her to her room in a bit."

"Well, Leonardo... What can I say? Anyway, here are two bottles for you."

"Thanks, Romi. Right now, I don't feel so anxious, but at night I can't stand it. How about you tell me if you want anything. I think there are some books and cassettes that might interest you."

"What cassettes?"

"A collection of underground rock bands."

"Bah. You know I'm not into that underground shit. But hey, do you still have the Kodak?"

"Sure."

"Want to trade it for the two piscos?"

"Perfect. And how's it going? They tell me you got yourself a new stud?"

I told him I was going out with Paolo, where I met him and everything else.

"Hey, and are you already cheating on him just like me?"

"Don't talk shit, man."

"I'm just kidding, babe. Don't act all bitter either."

"I'm not, I just don't like your little jokes."

"Why don't we go out this weekend? What do you say, want to take me out to the bars?"

"No, Leonardo. Hell no. I'll pass."

* * *

When I told Susana I was pregnant with my daughter Silvina, she exploded with anger. Lucero, for her part, recommended I have an abortion. Papá Ernesto actually rejoiced at the idea of having a grandchild. Paolo, Silvina's father, was also enthusiastic. He kissed me when I shared the news. He fantasized about our future family life.

What a difference from Leonardo's reaction when I told him I was expecting his child! The first thing he did was contact a doctor who performed clandestine abortions.

He took me to a gloomy doctor's office on Avenida Alfonso Ugarte, where the doctor subjected me to a curettage; the procedure turned out to be quite painful. Since I was already in my third month, the doctor literally tore apart the fetus inside me. I remember catching a glimpse of my son smashed to bits on a steel tray before the doctor threw him in the trash.

Before I left, I asked the doctor to give me the ultrasound showing the fetus he'd just dismembered. It was a black and white print of a small, coiled body.

"Doctor, I'd like it as a souvenir," I said.

He refused, saying:

"No, señorita, under no circumstances. There can be no memory of something that never existed."

I left the office in Leonardo's arms. We got into his Volvo and parked next to a park in Jesús María until my discomfort passed a bit. At home, I told Susana I'd been injured playing volleyball.

It's true: you could say I wanted a child. However, at a certain point, I became convinced that disposing of the fetus was the right decision. The child of an addict could've been born deformed.

* * *

I don't know how Leonardo found out I was expecting Paolo's daughter, but he started sending messages asking me to have another abortion. He said he'd recover, and we could get back together. After telling him to go fuck himself, he became furious. In a toxic email, he demanded I return some gifts, a few Burzum records and several books by Nietzsche and Schopenhauer. Plus, he demanded I repay him the money he spent on my abortion.

"You have to give back that cash," he told me. "Don't be a thief."

Leonardo continued to harass and even threatened to kill me. As a result, I wrote an anonymous letter addressed to the Lince police station. In it, I explained how Leonardo caused the accident that ended the life of a couple on the outskirts of Lima.

After some time had passed, Leonardo called me. He didn't mention the police. He just asked me to bring him more pisco.

* * *

Paolo moved into my house. It would only be for a short time until Paolo and I found a place. But Paolo didn't bother to get a good job. He spent the days watching HBO with Silvina. When I got sick of his attitude, I gave him an ultimatum:

"What did you think? You were just going to live off us? FYI, this ain't your house, where your stupid mother puts up with you. Don't think I haven't noticed you fucking around all day. And how you take advantage of Silvina to get away with it. And I'm saying this to your face: we're already tired of your laziness over here. If you don't get a job in a month, you're out of here."

Before the end of the month something happened: Valeria told me that, while she was taking a shower, through the bathroom window, she saw a small mirror attached to a stick. It was that asshole Paolo trying to spy on her naked. The very same day, with Susana's help, we kicked him out.

* * *

The guinea pig pen, made of wooden slats and chicken wire, had three levels. On the top were the pups. The middle one held the alpha male with ten females. On the first, my mother had separated the pregnant female who, due to her bad temper, would attack the others. In a second cage, the young males were separated by size into several compartments. The idea was not to let the bigger ones kill the smaller ones.

My mother fed the animals alfalfa and, when there was extra money, forage and a balanced feed. Her clients were mostly Andean migrants from the neighborhood who still ate traditional dishes. Mamá also raised a couple of black guinea pigs, whose young she sold to a shaman to do his cleansing rituals and spells.

Every time Susana prepared guinea pig, I would eat all the flesh from the head, including the brain, and look for the little bone they call zorrito. Then I'd put it in a bowl, serve myself Gato Negro boxed wine and down it all. My abuelita had taught me to swallow the zorrito. According to her, that way I would also have the sharp intuition of a guinea pig and no one could fool me just like that. Abuela also told me some black guinea pigs are witches, that's why the healers use them for macumba.

* * *

My mother didn't fully close the guinea pig pen. And the roof cats came down and killed several pups and a pregnant female. I remember I came home from work to find Susana crying for her animals.

Weeks later, when Susana slapped me and forced me to remove a piercing I'd just gotten on my tongue, I decided to take

328

revenge using her guinea pigs. I left the cage open and went out. This time, Susana blamed the death of the guinea pigs on Valeria, the only daughter who was in the house when the cats came down. That time, Susana gave my stepsister a tremendous beating.

* * *

I don't know why I felt guilty. So I took a bus to Chinatown, bought a pair of guinea pigs and brought them home.

"I won't be raising anything anymore," Susana said. "At the end of the day, guinea pigs have only brought problems. First, because of the dirty house, and now, because of Valeria. I think I went overboard. Besides, I was already getting tired. Lots of work, little profit."

"Mami, why don't we cook these two guinea pigs?" I asked. "They're perfect for a spicy stew. Papá Ernesto will love it."

That night, we all ate guinea pig except Valeria. Papá Ernesto ordered a crispy combo from KFC because guinea pig grossed her out.

* * *

Lucero's son was born with Down syndrome and the father, an emo from Los Olivos, took off. He was a horrible baby with bulging eyes, a boxy head and a permanent dim-witted expression. The doctors said he'd never get better.

I'd heard the mentally retarded wreck everything and that, once they discovered their sexuality, they masturbate in front of people. I read in William Faulkner's *The Sound and the Fury* that they used to castrate them. I wanted the child to die, so I left some marbles within his reach hoping he'd swallow them and choke.

* * *

My chibola Silvina got sick, and the doctor recommended she avoid contact with animals. We no longer raised guinea pigs, but Valeria had been given a kitten. I explained to her what the doctor had said, that it'd be best to give Granizo up for adoption. She, however, didn't want to understand. Her response was:

"Why don't you tell your deadbeat husband to take you to his house? Why don't you tell him to work and give his daughter a decent home? Leave my kitty alone."

It hit me hard. That same day I bought poison, mixed it with a can of Florida-brand tuna and left it near the cat. Then I blamed the neighbors. I reminded Valeria how they'd constantly complain about the cats fighting on the roof.

One night, while putting Silvina to sleep, I was thinking about how to get rid of Leonardo, who kept pestering me.

What would happen, let's say, if I were to put poison in his drink? Would he notice?

* * *

Leonardo called me. He asked for more booze. He said he had some jewelry from his mother to give me in return. So I bought a gallon of diluted rum from a shack on Jirón Zela, and Campeón rat poison, and went to his house with my daughter.

"This is for you to get rid of the mice," I said when I handed him the poison. "The other day, I saw rat shit in the kitchen."

"Thank you. Yeah, well, the mice and rats come in from the street. Also, with Natalia sick, it sucks trying to keep the house clean."

Then he said:

"Why don't you come in? I have some silver earrings. I hope it's enough to pay you back. Do you want to see them?"

Silvina and I entered.

* * *

The police concluded that Leonardo had poisoned Natalia and then took the rat poison himself. They found the bodies in a state of advanced decomposition and, since no one claimed them from the morgue, they buried them in a remote cemetery.

It was a long hike to reach Leonardo's tomb. Three hours through shantytowns and improvised settlements. I passed colonial walls, the tuberculosis sanatorium and the bomb-damaged prison. I found it difficult to find him at the graveyard. That's why I asked the guy in charge, an old man stricken with a terrible disease.

At Leonardo's grave, you could hardly make out his name on the stone. I spread out a traditional blanket on the ground and sat down with Silvina. Then I laid some flowers. A while later, thanks to the sudden heat, Silvina began to fuss. She couldn't stand to be there any longer.

Before leaving, I smashed the slab that marked the grave. And after making sure there was no trace of anything, I left.

Acknowledgments

I am extremely grateful to José Garay Boszeta for his tireless work and support over the last couple of years. Garay and I met when our mutual friend, the great author and editor of comic books, Jesús Cossio, visited San Antonio to give a presentation. After Cossio's talk, I invited a few friends to my house for pisco sours and chilcanos, and Garay struck up a conversation with me about translation. He told me about his dream of starting an independent publishing house primarily devoted to translations of Latin American literary works. Shortly thereafter, he founded Dulzorada Press and, to date, they have published a host of excellent titles including poetry collections from José María Eguren, Magda Portal, Raquel Jodorowsky and Fiorella Terrazas (aka Fioloba); a new version of Martín Adán's avant-garde classic novella, *La casa de cartón* (*The Cardboard House*) and Jesús Balmori's *Birds of Fire, A Filipino War Novel*, among others. I am honored to be a part of Dulzorada's impressive catalogue.

I am indebted to Lisa Carter, Creative Director of Intralingo (https://intralingo.com/), for helping to shape the final versions of the pieces in this anthology. Carter's keen eye, attention to detail and helpful stylistic suggestions greatly improved my translations.

Special thanks to my workout buddy and graphic designer extraordinaire, Susana Hernández, who designed the gorgeous cover of *Paciencia Perdida*.

I would also like to extend my heartfelt thanks to all the authors who generously agreed to grant me permission to translate their stories. This collection would not have been possible without their support and positive vibes. I know I must have been terribly annoying and pushy on Facebook, Instagram and WhatsApp trying to convince writers to believe in this project—apologies, hehe! Extra special thanks to Gunter Silva, my partner at *Stories from Peru*, for constantly checking in and providing helpful comments.

Many thanks to Asdrúbal Hernández, Founder of Sudaquia Publishers (www.sudaquia.net), for graciously allowing me to include two stories under contract from his publishing house. It's a pleasure to collaborate with Sudaquia, a leading publisher of Spanish-language literature in the United States.

Throughout the years, I've been lucky to count on the support of such great colleagues who have patiently listened to me geek out on Peruvian literature ad nauseam. I value the warmth folks from the University of Wisconsin – Green Bay and the University of the Incarnate Word have shown me. I also want to share my gratitude to César Ferreira and Luis Cano, two important mentors who constantly stretch my thinking on all things related to Latin American literature.

Mil gracias go to my good friends from the *Libros y copas* book club especially Cecilia, Sandra, Nelly, Cecy, Ketty and Héctor. I can't wait to hear their feedback after they dive into these stories!

An enormous thank you to my parents, Paul and Eliana, for their non-stop love and support. I truly appreciate everything they've done for me my entire life. I am particularly grateful for the time they spent going all over Lima to different bookstores tracking down titles I've needed for my classes, research and translations.

Lucas and Leo (los frikis), your support means the world to me. You guys have grown up so much since the idea of this book popped in my head. It's amazing seeing your different creative endeavors—I'm excited for what you guys come up with next. I am so proud of you both.

And lastly, I would not have been able to finish this anthology had it not been for Beatriz, my wife and the first reader of everything I write and/or translate. I really, really value your ideas and perspective. I love our life together. Gracias, mi diosa.

ABOUT THE AUTHORS

Katya Adaui (Lima, 1977)
Katya holds a master's degree in Creative Writing from the Universidad de Tres de Febrero. She has published several collections of short stories including *Un accidente llamado familia* (2007), *Aquí hay icebergs* (2017) and *Geografía de la oscuridad* (2021) and the novels *Nunca sabré lo que entiendo* (2014) and *Quienes somos ahora* (2022). Her works have been translated into English and Italian. She currently lives in Buenos Aires where she directs creative writing workshops. I should also add that she's the author of my niece's favorite children's book, *Muy Muy en Bora Bora* (2019).
Instagram: @katyaadaui
Twitter: @kadaui

Fernando Ampuero (Lima, 1949)
Fernando is a journalist and prolific author of over thirty books including the novels *Caramelo verde* (1992), *Puta linda* (2006), *Hasta que me orinen los perros* (2008) and *El peruano imperfecto* (2011), numerous short story anthologies such as *Bicho raro* (1996), *Mujeres difíciles, hombres benditos* (2005) and *Lobos solitarios y otros cuentos* (2018), and the poetry collections *Voces de luna llena* (1998) and *40 poemas* (2010). A graduate of the Pontificia Universidad Católica del Perú (PUCP), his career has seen him take leadership roles in the country's most prestigious news outlets like the magazine *Caretas*, the leading daily *El Comercio* and its cultural supplement, *El Dominical*. When he's not writing, you can catch Fernando walking or jogging along the malecón in Miraflores.
Instagram: @Fernando.ampuerodelbosque

Francisco Ángeles (Lima, 1977)

Francisco holds a PhD from the University of Pennsylvania and currently works at Yale University's MacMillan Center – Council on Latin American Studies. He's the author of four novels *La línea en medio del cielo* (2008); *Austin, Texas 1979* (2014); *Plagio* (2016) and *Adiós a la revolución* (2019). In 2015, he co-authored with Fernando Ampuero and artist Rocío Urtecho (aka Jugo Gástrico) the short story "double feature," *Hollywood en doble función*. For more than fifteen years, Francisco was co-editor of the literary magazine *El Hablador*. If you follow him on Instagram, you'll soon realize that he's something of a budding sommelier.
Instagram: @franciscoangelesss
https://www.elhablador.com/

Jorge Eduardo Benavides (Arequipa, 1964)

Jorge majored in Law and Political Science at the Universidad Garcilaso de la Vega. He's been living in Spain since 1991, first in Tenerife where he founded and directed the literary workshop Entrelíneas, and then in Madrid, his current city of residence. He has published two collections of short stories, *Cuentario y otros relatos* (1989) and *La noche de Morgana* (2005), as well as several novels including *Los años inútiles* (2002), *El año que rompí contigo* (2003), *Un millón de soles* (2008) and *Un asunto sentimental* (2012). His novel *La paz de los vencidos* (2009) won him the XII Premio de Novela Corta Julio Ramón Ribeyro, while his 2014 novel, *El enigma del convento*, was awarded the prestigious Torrente Ballester prize. He was a Scholar-in-Residence at the University of Wisconsin-Green Bay in 2011, making him a die-hard Packer fan for life. His latest novel, *Volver a Shangri-La*, was published in 2022 by Alianza Editorial.
Instagram: jorgeeduardo_benavides
https://jorgeeduardobenavides.com/

Miluska Benavides (Lima, 1986)

Miluska was featured in Granta Magazine's "Best of Young Spanish-Language Novelists" special issue in 2021. She's the author of *La caza espiritual* (2015) and a forthcoming novel titled *Hechos.* Miluska is also an accomplished literary translator and among the works she's published, I'd like to highlight her new translation of the French poet Arthur Rimbaud's *A Season in Hell* (2012). She received her PhD from the University of Colorado at Boulder with a truly interdisciplinary dissertation analyzing indigeneity through literary works and visual art from Mexico and Peru. I use her chapter on Martín Chambi's Andean photographs in my Cultural Studies classes all the time!
Instagram: @mkbenavides

María José Caro (Lima, 1985)

María José earned her master's degree in Communications from the Universidad Complutense de Madrid. She's the author of the short story collections *La primaria* (2012) and *¿Qué tengo de malo?* (2017) and the novel *Perro de ojos negros* (2016). The Hay Festival – Bogotá39 selected her as one the best Latin American fiction writers under the age of 39 in 2017. María José is also an avid tennis player and has been known to show no mercy on her opponents on Lima's clay courts.
Instagram: @majoclv

Luis Hernán Castañeda (Lima, 1982)

Luis Hernán (Ludo) is a professor of Luso-Hispanic Studies at Middlebury College. He's a prolific author and among his most notable works are *Casa de Islandia* (2004), *Hotel Europa* (2005), *La noche americana* (2011), *La fiesta del humo* (2016), *Mi madre soñaba en francés* (2018) and *El imperio de las mareas* (2020). In 2021 he published *Un escritor rural*, an introspective travelogue of sorts with ruminations on literary and cultural icons that run the gamut of figures such as José María Arguedas and Pedro Almódovar to Jean-Claude Van Damme. After spending several years in Colorado and Vermont, Ludo has become a true connoisseur of craft beers.
Instagram: @ludocastaneda

María Luisa del Río (Lima, 1968)

María Luisa studied Audiovisual Communications at the Instituto Peruano de Publicidad. She has published collections of flash fiction including *No mires atrás* (2006), *Parece una agonía* (2012) and the nonfiction works *Cusco Bizarro* (2008), *El Perú arde* (2011), *Hey, soy gay* (2014) and *La despensa del mundo* (2018). Her cookbook *Chia* was awarded the Gourmand Book Award in 2015. Her latest book *Máncora Blues* (2022) is an homage to the northern beachtown where María Luisa spent a lot of time in the 80s and 90s. She's also a well-known DJ, spinning eclectic sets all over the Barranco neighborhood of Lima.
Instagram: @djluisi

Oswaldo Estrada (Santa Ana, California, 1976)

He is the author of a children's book, *El secreto de los trenes* (2018), and of three collections of short stories, *Luces de emergencia* (2019), *Las locas ilusiones y otros relatos de migración* (2020), and *Las guerras perdidas* (2021). He has edited the volume *Incurables. Relatos de dolencias y males* (2020) with twenty Latin American authors who live in the US. In 2020, he won two International Latino Book Awards, as well as the International Latino and Latin American Book Fair Prize from Tufts University. In 2021, he was a finalist for the Doris Betts Fiction Prize. His book *Las guerras perdidas* won a Gold Medal (First Place) for Best Collection of Short Stories in Spanish at the International Latino Book Awards 2022. He is a professor of Latin American Literature at the University of North Carolina at Chapel Hill. A little-known fact about Oswaldo is that he's quite a singer; he can be found belting out boleros and valses criollos at post-conference after parties with or without the help of a few pisco sours and/or chilcanos.
Instagram: @estrada.camino

Yeniva Fernández (Lima, 1969)

Yeniva graduated from the Universidad Nacional Mayor de San Marcos with a degree in Library Science. She is most known for her fantastical storytelling in books such as *Trampas para incautos* (2009), *Siete paseos por la niebla* (2015) and *Los ríos de Marte* (2019). Her short stories have appeared in numerous anthologies including *17 fantásticos cuentos peruanos* (2008), *Disidentes* (2011), *El fin de algo: antología del nuevo cuento peruano* (2015) and *Arriba las manos: muestra de relato policial peruano* (2016). A serious film buff, Yeniva has also been a regular contributor to the Peruvian magazine, *Godard! Revista de cine.*

Hemil García Linares (Lima, 1971)

Hemil holds a bachelor's degree in Journalism and a master's in Spanish and Latin American Literature from George Mason University (GMU). He's been a Spanish instructor at GMU, Georgetown University and George Washington University. Hemil's publications include *Cuentos del norte, historias del sur* (2009), *Sesenta días para abandonar el país* (2011), *Aquiles en los Andes* (2015) and *El azul del Mediterráneo, un viaje ancestral* (2019). He has also edited numerous anthologies featuring a host of prominent contemporary Spanish and Latin American authors. His most recent collections are tributes to Gothic and horror writers such as Edgar Allan Poe, H.P. Lovecraft and Stephen King. A tireless promoter of Spanish-language literature in the Washington DC metropolitan area, he founded the Virginia International Hispanic Book Festival in 2017. A consummate cratedigger, Hemil's vinyl collection is the envy of many of us!
Instagram: @hemilgarcialinares

Bethsabé Huamán Andía (Lima, 1977)

Bethsabé holds a PhD from Tulane University, an MFA in Creative Writing from New York University and a master's in Gender Studies from El Colegio de México, A.C. She's the author of the following short story collections *Sábado pm* (2003), *Memento mori* (2009) and *La oscuridad del sombrero* (2017). Her works have been featured in several Peruvian anthologies including *Disidentes* (2011), *69. Antología de microrelatos eróticos femeninos* (2016) and *Sexo al cubo* (2017). Bethsabé is a professor of International Languages and Literature at St. Catherine University in Minnesota. She's a committed environmentalist and advocate for animal rights.
Instagram: @pecesitavoladora
bethsabeh.wixsite.com/bechita5

Alexis Iparraguirre (Lima, 1974)

Alexis received his PhD in Latin American, Iberian and Latino Cultures from The City University of New York and an MFA in Creative Writing from New York University. He has published two books of short fiction, *El inventario de las naves* (2005), which won the Premio Nacional de la Pontificia Universidad Católica del Perú, and *El fuego de las multitudes* (2016). Along with Francisco Joaquín Marro, he co-edited the science fiction collection *Esta realidad no existe. Antología de ciencia ficción por escritores del Perú* (2021). His stories have appeared in several important collections including *El cuento peruano 2001-2010* (2013), *Estados Hispanos de América. Narrativa latinaoamericana made in USA* (2016), *Incurables. Relatos de dolencias y males* (2020) and *Cuentos peruanos de la pandemia* (2021). In 2013, he was one of the 35 authors of "Latinoamérica viva," a selection of young writers of continental appeal and critical acclaim at the FIL in Guadalajara. Alexis is not only a voracious reader, but also a sci-fi and superhero TV shows and film enthusiast. By the time it takes an average person to binge watch three or four episodes of a Star Wars-related series, he will have watched the entire season and expounded on a myriad of theories concerning possible future plot twists on his social media feed.

Instagram: @alexisiparraguirre

Pedro Novoa (Huacho, 1974 – 2021)

At the age of 18, Pedro joined Peru's Navy (la Marina de Guerra del Perú), but left after five years to begin his university studies at the Universidad Nacional Federico Villarreal. After graduating he embarked on a fruitful literary career, publishing several highly acclaimed novels, short story collections, plays and poetry volumes. His book *Seis metros de soga* won the Premio Horacio Zeballos de Novela Corta in 2010 and the following year, his novel *Maestra vida* was awarded the Premio Internacional de Novela Corta Mario Vargas Llosa. In 2016, his story "Inmersión" won first prize in the XXVII Edición del Concurso de las 1000 Palabras, organized by the magazine *Caretas*. This piece was subsequently translated into fourteen languages. My good friend Pedro's life was cut short in 2021 after an intense battle with cancer, but his diverse and unique stories exploring the human condition will live on forever.
Instagram: @pedrofelixnovoacastillo

Karina Pacheco (Cusco, 1969)

Karina holds a PhD in Anthropology from the Universidad Complutense de Madrid. She's a prolific author of six novels, several short story anthologies and numerous articles focusing heavily on ethnic identity, racism and cultural studies. Her 2008 novel *No olvides nuestros nombres* was awarded the Premio Novela del Instituto Nacional de Cultura de Cusco. A few years later, her novel *Cabeza y orquídeas* (2012) won the Premio Nacional de Novela Federico Villarreal. She currently manages Ceques Editores, a publishing house based in Cusco which specializes in Andean literature, history and anthropology. Her most recent novel, *El año del viento*, was published in 2021. I should also mention that Karina's photos of the natural beauty of Peru's highland countryside are works of art.
Instagram: @karinapachecom

Romina Paredes (Lima, 1987)
Romina earned a BA in Translation and Interpretation from the Universidad Ricardo Palma and a master's in Audiovisual Translation from the Universidad Autónoma de Barcelona. She's the author of two short story collections *Famulus* (2020) and *Monstruos* (2022). Her short story "Kintsugi" was selected in an anthology of young Peruvian short story writers (Estruendomudo, 2021). A lifelong swimmer, Romina competed on Peru's national team for a number of years. As an admirer of the riot grrrl movement, Romina does not seek validation from the literary police. She loves dogs, beer, heavy metal, and walking barefoot. Her guilty pleasures include watching b-movies, the slap fighting championship and cute animal videos on social media.
Instagram: @rominaescribe

Richard Parra (Lima, 1976)
Richard has a PhD in Latin American Literature from New York University. He won the Premio Nacional de Literatura in 2021, Peru's most respected literary prize, for his exceptional short stories in *Resina* (2019). He's the author of the novellas *Necrofucker* and *La pasión de Enrique Lynch* (both published in 2014), the novel *Los niños Muertos* (2015) and the collection of shorter fiction pieces, *Contemplación del abismo* (originally released in 2010 and a 2nd edition which came out in 2018). His critical study, *La tiranía del Inca. El Inca Garcilaso y la escritura política en el Perú (1568 – 1617)*, won the Premio Copé in 2014. Richard's encyclopedic knowledge of all things heavy metal is astounding. He's equally insightful discussing stylistic choices in the works of Juan Rulfo or José María Arguedas as he is waxing poetic on the influence Danish vocalist King Diamond has had on American bands like Metallica and Slayer.
Instagram: @richardparra666
Twitter: @RichardParra666

Juan Manuel Robles (Lima, 1978)

Juan Manuel earned his MFA from New York University. In 2017, he was selected by the Hay Festival – Bogotá39 as one the best Latin American fiction writers under the age of 39. He is the author of the creative nonfiction book *Lima Freak* (2007), the novel *Nuevos juguetes de la guerra fría* (2015) and the short story collection *No somos cazafantasmas* (2018). As a journalist and editor, Juan Manuel's work has appeared in multiple publications including *VICE, Etiqueta Negra, Buen Salvaje, Letras Libres, El Comercio* and many others. *Nuevos juguetes de la guerra fría* is a master class in pop culture referencing—thanks to Juan Manuel I managed to max out a few credit cards while buying original *He-Man and the Masters of the Universe* action figures.
Instagram: @palidofuego

Gustavo Rodríguez (Lima, 1968)

Gustavo is the author of many novels including *La furia de Aquiles* (2001), *La semana tiene siete mujeres* (2010), *Cocinero en su tinta* (2012), *República de La Papaya* (2016), *Madrugada* (2018) and others. He has also released numerous nonfiction works, children's and YA books and the collection of stories *Trece mentiras cortas* (2006). In 2021, he published *Machista con hijas* (2021), which was based on his podcast of the same name and details his upbringing and the challenges of being a father in today's world. His most recent novel, *Treinta kilómetros a la medianoche* (2022) has garnered rave reviews and has been listed as a contender for best novel of the year by several respected Peruvian critics. I'm convinced Gustavo doesn't sleep since on top of publishing stellar books almost every year, he also manages to run the cooperative media enterprise Jugo de Caigua.
Instagram: @gustavoescribe
https://jugodecaigua.pe/

Claudia Salazar (Lima, 1976)

Claudia completed her undergraduate studies at the Universidad Nacional Mayor de San Marcos and received her PhD in Latin American Literature from New York University. She is the editor of two anthologies, *Voces para Lilith* (2011) and *Escribir en Nueva York. Antología de narradores hispanoamericanos* (2014). In 2013, she published her first novel, *La sangre de la aurora*, which was awarded the celebrated Premio de las Américas in 2014. Claudia was also the founder and director of PERUFEST, the first Peruvian film festival in New York. She is currently a professor at California State Polytechnic University at Pomona. Like many Peruvians, Claudia is fiercely proud of her country's cuisine. I have shared numerous meals with her at conferences in New York City, San Francisco, Chicago, Austin to name a few, and we always seem to end up at Peruvian restaurants.
Instagram: @clausalazarjimenez
https://claudiasalazarjimenez.wordpress.com/

Gunter Silva (La Merced, 1977)

Gunter studied Law and Political science at the Universidad Católica de Santa María in Arequipa and holds a master's in Literature and Creative Writing from the University of Westminster. He has published the book of short stories *Crónicas de Londres* (2012) and the novel *Pasos pesados* (2016), which was translated into Danish under a grant from the Danish Art Foundation. Gunter's works have appeared in diverse publications including *Latin American Literature Today*, *Suburbano*, *Letralia* and *Words Without Borders*. A tireless promoter of contemporary Peruvian literature, Gunter created the collaborative online portal *Stories from Peru* where many of the authors in this anthology were translated into English for the first time. I have taught *Pasos pesados* on several occasions and my students absolutely love it— I've even had students create playlists with 90s tracks referenced in the novel. He currently lives in London.
Twitter: @guntersilva9
https://storiesfromperu.com/

Jennifer Thorndike (Lima, 1983)

Jennifer is the author of two novels *(Ella)* (2012) and *Esa Muerte existe* (2016), both of which have received much critical praise. She has also published two short story collections, *Cromosoma Z* (2007) and *Antifaces* (2015), and appeared in numerous anthologies in both Peru and other Latin American countries. Her short fiction has been translated into English, Portuguese and Italian. The 2016 FIL in Guadalajara selected her as one of the twenty most oustanding Latin American writers born in the 80s. She currently works at the Myatt Center for Diversity and Inclusion at the University of New Haven. A confessed cat lover, Jennifer's feline photography is next level.
Instagram: @jen_thorndike

Diego Trelles Paz (Lima, 1977)

Diego earned his PhD in Hispanic Literature from the University of Texas at Austin. His narrative works include *Hudson el redentor* (2001), *El círculo de los escritores asesinos* (2005), *Adormecer a los felices* (2015) and *La procesión infinita* (2017). His 2012 novel, *Bioy*, received the Premio Francisco Casavella and was a finalist for the Premio Rómulo Gallegos in 2013. Diego also edited one of the last decade's most acclaimed anthologies of contemporary Latin American literature, *El futuro no es nuestro* (2008). Legend has it that whenever Peru's national side scores a goal, Diego's family and friends back home can hear his shouting despite the fact that he lives in Paris.
Instagram: @diegoganancia

Gimena Vartu (Lima, 1986)

Gimena Vartu is a pseudonym for María Inés Vargas Tunque, an author, poet and playwright. She has published a book of poems *Cura de sueño* (2012) and the short story collection *Fábula de los cuerpos calientes* (2019). Her play *Cachorro está perdido* (2016) was awarded the Concurso Nacional Nueva Dramaturgia Peruana courtesy of Peru's Ministry of Culture. Gimena currently works as an editor at the Fondo Editorial de la Escuela Nacional Superior de Arte Dramático (ENSAD). During her tenure at ENSAD, there's been a veritable boom in the publication of dramatic works in Peru.

Instagram: @gimenavartu

Nataly Villena (Cusco, 1975)

Nataly holds a PhD in Comparative Literature from La Sorbonne Nouvelle in Paris. She's the author of the coming-of-age novel *Azul* (2005), winner of the Premio Regional de Novela del Cusco, and the collection of short fiction *Nosotros que vamos ligeros* (2018). Nataly has also published a well-received work of literary criticism, *Mario Vargas Llosa, intellectuel cosmopolite* (2008). Her work as an editor has focused on improving the visibility of women authors as is evident in the anthology *Como si no bastase ya ser. 15 narradoras peruanas* (2017) and the online magazine *Las Críticas*. Although she has lived in France for the last twenty years, Nataly remains an important presence on the cultural scene of her native Cusco.

Instagram: @papillontoutcourt
https://lascriticas.com/

Julia Wong (Chepén, 1965)

Julia is one of the most prominent voices in Tusán (Chinese Peruvian) literature. She has published more than a dozen poetry books including 2021's *18 poemas de fake love para Keanu Reeves* and several short story collections and novels such as *Mongolia* (2015) and *Aquello que perdimos en la arena* (2019). A true citizen of the world, Julia has lived in California, Macau, Freiburg, Buenos Aires and Guadalajara besides living in different Peruvian cities. She currently resides in Lisbon.
Instagram: @juwk109

Carlos Yushimito (Lima, 1977)

In 2010, Carlos was featured in Granta Magazine's inaugural "Best of Young Spanish-Language Novelists" special issue. He holds a PhD in Hispanic Studies from Brown University. Some of his most representative publications include *El mago* (2004), *Las islas* (2006), *Lecciones para un niño que llega tarde* (2011), *Los bosques tienen sus propias puertas* (2014) and *Rizoma* (2015). His works have been translated into English, French, Italian and Portuguese. He is currently a professor at the Universidad Adolfo Ibáñez in Viña del Mar, Chile.

ABOUT THE TRANSLATOR

Gabriel T. Saxton-Ruiz is a Professor of Latin American Literature & Culture and Coordinator of the First-Year Experience Program at the University of the Incarnate Word. Before coming to UIW, he was Associate Professor of Spanish & Latin American Studies and Vice Chair of Humanistic Studies at the University of Wisconsin-Green Bay. He received his BA in Spanish and French from Virginia Tech, and his MA and PhD in Modern Foreign Languages from the University of Tennessee. His research interests include twentieth and twenty-first century Latin American literature, popular culture studies, cultural gastronomy and representations of violence in various types of cultural productions. He has published *Forasteros en tierra extraña* (2012), a study on contemporary Peruvian literature and political violence, and co-edited the monograph *La narrativa de Jorge Eduardo Benavides: Textos críticos* (2018). Saxton-Ruiz is also the Editor-in-Chief of *Stories from Peru*, an online magazine of Peruvian literature in translation into English. His scholarly articles and translations have appeared in diverse publications in the UK, USA, Cuba, and Peru including *Words Without Borders*, *Revista Hiedra*, *Palabras Errantes*, *Hispanófila*, *Latin American Literature Today* and *Revista Conjunto-Casa de las Américas*. He spends more time than he should crafting playlists packed with Elephant 6 oddities, Peruvian psychedelic chicha, yacht rock smoothness, Memphis soul grit, and NYC legends Interpol. Instagram: @saxtonruiz